Dirk's father was standing before him, steaming blue radiance. 'Don't be afraid, son,' he said.

'You're dead.'

The ghost was sad, at the brink of tears. 'I've been brought back to warn you. The Arc has to be returned. And soon.'

Dirk took the silver disc from his pocket. 'Then take it.'

'I can't. But there are others who can help you. They're on their way now, and they'll be here soon. The Arc is from another dimension, another reality, completely different from anything we know. It doesn't fit inside one mind. It needs all of you . . .'

'A. A. Attanasio's *Arc of the Dream* is a kaleidoscopic adventure, a potent piece of storytelling pulsing with menace, yet thoughtfully and gracefully rendered.'

— Roger Zelazny

By the same author

Radix
In Other Worlds
Beastmarks

For those who are

Nothing is more real than nothing.
– Democritus

Contents

When the Dead Cry

The land looked evil. Black rocks shaped like knives covered the earth. *Aa lava*, Donnie Lopes said to himself as he carefully stepped on to the frozen torrent. The lava was sharp-toothed as a ripsaw, and Donnie with his gimpy right leg stopped frequently and looked ahead to where the black flow slashed down slopes of scaly pines to the green sea miles away. Hell vents streaked with blistery colors leaked wisps of yellow smoke, and the air stank like a sewer. Above the steamy terrain and the bunsen blue of the ocean's horizon, the sky boiled with clouds. Sunlight splashed in evanescent puddles among the charred hills and the tormented oases of scrub trees. *No wonder the Polynesians thought this land belonged to the gods*, Donnie thought. *No one else would want to live here. Mountaintops, oceanbottoms, lava fields – the gods always get the crappiest real estate.*

Donnie was a seventeen year old from Honolulu on his high school's senior class trip to Mauna Loa, the biggest volcano in the world. Because of his withered leg, he had to forgo the hike along Devastation Trail with his classmates. He was supposed to sit in the ranger station and read about the rare plants and birds of the volcanic range, but after the others had left he had gone out to the back of the wood-slatted station and had found a trail of his own that gashed through the bristly shrubs behind the restrooms and emerged in this scorched landscape.

This trek wasn't as dangerous as it seemed, Donnie reassured himself. If he fell and lost his cane, he could always shout and holler and someone would hear him. He had spent his whole life being left behind because of his deformity, left to read books while others played ball or danced or explored. He had recently come to feel that he'd read too many books, that he knew more about what the world was supposed to be like than what it was.

Donnie's sneakered foot caught in the socket of a burst gas bubble, and he pitched forward. With desperate speed, he swung his aluminium tube cane in front of him and braced himself an instant before he would have collapsed on to the teeth of the lava. A puckish grin lit his round face. The trail his classmates had taken was much safer than the fire-chewed path he was discovering for himself here on the jagged lava but they wanted to move swiftly and cover the whole two-mile trail. He was content to pick his way across a few meters to a spot where the world looked as it had at the morning of time.

The toppling clouds swept the black landscape with fiery shadows, and from a scarp beside a ridge of ohelo shrubs as gray and twisted as smoke, something flashed. *Mica*, he thought at first, then immediately corrected himself: *Mica's a silicate, fool. It's found in metamorphic rock, not in an igneous flow like this.* His next thought was of bottlecaps and broken glass. The reaving clouds admitted more sunlight, and the flash burned briefly again, diamond-sharp as a star. The hot glint sat in a split boulder that looked like the charred hatching of a phoenix, and he edged closer to get a better look at it.

The nearer Donnie got, the more careful he had to

be, because the land tilted steeply downward. Even someone with two strong legs would have been in jeopardy, and Donnie moved gingerly and with a spry wisdom that he had earned from a lifetime with his cane. On the face of the sheer incline, he tested each step twice with the cane and descended far enough into the pit of sharp rocks to see that the sun-hot glint was not bouncing off broken glass or crumpled foil. The object looked about the size of a twenty-five-cent piece but oblong and blue-silver, and he was disappointed that it wasn't something he could recognize from this distance, because now he would have to go all the way down.

The brittle lava snapped under his weight, and his bad leg spun free. But his cane lodged firmly in a crevice, and his good leg braced itself on a firm jut of stone. He tottered briefly, the sweat of his strenuous effort flying from his face like chipped glass. He squatted, grateful that he was wearing his scruffy green denim pants, and cautiously crabwalked the rest of the way down.

The bright object was a slender metallic ovoid, cool to his touch and shimmery as a piece of the wind. He picked it up, and the sunlight fanned off it in a spectral smile as he turned it with the fingers of one hand, like a monkey with a strange fruit. It was featureless.

He put it in his pocket and began the arduous climb back up the ridge. Twice the ground crumbled from under him, and both times his cane stabbed into the fanged rocks and pivoted him back to his feet. At the top, among the tattered ohelo shrubs growing from the black sand, he took the object out of his pocket and held it up to the light.

Rainbows angel-haired about it, and a peculiar

feeling welled up in Donnie. The feeling suffused all of him at once like the rush of a drug but softer, more like a feeling of weather or time of day. He thought of October in an old forest, the ember scent of dead leaves glowing in the air, the sky amethyst, the day's last window, staring through cold vapors into the pins of the night, the depths that held all the stars, the void that encompassed all the days of every world, gleaming like a jewel.

Weird. He bent over to force more blood into his head because he thought the exertion of the parlous climb was affecting him. He rarely worked that hard, and the scintillations he had seen around the metal slug had to be the retinal flares of oxygen hunger. Same with the euphoria: A feeling like the end of the day in New England retreated as he caught his breath. He had not the slightest inkling that the object that he was holding was alive, let alone that it was a vaster being than himself.

The alien in his palm was terrified and in great pain. It was a 5-space being exquisitely bound to a precise point within the continuum, and by moving it, Donnie was killing it. Within its iridium shell, its brain was verging on panic. A conflagration of horror and confusion consumed it.

How strangely fearless the alien had felt when it had first entered this universe. Its jaunt was an act of play, at first an accident of evolution and then an exuberant experiment with its newfound ability to push outward. *Outward*! The concept was still bizarre to it – though here it was, outside 5-space, outside the pith. Of course, it had been stunned to enter so quickly a universe made of points. Within its 5-space origin, everything was one point, so its transition to 4-space was abrupt. It had evolved to

12

where it could trespass outward, and so it had – instantly. But the journey back home would be restrained by 4-space physics and so had to be gradual. The alien had known this at once, but the full implications were still too strange to grasp.

Time itself was new. When the alien first entered 4-space it was moving at light speed through this bizarreness called a continuum. Its sentience extended into the photon field and along the inertial contours of the universe, feeling the teeming points and all their connections. No point was separate or central. All points were radiant, luminous in the nets of their quantum energies. And all were scattered and scattering farther each instant. Light streamed among them, reaching outward in elastic fields of energy.

Any one of those points could have been a way back home. Each point of energy and inertial mass in the spacetime continuum was a monumental gateway of force, appearing to the alien as gleaming archways of bent spacetime winding through a tightening fibonacci coil to the iridescent gist of the subquantal dimensions. The alien selected a neutrino that was traveling alongside at the speed of light and focused its awareness on the tiny waveform. The silver lintels of curved space loomed closer as the mind narrowed smaller than the waveform – they were the spin properties of the neutrino. They appeared to the mind as glassy vaults that blurred by when the alien's consciousness focused to a point smaller than the foam of spacetime.

Immediately the being was aware of the song that was the map of its source. The coma of oneness opened before it, and the mind teetered to the brink of an infinite plunge homeward – then stopped. It

13

knew the way in. The way out was new, and it wanted to explore. It let the neutrino go, and its attention expanded outward again. That was its last chance to return home directly. After that, it belonged to the maze of creation.

Donnie wobbled at the edge of the lava slope, his shoulders slouched, his mind inspelled by the alien's trance. Like a plant listening to the rhythms of the earth, he swayed dreamily. The alien's story continued to rise in him with sap-force, and he saw the strange being as a gush of energy, a bolt of power that had burst from its world in 5-space, was spurting through the cold reaches of 4-space, and would soon fall back to the point of its origin in a fiery arc. That's what the alien was – an arc leaping across the void. Donnie shivered, and his mind melted back into that arc.

Spacetime was molten with radiation. Interflowing oceans of energy swarmed in the void, and the alien felt drunk to be a part of it. Its drunkenness was real. Moving at light-speed through the hive of galaxies, its energy was scattered by the gravity lenses of the stars, and the being multiplied into many beings, all of them bursting off in different directions – each of them was aware as the original and each alone with its own fate in the hungry darkness.

Here, finally, was where a story could begin, *Once upon a time . . .* – for this was where time as humans imagine it began for the alien. Here the raw blackness of space became a trajectory, millions of trajectories, one for each of the alien's gravity-refracted selves. Each trajectory through the fiery emptiness was a story. This story was the one path that led to earth.

14

In its fifth generation of star-lensing, one of the alien's numerous photon selves slowed to subluminal velocity and translated the inertial difference to a physical shape. The shape, structured by field patterns still directly linked with 5-space, took the form of an iridium-shelled titanohematite brain. Within the daedal interstices of the metal atoms, hypertubules connected the 4-space body of the alien with its 5-space home. When it decided to look for signs of its own kind, a mind that it could meet before its fall back to home, it used the infolded parameters of hyperspace in the subatomic matrix of its brain to scan for psychic fields in spacetime.

For every collection of points whose patterns generated sentience in this strange cosmos, there were signature waveforms in the photon field – electromagnetic auras of cellular potentials: Those were almost everywhere. But brainwaves were what the alien was seeking. Through the time-warped peepholes of its sensors, it was looking for mind. And mind was there – broken into multitudinous bits and flung throughout all of creation. Clusters of separate minds glittered in a gloomy vastness, crowding the psychic sensors.

It searched out one mind in the nearest galaxy, a mind that seemed most like its own. And it willed itself toward that consciousness.

The 4-space mind that the explorer had chosen to confront existed in protoplasmic form on a water world swinging about a yellow star on the rim of a galactic maelstrom two hundred thousand light-years away. The journey into the wheeling stars took a quarter million years, but the alien hardly noticed, for it was in empathic trance with the mind that it had selected.

First of all, the mind it had chosen was really many minds, a blowing of radiant atoms, iridescent as the pith of 5-space. Each atom was one creature, a part of the song and a three-dimensional being, bright and glowing – and then gone. The bodies lived for a while – and then dissolved and were gone. But not really gone. The light cone of each individual's existence persisted in the vacuum field that permeated the continuum. The waveforms of each atom, each body, each mind continued to exist and change in the 4-space expanse of the cosmos that surrounded the three-dimensional world. Some of the waveforms in the vacuum field interacted with three-dimensional creatures again, and for all those bodies that dissolved, blinked out, and became ghost lights, new flashes of the song appeared, and the fire-flicker rhythms among the millions of comings and goings of individuals sang of the savage rapture of life, the travails of awe, and the harrowing abundance of time. It sang of the sun's incandescent passion for the night and the creaking stars. It sang of the alien poised in the night's depth, light-years deep, rising toward earth to share in the song.

Dolphins and whales! Donnie thought from the core of his trance and nearly quivered awake with the recognition. For an instant the boy's self-awareness flared brighter, and he saw himself against the heights of the sky, the lava field around him gray with translucence, a thick fog of rock. The air was drugged with the sulfur stink of volcanic vents, and he tried to pull himself awake through his nostrils. But that didn't work. The alien was too strong, and muscles of whale-music closed the lock of the trance.

'Insideout,' the sea-animals called the 5-space

mind whom they sensed approaching them. That's what it felt like to them, leaving the songfulness of the pith and being flung through outer space at the speed of light. Insideout was impressed by their awareness of it, and it used its hyperspace field to reach more strongly through the distance between them. They were clearly one mind in a spray of many minds, and their intelligence fascinated the alien.

The songful water creatures understood trespass between worlds: They had left the sea once. They had lived along the tumbling shores and jarred rocks in tangles of grass and mud. And when the mud had dried and the sun had begun to eat everything, they had come back, stronger and wiser for their trespass. The song had begun then.

Insideout swam with all the tribes: They were cetaceans – the dolphins and the whales whose huge, complex brains held the light of a magnified reality. The alien called them by their own whistle names. It communed with them through its hyperspace window, appearing in their minds as a disembodied and remote presence at the fringe of voice. Though it was physically light-years away, the titanohematite brain was closer to the dolphins and whales than the spume in their clutching airholes. The 5-space core of the alien at that time was actually touching every point in the universe, and it could put its consciousness anywhere.

It put its mind on earth and learned from the cetaceans how to radiate – how to sing in this flying-apart universe. By the time it arrived near earth, hundreds of millennia later, its song was a bliss of sharing: It sang of the bedazzling pith and the tranced oneness of 5-space, which the whales called yes-out-of-mind. It listened to the earth songs in an empathic bliss that melled its consciousness with the collective unconscious of the cetacean psyche. And it knew the gauze of a physical body, the dust of eyesight, and the absorption of sounds pictorializing a benthic world of up and down.

This liberty of mind flowed over generations, riding the crest of life right through the rendings of death, unimpeded for over two hundred fifty thousand orbits of the water planet about its yellow star. Abruptly, toward the very end of its journey, another mind from among the many minds on this planet intruded aggressively.

Insideout, whose point-awareness was fixated on the cetacean psyche, would have ignored this songless mind except that it appeared so suddenly, filling every pock of the planet with its radiation. The serenity of the blue world, which had been luring the arc, all at once blared with screaming energy. Radio noise and microwave sirens swirled about the planet like the aura of a small star, and Insideout thought that its approach had somehow triggered this global response. It filtered the radio flux and listened to military frequencies, radar beacons, and soap operas long enough to be certain that it had nothing to do with the radioactive frenzy that was blazing hotter as the alien approached.

The being responsible for the noise was a dim, chittering mind whose thronging spindle-limbed bodies were everywhere on the planet's exposed land.

From inside his trance, Donnie saw a magic kaleidoscope of people: prismatic faces, ghostly bodies, fluttery snapshots of bright cosmetics, spike-heeled shoes, cuffed trousers, and padded shoulders.

18

Images from the fifties ruffled before him like reflections on water, and he desperately tried to mentally seize hold of any one of these familiar shapes from the past, hoping to rouse himself from the alien's spell. Fin-backed cars streaked by, suburban houses appeared and vanished – and he was growing smaller, shrinking back into the alien's trance. *I'm Donnie*! he shouted to himself. *I'm Donnie Lopes*! He was afraid of losing himself among this jumble of human faces glittering with makeup and the silent animation of lost conversations. *Let me go*! he screamed, but Insideout could not hear him, and his noise dwindled into the neverness of the alien's grip.

Humans were without a song, Insideout realized. Only their machines created jangling distortions in the photon field, and their machines made little sense to the alien. It finally ignored them and put its attention back on the sublime blue peace of the cetaceans.

While Insideout's mind was exploring earth, its iridium-shelled, titanohematite-cored body was decelerating by using its internal hyperfield to siphon some of its inertia out of spacetime and into the multiverse. But the accuracy of its map of the continuum was fractionally off, and Insideout missed earth and plunged toward the proton wall of the sun.

On its three-hour detour back to the blue planet, Insideout took time from its rapport to calculate how long it would remain on earth. The stay could hardly be indefinite because the alien's connection with 5-space demanded that it stay in motion within the expanding field of the continuum. Its interlope could last only three rotations of the planet. Then it would use the infinite power of the arc to return home. Any longer and the hyperfield in the atomic spaces of its brain would collapse into the flux of spacetime and the alien would be trapped in this weird, exploding reality, where one was many, each radiating a psychic field for a small time and then – blinking out and becoming eerie, bodiless light cones.

Insideout had sometimes wondered about the light cones. The wraiths of past light interacted endlessly in the vastness of the vacuum field – and Insideout realized that the waveforms generated by the three-dimensional creatures never dissolved or blinked out. Light within the tesseract range of the continuum was forever. And it was there, among these shapes of light, that the alien would be stranded if its hyperfield collapsed. The thought of enduring endlessly in this blasted apart cosmos was terrible, and Insideout was glad when its attention was diverted by a close-up view of the planet's surface.

Pastels of radio emissions covered everything, and the alien shifted to gravitational light to see through the smog of radio and microwave noise. The land surface of the planet was mostly wasteland, yet even in the most desolate regions of rock and ice electromagnetic pollution from the radio animals seethed. Insideout was grateful for the weak graviton current of the planet, which revealed the landscape dimly but without distortion from the electronic yammering, and it avoided the wide land masses. The dolphin-sized, narrow-shaped beings filled all the river crevasses and plains of the planet, cluttering the surface with their concrete and electrical excrescences. Fortunately, most of the surface was water, and in the water were the cetaceans, whom Insideout had traveled light-years to greet.

The arc circled the globe twice, scanning in gravitational light for the right place to land. The seabed was too unstable: Creatures came and went down there, and most of the currents were strong. The ice sheets of the poles looked good, if it could find a niche away from the wind. Insideout was banking toward the bright haze of the frozen Ross Sea when it saw again the largest mountain on the planet, and it changed its mind. The mountain was more inviting because it was surrounded by the warm waters the dolphins loved. Insideout had rejected the site on its first flyby because of the electrical clutter there, signifying again the presence of the photon-loud but otherwise songless animals that the alien had come to fear: There was a sinister texture to their thought-waves, and the jumble of radiation that they were dumping into the photon field was apallingly centerless and growing louder with each orbit.

Now, however, its urgency to match the inertial frame of the earth and experience union with the cetaceans before returning to 5-space overrode its anxiety, and it decided to ignore the radar-howling creatures and land at a site on the planet's biggest mountain, somewhere out of reach.

Insideout selected a rock slope that appeared luminously empty in the gray fabric of gravity light – a barren lava field overlooking black, devastated miles of crusty magma. Barring a freak meteor, the site looked safe from change for centuries, let alone three days.

The sight of the familiar terrain roused Donnie Lopes toward consciousness again. Sunlight was pressing on the land. For one clear moment, Donnie was himself once more, holding the arc in his hand. Only an instant had elapsed since he had climbed

21

out of the lava kettle, and the soulful bellies of the clouds were still hung as they had been when he had first held the arc up to the light. *Please, let me go*, he whimpered from inside the ice of time. Fear scampered in him. Where were the world's old noises? Why were the birds he could see stuck in the air like pieces of the sky that had been punched out? *Please, please*, he cried and fell back into the alien's dream.

The arc released its expendable inertia to the hyperfield and fell to earth. The iridium-shelled pod flumped on to the black sand among fists of igneous rock, and Insideout melled at once with the morpho-genetic field lines of its old friends in the sea.

Alone inside a dolphin body, in the green sea, it knew again in-ness, and it was inflamed with joy by the ubiquity of this intensely primal feeling: Once more, it was in. Only here in this strange reality, each being had its own in! *Each has its own Point*! A numinous feeling gripped Insideout – and it prayed in the click language of its hosts:

'Glory of the Great One – glory to You, the Many. A brief instant ago it seems I hung far yet erect in the fixed attention of the pitch, undreaming, with all the one, younging as my life became the hopeful dark, as Being has willed, O as Being has willed from the Last! Great One – you are here! Even in this scattered world, you are here!'

The dolphins shoaled at the surface, spinning with giddy energy in the mellifluous and mysterious presence of Insideout. They sang a soft-eared song as serious as play about the fire of becoming, and the alien was touched.

'You songful ones are like me – so yes-out-of-mind and all one, yet – yet so separate, so far from the pith

22

and not one at all! How can this be? You are one only in song!'

All at once, as if in reply but with violent impersonality, the high blue air of the sky tore by like the wind, and Insideout was flung beyond organic bonding. Silence zenithed in the direction of its plummet, which also felt like a wild ascent. And that's when it recognized that it was going to die.

The arc had been moved! Insideout was churning with the expanding knowledge of what had happened: Some animal had moved its physical form! It could see the beast in electromagnetic light – one of the radio noise creatures, climbing clumsily over the black rocks, the arc in its hand.

Donnie saw himself climbing up the rocky incline, and when he reached the exact place where he was standing now, the trance imploded and all memory of the alien's memory was snuffed out in him. He stood like a flash of rain, all awareness of Insideout falling out of him.

Horror quaked through Insideout as it realized that it was truly going to die. The arc was now broken. The hyperfield itself could not be moved and was still there on the lava field suspended in the suds of the continuum at the exact point where the arc had entered the inertia frame of the earth. Unless the titanohematite brain was returned to that precise point where the connection to 5-space was waiting, the hyperfield would weaken and in a few days smear away in the expansion of the universe.

There was no death in 5-space, only here – and here is where the alien's only way home was being torn apart by the bloating fields of the cosmos: It would have to make its own peace with death. But what did that mean? Its mind unspooled its calculations. When the hyperfield collapsed, the arc would convert into pure energy. It would become light again – but would it be conscious? How long could it live without its bond to hyperspace? The question took longer to ask than the time the answer offered – and it retracted from its thoughts, stung. Its own intelligence mocked it. It was going to die.

No! It commanded itself to find again the animal that had moved it and to reach into the being, toward its pith, and communicate its need.

A cramped, skullbound sensation squeezed it like the birthhold, and it pulled away in a huff of fright.

The screaming sky sheared through it. The inertial rip in the hyperfield, though still miniscule, was excruciating, a dizzy anguish that was getting worse as its metallic brain was moved farther from the hyperfield. Hurt mangled its perceptions, and it reached again, more desperately, for the animal that was moving the arc.

A smothering terror enclosed it and fisted harder, pressing out all sensations but a muffled smudge of sound and a pale leaking of light. This animal was so wee-minded that were barely room to feel anything but the blood of the beast welling in its loops.

Insideout wanted to lift away from this seizure of numb flesh, yet it knew it couldn't. Until the arc was returned, it had to go on, deeper into the mute flesh of this being. Moments collapsed and sprawled. Sinewy thoughts flexed with aching slowness.

The dolphins called after Insideout in fiery tatters of song, startled by its vehement withdrawal. It went on, ignoring the song. Pulps of visceral feeling globbed thicker and swathed its wounded core. Thinking dimmed. Yet Insideout went on into the animal darkness, deeper into the deathable kingdom.

The mind that it encountered was too small to contain the alien's presence. Unlike the cetaceans, these creatures had no group unity. They were a swarm of pinpoint minds. Even the light cones of the physical bodies that had dissolved went on in the vacuum as distinct waveforms, melling into each other much more slowly than the light of the cetaceans.

Desperate to save itself, Insideout forced its sentience into the tiny psyche of these loud creatures. Forty centuries of human thought funneled into it in a luminous frenzy. Donnie's body, vibrantly contoured in infrared colors, appeared before it. Three other human bodies, chromed in hot light, were visible beyond Donnie. Four human shapes confronted the alien. To communicate with these organisms, it would have to use all four bodies.

Space glittered with icy motes as information about these beings was culled from the human light in the vacuum field. The viscera of physical bodies swathed the alien's senses, constricting its awareness to the one creature holding the arc. This was the one it had to reach. Donnie looked as if he were made of mirror pixels: Each of the millions of gleaming mirrors was a window on an instant in the creature's life.

Almost gagging with claustrophobia, Insideout peered into the windows and saw Donnie's life. The waveform in the vacuum field that had blinked on with the DNA of Donnie's first cell, when the boy was conceived, was a cruel consciousness, a minatory waveform. Staring across the tesseract range through that waveform, Insideout saw a sooty red vista, heard screams, felt rage and fear. War. This waveform's last physical shape had destroyed other

25

human bodies, and it itself had been destroyed by its own kind. The fear imprinted on that waveform matched the clangor of the alien's own terror, and it wanted to pull away. But to live, it had to go on. It shifted its focus to the waveform's present three-dimensional shape. The atrophied left leg felt numb. The natural flow of energy had been cut off there shortly after birth by an invasion of poliovirus. The rightness of the body was wrong. Both parents were waveforms in the vacuum, their bodies gone, dissolved after they were shattered by a car accident. All recent memories were of the Home – limping among other orphans, reading, hobbling among classrooms, reading –

'What'd you find, stooge?' a voice cracked Donnie's reverie, and immediacy screamed back on him. The sour egg stench from the volcanic fumaroles and the sight of the blasted terrain jolted into place, and he looked toward the voice with a dazed expression.

'You stoned?' a blond face with sunstreaked, windcast hair and a mischievous smile asked. That was Dirk Heiser, the class tough. He was lean and restless as a leopard, and he wore a flouncy white shirt with a wide collar like a pirate's, open to his navel to reveal his taut stomach. Dirk reached out and plucked the bright object from Donnie's fingers. 'What have we here?'

'Hey, I found it!' Donnie shouted, and he snatched at the silver disc.

Dirk tossed it in the air like a coin, and it shuffled sunflashes and opals. 'It's mine now, stooge.'

'No! I found it!' Donnie was yelling – something he had never dared with Dirk before. Remotely he was awed by the airy twilight feeling that had come from the object and that had led to this defiance.

26

'Give it back to him. Dirk,' a woman's voice called from the bushes. A scrawny girl with a long-eyed and sharp-boned face appeared behind the leering bully. Her dark, fluffy hair was flattened at the back, and black sand smudged the shoulders and elbows of her red pullover.

'Go sit on it, Sheila.' Dirk fit the reflectant shape to his eye, monocle style, and with one hand pushed Donnie backward.

Donnie staggered to the edge of the scarp, and his bad leg went out from under him. He slid into the pit and immediately stopped his fall with his cane. Gravel chuckled down the long slope.

'I don't like to be yelled at, gimp,' Dirk said, bending over to confront Donnie face to face. Donnie saw himself in the bauble gripped by Dirk's angry eye: The horse of his face in the curved surface was snorting with fear. With a grin that revealed backward bent teeth, Dirk grabbed the cane and yanked it from Donnie's grip.

Gravity jerked through Donnie, and his hands clutched at the sharp rocks jutting from the brim of the slope while his good leg scrambled for footing. He ignored the hot pain of cut nerves in his fingers and held the frantic weight of his body until his leg found support.

'Dirk!' Sheila protested and bent to help Donnie.

Dirk shoved her back. 'Get away.' He hooked the cane to a branch of a wispy ohelo and held the other end out for Donnie. When Donnie reached for it, Dirk swung it away. The bully laughed as Donnie fell back and the air gasped out of him. 'You still have the stuff I gave you last week?'

'Sure,' Donnie wheezed. 'What would I do with it?'

'Some gimps might not like holding hot goods,' Dirk replied, waving the end of the cane before Donnie. 'Some gimps might get the idea of turning it in. But you wouldn't do that after all these years, would you?'

'Dirk, the stuff is still in my locker – just like you gave it to me. Two watches and a car radio.'

'Good.' A dark smile shadowed his face. 'Then I won't have to rough you up.'

Donnie whined, sweatdrops standing out on his face like the heads of pins. 'Help me up.' His eyes reached for Dirk. 'Please.'

The shadow of Dirk's smile flitted away. 'See you downstream, fool.' He left the cane where Donnie could reach it and backed off.

Even with his hand on the cane, Donnie saw that he was going to fall. His shoulders were icy with fatigue, and he couldn't pull himself up except in wild, lurching movements that would snap the branch holding the cane. He hung there quivering, a whimper opening from the center of him when he saw that he was going to take a beating.

Sheila looked at Dirk with pinched eyes and rushed away over the gnarled ground. Dirk flicked his middle finger at her and dropped the silver disc from his eye. He caught it below his hip. 'Women,' he said with resignation. He faced Donnie, whose round face was shivering. 'They don't understand, do they?' He walked the long coin between his fingers, grinned at Donnie like a bat, and walked away.

Dirk caught up with Sheila at the ranger station, a building of gray planks and unlathed treetrunk posts supporting a sun-battered shake roof. The place was empty except for a husky Hawaiian woman behind a counter of pamphlets about exotic birds and plants. Sheila was striding across the gravel parking lot to the charter bus that had brought their class to the volcano park when Dirk took her by the wrist. 'Hey, slow down.'

'Let me go,' Sheila said with clenched intensity.

'What's the matter?'

Before Sheila could say anything there was a shriek from beyond the blossom fired shrubs as Donnie Lopes took his fall and began crying from the lava field. 'You're cruel,' she said with flat indignation and turned to walk toward the bus.

'Me?' Dirk followed her, his arms open at his sides as if to reveal his obvious innocuousness. 'You don't know Donnie Lopes, sister.'

'He's a gimp, Dirk,' she said without breaking her stride. 'You beat up on a gimp.'

'So what? He holds stuff for me. I got to keep him in line or he'll think he has something on me. What do you want me to do? Go back and apologize?'

'Don't shock me.'

Dirk took Sheila's arm again, and she stopped to face him. The woman at the ranger station hurried out of the building toward Donnie's cries. Dirk shrugged. 'Okay. I was too hard on him. I'm sorry. I can't stand the sight of him limping around studying rocks and plants like he's some kind of scientist. He give me the creeps.'

'You give me the creeps,' Sheila said coldly and pulled her arm from his grip. She had been warned about Dirk. Her brother was the gangleader of the Mokes, a dangerous streetgang of mongrel youths that Dirk had been dealing with for the last year. The Mokes sometimes used him to move stolen goods because he knew most of the reliable fences in town. Her brother had told her that Dirk was an angry clown and bound to make a fool of her. He was right. 'I don't want to be with someone who steals from gimps.'

'Steals?' Dirk's face was wide with incredulity. 'I never stole anything from him.'

'Then what's that metal thing you took from him?'

Dirk reached into the thigh pocket of his safari pants and pulled out the silver ovoid he had taken from Donnie. 'This piece of junk?' He held it out to her, and his fingertips felt chilled and the air around it looked burnished and scratched with hair-thin rainbows. 'I don't even know what it is. I'll give it back to him if it makes you feel better.'

'You want to make me feel better?' She stepped away from him. 'Leave me alone.'

'I would if I could.' He sidled up to her. 'You know I'm hung on you.'

His gentle tone mollified her anger, and she didn't stop at the bus but kept walking to an asphalt path that winded through a brake of banana trees. The arrow-shaped sign there read 'Lava Tube.' Dirk had a golden scent about him – a woodmeat odor Sheila liked – and when its damp sawdust fragrance touched her, she calmed enough for him to take her hand.

They strolled without speaking down the switch-back path under boughs of red ferns and along lava walls glisteny with moisture and splotched with yellow and blue-green lichen. The lava tube appeared ahead, a dark tunnel loud with the echoes of some tourists at the far end. The darkness was cool and silken as the inside of a cloud. Dirk drew

Sheila closer and was bending to kiss her when a thick hand gripped his shoulder.

'Mistah Romance, you sold trouble.'

The voice was gruff, like what a boulder might sound like if it could talk. Dirk faced about and in the blackness saw the denser darkness of two large men.

'Sheila, walk,' the boulder said.

'Limu, leave him alone,' Sheila said in a quavery voice.

'Mistah Romance romances more than babes,' Limu's gravel voice crunched on. 'The Mokes say break his nose. Poetic justice. You catch my drift.'

Terror quaked like a choking duck in Dirk's chest, and he couldn't get his voice to work. He had heard about Limu and his silent partner, Chud, two legendary Mokes who had done time as juveniles for murdering a cop ten years before and had gone on to become hitmen for the Japanese mob, the dreaded Yakuza. 'Hey, what's the problem?' Dirk asked, and his voice sounded like tinfoil.

'The problem is – you feel good and the Mokes not.' Limu's thick voice chewed the air around Dirk, and he could smell something like squid on the big man's breath. 'You burned the Mokes, toilethead – now we gonna unscrew your face.'

'Hold on!' Dirk squealed. 'I never burned the Mokes. They don't like what I gave them, give it back. I'll get their money for them.'

'Oh yeah, you find the money all right – wit' interest, toilethead.'

'Sure,' Dirk agreed, the word smoking up from the hot ingot of his stomach. 'Anything the Mokes want.' Dirk's eyes had adjusted to the dark, and he could see the golf clubs that Limu and Chud were carrying.

31

Their shaven heads looked like the silhouettes of footballs.

'What's going on?' Sheila wanted to know.

'I sold the Mokes some snow and they think it's been stepped on.'

Sheila stared at him with plangent surprise. 'You don't deal drugs, Dirk.'

That was his reputation: He was clean. He never touched drugs. The street noise said his mother was a junkie. He shrugged off Sheila's disappointment. 'I was helping a Hotel Street girl. She'd lifted it off a sailor. It was no good for her. Money's kinder.'

'We want a grand, toilethead.'

'A grand?' Dirk looked to Sheila as if this were a joke. She was white as a pulled blind. 'The snow cost them two-fifty. I spent a hundred of that already but I can borrow it back. I ain't got a grand.'

'Then you won't have a face, neither.' The head of Limu's gold club came up swiftly under Dirk's chin and clacked his teeth together forcefully, sharply nipping his tongue. 'You took one bad step, toilethead. Now you gonna pay. Either wit' money or wit' pain. You decide.'

Dirk swallowed the gummy taste of blood from his cut tongue. 'I'll get the money.'

'Tomorrow.'

'We're just getting back to the Home tonight. How can I get up that kind of money in one day?'

The head of the gold club pushed tighter against his throat, gagging off his breath. His hands moved to pull the club away, and the other club came up between his legs just hard enough to send a jolt of nausea from his groin to his scalp. 'Tomorrow in the playground – or next time we see you, it won't be to talk.'

The gold clubs fell away, and Limu and Chud turned and slouched into the darkness.

Sheila stepped closer. 'Are you all right?'

'Yeah, I eat pain.' One hand massaged his throat, the other clutched the throbbing ache of his crotch.

'What're you going to do?'

'Get the money,' he said, though he couldn't imagine how he was going to pull together that much cash so quickly.

'Was the coke bad?' Sheila asked.

His look was indignant. 'It was a real bride. I wouldn't've touched it otherwise.'

That news deepened Sheila's frown. 'Then you're in bad. They want to break your face, don't they?'

Dirk walked out into the sunlight, and the plaited scents of water-rubbed rock and blossoms gentled him. 'So why're you hanging out with me?'

'My brother says you're a bad time,' she admitted. 'But you know me – I never listen to anybody but me. Come on – let's get back to the bus.'

Dirk didn't move. While holding the pain in his pants, his hand touched the object he had taken from Donnie and was carrying in his thigh pocket. A peculiar feeling streamed from it into his hand. A worshipful sensation, like the indigo dark of trees at dusk, whelmed through him, and his hurt seemed tiny by comparison. Suddenly, he wasn't in his body anymore. He was lofting through a darkness chained with stars. And though the air was very cold, black as oil and filmy with rainbows, a boast of euphoria swelled through him.

Insideout's scan lasted about six seconds. While Dirk was entranced by the magnetic stimulation of his midbrain, the alien replaced its images of Donnie with those of Dirk. In the exchange, it saw them together: At lunch in the high school cafeteria, Donnie reading while he ate, oblivious to the clamor around him, and Dirk leaning across the table to sprinkle Donnie's soup with fishfood from biology-class; Dirk sitting behind Donnie on the bus, pelting him with paperclips, slyly tying his shoelaces to the seat post and dropping to the curb with laughter when Donnie tripped and couldn't get up before the bus pulled away. Inside the laughter were more cruelties, memories of trapping Donnie in his locker, rigging a ball bearing in the tip of his cane in the middle of the night, and dropping insects into his ear while he slept.

Dirk hated Donnie because they both came from the Home – Oahu State Boys' Home – and the sight of Donnie staggering around had filled his days for the last eleven years, since Mady, Dirk's mom, was sent to prison for prostitution and he was committed to the Home. He had been six then and used to wandering: Mitch, his dad, had been military, and before he was chopped to pieces by a land mine in Nam, leaving them stranded in Honolulu, he had taken them with him to Germany, Alaska, Virginia, and the Philippines. Dirk grew up a stranger in the world, and Mitch saw to it that the boy learned how to hold his own. He taught his son hand-to-hand combat when he was three, and he instilled in him a predatory watchfulness before the boy could even speak well. An animal genius possessed the boy, and he excelled at shattering pine boards with his hands and kicking water balloons dangled above his head.

If Mitch hadn't died three years later, his disciplines would have shaped Dirk into a Marine. That's what Mady told the teachers who called her to the schools because of Dirk's brawling. Dirk went to five different Oahu elementary schools in two years. The rage of losing his father was uncontrollable, and since all that was left of Mitch was the merciless fighting style he had passed on, he fought.

Dirk spent the rest of his childhood perfecting and augmenting the skills his father had taught him. Thinking back on it, as he often did during the long bus ride from he Home to school that passed the gates of the military base where his father had served, he was glad for his fighting heritage: That was all that kept him whole when Mady went bad after Mitch was lost. Alcohol and pills cut the grief of enduring without Mitch, and Dirk spent a lot of time on the street running purchase errands for Mady and her clients. A six year old copping pills on streetcorners lured perverts from every rathole in the city, and Dirk became proficient at warding off threats and inflicting injuries.

By the time Mady was busted and jailed, Dirk was a street viper, spindly from malnutrition and venomous with rage. His face was clenched in a defiant scowl, even in sleep, and his furiously scrawny body had muscles like razors. He terrorized the other kids, even the senior boys and the social workers because, small as he was, no one could stand up to him when he was enraged. Fury jagged in him like lightning and moved him faster than most people could think.

Six older boys, blighted by child abuse and toughened from years of vengeance, ganged up on Dirk in the lavatory during his first week at the Home. Three were hospitalized. Shoved into a urinal, which was bigger than he was at that time, Dirk spun about on the wet, scooped ceramic and gouged the air from the lungs of his nearest assailant. His flash-stab

35

forced fingers under the boy's sternum and touched his heart with a pain like the silver tip of an acetylene flame. The kid curled up like a torched insect, but that happened so swiftly that the other five boys didn't recognize the dark skill they had just witnessed, and they assaulted him. The scowling wastrel whirled, whip-punching testicles, elbowing a kidney, kicking a knee to splinters, biting a half moon of flesh from an arm, and slicing the cornea of an eye with a precise finger flick. No one in the Home ever threatened him again.

Dirk, of course, didn't require threats to vent his rage, and soon he had used his terror to buffer him from the Home: Other boys made his bed, completed his chores, prepared his homework, and helped him to hawk the drugs he scored from his old street contacts. This was a smooth arrangement for him, until Mady got out of prison four months later and left the islands without him. He didn't blame her. She had married Mitch when she was sixteen. That was in Stuttgart, where she had grown up near the military base. She was a war baby, fathered by one of the many occupation troops who had used her mother to flash their lust, and life for her in Germany, especially after her mother's suicide, had been grim. It was a tired story. Dirk knew all about it. When Mady was drunk, that was all she talked about.

Dirk was glad he wouldn't have to hear that anymore, but he despaired at being kenneled in the Home until he was eighteen. His despair made him sloppy, and the Home counselors caught on to his drug trade and called in the police. Not much the police could do to a seven year old, but his street contacts deserted him, and the counselors isolated him and kept him from abusing the other boys.

Denied human targets for his vehemence, Dirk turned on the inaminate world, breaking windows, clogging toilets, and scrawling obscenities on the walls. Punishment fed his furor, and eventually he was sedated. He was on and off medication for the next six years, examined by countless psychiatrists and childcare specialists and finally abandoned as incorrigible. By then puberty had assailed him, and he found a new outlet for his violence.

Ruddy blond, with eyes pale as water, thick-shouldered and tall, Dirk was attracted to women from the time he was twelve. Several times a year he'd run away from the Home and seek out the contacts Mady had made in Waikiki. Most of them had left the islands or gone to prison, but friends of friends were always available for a boy as ruthlessly handsome and aggressive as Dirk. He ran purchase errands again for the prostitutes on Hotel Street, and they paid him in favors, which for Dirk at the age of twelve was better than money.

By the time he was fifteen, though, he was tired of sex and became intrigued with love. His first lover was a social worker at the Home, a woman in her early twenties with hair the color of a violin, eyes the subdued gray of clouds, and a voice like the northern lights, bright, shifty with moods and colors, and far away. Her name was Tina, and Dirk fell in love with her beauty and her tranquil equanimity – a sureness of character that he had never witnessed in any of the girls on Hotel Street.

Tina's attraction to Dirk was purely animal magnetism. At fifteen, Dirk was a rangy, sandy-haired boy with eyes of crushed glass in a face hewn by summer sunlight. They made love in the attic storage room among shrouded hulks of unused furniture, dim mirrors, and tiger shadows from the window sill.

For the six months that Tina was his lover, Dirk's mischief was curtailed. The Home counselors initially thought he might be sick. When they finally came around to believing that the hellion had made a change of character, Tina left to seek her fortune in LA, and Dirk was bereft. Rejection did not mix with his innate animal outrage, and he railed against love and women in his graffiti and aloud, in feverish ranting, whenever he was reminded of Tina. From then on, Dirk was determined to love only for convenience.

Sheila saw him shivering, his eyes glazed like blue mints, and she assumed he was trembling with fear of Limu and Chud. She knew then she had been a fool to go for this bullying and deceitful loverboy. She had been attracted to him by his brash good looks and his perpetual bravura – though now she saw how shallow that act was. A pang of pity lanced her remorse, and she shook her head sadly, more for herself than for him. Now she'd have to find someone else for good times.

Dirk's trance drifted off like a cloud shadow. He was again standing in white wine sunlight, surrounded by mossy walls of black rock and long, bashful green giraffes of ferns. He saw Sheila walking away, but he didn't care. Like a crescendo of alcohol, power surged in him. A sound like the music of icicles chimed from the sky. He wondered what was happening to him and suspected that somehow whatever was happening, it might be coming from the silver disc Donnie had found. But how could that be? This was just a piece of metal, not much bigger than a bottlecap – how could it make him feel anything?

He turned to follow Sheila back to the parking lot, a shout of amazement beginning in him before he saw Limu and Chud watching him from the mouth of the lava tube. In the sunlight, their shaved heads and faces looked like lacquered wood. Limu, barefoot in red nylon shorts and sleeveless undershirt, was leaning on his golf club, sunlight peeling off the globes of his shoulders in a sweaty gloss. His squashed face was chuckling. He thought Dirk had been shuddering with fright. Chud, who stood behind him with his golf club across his bare shoulders, stared with the impassive ferocity of a tiki god.

Dirk flicked his shoulder back. *Let'm think I'm scared*, he told himself, as the incredible trance he had just experienced shrunk to a smell of cider-turning apples and a dewy feeling in his lungs like after a long cry or before a thunderstorm. He didn't know what had happened to him. The disc had shocked him, not with electricity but with some colder and more ethereal force. He still felt it. The faceless coin in his fist hummed icily, and an exhilaration pungent as autumn smothered all fear. When he passed the hoods, he stared far into their eyes, into the back of their heads, and the frost light of his gaze made them both flinch.

On the flight back to Honolulu, Dirk was sternly reprimanded for pushing Donnie Lopes down a lava slope, and he had to sit in the front row of the place facing an airlines ad with the vice-principal and without a window to stare out of. He fell asleep. While he slept, the disc in his pocket hummed at a pitch far above human hearing, and he dreamed that his father was sitting next to him. *An orphan's dream*, he recognized right away, and in a fitful lurch of lucid dreaming, he tried to wake up. His body didn't respond.

'Relax, son,' his father said. He was a bear of a man, a Marine staff sergeant with razor blue eyes, a dented chin, and a prizefighter's brow. 'This isn't a dream.'

'Come on, Mitch!' Dirk barked as he usually did when the yearning dreams wouldn't break off. 'You're dead. You've been dead twelve years.'

'That's right,' the thick-armed man agreed. He was wearing camouflage fatigues and combat boots. The remnants of green and black war paint were smudged at his ears and along his crewcut hairline. 'Shrapnel severed my aorta outside Hue and I was zipped in a bodybag and flown home to Indiana. That was twelve years ago. Twelve easy years. Until you picked up the arc.'

'You mean this thing?' He took the silver disc out of his thigh pouch, amazed at the lucidity of the dream. 'Donnie Lopes picked it up.'

'You took it.' His gruff features were wrung, and he looked sad as a hound.

'So what? What's the problem?'

'You're holding an arc.'

'You mean like Noah?'

'No. I mean like electric arc.' Concern smoothed his father's voice: 'Dirk, you're holding a live wire. That silver disc isn't an object. It's a force, like electricity – only a lot stronger. Unless you return it to exactly where you found it, a lot of people, including yourself, will be killed. The whole island is in danger.'

40

'Oh, Christ. Why am I dreaming this?'

'You're not dreaming it. This is real.'

'But you're dead.'

'I told you already. I am dead. I was killed in Nam. But the arc has brought me back.'

'That's crazy.'

'I know it must seem that way to you.'

'What'd ya expect? This is crazy.'

'Just think this over when your body fits again. There'll be signs soon enough, and you'll see I'm right.'

Dirk took a moment to assure himself that this *was* a dream. He reminded himself that he was asleep, next to the vice-principal, on his way back to Oahu. 'Why you?' he asked the ghost. 'What's really going on here? What kind of signs are you talking about?'

The sergeant sighed and sat back deeply in his seat. He ran a blunt fingered hand over his weather-worn face, and a tear glinted in the corner of one eye. Dirk flinched with the anxiety that he was going to ask about Mady, Dirk's mom. Instead the silence thickened.

Finally: 'I knew you wouldn't understand.' He shrugged his hands. 'Who would? I can't help you.'

Dirk's incredulity wavered. 'Hey, just tell me what's really happening.'

His father looked at him with woeful eyes, all the more terrible in his coriaceous face. 'The silver disc you're holding is an arc between dimensions. It connects this world with a reality utterly foreign to us. It must be returned to the precise coordinates where it appeared.'

'Why?'

'That's where its home is. The dimension it comes from is smaller than anything you can imagine, son.

41

Smaller than an atom. You've just moved the arc a universe away from itself. And if you don't return it, it'll explode with a force that will make a hydrogen bomb look puny.'

Dirk stared deeply into his father's face and recognized the strength in his features from every lovelong memory he had of the man. 'Why didn't you tell me this back there?'

'I couldn't. The arc is too big for one mind.'

'What's that mean?'

'There are others, other people the arc had to touch in order to talk with you here.'

'Wait a minute. Are you really my dad or what? Are you some kind of alien?'

'I'm not an alien,' his father responded in a rueful tone. 'You are, Dirk. As long as you're holding the arc, you're in its field of influence.'

'Then why don't I just dump it?'

'That would be stupid.' Anger flashed in his voice. 'I told you – it's going to explode unless you return it.' He turned away again, and the air faceted around him, flashing to bezels of blue fire. His father looked surprised and stared at Dirk with hurt alarm. 'Stay alert now, son.'

His last word taffy-stretched into a sixty-cycle hum as his body solarized to a spectral outline, the keyhole shape of a sitting ham, seething with light. And the whole dream zoomed into his brightness.

Insideout decided that this attempt to communicate with this organism was not working. Every other attempt had failed, too, because the titanohematite brain was wracked with pain. As the arc moved farther from its hyperfield, the ripping hurt intensified. In its desperation, Insideout had used one of the disembodied light cones in the vacuum field about Dirk. That waveform was Dirk's father. Free of three-dimensional limits, the ghost was easy to communicate with in 4-space. But getting the ghost to convey clearly the alien's message was harder: The emotions between father and son were befuddling Insideout's intent.

After the light cone's apparition in Dirk's brain disappeared, Insideout attempted to speak with him directly. But within the tesseract range, time prismed language in odd ways, and when the alien's anguished voice spoke from the glare of the dream it said. 'Myn herte is sore afright! Help me, Dirk. Stille thy mind. Lusk fer me. I am no false dissimilour. I am no heigh imaginacioun. I am y-falle from mine own soveryn werld. Alle I ask in felawshipe is lusk.'

The brightness of the dreamlight dulled to a color like cold cement, and Dirk fell asleep.

To speak with Dirk, Insideout needed three other humans to carry the spillover of its 5-space consciousness. The clawing pain of its sudden separation from the hyperfield had kept the alien from focusing on these three, and it had manifested among them unconsciously. Once its brain's pain-buffers began to come on, though, it looked about to see where it was.

The human tesseract range was a landscape of fire. Unlike the cetacean tesseract, where light cones converged to the one beaconlight of the species, the human light cones wheeled against black infinity as a cyclone of individual waveforms. Insideout's 5-space mind touched the clustering whorl of human-light in four separate places. It was reluctant to let go of Dirk, and so when it focused its awareness on the three other humans it was touching, it took him with it.

Dirk dreamed that he was flying around the world, his arms and legs spread over a ball of wind. The earth spun below him, huge and feathery blue. The ball of wind plummeted, flashing through clouds, blurring to a lightningstroke dive – and with a bone-stunning jerk, bouncing off the ground. He zipped up through the clouds, past the blue tatters of the upper atmosphere, and toward a blizzard of stars. He plunged again, slower, and he saw cities and highways strung among green hills before he streaked to the ground and bounced back into the clouds.

On the third fall to earth, the ball of wind carrying Dirk dropped slowly enough for him to see sharply where he was: a mighty brown river looped through craggy terrain, and glossy green fields of rice patch-worked the lowlands. Water buffalo and barefoot, straw-hatted farmers trudged in the river mud, dragging plows, and a village of dried mud and reed roofs peeked from among the river hewn hills.

Asia, Dirk thought, and his self-awareness slowed the dream even more. He glided over hills of yellowed trees and bamboo-thick gorges and circled down toward the snug village.

'Demons!' the old woman squawked. She was a bent, iron-haired Chinese woman with a face like a shucked pecan. She hobbled quickly up a dirt road, past stone houses with reed roofs. 'Demons!' she repeated. She was leading a militiaman, a skinny youth in sand-brown shirt and pants with a leather belt, black slippers, and a militiaman's cap with a red star above the bill. He followed at a leisurely pace while the crone hobbled up the dusty, sloping road, past the communal vegetable patch, toward a grove of shimmering poplar trees.

At the grove, the militiaman went rigid, and alertness jumped in his face. A lattice pyramid made of boulders, rocks, and pebbles rose majestically above the stone-littered field beyond the trees. He closed his eyes and looked again. Right before him, where a few hours earlier there had been an empty field, sat the perfectly exact joints of a pyramid with a sizable boulder at the apex. The poise of the rough rocks on each other was so precise that the shape of the pyramid seemed as though it had to be supported by iron rods.

The old woman muttered, 'It's demons,' and shuffled backward into the trees.

The militiaman stepped closer, his head craning to see the wonder, which reached as high as the tree crowns. Birds alighted on the rock-balanced vertices and glided through the empty faces. He walked around one of the slanted rock columns and then timorously lifted a hand and touched a stone.

The pyramid collapsed in a brattling avalanche that sent rock chips flying. The militiaman ran into the trees with his arms over his head, and the old woman threw her hands into the air and cried: 'I told you! It's demons!'

When the militiaman looked back, the field was strewn with rocks, no different than any other stony lot. He stared at the empty field with eyes like dice dots and then at the crone. They scurried back down the hill, never noticing the elderly man with beard and hair like cobwebs and merry eyes who watched them from among the trees.

Jiang was older than the crone who had brought

the militiaman to see his handiwork. The gods had cursed him to outlive his family, who had all been lost in the wars of the century: The civil war took his firstborn, the Japanese invasion deprived him of his daughters, the Communist victory killed his wife and their one son, and he hadn't seen his grand-children in the ten years since the end of the Cultural Revolution. In the village they called him the War Sage, for he had given so much to the jaws of history he had to have grown wise on his losses. In fact, he had only grown tired.

Jiang lived alone in his hut at the end of the village near the nightsoil ditches. He no longer minded the smell, and the flowers and dragonflies were more profuse here. His place seemed appropriate to him because he had no skills to serve the village except his strength, which had thinned like smoke since he lost his grandchildren. He felt like refuse, everyone else in the village was so industrious. His most strenuous job was to gather small rocks to repair the village fences. Most days he just sat in the poplar grove stripping and splitting reeds the villagers brought from the marshes for use on their roofs. Oftentimes his weak hands barely had the strength to do that, and he lay back in the tremulous shadows and dozed.

Today his bones had been damp with weariness, and while he slept he dreamt that the village needed many rocks to partition a new field. But he couldn't move from where he lay. He was a gray, old mouse, and he couldn't budge from where the grass-matted tree roots cupped him kindly. Instead, the stones moved. When he looked at them they jumped like toads. His blood whispered, *Sleep*, and he couldn't move, but the rocks were singing in his head: 'Each

46

of us once was a star!' and when he looked at them they twitched. In the dream, he made the stones hop on to each other, thinking to make a pile. The stones hopped and clattered, sticking together like dough, until they had stacked themselves in four great columns higher than the trees. The columns leaned in toward each other, and he thought they were going to collapse. Instead their tops clunked into each other and stopped, forming a pyramid of air with stone edges.

Jiang had flickered awake, shivering still from the remarkable clarity of his dream. And there was the pyramid! His heart kicked, and he jolted alert, leaning forward with the cocked hammer stillness of a lizard. At that moment he heard the crone, the busybody with so many grandchildren she had nothing better to do than meander through the village spying and gossiping. She was shouting about demons and leading one of the young soldiers to Jiang's field. That was when Jiang saw that his dream was real, and he almost soiled his pants. What was going on? Sorcery? Demons? He had always scoffed at such notions – yet here was proof of the miraculous.

After the crone and the soldier left, he looked at an ankle-sized rock and willed it into the air. It bobbed up like a fisherman's float and spun gracefully before him. He dropped it at once and leaped back like a firestung monkey. Dreadfully, he tried again. He concentrated on a larger rock, willing it to rise – and it shot into the treetops like a kite.

His mind whirling with astonishment, Jiang lowered the boulder. A smile lifted through the heaviness of his face for the first time in many years, and he brought his trembling hands together in amazement and humble acceptance. Stones were indeed the memories of stars, filled with light in their depths, swirling with light in their cores, like dark wells too deep to sparkle.

'She's changed, Doctor Lefebvre,' the matron said. 'She's fully alert now – and she's asking for you.' The matron was a stout woman whose robust physical stature was emblematic of her psychic fortitude. Her stern eyes had faced down every kind of madness over the last thirty years, and if she said that the girl had changed, it had to be true. But how could that be? The girl was a congenital schizophrenic: She had a biogenic disorder of her hippocampus – a somatic brain dysfunction that was irreversible.

'Where is she now?' Dr Lefebvre asked. He was sitting at his cluttered desk in his cramped, windowless office. He had been filling out medication schedules for his thirty-two patients when the matron came in and announced that the girl's catatonia had abated. The digital clock on his file cabinet blinked to 5:32 A.M. – less than half an hour before his morning rounds began – and he still had numerous forms to complete.

'She's in the east courtyard,' the matron replied. 'She wants to see the sunrise.'

Dr Lefebvre put his pen down and stood up. He was a narrow-bodied man with a black mane prematurely gray at the temples, a thick nose, dim chin, and tristful eyes. 'This is unbelievable,' he said, donning his white, knee-length medical coat and touching the knot of his tie to be sure he had remembered to put it on. 'I must see her at once. Will you begin my rounds if I'm delayed?'

48

'Of course.' She followed him out of the office and at the door took his arm in her sturdy grip. 'Is it possible she has been misdiagnosed all these years?'

Dr Lefebvre stared into the matron's broad face with a mystified frown. 'If so, then maybe we're the crazy ones.'

The girl was in the courtyard as the matron had said. She was sitting on a stone bench whose side was graven with letters worn by a century of weather: Avignon Hospice d'Aliénés. An old-style gas lamp fitted for electricity cast a wan luminance over the courtyard, illuminating a cobbled path bordered by a mesh of flowers – puss willows, primrose, spurts of daffodil. Behind the stone bench, a huge chestnut grew, its sugary blossoms littered the ground, and some were in her blond, jarred hair. She heard his step on the cobbles and turned to face him with her green, lemur eyes.

'Good morning, Reena,' Lefebvre said, suppressing his amazement. The girl was twenty-two years old, but she had never appeared womanly – until now. Her movements were always slurred, and she rarely responded to a greeting. Her face, which had been impassively slack before, was bright with sapience, and her gaze was vivid and animated, wholly unlike the flat stare he had become accustomed to. 'May I join you?'

'Yes, please,' she responded in a dulcet voice he had never heard from her. 'I was hoping you would come, but I didn't really expect it. I know how busy you are at the beginning of your day.'

Lefebvre could no longer hide his astonishment. He sat down as slowly as a man in free fall and seemed to hover above his seat on the bench, his jaw loose, his dark eyes searching her face. Self-consciously, she put her hands to her sleep-wrangled hair, and a tinge of a blush was visible even in the crinkled electric light. 'Reena – what's happened?' he finally asked.

'I don't know, doctor.'

'Yannick – please, call me Yannick.' His voice was airy with surprise. 'I've know you for ten years now, when I was just a resident here. I've never seen you like this. I can't tell you how happy it makes me.'

'Have you changed my medication?'

'No. You're still receiving the same antihallucinogen we began six years ago. One of its side effects is torpor, yet I've never seen you more lively. When did this begin?'

'I had a dream,' she said and put a warm, almost magnetic hand on his. 'A wonderful dream. I was inside other people's minds. I was feeling what they felt, thinking what they thought.'

'Were these people you know or imaginary?'

'At first I didn't know the people. They were strangers – foreigners. One was Oriental, the other I think was American. They were men. The Oriental was elderly and sleepy. The American was a teenager, full of hurt.'

'But then you dreamt of people you know?'

'Yes, I dreamt of you. I was sitting in your office, at your desk, writing down your patients' names, their drugs and doses. I woke after that, and my mind was clear. I've never felt this clear. Doctor – Yannick – do you think I'm better? I mean, do you think I'm cured?'

'I don't know, Reena.' He clasped her hand reassuringly. 'We will have to do tests. We'll begin at once, with a blood sample. Do you mind?'

50

'No. But I would like to sit here for a while and watch the sun come up. This is the first time I've noticed it. May I?'

'Certainly,' he replied, standing up and feeling light-headed. 'I'll make the arrangements.' He took her chin in his hand and grinned affectionately. 'Reena, this could be medical history.'

He walked away, her quiet smile glowing in him. *What's happening to me*? he asked himself as ballast for his euphoria. *Congenital brain dysfunctions don't just heal. This is impossible.* Her condition had obviously been misdiagnosed. With a pre-Adamic uncertainty in the absence of his journals, he reviewed the few known cases of self-integrating psychoses – but none of the symptom profiles matched Reena at all.

At the end of the garden, he looked back. She was gazing at the green copper filaments of dawn beyond the wrought iron fence of the courtyard, beyond the rooftops of Avignon in the Rhone Valley below – gazing with wonderment, and he shared that wonder. Today, dawn was a vast rent in the blackness of space through which the fire of creation was burning away the night.

'Wake up!'

Howard Dyckson shuddered free of sleep and looked startled to find himself in his artificial leather recliner with a warm beer between his legs and the ten o'clock news muttering on the color console. 'We've won, Cora!' he shouted at once.

'Calm down, already,' his wife said from her rocker beside him. 'You were just dreaming. Yelling in your sleep. The neighbours'll think we're arguing again.'

51

'Cora, I tell you we won!' Howard lurched forward as his recliner righted itself, and his beer sloshed on to the carpet.

'Howard! The rug!' Cora put down her crossword puzzle, seized a handful of tissues from the vinyl-topped sidetable beside her, and got down on her hands and knees to blot the spilled beer.

'Forget the damn beer,' Howard yammered. 'We've won! We've won the fucking state lottery!'

'Stop that!' Cora scowled at him from the floor. 'You know I can't stand foul language.'

'Aren't you listening to me?' Howard shrilled and bounded to his feet. 'We're millionaires!'

'Howard, you were dreaming,' Cora said with grievous explanation. 'We're flat broke, remember? You lost your unemployment check at last Saturday's poker game. We had ketchup sandwiches for dinner. It gave you a nightmare.'

'This was no nightmare, Cora.' Howard paced before the TV set, running his hands through his thinning hair. He was a gangly man with a rusty mustache and callused, grease stained hands from fourteen years of working at the Caterpillar plant outside Peoria. The stains were still there, though he hadn't worked in over six months. His large-featured face, usually saturnine until he was drunk, was luminous as a child's. 'I bought a lottery ticket with my cigarette money last week. Tonight's the drawing. I saw them pick our numbers.'

'You were dreaming, Howie.'

'I tell you, Cora, it wasn't a dream. It was as real as . . . as me standing here with you. I was in the lottery room. I saw the drawing – and I saw the numbers. It's ours, I swear it.'

'The drawing's happening now. How could you have seen it?'

'I saw it.'

'Then it'll be on the news,' Cora said and resumed blotting the beer from the rug.

'Fuck the news,' Howard said, striding into the kitchen. 'I'm calling the lottery.'

Cora pursed her lips grimly. Since Howard had been laid off, his need to gamble had gotten far out of hand. If he had been any good at gambling, she would have been more tolerant. But he never won, and their credit had been exhausted months ago. Her part-time salary as a diner waitress, his unemployment check, and the charity of friends were all that kept food on the table. And this week there was very little food because of his compulsion. She was grateful now that she could not have kids. For the fifteen years of their marriage, she had prayed for children, arranging for a high mass each time she found a new fertility doctor who gave her any hope. She and Howard were thirty-eight now. Older than Christ. All hope was gone, but at least their children wouldn't have to help carry the cross of their poverty.

She heard the phone clatter to the linoleum in a ringing bang, and she was up on one knee, on her way to the kitchen, when Howard appeared in the kitchen door. His face glittered with sweat and his mustache twitched over a smile that showed all this thick teeth. A scream widened in her.

Oahu State Boys' Home was an antique, gingerbread-colored building that had been built by missionaries the century before, not as an orphanage but as an asylum for the mentally ill. It was located at the east end of the island, which in the last century had been virtually unoccupied, and it still had bars – floriated wrought iron grille work – on most of the first-floor windows. An eight-foot wall of lava rocks encompassed several acres of royal palms, banana trees, and jasmine shrubs. A playground for the younger kids adjoined the sprawling building, and a pond green with algae gleamed in a far corner of the grounds where mongoose from the sere hills came to drink with the sea wind.

All memory of contact with the alien had drained from Donnie when Dirk took the arc, and the boy was sullen with the oppressive sense of having misplaced something important. Dirk Heiser ignored him on the long ride back from the airport in the Home van that Mr Paawa, the Home counselor, was driving. Mr Paawa was a huge man with perpetually joyful eyes, fingers like cigars, and the girth of an ancient oak. He had once been an orphan at the Home, too, and when there were disciplinary problems, he was the one the other counselors turned to because there was a legitimacy to his authority that the others could never even approximate. When he heard from the high school vice-principal what Dirk had done to Donnie, he grabbed Dirk by the front of his pirate blouse and lifted him off his feet with one hand. 'What you wen' do that for, brah?' he asked the boy in his angry pidgin. Dirk had made no reply, and the large Hawaiian, with a look of disgust, put him down and ordered him to sit in front so Donnie would have the rest of the van to himself.

The arrangement satisfied Dirk because now there'd be less chance of Donnie attempting one of his bizarre and lethal acts of retribution. During the eleven years of their tormented relationship, Donnie

54

had openly defied Dirk only once – today, on the lava field. That was why Dirk had been more cruel than usual: Donnie had broken the rules, and that frightened Dirk. Over the years, Donnie had frequently and vehemently attacked him, but always surreptitiously. Three times Donnie had almost killed him.

Once, when Donnie had rigged the toilet to mix explosive chemicals when it was flushed, Dirk had escaped because he'd seen vapors fuming from the swirling water. He dived out of the stall a moment before the toilet bowl burst apart with a stunning boom. No one believed his story about the explosive chemicals, and he was punished for flushing fireworks.

Another time, Donnie had concocted his own curare, tipped a bent needle with it, and taped it to his shoulder under his shirt. After Dirk slugged him there in his daily endeavour to strike the righteous nerveblow that would numb Donnie's whole arm, his hand swelled up as black and rubbery as an eggplant. He spent two days in the hospital sweating a possible amputation, and Donnie claimed it was purely accidental. The poison-tipped needle was his invention for numbing lab animals for vivisection in biology, and he carried it in a specially tailored shoulder pocket so he would never accidentally misplace it. Dirk wailed when he learned that the counselors actually believed Donnie.

The gimp was a genius at designing fatal accidents. Like God, there was no trace of him in his best creations. Most recently, shortly after Paawa hit upon the vicious idea of rooming Dirk with Donnie in an effort at bringing Dirk's cruelties out in the open and so collect sufficient cause to have him transferred to the Correctional Facility, Donnie acquired a pet rat. Dirk slept restlessly for six weeks, waiting for Donnie to slip the thing in his pajamas while he was sleeping. Then one lazy Sunday morning he got up as usual in the last half hour before the kitchen was closed and went into the shower room to *his* shower, the one with the forceful spray away from any drafts. When he turned the water on, a sizzling torrent of army ants rushed up his arm and began to eat his brain. He was being electrocuted. He couldn't scream. He couldn't even breathe. Another kid saw him and used a mop to break his hold on the metal spiggot, and he writhed on the tiles for minutes with flurries of insects scurrying through his body. Later he was told that he had almost died in a freak accident. An electrical line inside the wall had come into contact with the shower's metal pipe when its insulation had been eaten away by a rat.

Dirk was certain Donnie would try something after the incident on the Big Island. He'd have to be alert once this ride was over, but for now he could afford to ignore him.

Donnie didn't look that bad – his clothes were hardly ripped, and he wasn't bleeding, only bruised. Donnie knew how to fall if he knew anything.

During the ride to the Home, Mr Paawa lectured Dirk on Christian fellowship, but Dirk's gaze was lost in the traffic on Kalanianaole Highway as he pondered the strange dreams he had endured on the flight back from the Big Island.

The vivid dreams made no sense to Dirk except as a fallout of anxiety from the threat of Limu and Chud. His tongue throbbed with swollen hurt from having bitten it during his encounter with the two hoods, and he massaged the cut reflexively with his teeth while he considered his options. After a moment he realized there were no options. The snow he had sold the Mokes had been good. He figured that was just their lame excuse for shaking him down. He had a hundred fifty dollars left from his drug sale to the Mokes, and he had a hot car stereo tucked away in Donnie's locker, though he wouldn't get much for that since he had damaged one of the speakers when he had ripped it out of an unlocked car in Waikiki. He also had a couple of watches that he had stolen from beach blankets, almost worthless black plastic digitals. He could return the clothes he'd bought with the Mokes' money, but his wardrobe was impoverished as it was, and this was the Age of the Smart Dresser, when packaging trumped all strategies for winning girls. Watching the sea glimmer under serifs of red cloud, he knew he couldn't get a grand together, even if he had a week to do it. His only realistic option was to stay in the Home, find a way to get the two hundred fifty dollars back to the Mokes, and beg them to withdraw their seven hundred fifty dollar penalty.

The thought of begging the Mokes galled Dirk, and by the time the sea cliffs near the Home appeared he was scheming up bold ways to get the money. For some years he had toyed with the idea of a ski mask bank robbery, though he had never been desperate enough until now to consider it seriously. This would be the last year that he could pull off such a stunt with his juvenile status as insurance in the event that he fumbled and got caught. He was designing a handgun of balsa and shoe polish in his mind when the van turned off the highway and the caldera of Kako Crater overlooking the Home swung into view.

Mr Paawa dropped Donnie off at the dorm entrance at the side of the building, but he held Dirk back with a firm hand on his elbow. 'Listen up, Mistah Tough Guy,' the counselor said. 'Roughin' up cripples is easy. But what you t'ink you wen' do when you walk from here next year – eh?'

'Survive,' Dirk said and hopped out of the van. He watched Paawa drive off and he lingered on the driveway, staring west through a stand of leaning palms at the flame-horned crater. The bronzed sky returned to him something of the autumnal feeling that he had experienced when he had held the silver disc that he had taken from Donnie. That feeling had been strong, and if he had not been terrified of Limu and Chud, he might have paid it more heed. An *arc* his dream-father had called the disc, and he smiled at the absurdity of that. By now he had completely convinced himself that the encounter with Mitch's ghost was indeed a dream and that the weirdly dizzying trance that had momentarily disoriented him outside the lava tube was a fear reaction to the shock Limu and Chud had so expertly induced. He reached into his pocket and took out the arc (that was as good a name as any, he figured). In the crepuscular light, it appeared almost blue and again grained with rainbows. It was quite beautiful, and he wondered what it really was.

A hideous scream pierced the twilight. It had come from the dorm wing, and Dirk rushed in to gawk. The scream shrieked again, this time more strangled and grievous, and he followed it swiftly up the metal stairs that smelled of chewing gum to the room he shared with Donnie where a gaggle of younger kids crowded outside the door.

Dirk shoved his way through the blanch-faced kids and found Donnie pressed up against the wall with his back to Dirk's color poster of a hydrogen cloud, the handle of his aluminium cane held to his tragically downcurved mouth. His eyes were startled and watery. Dirk looked to where he was staring, and a gag of horror throttled him. Lying on Dirk's cot was a Scot terrier and a black cat – Hunza and Peppercorn, the Home pets – their bellies sliced open and the slithery ropings of their guts unraveled around them.

Dirk knew who had done this and knew their demonic intent. The Mokes meant to do more than punish him. They were going to torture him. Now it was terrifyingly clear to Dirk that they never intended for him to pay them the grand, and Dirk was pondering that when Mr Paawa, grunting with revulsion at the sight of the carnage, grounded Dirk for the rest of the spring break. The Home was no sanctuary. It was his trap.

Dirk carried a shovel and the animal corpses wrapped in the bloodied bedsheets out into the back field by the pond, but Donnie, who had been the animals' caretaker, insisted on burying them himself. With his weak leg, he had difficulty digging up the weed-matted earth, yet when Dirk tried to help he shoved him away. In the darkness, lit only by the distant lights from the Home, Donnie's slippery face had the sheen of a blister. 'Get out of here!' he shouted. He raised the shovel. 'Get out or I'll kill you!'

Dirk plucked the shovel from Donnie's hands and pushed him to the ground. 'You're not killing anybody, gimp.'

'You killed the animals,' Donnie said bitterly. 'The

people you steal for killed the animals. And now I'm not helping you anymore. I'll go to the police and give them what you stole.'

Dirk raised the shovel like a spear and heaved it. Donnie screamed, and the shovel dug into the earth next to his ear. 'Look, gimp, I didn't kill those fucking animals. The people who did are crazy, and if you turn me in, I'll see they get you.' He stooped over Donnie and snarled, 'Understand?'

He hoisted Donnie up, placed his cane firmly into his hands, and pushed him toward the Home. 'You get out of here,' he ordered. 'I'll take care of this.'

Donnie stared furiously at him, and Dirk could see a hideous vendetta forming in him, his eyes twitching as the rat of his brain shivered with rage. He turned abruptly and limped off.

Dirk dug furiously, attacking the earth with furor. He made the hole deeper than necessary because he couldn't stop the maniac strength volting through his limbs. He threw the linen-wrapped carcasses into the pit and heaved the earth over them. As he was stamping the dirt of the finished mound, grunting lopsided cries of anger and hurt, a voice swooped over him from beside the pond: 'You shouldn't be here, Dirk.'

Dirk whirled about in a horrific spurt of recognition. His father was standing at the lip of the pond, dressed in jungle fatigues and combat boots, dusk light stretching through him ice green and smoky red, though the night was black as space. Dirk screamed and reflexively threw the shovel at the ghost. His father caught it with one hand and stuck it upright in the mud. 'Don't break down on me now, boy,' his father admonished him. The luminiferous haze misting through him slimmed away, and he stepped forward solid as a policeman. 'Hold on.'

Waves of fright tumbled through Dirk, and it took all his strength to keep from collapsing under the impact of his fear. His blood was whistling in his ears as the coil of another scream began to unwind.

'Calm down, Dirk. I'm not going to hurt you.' The ghost stepped forward, the tasseled grass bending under his boots, and the drum-music in the boy's head boomed louder. 'I'm here to warn you. The arc has to be returned. Now. Or you are doomed – and a lot of other people with you.'

'Who are you?' his lungs squeaked.

'I'm your father – back from the dead to warn you. Return the arc. Right now.'

'How?' Dirk's breath leaked out of him.

'Find a way.'

The pallid, tremble-lipped boy waved his arms before him. 'No,' he moaned. 'How have you come back?'

'The arc brought me back, son – to warn you.'

'How do you know about the arc?'

'The arc's using *you*. Dirk. Your body's an antenna. The arc's using you to receive me.'

'From where? What're you talking about?'

'I'm all around you, Dirk. So are all the dead.'

A shout jumped from behind Dirk, and he glanced over his shoulder to see the beam of a flashlight star-webbed in the tarry darkness. When he looked back to his father, the ghost was gone.

'Mitch?'

'I never hit no boy in this Home,' Mr Paawa's voice grumbled from behind the glare of the approaching flashlight. 'But if you don't get your ass inside from now, I'm going to deck you.'

'Mister Paawa,' Dirk pleaded in a mournful tone, 'you've got to help me.'

'For sure.' The large man stepped up to Dirk with quick, long strides and grabbed him by the collar of his shirt. 'If you hurt Donnie again, if I even see 'em running from you, you found big trouble, boy.'

'Mister Paawa, I'm already in big trouble. You've got to help me.' Dirk's face was bleached with fear, and his hands were trembling.

'What's wrong with you?' the big man gruffed.

'I don't know.' Dirk covered his face with his quivering hands. 'I think I'm cracking up.'

'Tell it to the doctor.' Mr Paawa thrust Dirk toward the Home. 'Ey, move! More trouble from you and you're outta here. You think you're so radical, maybe you can make a home in the JD cage then. That's where you belong. See you pressure out there.'

Dirk shuffled back toward the Home, head hung. Mr Paawa thought he was contrite, scared of the older man's size and brusqueness, and the counselor felt he had done his duty. Dirk went straight to his room, ignored Donnie, who was sitting hunched over his desk, and clambered into the upper bunk. He lay there with his clothes on and no bedsheets. He ignored the revulsion that he was lying where Hunza and Peppercorn had lain dead. Donnie had opened a window to air out the stink of the gutted animals, and the draft slinking through the room carried the hallway's scents of ammonia and dried chewing gum. The familiarity of the odors mixed poorly with the vertiginous horror that had opened in him beside the pond. He stared at the hairline fractures in the ceiling, wondering what had brought this madness upon him and to what hell it was leading him.

'Dirk,' Donnie's voice whined from beside him.

Dirk whirled about and was halfway to a crouch when he saw that Donnie wasn't armed.

'Don't be mad, okay?' Donnie pleaded. 'I didn't tell Paawa anything. Your stuff is safe in my locker. I was talking hot before. You know, I loved Hunza. I always thought Peppercorn was a little weird. The way all cats are, I guess. But I never wanted anything bad to happen to him.'

Dirk slumped backward on the bed, exhaled his relief, and rolled his head to the side. He looked into the red filaments of Donnie's wet eyes. 'Forget the animals,' he said. 'There'll be others.'

'You're not mad at me anymore?' he asked in a voice burred with anxiety. The sight of his twitchy face only heightened the thundering terror in Dirk. What was the gimp setting him up for?

'Go to the game room and watch some TV,' Dirk ordered. His heart felt like a fist banging to get out.

'You're not going to scare me tonight when I'm sleeping, are you?'

'What about *you* scaring me?'

Dirk's face was pale, and Donnie realized that he was scared. 'You're really shook up,' he said with a tinge of amazement.

Dirk shut his eyes, and the darkness was nerved with a beaded light like the skin of a reptile that breathed brighter and darker with the mad cadence of his heart. 'Forget about me, Donnie. Just get lost.'

'You want me to get you some new bedsheets?'

'No.' Dirk sat up, his head in his hands, and he could feel his madness buzzing in him, angry for a way out. 'Get lost – now, gimp!'

Donnie spun away, pivoting on his cane, and was at the door when Dirk called out: 'Hey, hold on.' The bully dug into his pocket and took out the silver disc that he had taken for himself on the Big Island. 'You want this back?'

Donnie frowned at him, puzzled. 'What is it?'

'Aw, forget it.' He waved Donnie off, and the boy hurriedly limped away. 'Fuck,' Dirk said softly, as though praying. 'What the hell *are* you?' He looked closely at the arc, studying it for a seam or a pin bolt, anything that would hint of its construction. The metallic surface was flawlessly smooth. An opalescent whorl gleamed like a fingerprint as the electric light from the desk lamp reflected off it.

Dirk returned it to his pocket and turned to lie down again, but what he saw on his pillow skewered him with fright. Bleary with anguish, glistening with a shiny force that swirled like hot oil, a face was pushing out of his pillow. Terror cramped in his heart as he recognized the greasy features of his father, his lineaments straining for breath.

Howling, Dirk fell from the bunk and bounced off the floor and out the door. Whimpering incoherently, he dashed down the hall. Donnie, who was stepping out of the game room with his face in a comic book, collided with him, and the two tumbled to the floor. Dirk was frenzied, hysterical with alarm, and he thrashed to his feet, boosting Donnie out of his way and bolting down the hallway and into Mr Paawa.

With one glance at Donnie sprawled on the floor, groping for his cane and Dirk feverish to get away. Mr Paawa saw enough. 'You asked for it, bully boy!' he roared and slammed Dirk against the wall. 'What eye you want me to blacken, eh?'

'There's a face on my bed!' Dirk screamed.

'Watch *your* face, bully boy! Let's see how you

fight wit' someone who isn't a cripple.' Mr Paawa feinted with his left, and Dirk instinctively dodged and caught the counselor's right jab with his jaw. His head snapped back, his eyeballs rolling white, and Mr Paawa grabbed his body as he slumped. He draped the boy over his shoulder and carried him back to his room. 'He won't *ever* touch you again,' he told Donnie as he strode past him.

Mr Paawa lay Dirk on the top bunk and lifted the pillow off the bed. It was glossy with something like snail slime, and he threw it to the floor. He shook his head at the unconscious youth. 'You're one sick kid.'

The big rocks danced, and Jiang rang with life. Afternoon sunlight slanted through the tall trees and lay calm and still among moss-shawled boulders. Two of the boulders danced in the brassy sunlight – huge, gray-green bulks of rock pranced, swayed, and pivoted around each other, coughing like an earthquake and filling the air with the damp, cold scent of the soil they had hidden, a fragrance like the breath of a glacier. Jiang breathed deeply of the loamy redolence, his withered visage gleaming with pride. One of the boulders grazed a gnarled pine, splintering the trees and sending the old man flopping to his belly to avoid flying shards. The breath whooshed out of him, and the dancing boulders boomed back to stillness, one of them cracking open with a rale like dynamite.

Jiang peered up timidly from where he lay. This power was new in him, and though he exulted in it, he hardly understood it and had no idea what to expect. He rose slowly, dusting off his baggy gray trousers and gray Mao jacket. Where the boulder had split, a fossil was visible in the grain of the rock. Jiang approached it and touched the fern-shaped skeleton of the broad-headed fish very gently. What had become of him that he could open the hearts of rocks?

Until a few hours ago, when he had awoken from his dream of moving stones at will and had discovered that he *could* move stones at will and had shocked himself into a watchful reverie by building a pyramid of poised stones only to alarm the old widow and the militiaman she had brought as a witness, Jiang had felt doomed. He was old, already a teen when the last dynasty was overthrown and China's first republic established at the beginning of the Christians' twentieth century, and he had been enfeebled by a long life of manual labor and tragedies. He himself had felt like a rock melting among roots.

The dream changed everything. For the last few hours, Jiang had been feeling stout and spry, centered between sky and sod, burgeoning with power the way a flower fills with sun. The power had lifted him to his feet and marched him spritely away from his village and down the dusty road, east, to here, where thrusts of rock leaned against each other like drunks.

And the power wasn't through with him yet. Demon or god, the power lifted him like a feather. His legs and feet filled with vigorous strength and gusted him over the earth. He waved farewell to the fossil fish, the ocean of time between them like an unfocused stare. A wind-teased mist blurred his sight, and he wiped his eyes with his thumbs so he could see where he was going. Not that it mattered:

The power muscling through his legs seemed to know precisely where each footfall belonged. Old pines swung past like gibbets, the stony path smeared under his black slippers, and his body felt awake and lively with seething joy.

Jiang placed his mind ahead, contemplating where it was that his new strength was carrying him. Behind him was everything he wanted to forget: The village where he had been born, where he had lost his parents to famine, where he had lost his children to war, where he had lost himself to the debts of the past. Wherever he was going was better. Even death was better.

Beyond the rock-staggered hillside at the edge of the village, the land leveled and unrolled to the horizon in fields shimmering with young rice. Jiang laughed to see the green distances polished by the wind, and his laugh was like the chime of a bell. Workers looked up with their fates muddy in their hands and watched Jiang rushing by. No one had ever seen anyone moving so swiftly, let alone a wizen-faced old man whose wispy beard and smoke-thin hair were streaked backward by his speed. Water buffalo stopped their dolorous trudging, and farmers shouted and pointed until the galloping old man was out of sight.

With his heart in the weather, Jiang felt like a cloud in the rivering sky, drugged on the pollen scents of the fields, mindless for the first time in recent memory of the many years that had sped from him so airily. The paddies bounded away behind him, and orchard trees bristled along the roadside. He pointed his mind into the red jeweled tree haunts, and an apple swooped toward him like a bird. He snatched it out of the air and took a crisp bite in midstride.

Demon, you cannot drive me crazy! He munched the apple, grinning. He was lewd with incredulity, sexually stoked with the amazement of his demonic possession. *Carry me to the end of the earth if you will. As long as you feed me, I will laugh*!

Strength shouted in him, and his heart gulped, not with fatigue, but with esctasy. When he looked up at the clouds, they were the skywriting of the gods, waiting for his editing. He could will a cloud to vanish, and it puffed away before his eyes – until he pulled it back together in a lathery tumult of thunder blue billowings. Lightning stabbed the cloud, and rain streaked from the sunny sky. But he didn't get wet. The rain peeled around him, fuming away like the wake of a fast ship.

When he looked to either side, the world was tangled in itself like good and bad luck: A pond and its rocks like a sunken city, a rare hillock of woodland tatty with dead leaves, bamboo, and shrubs, rocky fields where the farmers were too entranced by five thousand years of hunger to look up. The land was the same China he had always known, a rag of stones and mud and tattered green. Yet the land shone, rubbed bright by his speed.

A truck laden with woven baskets filled with the seagreen brains of cabbages appeared around the bend in the road, traveling east and trawling a balloon of dust behind it. In moments, Jiang was alongside it, the dust whirling around him but not touching him. He waved to the lazy-eyed driver as he came up beside the cab, and the man hung out the window in mute amazement. The truck accelerated to catch up with the old man, but Jiang surged forward in a blue of speed that left the rackety truck clattering far behind on the rutted road.

Untainted by weariness, Jiang would have continued devouring miles until he reached the sea, but eventually the power dimmed in him. He slowed to a stroll and soon thereafter found himself plodding down the dirt road by his own weary strength. He stopped and sat beneath a shabby tree. Over the western hills, the sun was closing its wings, and the minutes of twilight were gathering in purple clouds.

Jiang felt wrung, older than he had ever felt. The marvelous power that had carried him so far from his village was utterly gone, and momentarily he experienced a spasm of horror at the unnatural force that was possessing him. The absence of facts gaped like a wound, and he waited for the pain of his ignorance to overcome him. Instead, he slept.

The dawn sun quivered like a gong, and Reena sat up straighter on the stone beech under the chestnut tree. Her bones felt like old plumbing, knocking in her with a pressure that wanted out. Voices gurgled from inside her, growing louder with the blue morning. Her hands went to her head as if to feel out the damage there. It was happening again. She was going mad. Within the impenetrable crucible of her skull, bubbling voices were bursting into words.

The oddity was, she *understood* these voices. They weren't speaking the glossolalia she had sometimes heard before, which had sounded to her like gibberish. These new voices in her head were speaking French – some as clearly as Yannick and some as garbled as the other patients.

A terrible revelation unfolded in her as the chapels,

chimneys, and rooftops of Avignon vanished in the brightening and the trees rose from the hills younger and the clouds began their silent conversations – a new day, a new life: She was hearing the thoughts of the people around her!

At first she thought her revelation was really a resumption of her insanity. Birds were jabbering their matin songs in the courtyard, and the childhood of the day was lively with the clatter of dishware and the murmur of the cooks in the kitchen behind the courtyard. Yet – beyond the moist voices of the birds and within the muffled kitchen noises – she heard people thinking. There seemed to be basically two strains of loud thoughts, both incredibly clear, unnaturally clear, as if distance could not intervene on their clarity. The first thoughts she identified were jaunty, like the birds throwing themselves on the wind: She recognized the sound and feel of the cooks in the hot weave of breakfast fragrances, and she felt Yannick and the matron, feeling awkward with what they had just seen of her: 'Her life has been locked up until now,' Yannick was saying while thinking. *Not just incommunicado but somehow bound in the roots of her blood.* 'What could have freed her?'

The other strain of thoughts was sad, desolate, and pervasive, like the gloomily purple color of twilight when the radioactive energies of space become briefly visible. That was the *duende* of this place. That was the depraved, crazy, embittered energy of this place, disconnected from the outer world – a hellishly interior energy jumping about in her nerves so fast it could never be controlled. She thanked God that wretchedness was over. That was not her anymore. She was free of that – for now.

70

'I'll bring her down to the lab right away,' the matron said, and her voice was so distinct that Reena looked over her shoulder for her. Of course she was alone in the courtyard. The upturned face of the circular walk was sweaty with dew, and the banks of flowers were still unlit.

She stood up, and the deadfall rhythm of her steps on the cobbles mimed the futility of her own thoughts. What had brought her to this? Wasn't it better to have been the way she was, asleep in her flesh, her mind held still by the magnet power of the earth, all thoughts dragged from her hold the way the body was dragged at the end of a life? What good was her mind awake if she was forced to be lidlessly alert to the tortured soul of this maimed planet? She concluded that she was the Devil's pawn.

Hearing the redundant, torpid mutterings escaping from the hospice like heat, the dark breathing, the goblin chatterings, and occasionally the breezy clarity of the thoughts of the cooks, she felt like a ghost looking for its head, wanting its skull to shut out the astral noises. The furious, uncontainable lightning of the hospice crackled its ceaseless static in waves of intensity. After a while she realized that she could dim the noise for a giddy moment by placing her attention outside of herself. She had never had attention before, and that was as eerily new to her as the telepathic gnatterings.

Reena returned her concentration to the trance of light widening over the city. The sun-daubed hills outside the iron fence glowed with the exhaled mists from the city. Staring at the industrial froth lifting with the solar tide, the cacophony of voices in her head hived off. Her mind was clear again, though,

71

deeper within, echoes were turning in the wells of her ears.

'Reena,' the matron called from the doorway to the hospice. 'Will you come with me, please?' *The poor dear looks troubled. I hope Yannick didn't alarm her.*

'It's not Yannick,' Reena said, turning away from the factory plumes. 'It's the newness of all this that's troubling me.'

The matron's face wobbled, and Reena realized that the older woman hadn't spoken aloud her thought about Yannick. The matron crossed herself, and Reena felt unholy. 'Come with me, Reena,' the large woman said in a small voice.

Reena concentrated on the sherbet-green walls of the corridor so as not to hear the matron's reaction. Inside the building, the numerous voices of the hurt minds moiled in the dark holes of her head, and she was glad to be able to shut them out.

The sharp radiance of the lab with its medicinal odors, chrome fixtures, and old, white marble countertops made concentration oddly more difficult, and she frowned with her effort to keep out the voices like a tree struggling to hold back its buds. *She looks like she's in pain,* Yannick's voice bloomed loudest. *Maybe skipping her medication this morning is not a good idea after all.*

'I'm okay,' Reena announced in the doorway. 'I'm sure it's not just a lapse in my medication.'

'What's that?' Yannick said. He was sitting on a stool at a counter with a microscope, a rack of syrettes, and stoppered flasks with cider-bright samples of urine.

Reena entered, and Yannick noted the self awareness in the poise of her stare. The green, sacklike

72

hospice dress she wore seemed incongruous with the clear, direct feeling in her face. 'I do feel clearer,' she admitted. 'And this dress does look ridiculous, doesn't it?' She looked at herself in the shiny surface of a thermoclave and plucked a chestnut blossom from her yellow hair.

'I haven't said anything to you,' Yannick told her and glanced at the matron, who was standing in the doorway looking troubled.

'Doctor – ' Reena said, facing him and then stalling at the sight of his puzzlement. The dark voices surrounded her like the muted pealings of a sunken bell.

'Call me Yannick, please,' he insisted. 'We've known each other long enough,' *Though now I hardly think I know you at all.*

'That's just it, Yannick. ' She stepped closer. 'I hardly think I know myself at all.'

Yannick sat up taller. He stared haplessly at Reena, then dismissed the matron with an urgent wave. *It isn't possible that you're reading my mind. Telepathy is a fantasy.*

'I *am* hearing you in my mind, Yannick.' She stared at him with the timidity of a squirrel. 'I don't believe this is a fantasy.'

A mishmash of wonder, fear, and disbelief filled Yannick and yanked the strings of his face. 'Hold on now!' he cried to himself and rested his head in the gap between his thumb and forefinger. He struggled to control the hysteria toiling in him. *If you can really hear my thoughts, Reena, I want you to say to me, 'The moon is blue once every three years.'*

Reena experienced a flash of excitement so sharp it was painful, as though somehow a match had been struck in her heart. She heard his voice ringing in

73

her mind with his stupendous awe – but behind that furious wonder, she felt something else in him. That something was smooth, cool, and shatterable as porcelain. It was his sanity. It was the bowl of his mind, as tangible and forgotten in its usefulness as the pan of the brain. The words he wanted her to speak rolled heavily in her like dense ball bearings. If she spoke those words, they would leap out of her fast as bullets, and their impact would blast him to bits. 'I can't!' she said in a flogged breath and covered her face with her hands.

Yannick slumped. *What's really happening here?* he wondered. Hadn't she just read his mind? *Of course not, you bumpkin. You're projecting your fantasies again.* A twinge of foolishness forked him. *A shrink's nightmare*, he laughed to himself and reached out for Reena. 'It's okay,' he said with his soothingly familiar patience. 'Just calm down. I'm impressed enough that you're even talking with me. You don't have to read my mind.' He gently pulled her hands from her face and peered into her tear-gleaming eyes with a grin. 'I'm the one who's supposed to be reading your mind. Come on, let's take that blood sample.'

She smiled back. Listening to him think had been like budging open the fire door to Hell one raging inch, enough to hear the mind's cringing torment with her bones. She *was* the Devil's pawn. But now that he was safe from her, she was as calm with him as though the world around her had never opened. She didn't want to hear thoughts. She focused on his dark, clear eyes with their steady knowing that now, she knew, knew nothing at all.

* * *

74

On the ride out to the airport, Cora hardly believed their luck. It was night, and the dark miles to Chicago were too familiar, too bleak with used car lots lit by strings of silver bulbs and all-night supermarkets in their haze of halogen spotlights to be anything special. Their old credit car, which had died months before in the pit of their poverty, was alive again, and Howard used it to buy two first-class airplane tickets. The jangling telephone back home was unplugged, and the reporters had been left behind, reduced to interviewing the neighbors. The car ride was silent, both of them too numb with disbelief to do more than drive and listen to country and western on the radio. Even the announcement on the radio news of their big win – ten million dollars big – sounded like someone else's luck. Only after they'd grinned their way past another gauntlet of reporters at the airport and the jet had taken off, lofting them deeper into the night, did their fortune seem real.

With the help of the airline's personnel, they had deceived the reporters into believing that they were bound for a getaway holiday in Miami Beach. At the gate, they had been secretly taken to a jet scheduled instead for Las Vegas. That had been Howard's idea. He felt he was on a roll – a feeling that she for the first time acceded was justified – and what better place to keep a roll going?

Cora stared down at midnight America. The ember lights of cities and towns scattered in the darkness glimmered like the dropped sparks from a comet's tail. A few hours ago they had been down there, as hopelessly fixed in their fate as those tiny lights were locked in darkness. Like everyone else, they had been dropped out of nowhere to burn their lives out where they found themselves. Now – and so suddenly – they were above all that. What was happening to them? Where were they going?

In the black reflection of the window, she saw her face. She had never considered herself beautiful, though she knew she was attractive. Or at least once she had been attractive, twelve years before when she had worked as a hostess in a fine restaurant on the north shore of Chicago. There had been no end to the compliments and passes from men in those days, and she laughed to herself now to remember how it had annoyed her.

She took out a small makeup mirror from her bag and looked at herself. The fifteen years of her marriage to Howard and her job as a diner waitress glared at her from the fatigued flesh around her eyes – brown eyes, brown hair, brown age blotches that had once been freckles. She snapped the mirror shut and put it away. She was older than she could ever have admitted until now. Funny, she thought, how one has to afford to be honest.

Howard was dozing beside her, and the well-recognized sight of his long face open-mouthed with sleep brought a smile up out of her. She wondered for the first time since the franzied miracle of winning the lottery had swept the two of them away how he had been so sure that they had won before the news had come on. Howard's wild hunches were always wrong. She shook her head and closed her eyes. Maybe that's why he was right this time. Even bad luck goes bad.

Howard knew it wasn't luck. He had seen the lottery number drawn. He had actually been there, minutes before the actual event occurred. The numbered styrofoam balls had been a cloud of motion in the hopper. One by one, with wincing eagerness, he had watched his numbers pop into the plexiglass display tray. He was convinced that somehow he had seen the future – somehow he had gone past the fabric of his skin and the seeps of seconds into minutes and had lived briefly in the future. *Is that possible?* he had asked himself continually since.

Nothing had happened during the frenetic events after winning the lottery to explain this weird experience. The real world closed in fast as a bear trap and the only escape seemed up. But once he was airborne and bound for the world's gaudiest laboratory of chance, he began to ponder his future vision.

His thoughts skittered across the surface of his mind as wild as that crumb of phosphorus he had once seen dancing on water in high school chemistry. Nothing connected, and he dozed. The retinal pastels under his closed lids trembled to a view of white waves shrugging toward shore, dazzling with sunlight on the sands. Diamond Head cut its distinct silhouette from a sky of towering, tropical clouds.

Hawaii? he puzzled, gawking through, his sleepiness at the tangy sunlight on the green water. He willed himself away from that unexpected scene and imagined himself in Las Vegas.

The chattering neon appeared at once. A roulette wheel whinnied before him, dice galloped, cards snorted their shuffles. This was the dream he wanted. The voltage of images crackled brighter in the vacuum of the dream.

Donnie Lopes juddered awake. A milk-blue light filled the room, and the bunk above him, where Dirk Heiser had been laid out by Mr Paawa, was bucking.

Donnie groggily sat up. The air was refrigerated, and he realized that it was the cold that had awoken him. He pulled his blanket off the cot, wrapped it around himself, gripped his cane from where it was hooked on the headboard, tapped it to be sure Dirk hadn't rigged it, and stood up.

Something was happening. Dirk was shrouded in his blanket, hunched over like he was heaving. Gray-blue light, like the static channel of a TV, squinted from under the blanket.

'Dirk?' Donnie called, softly. 'You okay?'

The shambling shape under the blanket trembled violently, and the icy light winked brighter. An Arctic chill swelled through the room.

'Dirk, what's happening?' Donnie said, louder. 'Come on – you're scaring me.' He reached out and pulled back the blanket.

The room blared with lightning, and Donnie's heart stopped. Dirk was writhing under gruesomely tendriled masses of gooey fire. His face, with his eyes open and bald, was glossy and just discernible beneath the leech gills of the viscous flames. The hot ichor pulsed and swelled and bulged like the ruffled skirts of a dayglow jellyfish, casting a blue shadow into the darkness around it. A scream twittered in Donnie's throat when the whole wriggling mess reared up with Dirk's limp body hung in its mucila-ginous webs.

Donnie's brain thought to flee, but his muscles, soaked with terror's gravity, were too slow. A napalm coil unwound from the abomination and whip-clutched him around the throat. Frosty pain made his viscera jump in his rib-basket, choking off his scream, and plummeting him into a blackout.

The luminous tentacle gently lowered Donnie to

the floor and covered him with his blanket. Then, hunched over, with a blanket hooding it, the fiery cold being lurched out of the room dragging Dirk in its fibrillose grip and leaving a slime trail that whirled away in silvery tufts like tiny, vaporous ballerinas.

On the roof of the Home, the monstrosity collapsed, and Dirk was spewed on to the tarpaper. The glop wrinkled into a puddle and began immediately to percolate to a new shape.

Dirk stirred. His muscles were stringy and slack, and his head felt like an empty butane lighter snapping sparks but not lighting up. The last thing he remembered was the horrible apparition of his father's face rising out from his pillow. A jolt of panic shook him – and then he remembered running, his fright galloping with him inside his heart, his whole body humming like a grenade – and finally, Mr Paawa.

Dirk touched his jaw where he had been hit. It was tender, but he could tell from the superficial sting that the flesh was hardly bruised. He sat up and noticed he was on the roof. An electric shine salted the darkness, and when he looked to see where it was coming from, a mow of panic stretched his face flesh tight against his skull.

Dirk's father was standing before him streaming blue radiance. 'Don't be afraid, son,' the ghost said in a voice from the far end of a tunnel. 'You're not cracking up. I'm real.'

'You're dead.' The words spoke themselves again, flung out of him by an appalling upwelling of dread.

'That's what I've been trying to tell you, Dirk.' The ghost was sad, at the trembly brink of tears, and that softened Dirk's alarm. 'I've been brought back to warn you. The arc has to be returned. And soon. You've seen enough signs now. You must believe me.'

'Mitch . . .' Dirk swayed to his feet groggily and reached for his father.

'Don't try to touch me. I *am* just a ghost.' A tear glinted along a seam of his face. 'You look good, son. You look strong. I bet the girls go for you.'

Dirk took the silver disc from his pocket. 'This is what's making everything crazy, isn't it?'

'That's right.' He nodded with melancholy regret. 'If only you hadn't touched it, I wouldn't be here now.'

'Then take it.' Dirk held the disc out.

His father's eyebrows curled wistfully. 'I can't. I'm just an empty shape. But there are others who can help you. They're on their way now, and they'll be here soon.'

'Who are they?' Dirk returned the disc to his pocket.

'You've seen them. There are three of them. The arc is touching all of them the way it's touching you.'

'You mean those people in my dreams?'

'They're not dreams.'

'Who are they?'

'People. I've told you – the arc is from another dimension, another reality, completely different from anything we've known. To get back to where it came from it has to be returned to the exact spot where Donnie Lopes picked it up. The arc's been trying to tell you this, but because it is from another dimension it doesn't fit inside one mind. It needs the others to reach you.'

'Okay, it reached me,' Dirk said with conviction. 'I believe you. Let's get it back.'

'How?'

'We'll catch the next flight to the Big Island.'

'You've got the money for the ticket?'

'Sure. I've got a hundred and fifty bucks.'

'Where?'

'In my desk – in my room.'

The ghost shook its head and sighed lamentably. 'The Mokes who gutted the cat and dog took it.'

Dirk looked ill. 'Christ. What're we gonna do now?'

'You may have to steal a boat.'

'Me? Aren't you gonna help?'

'Dirk, I'd do anything I could for you.' He wiped the tears from his eyes with his palms. 'But this will be the last time you see me.'

'What?' Dirk was getting dizzy. 'Why?'

'The arc is through with me. I've got you to believe. That's all it wanted me for.'

'But that's not fair. You're my father – ' Dirk's mouth groped for what to say.

'I am your father. And I love you, son.' His shape warbled like a heat mirage.

'Hey – hold on!' Dirk dashed forward and grabbled at the image. Icy froth scattered in his grip. His father's face hovered before him briefly, drained of color, blind flesh except for the eyes, luculent and imploring, dwindling to twin sparks like a star split by gravity millions of miles away.

Dirk held his shivering hands open before him, the fulgent ether smoking off his fingers. The coolness of the apparition wafted up into the warmth of the tropical night. A moment later, he was alone on the rooftop. He sunk to his knees under the weight of his dismay and stared out over the brink of the roof, past the black silhouette of Koko Crater, to the glittery brain of Honolulu.

Every thought that came to him seemed big like a cardboard toy, flat and lifeless. Pulsating with nameless feelings, he knelt for a long while, until memories of the three people he had seen in his recent dreams returned to him with a gleam like the solidity of furniture. He sat cross-legged and reviewed those dreams.

These weren't dreams, he realized at once – they were empathic, even telepathic experiences. That made him sit up taller. *Empathic*. What classroom had that word escaped from? He made fists until his fingernails bit his palms, hoping the pain would remind him of his creaturely self. The new thoughts beginning to open in him seemed more muscular. He stared hard toward the earth's far rim, where the constellations were tipping into the sea. His thoughts reached farther, around the whole earth turning in its empty bed to an old man in China, a woman in France, and a silent majority couple who were six miles above the American heartland. Who *were* these people who were invading his mind?

The answer unfurled in him like the beatitude in a shot of whiskey: He saw himself holding hands with the others in a circle that was as much a square, and in the center was the silver disc clinking its rainbows. That scene was but a glimpse, yet the accompanying thoughts were effulgent with abrupt insights. He and the others were being linked together by an alien.

His father's ghost had been right – this thing was too strange to grasp. He was just a high school kid. How was he supposed to use the welter of bizarre images that made him feel as though his brain were bulging like some balloon-headed future man? He couldn't think everything that had to be thought. He needed the others.

Reena was the one he felt closest to. She was pretty. And though she was five years older than he, that didn't matter to him. Her face appeared in soft detail, fired with red and blue spectra, and a bubble swelled in his chest. All the rancor that had pickled his heart since Tina had left him two years ago vanished. Brightenings of feelings stirred in him as he studied her features – the devilish angel breadth of her eyes, her hair the feathery yellow of goldenrod or grass heads, sexily tousled, and the wings of her nostrils alert, widening and relaxing around a breath with a smell like snow.

The generalized awareness continued in him, informing him that she was the bond with the others and even with his own power. She was the one that the arc was infusing with telepathy. Even now, he sensed her sensing him.

She was back in the courtyard of the hospice, a small bandage in the crook of her arm where Yannick had drawn blood. Other patients were there, too – vapid-faced people in green smocks, sitting open-mouthed on the stone bench under the blooming chestnut, the clear, almost white morning light lying on their tongues like wafers. Reena was at the iron fence, staring through the bars at the wooded hill that sloped down to the highway. A terrible sense of loneliness pervaded her. Though the thoughts of everyone around her were filtering through her, she couldn't connect meaningfully with any of them. If she had confirmed with Yannick that she could read his mind, he would have been damaged, she was sure of that. But what was she to do? What was this curse that had lifted her out of her stupor only to cast her adrift in a nightmare of disembodied thoughts? Where was the Devil within her.

Hi, Dirk said into his reverie of Reena and was surprised when she started. *Don't be scared. I'm a friend.*

'No,' she said aloud to the invisible being. 'You're the Devil.' She could feel the inside of Dirk Heiser's presence – she could feel the fright in him, the rage that had clubbed and smashed all laughter in him to a prank. He *was* the Devil. And she feared him. 'Get behind me, Satan!' she cried out – and the matron stared at her from under the chestnut.

Reena looked about at the numb faces in the courtyard and the nurse guiding an elderly patient on the cobble path toward the rose arbor. Dirk's bestial presence choked her with fear. The goblin noises in her head intensified until she focused on the breeze sizzling through the treetops and the hornets like points of lensed sunlight jittering among the flowers. *Why are you haunting me, Satan?* she asked in her mind through a flurry of panic, and Dirk understood her: It didn't sound like French or English, just pure understanding sharply edged in fear.

I'm not Satan, he insisted. *My name's Dirk.* Excitement threaded through him, and he didn't know what to say next. *I'm not sure exactly what's going on – it's all new to me, and it's just beginning to make some sense. But you have to understand, you're not alone, Reena.* The sound of her name coming from him was like a gentle shock for both of them.

84

Where are you? she asked, pressing her forehead against an iron bar to assure herself of her wakefulness.

I'm in Hawaii, he answered. *Do you know where Hawaii is?*

Far away.

Can you see me?

No.

Well, I can see you. You're beautiful. That thought had slid away from him before he knew what he was saying. He blushed, and he felt that emotion skip into the telepathic bond, and that made him blush more hotly. *Look, I'm not the Devil. I know I must feel that way to you. I'm a pretty rude guy – but I'm not that heavy. It's an alien that's given us these weird powers. Some kind of being from another world needs our help. I don't think I can explain because I don't really understand. But I can see you, I guess because the alien has given you telepathic power. Do you understand?*

No. I don't understand. She squeezed her eyes shut, hoping to see something of where this loose voice was coming from. Neural light freaked behind her lids, but no images appeared. *The Devil is full of deceptions. I don't believe you.* How could she think otherwise? She could feel the hurt in him as wounded as the sea. To her he was a phantom glaring with the anger of his own powerlessness. He was a scream wanting her body for a gag. 'Get away from me, Satan!' she shouted.

Dirk's mind scrambled for some intelligent reply. *I don't know what to say to convince you, lady – but I'm not the Devil. You've got to believe me. I know that's hard for you to accept, because you've been bonkers for so long. But you've got to trust me. This*

85

alien is trying to talk with us. I need your help ...
He broke off when he realized that Reena was no
longer hearing him. The bond between them was
fraying. In the next instant, his mental view of her
dulled, then darkened to the granular blackness
behind his closed lids.

Dirk opened his eyes. The fuel of his attention felt
spent, and the starry sky above the Home looked like
a huge mirror crushed to grains. *What's happened?*
he wondered, and knowledge shivered up in him.
The bonding with the others was intermittent
because the alien was parametrizing oddly in spacetime. 'PuhRAMuh-try-zing – what the hell does that
mean?' he asked aloud in a jet of anger.

A clogged feeling gummed his lungs, and he
clutched at his throat as words began to force themselves into his mind. *Parameter is the way a thing is
measured*, he heard his own voice speaking inside
of himself. *The arc is measuring itself against the
coordinates of spacetime. But the isometry – the
mapping – of the arc's 5-space coordinated to earth's
4-space coordinates is imperfect. So there are going
to be discontinuities – gaps – in communication
between the arc and its earthly counterparts.*

'Oh.' Dirk's lungs had cleared, and he sat empty
and replete as an urn. There was so much more for
him to understand, so much more for him to contain
in the squeezed space of his clasped skullbones that
a pang of hopelessness stabbed him. He sat mutely
for a while, watching the sky turn.

The disc was back in his hand before he realized
that he had reached into his pockets for it. *Arc*, he
thought. 'Arc,' he said aloud and turned the object
in his fingers, brightening with the marveling perception that this small, faceless coin was everything

that he and the rest of the universe was not. *Bizarro*!
he thought, remembering the sadness of his father's
ghost and the anguish on Reena's face. Those memories rang an adamant strength in him. 'I'll get you
back, sucker. If it kills me.'

The force of that commitment soared through him,
and a chamber opened in his mind. Mistings of
thoughts whirled out of that chamber and congealed
to knowing: He understood then, with flashbulb
suddenness, that everything his father had been
trying to tell him was already inside him, waiting to
be known. The arc was touching him with the same
suffusing, alien power that he had witnessed in his
visions of Reena, Jiang, and Howard. He was one of
them, stupefied as they all were by the strength of
the arc. Reena had the power to hear thoughts. Jiang
could move objects with his mind. Howard had a
way of touching the future. And Dirk's strength? His
strength was knowing. He felt the answers to all
their questions within him, coiled tightly like
mighty springs waiting for his needful alertness to
trigger them.

He floated to his feet like a man underwater.
Speechless with power, he gazed up at the exhaled
light of the stars and the vast surplus of black
emptiness and wondered how all this mystery could
pivot on him. The archaic nerves in his brain didn't
seem adequate to the task. And they weren't. He saw
then why his dead father was crying for him. The
loops of his body, the sparks of his mind were parts
of a machine straining to execute the commands of
something unspeakably alien. His whole engineer-
ing, the whole assembly of himself, no longer
belonged to him. He was possessed.

In an Alien Way

Mile by mile, through fiery green conifer forests, among blue hills, and along the serpentine canals that spread from the mighty Yangtze River like whiskers from a dragon, Jiang journeyed east. Overnight he followed the railroad from the Wuhu to Nanking, the gravel spinning beneath his swift feet, the silver tracks ribboning with starlight and occasional station signals. Ponds and lakes flew by, and in the darkness he sensed them by their perfumes.

When trains approached from ahead, Jiang skidded down the rail bed to the dirt wagon road beside the tracks. The thicker darkness there unsettled him. His tremendous speed burnished the dark air with electric brush lights. Puffballs of green luminance pranced around him and whirled away into the starry night. And his body and limbs were flecked with tufts of gold energy that came and went of their own accord.

Jiang ignored these will-o'-the-wisps and stayed in the clear space of the rail tracks as much as he could. No trains approached him from behind. The mint scent of the waterways in the riverine basin that the railroad followed replaced all thoughts. He was the journey that was energizing his body. Only rarely, when the wind shifted with the smell of valley grasses stained with the nightsoil of a village or a trestle bridge aimed him over a black span of water and the ghost sparks swirled in the encompassing darkness, did he wonder what was happening.

At sunset he had dozed off under a shaggy tree, and he had dreamt of a youth – a white devil with sun-crayoned hair and eyes pale as ice. 'Dirk,' the dream youth had called himself. He had a smell like wet wood. Actually, when Jiang thought about it, he realized that the youth had not said anything. The dream had been of Jiang's dead family. Wife and children, brothers and sisters – all those chewed up in the jaws of history – were there in his dream in a place as clangorous and dazzling as lightning. They were weeping. One of his children – the son who had been killed with his mother, Jiang's wife, by a wayward shell during the Communist liberation – broke free of his sobs to tell him the name of the white devil who was standing among them, gawking at Jiang.

'His name is Dirk, father,' he had said through the drenchings of his grief. 'He is the one leading you away from our home.'

The great sorrowing among all the ghosts troubled him, and he tried to comfort his son. 'You should be happy on Sandalwood Mountain now and not grieve for me. I am still part of the toiling world. I must go where the world takes me.'

'Father – ' His weepy voice melted into the keening of the others, and he had to gasp deeply for breath to go on: 'Father, he is not of this world.'

'But, son, he is a white devil. Look at him. He obviously is of this world. He is a youth from Golden Mountain.'

His son made no further reply. He and the others moaned and wailed, all in a trembling circle about the white devil. And the youth just stared at him with a stupid look on his face.

What do dreams mean? Jiang queried himself to

89

keep his mind off the sparks of gold fire moth-fluttering around him. *The ancients taught that life itself is a dream.* That was what his father had often told him in those fargone days of his childhood. His father had been a scholar, and that was why Jiang had grown up with no useful skill. He had managed to learn some of the one thousand characters necessary for reading and writing but barely enough to be literate before his father made the journey to Sandalwood Mountain, rushing there prematurely on the wave of famine that swept the countryside in the ninth year of Jiang's life. From then on he worked as a laborer, but always he cherished the few, valuable shards of knowledge his father had bestowed on him.

His father would have known the meaning of the dream. Jiang felt fortunate that his father's ghost and the ghosts of his ancestors were not in the dream. Only his own family was there, those who had known him as a man. *But why were they weeping for me?*

No answer came to him, and he thought very little more about it. The wet wind running beside him was the companion he preferred to thoughts, which only muddied his mind. Besides, the more he thought, the slower he went and the more exertion he felt. With his attention on the glassy rails of the tracks, he was a machine streak, easeful, serene, resting as even eagles rest on rings of wind. What did it matter where he was going? What did it matter what demon was carrying him? Was this demon any stranger than an aircraft bomb wailing its doom-scream across the sky or an enraged mob in full glitter trampling children and animals in their mindless frenzy? He had witnessed both and more. Those

90

horrors lived in his bones. But bones are dumb and eventually broken to the dirt that feeds plants. *Life is a dream faster than the fleetest imagination. Demon, carry me on and on. I am an old man and have nothing left to leave behind. I belong wherever I am.*

But Jiang really didn't feel like an old man anymore, and that was the chief reason why he did not object to the demonic force empowering him. The ice age that had been leaning on his shoulders had lifted, and he felt younger and more alert than ever. And here, in the stomach of night, he was the one living thing left on earth.

A train mourned from around the bend, its headlight finally appearing like the low doorway of the moon. Jiang leaped down the embankment and flitted among rasping bushes into darkness. Atoms of sunlight breezed off of him, flustering in the eddies of speed at his sides. A few of the hot motes drifted past his line of sight, and Jiang's mindless rapture was jolted. The burrs of light had faces!

Jiang slowed and looked about him. The clots of fire whipping off of him were scattering in the wake of his rush and settling like weed tufts on the ground and on the black-soaked branches of shrubs. He was still moving too swiftly to see them clearly, but when he slowed there were less of them to see. At last he glimpsed a few that were drifting slightly ahead of him, and he saw with a fascination that slowed him almost to a stop that each spark *was* a surly face buckling with cruel laughter. The train bellowed by, and its wind snatched the imp faces away, hurled them into the night.

The burn of a blizzard scalded Jiang's whole body. He looked down at his arms and legs. In the dark there was little to see. A cry sharpened in him, but he did not utter it.

He tried to run again, and the boostful energy uncoiled in his legs and sent him dashing over the dirt road. When the fiery flecks gusted about him again, he avoided gazing too closely at them. He was a crazy pony, racing for nowhere, night-mad, busy as the stars flying through the blackness. Fire-points skirled off of him like electricity breaking free and breaking up. His heart drummed its bravery. And horror and awe danced in him, old partners who needed no conversation.

Dawn clouds crumpled the darkness like a used up stencil. Dirk Heiser, who had sat up all night on the roof of the Home pondering his fate, waited until the last star vanished before wearily standing up. He was still clutching the arc in his right hand, and he held it up to the orange clouds in the east. The colors around it seemd to have changed. Instead of rain-bows, purple whiskers of light brushed the air, trembling with the micromovements of his muscles.

Dirk put the arc in his pocket and ambled back to his room. Donnie Lopes was asleep on the floor with his blanket over him. Dirk nudged him with his sneakered foot. 'Hey, your bed's two feet away,' he said with an edge of his customary gruffness. 'Think you can crawl that far?'

Donnie winced awake and sleepily regarded the floor and then his cot. 'I had a nightmare,' he groaned and clumsily rose to his knees.

'Yeah – me, too.' Dirk took the aluminum cane from where it leaned by the bed and dropped it next to Donnie. The sight of the handicapped kid, tottery with sleep, laboring to stand, inspired Dirk with abhorrence – his usual odium for all weaknesses, because life belonged to the strong. But for the first time his hatred balked, and a lenient mood flowed in him. Lit with unexpected caring, Dirk amazed himself with the perception that he was no different from Donnie. They were carnal accidents, bound by loss to the same unbegun future. They were orphans left in the care of strangers to excavate their own lives from the afterlives of their parents. Life itself was fierce and pure, instinctual. Cruelty was the impulse of the beast unfettered from instincts. Only humans had that freedom, that curse of choice that could turn the ferocity of life back on itself.

These thoughts called a silence over Dirk's acrimony, and he bent to help Donnie. As he lifted him under his arm on his weak side and guided him into his cot, Donnie gaped dubiously at him. 'Are you all right?'

Dirk's old disgust flashed again, and he dumped Donnie on his bunk. 'If I was all right, would I be here with you?'

'What time's it?' Donnie asked, the cups of his eyes wet with fatigue.

'Forget the time,' Dirk said gruffly, carefully placing the cane beside the bed. 'It's spring break, remember?'

Dirk's usual rancor for Donnie slimmed away, and the affection he felt for the bleary-faced kid amazed him. *Nothing like a ghost to turn your head around*, Dirk said to himself. The horror of the previous night had quelled to a stunned acceptance of his crazy destiny. He had no heart anymore for his petty fears or annoyances.

He went to his closet and took out his blue denim duffel bag with **WHOP YOUR JAW** stenciled in red balloon letters around a dazed, boot-chinned cartoon head resting on a street curb with knockout stars and comets whirring about it. Into the bag he dumped his entire drawer of clean underwear and socks. He selected several of his favorite silk shirts and a pair of French-seam jeans and put them in the bag too. Dirk prided himself as a sharp dresser. For the last couple of years, he had spent all the money from his thefts on second-skin shirts, filament-on-cotton jackets, and primitive print underwear. He wasn't afraid of any bad situation, as long as he looked good.

At his desk he saw that the ghost had been right: the Mokes had cleaned him out. His money was gone. He rummaged through his clutter of coral chunks, belt buckles, pen knives, decals, and clippings of motorcycles and decided to leave it all behind. He took out his two copies of *Penthouse*, buried them in his bag, then thought better of it and put them in Donnie's desk drawer.

After removing the arc and placing it carefully in the side pouch of his bag, he took off his clothes, which he had worn all day yesterday and through the harrowing night, and dumped them into the pile of laundry in his closet. For the work at hand, he decided he'd wear his western boots, black ninja drawstring pants, and a tight black T-shirt with a wide neckline and slant-cut short sleeves to reveal the muscles he'd spent the last five years eating pain to build.

The large shower room was empty, and he turned on three of the showers and trained hot water on him. In the midst of his lather, a voice called to him. 'Can't you hear me?'

He whirled about, squinting through the sting of soap in his eyes, and saw no one. He pressed his face into the shower spray to clear away the soap, and the voice returned, 'Where are you? Satan – hear me!'

'Reena?' In the noise from the showers he hadn't recognized her voice. 'Hey, I'm right here. What's going on? Are you all right?'

'I'm not all right. This is horrible. Where are you? Can you see me?'

'No, I can't see you. I'm taking a shower. What's horrible?' He shook the water from his face and turned around to see one of the younger kids swathed in his bath towel standing in the doorway to the shower room, looking at him with a querying frown.

'Some people like to sing in the shower,' Dirk told him, reaching for his towel. 'I like to talk.'

He wrapped the towel about him and jogged back toward his room, listening intently along the way. His self-consciousness before the younger kid had squelched his tenuous link with Reena. He needed to sit down and concentrate.

Mr Paawa was waiting for Dirk in his room. He had Dirk's duffle bag in hand and was rummaging through it.

'Hey, you got a warrant or something?' Dirk said indignantly when he strode into the room.

'You goin' on vacation this summah, eh?' Mr Paawa asking in an uncharacteristically soft voice, dumping Dirk's clothes on his bare cot. 'Get dressed.'

Donnie was still snoozing on the lower bunk. Mr Paawa stooped over to be sure he was still breathing and unhurt. After Dirk put on his underwear, drawstring pants, and T-shirt, Mr Paawa escorted him barefoot out of the room. 'Mistah Leonard wants to see you, tough guy.'

Mr Leonard was the Home supervisor. He was a bald, paunchy man who loved kids and made a great Santa Claus, but he'd never had any sympathy for Dirk. For the last two years he had been striving to have Dirk transferred to the State Correctional Facility for Youths, affectionally nightmared by the Home kids as the Clam: Once it took in an offender, they never came back to the Home. Mr Paawa had taken Dirk on a tour of the Clam a year ago, thinking that the grim lockup would scare some righteousness into the bully. Dirk brought along cigarettes and slipped them to the gang members he recognized from school, and they joked about going straight. To hell. The cramped, sour-stenched, and filthy cells seemed no more horrible to Dirk than the tight and uncomfortable space within the fitted bones of his skull.

Mr Leonard wasn't in his office yet, and Mr Paawa made Dirk sit on a stool in the corridor to wait for him. The stool was situated near the glass-paned door of the office where Mr Paawa or one of the secretaries could see him at all times. There was also a window that gazed out on the playground.

While waiting, Dirk listened deeply. Somewhere inside of him was Reena's hysterical voice. He could feel her like a jarred loose memory, haunting closer. He stared at the windowsill, flattened his attention against the notched, whelked, and pocked surface where other delinquents had scored their rage, and he heard her.

Dirk!

The urgency of her cry yanked him free of his senses, and he was abruptly rushing through a tunnel of charred light toward a figure standing in a bare room. The green-smocked bulb in a cage high

96

above her head filled the cubicle with mustard yellow light. The only furniture was a spread open bedroll and a pillow.

Reena, I'm here, Dirk announced, finding himself hovering mothwise about the stark luminosity of the bulb.

She didn't hear him. A pain like a tight-fisted apple was lodged in her chest. It was her despair. She didn't understand at all what was happening to her. The thud of her heart in her ears was a demented graffito against the wall of white noise that was a mix of everyone's thoughts.

Solemn, solemn, solemn – splendidly solemn.

God plays with dirt! Look at us! The splendor of his mud!

Teenie weenie meanie curled in its shell –

She's distressed. I must put her back on medication. It's the only fair thing to do.

That was Yannick. He was watching her. In the green room, under the brown light, the mad often did their dance. She wouldn't dance. She would just stand here and face him. He was behind that slot of mirrored glass in the door. He was watching her to see if she would dance. She focused on the flaked green paint on the door jamb where others before her had scratched to get out. The scabby wall was a terrain vivid enough to block the mutterings of the insane.

Reena! It's me, Dirk!

Tick-tock, mock-knock, dock-cock – help me!

Monkeys in the oaks of Bashan – elephants in the toilet – if the baby's not ready by dawn, then we'll just have to boil it.

She would stand there, brimming with Hell's

noise, until she stared herself free. The paint on the wall was chipping from the force of her gaze.

The door opened, and Yannick entered. 'Reena, thank you for waiting here for me.' He looked sullen, and his right hand was in his pocket.

'I'm not mad anymore.' Her voice sounded clouded.

'Something is distressing you.' Yannick's long face bobbed closer. 'Why are you frowning?'

'You're going to medicate me again.'

'You're much better than I've ever seen you, Reena. But you're troubled, aren't you! I think you're hearing voices. Is that so?'

She shook her head and backed away from him. The matron appeared in the doorway with a glass of water.

'We've talked about the voices before. You don't have to be afraid with me. I understand.' Yannick removed his hand from his pocket. He was holding a vial of tiny pink pills. 'These will help you. They'll make the voices disappear.'

'But I don't want the voices to disappear,' she blurted and skipped past Yannick. 'This is Satan's world. The Bible says so. Don't you see? He's the only one who can help me.'

The matron put out her thick arm to stop her. Reena stared into her glowering face and shouted 'No!'

The matron's face went simple, and her arm dropped. Reena dashed right past her and ran with all her might down the hallway, up a flight of stairs, and into the courtyard.

Amber sunlight fell in coins through the leafy chestnut tree. Vapor trails thin as scars etched the late afternoon sky. A whole day had been spent dissolving into the voices in her head. Hard to believe now that just this morning she had thought she was cured. She anchored herself to the iron fence and laughed.

Ask the sun and the moon and the stars. Go on, ask them. See if they care.

Reena, calm down, already. I'm back. You're not crazy. Not anymore. And I'm not Satan.

Where's my bifocals? Where's my ink? By the Devil's teeth, what good is memory if I can't see or write?

The white owl! God, it's eating me!

A hand rested on her shoulder. She lurched about, skittery as an animal. 'Relax, Reena,' Yannick said. 'You know I want what's best for you.'

'Why did you put me in the room?' she asked, her eyes hot.

'You haven't eaten anything all day. You've been very active, pacing the halls, returning to this fence time and again. I thought you were being overly stimulated. I could have given you a tranquilizer. Instead I asked you to sit for a while in a bare room to see if that would calm you down. And it hasn't.'

'So now I must take the tranquilizer.'

'No. I'm not going to dope you.' He took out the vial of pink pills again. 'This is a new medicine. It won't make you tired. It will just stop the voices.'

'What if I told you that the voices I'm hearing are the thoughts in other people's heads?' Her eyes were green as reef water.

'We've been through that, Reena. This morning, remember?'

She had backed out then, she remembered. Somehow she had reached tenderly into him then and had felt the measured pace of his mind – and she had sensed the terrible thunder laggarding behind the lightning of revelation that she had almost struck him with. That thunder would have shattered him, she was convinced. She liked him too much for that.

He shook out one pink pill and held it in his palm for her.

She nodded imperceptibly and took it.

After she had swallowed it, he patted her cheek. 'Now just rest here for a while. Everyone else is eating dinner. I'll see that your meal is kept warm, and you can have it later. I have to go now, but I'll see you first thing in the morning. We'll have a long talk then. Okay?'

He left, and she stared up at the vapor trails that were pinking with the sunset to veins in the sky.

You're not crazy, Reena. You don't need that pill. Dirk was giddy in the stretched light that connected him with Reena's lifeforce. The rapture of their bond ached in him like wisdom. The alien's presence expanded through him with intimations of understanding. A plenitude of knowing opened. *I can help you,* he told her with conviction.

She shut her eyes at the sound of Dirk's voice. He sounded so different from the blatherings of the other voices. He sounded closer, alert, deeply alive. He was the supreme demon.

Look, if you want to, you can pull the plug on this drug, Dirk's voice continued in her. *I feel like I know how. We can try. It's the only way we can keep in touch.*

The intimacy of his presence assuaged her fear. She could feel beyond his vicious exterior, which was all she had sensed of him before. Deeper than the brash insensitivity that had felt to her like thistly fright and drumming anger was a composure warm as fleece. Soothing, almost plaintive, a song cadence glittered from the depth of his being. Reena listened to its broody calling, lonely and weird as a wolf song but at the same time remindful of the silkiest breezes of spring, sweet with the scent of miles of grass. She sat down on the mossy ground with her back against the iron fence. When the pill took hold, she would lose this contact – and without the voices, she would be wholly alone. Even Satan was preferable to the void that she had lived until today. 'What must I do?'

Dirk's mind reeled. He was hearing the lonely song, too. It was voluptuous as a crystal. It was the diamond body grindstone of heaven, crushing the grains of time into seconds, shattering his ignorance into thoughts and words and a feeling as dilapidated and glorious as sunset. *Keep your eyes closed. That'll help to turn your telepathy on yourself. Look for the drug. You'll see it.* Those thoughts were the alien's, steeped in heavy silence, hurtling into his mind from out of nowhere.

Reena complied to the suasive voice, imagining herself looking inward. Instantly, the dark behind her lids lit up with a platinum radiance like moon-light, and silence squeezed her.

This is the light of your body, Dirk's smooth voice informed her. *Everything living glows. You're in the heat of that now. So think about your stomach. You haven't eaten all day. You'll find the drug pretty easily.*

Her attention settled under her breath to the pit of her stomach. The silvery luster of her closed eyes flickered with spark-points, crimson and azure and looped in a fine tracery of vibrations like golden threads, and she knew without hearing Dirk that this was the pink pill shredding into molecular strings. Her attention had shrunk into this kinetic frenzy, and she could see the very atoms of the drug heat-wobbling in the golden nets of the molecular bonds.

Dirk was closer now than words. He was the knowing within her. *Am I mad?* she wondered – and the silence ripped apart. The world around her screamed like a wounded mammoth. The wind in the chestnut howled, and the litter of noises from the kitchen avalanched over her.

Hey – concentrate! Dirk commanded. Frantic energy from the alien grew into thoughts and under-standings like a timelapse film of a crystal garden. *Forget what's outside of you. Focus inside. You can do it, Reena. Hurry, before the drug reaches your brain and shuts me out.*

Intently, she pulled her attention inward again. Sounds muted, and she was alone once more in the soft glare of her biofield. Attention honed to the remote effervescence in her stomach, and she found the red and blue speckles unwinding their golden loops. Only now, there were masses more of them – a swirling cloud of confetti lights in a gold haze.

The knowledge of what to do next was there, astonishing her with its immediacy. She had to go into this festival of molecular unravelings. Like a parachutist, she descended into the bustling cloud. Vison dazzled with barbed lights and the swirly mist of sunlight. The sunlight was the bond energy – and the spurs of fire were the atoms themselves.

The wavering intensity of the molecules blurred her vision, and the soft background haze abruptly resolved to jangled colors of geometric plates and amorphous blobs incandescing with ultraviolet ghost hues. *Hemaglobin, glycolytic pathways, por-*

phyrins, mucopolysaccharides, glucosamine . . . The identities of the shapes proliferated in her stunned consciousness like the mad voices that had been haunting her all day. She was losing balance.

Just look at the drug, Dirk insisted. *It's like soccer. Forget the audience. Pay attention to the game.*

Dirk's voice snapped her free of her dreaminess, and the confusion of shapes and chromatic motions hazed back into fog. The drug's chittering sparks reappeared, hotter and more crowded than ever. She glided into the midst of it and began compressing the fiery motes with her will.

The cloud of sparks broke apart only in certain ways, like fabric ripping along its grain. Carboxyl groups dispersed in fluffy trails of CO_2. The cloud thinned, and quakelike waves surged through the tangle of the drug's cell-receptor enzymes. Rainbow chips cluttered around the magenta sparks, snapped into tiny boxes, and were swept away in the colorless wind of the plasma current: The iridal cubes were open-chain aldehydes locking into methylated molecular cages that trapped the drug so that the blood could swiftly carry it away to be filtered out in the liver. The reaction accelerated like a crumbling house of cards as one molecularly boxed group dislodged several others.

The reaction would carry itself from here, and she withdrew. Bird chirrups whistled from the chestnut and the wooded hills behind the fence. The pastel thoughts of the cooks drifted from the kitchen with weary images of the bus rides to their scattered homes. Gruff mutterings spilled from the mangled minds absorbed in their eating. But these noises were no more intrusive now than the trillings of the nesting birds. The journey into her blood had granted her some control.

You're getting good, Reena, Dirk said in his lambent voice. *I'm proud of you.*

She opened her eyes, and the sky was syrupy with the day's last light. Was she blessed or cursed to have lived this day? The first shivering star waded through the sky's ethers. Impermanence blazed among the twilit clouds, and something of the supernal order she had just known stretched through her. *What's happening to me?* The silence of the encroaching night offered nothing. *Dirk – can't you tell me? I've been asleep all my life – and now . . . Now I'm more awake than anyone around me. Except for you. Who are you? If not Satan – a sorcerer? Have you made a pact with Satan? Is my mind given back to me in exchange for my soul?*

Reena's imploring face filled all of Dirk's awareness. Her vivid green eyes above sudden cheekbones were startling. Her bright hair, wrung like seaplants in the evening breeze, her nose sun-cut across the bridge like the start of a blush, and the sad curl of her lips above her strong chin where features from a love-harrowing dream.

'Heiser!' Mr Paawa's voice jolted him free of his vision. 'Move it. Mistah Leonard's waiting.'

Dirk jerked upright to find himself sitting on a stool in the corridor of the Home. He sagged into his acceptance. *Mind is the transparency of the body*, his own voice said in a wet whisper. He wondered from where. *And the body is the unconscious of the world.*

He ran his fingertips over the battered windowsill before him, wanting to imbue himself with the texture of the present. The electric tension of the alien's possession slackened, but the supernatural knowledge that had possessed him when he was with Reena persisted. The braille of graffiti etched and battered into the sill was translated by the pressure at his fingertips into neural impulses that were becoming spurts of acetylcholine in the parasympathetic nerve endings under his fingerpads. The acetylcholine itself was then hydrolyzed by acetylcholine esterase, and it was this esteratic compound that overcame the electrical impedance in the synase and continued the nerve impulse on the brain where . . .

'Are you alive?' Mr Paawa's mouth was beside Dirk's ear, and his loud voice pierced Dirk's cerebral spell.

He blinked up at Paawa like a man out of a trance.

'What're you on?'

'Nothing. I was daydreaming.'

'Save it for school. I want you to pay attention to what Mistah Leonard has to tell you.'

Dirk stood up. As he rose, his glance flitted out the window, and he saw Chud and Limu standing in the playground in the skeletal shade of the jungle gym. Freezing voltage aborted his movements, and he stood there staring through the window at the two hulking men.

'Move your tail, Dirk, or I'll drag you in there — you hear me?'

Dirk pulled away from the window and followed Paawa into the office. He figured he must have been entranced deeply because the clock above the secretary's desk said nine o'clock. Hours had lapsed. Mr Leonard was bent over his desk, scribbling something, his bald pate liver-splotched and freckled. He looked up with clamped jaw and tensed eyebrows.

'Dirk,' he said with a solemnity reserved for condemned men, 'I had you sit out there for two hours so that you'd have the chance to think over just who you are and exactly why you're here. What've you come up with?'

Dirk shifted his weight, but his gaze never left the supervisor's level stare. The crystal music in his head crushed his stupefaction into measured sounds: 'I'm a ward of the state,' he said in a lucid tone that neither he nor Mr Leonard had heard from him before. 'That's an alienating position for any youth to be in. I'm no exception. My displays of violence and recalcitrance are symptoms of my anomie. Reflecting on it, I really regret the difficulties I've caused you and the staff in my struggle to come to terms with my destiny.'

Mr Paawa, who had been watching from behind, stepped closer and exchanged an amazed stare with Mr Leonard.

'Anomie?' Mr Leonard asked. 'Do you know what you're saying, Dirk?'

'Of course.' Dirk looked at Mr Paawa, and his joker's grin revealed his backward bent teeth. To Mr Leonard he said, 'Anomie is Greek to me.' He chuckled, and the weird intelligence in him flexed like a muscle. 'Anomia meant lawlessness to the Greeks. I guess I have been lawless, at least by your strictures. Less sympathetic people would have incarcerated me by now. But you've tried to see it from my viewpoint. And I'm grateful. I'm the child of a prostitute and a soldier who was killed in an unpopular war. What does that make my heritage?'

'Don't get smart with us,' Mr Paawa said, his bull neck bulging.

Mr Leonard held up a restraining hand. 'I'm

pleased to hear you speak so intelligently,' he said, squinting at Dirk. 'You've obviously given this some thought. If you'll back your words up with consistent action, I won't be forced to take the drastic steps that I was prepared to take this morning.'

'You're in trouble, boy,' Mr Paawa interjected. 'You memorized a cute speech for us, but that won't erase all the mischief you've made or the suffering you've caused Donnie Lopes.'

'Donnie's handicapped, Dirk,' Mr Leonard went on in a less threatening tone. 'But he tries to pretend he's not. He won't take a room on the ground floor with the younger kids. He wants to do everything everyone else does. You should be looking after him, not tormenting him.'

'If we had enough room,' Mr Paawa said, standing close to Dirk, 'we'd isolate you. Like a germ.'

'The other kids in the Home in your class are more afraid of you than he is,' Mr Leonard added. 'So you see, we have no place to transfer you – except to send you down to the Correctional Facility. Would you want that?'

Dirk had listened patiently. At every other dressing down, he had glared defiantly or smirked or watched with torpid indifference. Now the attentive, concerned expression on his face was so unexpected, it galled Paawa. 'I've turned over a new leaf. I'm reformed. Emendated. New and improved.' His smile showed molars. 'These are my last ten months in the Home, and I intend to be exemplary in my behavior.'

'If not – ' Mr Paawa wound up toward a threat, but Mr Leonard stopped him with a blunt stare and an avuncular smile.

'I'm glad to hear that, Dirk. Of course, we'll be

107

watching you closely. But I have faith that this time you really will keep your word. Don't disappoint me.'

Dirk nodded, and with a charmed wink to Paawa he left. As soon as the door closed behind him, Mr Leonard's calm smile darkened to a frown. 'Something's up. I don't know what.'

'He's hiding something,' Paawa quickly agreed. 'I know that boy. He's hiding trouble.'

'Maybe. Perhaps we'd best check his locker, search his room, see if he's gone back to fencing hot goods. This time, though, it will be a matter for the police.'

Dirk had paused in the corridor to look out of the window at the playground. Chud and Limu were still there, and he knew he had no choice but to go down and meet them. But first he had to get the arc.

When Dirk entered his room, Donnie was crouched over the spilled contents of Dirk's duffel bag, sorting curiously through the clothes.

'What you looking for, Sherlock?'

Donnie, still in his red pajamas, popped up so suddenly that he lost his balance and fell in a spraddle over the scattered clothes. 'Dirk, I'm sorry. I woke up and saw all this stuff on the floor.'

'Yeah, Paawa got tough on me this morning.' He held out a hand to help Donnie up, but Donnie ignored it and lurched upright on his own.

'I didn't touch anything, really. I was just looking. Want me to clean it up?'

'Nah. It's my mess.'

Donnie looked at him like his hair had turned to pinworms.

'Look,' Dirk said, shoving his spilled clothes back into his bag. 'I'm sorry about yesterday. I was pretty cruel to you, wasn't I?'

Donnie shrugged. 'I'm used to it.'

'Yeah, well, it won't happen again.' He felt the chilled ovoid of the arc at the bottom of his duffel bag, and he closed his hand around it. His whole body shivered, and Donnie, who was watching him, sank deeper into bewilderment. To avenge the deaths of Hunza and Peppercorn, he was hatching a lethal reprisal that involved finding an AIDS-infected syringe.

'Hey, Donnie!' a red-haired, freckle-mottled kid shouted, sliding into the room. 'The Mokes are in the playground, and they're – ' He skidded to a stop when he saw Dirk and started backing out.

Dirk slung his duffel bag over his shoulder, picking up his stub-toed western boots, and smiled at Donnie. 'See you downstream, buddy.'

'The Mokes are in the playground, Donnie,' the redhead jabbered excitedly after Dirk walked out. 'They're asking for Dirk. Looks like they're gonna break his face.'

Dirk lag-stepped outside the door to step into his boots, overheard that, and smiled. The arc in his fist was an icecube. He swagged vauntily through the camphorscented hallway and down the sepia-lighted stairs. He pivoted into Carry Tiger to Mountain, a tai chi movement, whirling his duffel bag under the red glare of the exit sign, and burst through the push handle door into the wincing brightness.

While his eyes adjusted to the brash light, he reached inward for the new strength that had carried him when he had been with Reena. It was there. Glisteningly cold, not just in his palm but in all the hollows of his body, the alien power was closer than ever.

Dirk's attention huddled under the spiking rays of

his squint against the morning sun, and he focused the alien's alertness on to itself: *Who are you?* he asked.

Inertia smeared through him like the tug of a fast elevator. Sound liquefied, and astonishment gasped to fright as Dirk became aware of the alien's consciousness. It shivered with the sensation of I. It was inside him, watching him, like the still eye of a falcon hanging over everything.

By the time his sight relaxed to the hot brilliance of the outside, Dirk was drumming with bravery. He ambled across the asphalt and the red dirt of the playground in a casual gait, free as a poem. He admired the cat briers that had climbed halfway up the backstop, their leaves flapping through the wire mesh like hot green tongues. He traced the momentum of the clouds over the deep-keeled hills, feeling their soundless power billow in him. And he faced Limu and Chud with evangelic calm.

They were wearing sandals, baggy trousers, and gaudy aloha shirts that clung to their bulks like rumpled Christmas wrappings. 'You lookin' happy,' Limu mumbled. 'I hope it's real. For your sake.'

A stink, of mundungus or spongy punk tinder, tainted the air around the two Mokes. 'Clowns make me laugh,' Dirk said.

Chud jumped forward like a truck slipping gears, and Limu stopped him by slapping a hand across his chest as thick and brown as a steak. 'You got the money?' Limu asked.

'What do you think, coconut head?'

Dirk's eyes were animated, his body springy as a prizefighter, and Limu figured he had to be packing to be so cocksure. But in his drawstring pants and tight black T-shirt there was no place to hide a gun.

It had to be in the duffel bag. After this brief assessment, Limu's fist flashed out and up from his hip.

Dirk saw Limu's weight shift before his hand even clenched, and he easily dodged the blow by pulling back his head, not bothering to budge his feet. In the instant that Limu was off balance, Dirk sprang forward and whipped open his arms into White Crane Spreads Its Wings.

The blow hit Limu with thunderstroke force, and the big man flew backward into the dirt. A cheer burst from the kids who had gathered to see the confrontation. Whistles and jeers slashed the air.

Dirk pranced on the balls of his feet, but his strength had suddenly and thoroughly drained out of him. He felt blown out and fragile as a lightbulb. *What happened*? A hot filament of fright burned the length of his spine when he saw both Limu and Chud bounding toward him. He ducked toward Snake Creeps in the Grass, but his knees buckled.

Chud seized Dirk by his hair and jerked him briskly backward so he was sitting in the dirt. Limu grabbed him under the jaw and stood him upright. 'Toilethead t'inks he knows goong foo,' his tense breath spat in Dirk's trembling face. 'Get 'em in dah car.'

Dirk's arm twisted behind him with grotesque pain, and he was shoved toward a battered, rust-freckled car. Shock gripped him more severely than the searing pain in his sholder. Where was the alien? What had happened to the algid strength of the arc? the fire in his shoulder fanged up into his neck, and he howled loudly. 'Hey, let up!'

'Too late, toilethead,' Limu gnashed through clenched teeth and wrenched the car door open.

111

The pain stabbed sharper, and gruff hands spun him about. He saw the crowd of boys, their slack-jawed faces stunned loose from their voices. With roundeyed fascination they gawked to see the Home tough being taken out like a bag of garbage.

Dirk's haggard eyes glimpsed Donnie in the throng, his oil-shiny face merry with satisfaction. He leaned on his cane and waved with his fingertips like a grandmother. Then a hand fisted in Dirk's hair, yanked his head back, and slammed it against the windowsill of the car door.

Pain cracked his senses. Darkness, velvety with motion, enveloped him. He was dropping away like a calved glacier, falling free into an astral ocean of chilly black fire. Pain dimmed away, laughing voices faded, and he was alone in a lively darkness.

Weightless, plummeting, soaring, and blind, Dirk shed himself. He was dipping and drifting like the changing notes of a song. He was still as the center stretched on the rack of a snowflake. He was unintelligible. And he was the conversation in a heart.

Weird. A thought icicled in the dark, and the cold touch of the thought infused Dirk with its Being. He was moving. The very sensation of moving seemed frightfully unique. Operatic voices were screaming chromatic scales. *Neutrino static,* he thought. *Gamma and X-rays shrieking through me.*

He was in space. Of course. Everything was flying through space – though all his life he had thought of himself as on a planet, insulated from space by the sky. The sky! The thought was risible. The sky was a film of mist on the earth. It protected very little. But within that little was this mind called Dirk. A point in itself, a weird simulacrum of the pith, the singularity of 5-space. Even here in this flying apart universe with its 3×10^{78} points – quark-groups, leptons, and gauge particles – the memory of oneness persisted in a pathetic thing called Dirk.

Almost five billion skull-locked minds like Dirk! The horror of those estrangements shook the alien consciousness free of its empathic bond with earth's biofield. Knots of galaxies sprawled like electric macramé in the darkness. The galactic streamers coiled into seemingly endless emptiness. That emptiness was the truth of this radiant universe. Without it, there was no radiance. Yet with it, darkness filled all absence, existence spent itself in waves, and each embrace was hollow.

Insideout despaired that it would never go home. It needed a new way to talk with Dirk. The known dead were too full of kindnesses and old loyalties. It needed to find another image in the vacuum field, someone more neutral. Biographies rushed up from Dirk's recent classroom memories – Lincoln, Einstein, Shakespeare – So many ghosts to choose from! So many bodiless minds!

That was the alien's real horror: It was trapped in this disintegrating universe! The wholeness and timelessness of its 5-space home were lost, and now it was only a wee, ephemeral whisper in an immense vacuum. It was disappearing!

No – not yet. That was carryover fright from its bond with the humans. It was still embroidered with feelings from those many pulsing minds, and the pattern was a bewildering intaglio of sensations: hungers for food, sex, and dreams while radiation chipped and frayed the genetic sequences and the cell noise mounted to the cacophony of old age. And at any time an inanimate object could fall out of the sky and smash a skull into nothinged disorder.

So this was survival – making sense out of non-sense and finding hope in emptiness.

In the blood-drumming dark, Dirk waited. He was alone. The blood cusping through his heart thudded more loudly. The wild hope that the alien was gone gushed in him like a blowtorch, and he tried to rouse himself. But his muscles wouldn't work. He remembered Chud and Limu dragging him from the playground, and he struggled to wake up.

'Relax, Dirk,' a windy voice flapped in the blood-moaning silence.

The dark went smoky, and the vaporous shadows sparkled with crystal flakes of light. Dirk sensed that he was in the emptiness of an enormously vaulted space. Sparks flurried throught the widening dark, and a human figure appeared ahead. When it walked out of its shadow, he saw that it was Edgar Allan Poe. He recognized his domed forehead, long hair, and panda-sad eyes from the cover of his English Lit text.

'You have every reason to be terrified,' Poe said in a lugubrious drawl, 'yet I want you to remain calm.'

Dirk pushed with all his might to flee, but he was immobile, hung like a wasp nest in the dream-space, busy with fear. Poe strolled closer, tilting drunkenly, and stood unsteadily before him, his hands in the pockets of a long black coat buttoned to the throat of a disheveled neckband. His large eyes were bloodshot and filled with the starlight of tears.

'Who are you?' Dirk asked, even though the knowledge that this was the alien loomed in him.

'Insideout,' Poe said, and his forehead bulged and split like a popcorn, gray brain matter bursting forth in veiny lobes.

114

'Christ!' Dirk shouted. He was transfixed by the nightmare, and he watched unblinking as Poe's husked brain dangled before him and then withdrew in a slug-slither back into the shell of his skull.

Poe bowed with a courtly bearing that nearly collapsed into a drunken sprawl. He righted himself shakily. 'Forgive me, please.' He put his trembling fingertips to his sweaty brow. 'This is all so frustrating. But at least you know my story.'

'Yeah, you wanna go home. So why don't you just get me outta here and we'll hop to the Big Island?'

'I can't help you.' Poe dolorous face wearied sadder. 'My mind is weakening. The hyperfield is so far away, simply to stay alert requires supreme effort. I am reduced to a witness. All other effort is madness. I'm drunk with confusion. I thought you would be able to carry my full awareness – but I can only be partially with you. The rest of me is scattered hither and yon.'

'What're you tellin' me? You can't help me? These guys are gonna kill me! You understand that?'

'Too well now, I'm grieved to say.'

'Then *do* something! You've got an old Chinese guy juggling boulders. Give me some of that power.'

'I can't. Don't you see? I'm not all in one place.'

'That's stupid. You've come from another world and you can't even get it together to save yourself? Stupid. Stupid. Stupid.'

Poe's pony eyes closed, and he slowly turned away. Insideout collapsed the dream. Direct communion was impossible. The alien's mind had refracted in 4-space into four parts, and the part it needed for empathic communicating was in an insane asylum in France.

Dirk drifted gratefully away from the alien's influence and curled into the luggage of his body, half-asleep. The tread of his heart paced his fright. On one side of his dozing consciousness, the Mokes were freighting his body to somewhere convenient for murder. On the other side, sleep ranged through darkness toward the slender gray light of a dream.

He shoved himself toward wakefulness and was yanked backward into the molten blackness of sleep.

Night broke into sabers of dawn. Jiang had been racing east for hours, and though he felt no fatigue, he was hungry. Darkness was sinking back into the earth, and the terrain that was appearing in the dewy, lilac shadows was unfamiliar to him. A becalmed junk drifted on its reflection in the Yangtze. Closer to the rocky shore, another junk was turning as the men poled toward deeper water, and by that Jiang knew a village was nearby since even to his village's furious bend of the river junks often came to shore in the evening to trade their catches for village produce. He willed himself slower, and the power in him dimmed away, leaving him small and slow-stepped among a stand of bristly pines alongside the rail tracks. No station was in sight, but by staring through the scrawny trees in the direction opposite from where the junk was poling away, Jiang noticed a wheel-rutted dirt path bending around a stony, weed-stubbled hill. He sauntered in that direction.

Beyond the hill was a one-street village of clay walls and mud-packed tile roofs. He was approaching it from the back, where the village had dumped the stones from their fields, and this reminded him of his own rackety hovel that faced the nightsoil fields on one side and the rocky lot on the other.

116

Unhewed firewood and tangled sorghum stalks lay stacked between a pig sty and a chicken house, and tasseled rows of green corn grew in a field beside a tool shed. The verdant sheaves trembled lustrously in the morning breeze, spurting with birds hunting insects among the stalks.

Outside the bamboo wall of her courtyard, a woman in the black, baggy pants and padded jacket of all village women was winding plant fibers into twine by spinning a wood block dangling from the cord of the vegetable string. The fragrance of steaming dumplings fluffed from behind the courtyard wall, quickening Jiang's elderly stride.

'Good morning, young woman,' Jiang said. She was no young woman – her hair pulled back severely and knotted at the back of her head was clawed with gray – but she accepted the compliment by not contradicting him.

'Who are you, old man?' the woman asked, glancing up briefly from her tedious spinning.

'A wanderer.' He lifted his face to the trees with their green tattered buds like burst firecrackers. The heart of spring had always been Jiang's favorite season. Winter stilled life with cold; summer flaked rocks with heat; but spring brought the rain in turbulent, immense mushrooms of hot air.

'There are no wanderers anymore.'

'I am a wanderer. And I've come from far away.'

'From the western hills to judge by your accent.'

'Indeed so, young woman. I am from the White Cabbage Village near the Yangtze Gorges. I have been traveling all night, and I am very hungry.' Carved into the lintel of the backdoor was the 'tai chi' – the two interlocked fish that symbolized the cyclic flow of creation – a leftover from the ancient order before the 'change of sky' brought the Communists.

'We have nothing for you here, old man. This village is too poor for handouts.'

'Handouts?' Jiang looked astonished. 'I never accept handouts. I work for my food.' He slapped his chest to show his strength, and a smell like thunderstorms puffed off his gray, use-sheened jacket. 'Perhaps I can work for you?'

The woman glanced up again from her spinning and shook her head at the sight of Jiang's wizened face and broad but stooped shoulders. 'You look like you were indeed strong once, old man. But now what could you do for me that my own grandfather could not do as well?'

'I am old, but I am not as enfeebled as you think. What work needs to be done?' He stared down the long gully that was the main street and saw in a glance the entire tapestry of the village's work: A buffalo disconsolately pulled a plow in a field abutting the street; in the same field barefoot children were spreading nightsoil with long-handled ladles; several women sat on their knees in front of their adobe houses pestling millet: naked toddlers played with twigs in a ditch; and a young man was industriously repairing an adobe wall that the spring rains had hammered back into the earth from which it had come. This crumbly village was so very much like his own that he felt he knew who lived in each of the battered houses.

The woman before him untied the newly made twine from the wood block that she had hung from the fibers and had spun to twist the filament together. 'My husband left before dawn to trade my pastries in the next village, and he had no time to

118

finish his chores. Do you think *you* could chop firewood or untangle sorghum stalks or grind corn?'

Jiang slapped his hands together. 'Prepare my breakfast, young woman,' he said with a cunning smile. 'When it is ready I will be done.'

'Done with what?' the woman asked derisively. 'Your daydreaming?'

'Prepare the breakfast,' Jiang said more sternly and walked past her to the side of the house and the stacked logs by the animal pens. Jiang wasn't sure what he could do, but the long night of running with the wind had convinced him that he could do anything he had to do. From here, he was out of sight of the street, and no one would see the devilish power he was going to unleash. He bent over and put his hands under the top log. It was heavy. When he glanced over his shoulder, the woman was watching him with a skeptical frown. 'Don't you have work to do as well?' he asked.

She pursed her lips impatiently and walked behind her bamboo wall into her house.

As soon as she was out of sight, Jiang imagined the large logs lifting into the air and shattering into splinters. Nothing happened. He willed the logs to stand up and burst apart. Again, nothing. He knit his brows with concentration, forcing his will into the grain of the wood and splitting the logs apart. Nothing at all happened.

Frustrated, he looked up to see the sun like a vast balloon rolling along the hills. 'Where are you, demon?' he asked softly and turned toward the stack of sorghum stalks. The brittle stalks were hopelessly tangled. Unmeshing them would take most of the day. In great detail, he imagined the whole stack flying into the air, scattering apart, and settling to

119

earth in a neat pile. With clenched fists, he willed that this be so. His temples throbbed the vigor of his intent, but the dry stalks sat inert as a stack of dry stalks.

Jiang paced impatiently past the stalks and firewood, past the pigs greedily feeding on their slop to the stone corn mill. The mill was out in the open in a circle of stamped earth beside the cornfield. In large wicker baskets, ears of corn waited to be husked and the kernels shucked. The mill itself was a crude grinding stone laid flat on a column of fired clay bricks. Three wooden poles were lashed to the stone, and even with his full weight against one of the poles, Jiang could not budge the stone.

With arms outstretched, Jiang visualized his power streaming out of him and into the wicker baskets, yanking the ears from their husks and the kernels from their cobs: Cobs and husks danced into separate piles in his mind, and the kernels whirled through the air and into the furiously spinning mill. His arms shook with the vividness of his wishful command, and a passing villager stopped to watch him.

Jiang lowered his arms and slumped against the mill. The villager went his way. Alone, Jiang muttered to himself, 'You old fool, you cannot command a demon.' He put a hand over his empty stomach and shuffled toward the path out of town. At the weed-frayed end of the grooved road, he willed his speed back into his legs, and his skeleton lurched as if trying to rip free of his flesh. A cannon boom resounded behind him, and he jumped about in fright to see the firewood logs lathing in midair and cracking apart into sticks that spun like batons and clattered into a neat pile on the ground. A demonic hissing filled hearing as the sorghum stack leaped from the ground, unraveled in midhop, and dropped into a precise stack. Jiang looked to the mill in time to see the corn launch out of the wicker baskets and explode in a vortex of kernels, cobs, and husks. The cobs and husks collapsed into separate heaps, and the golden kernels streamed into the mill. With an eerie scream, the grinding stone spun, crushing the kernels to cornmeal.

Jiang shivered violently. The power was his to control after all! He limped back to the woman's courtyard on wavery legs and met her as she fearfully stuck her head from around her bamboo wall. 'What was that noise?' she asked in a splintery voice. 'I thought it was an earthquake and hid under my bed.'

Jiang laughed – his first laugh in years and years – and the laughter invigorated him like an elixir. 'Young woman, that noise was just this old man finishing his chores. Is my breakfast ready yet?'

The woman stepped out of her courtyard and gaped in astonishment at the cleanly hewed wood and meticulously separated sorghum stalks. When she turned about and saw the baskets of corn empty and the cornmeal sitting in the clay bowl under the mill, she shrieked. 'You're a demon!'

Jiang's laughter collapsed to a frown. 'A hungry demon, woman. Have I not done what you asked of me?'

Villagers were gathering and muttering, wondering what all the commotion was about.

Jiang leaned closer to the stunned woman. 'You must tell them nothing until I am gone. Feed me, and I will leave you in peace – understand?'

'Miller's wife,' one of the villagers called. 'What was all that noise we heard?'

'How should I know?' the woman asked, ushering Jiang into her courtyard. 'An earthquake – or one of the government's airplanes. I don't know.' As soon as Jiang's back was turned, she signaled with a tilt of her head and a fearsome grimace for the villagers to get help, and two of the younger ones dashed off immediately.

At a small table under a latticed window of translucent rice paper, Jiang was seated and served steamed dumplings, salty soybean milk, and unleavened pancakes chopped up and quickly fried with mustard greens and white cabbage. He thanked the woman and ate with gusto.

She watched him with twittery eyes as she prepared tea. The villagers were still outside her courtyard, marveling at the perfectly hewn wood, separated stalks, and ground corn that just the night before the woman had loudly berated her husband for not having started on. Their mumblings drifted into the narrow house.

'What will you tell them when I am gone?' Jiang asked.

'The truth,' she answered and poured him tea in a thin blue cup without a handle.

'And what does the wife of the miller believe the truth is?'

'That you are a demon.'

Jiang sipped the tea and lowered his lids with satisfaction. 'That's what I figure, too.'

The woman's nervous eyes widened. 'You don't know yourself?'

'Not at all.' He relished the tea, letting the steam unfurl under his nostrils. 'I woke up yesterday from

122

a nap and this new strength – this magic – was mine.'

'Oh, then it is certainly a demon who entered you while you were sleeping. You must see a priest and have it driven out. It could ruin you.'

'Thank you for your concern, miller's wife. But I am an old man. Life has already ruined me. Besides – the demon cuts firewood pretty well, doesn't he?'

The mutterings outside the courtyard intensified, and one of the village cadre leaders entered with a youth carrying a rifle and wearing a cap embroidered with a red star. 'What is all the commotion we've heard from your house, miller's wife? And who is this stranger you're feeding in your home?'

Jiang rose and bowed. 'Forgive me for making such a racket,' Jiang said. 'I simply did some chores for this woman, and she has rewarded me with a fine breakfast.'

'He has chopped all the firewood, sorted the sorghum stalks, and ground the corn for me,' the miller's wife said in an excited burst, 'all in an eye-blink!'

'What are you blathering about?' the cadre leader asked angrily. 'Do you think I'm a fool?'

'You can see for yourself,' the woman insisted. 'All in an eye-blink! Didn't you hear the noise?'

'Who are you, old man?' the cadre leader queried, studying Jiang closely but seeing nothing at all unusual in his features, dress, or manner.

'I am Jiang Cheng-yu from the White Cabbage Village of the Yangtze Gorges.' Jiang bowed again. 'I hope I haven't alarmed you. I'm just passing through.'

'On your way to where?'

'Wherever my feet take me.'

'Don't be flippant with me, Jiang Cheng-yu,' the cadre leader snapped. 'You will find yourself in trouble with higher authorities if I don't get very clear answers to my questions.'

'No disrespect is meant, sir,' Jiang said, bowing again. 'I don't know where I am going. I am a wanderer.'

'There are no wanderers,' the headman insisted. 'Where are your travel permits?'

'I have none.'

The cadre leader squinted. 'Then we will have to take you to the district police so that they can decide what must become of you now that you've wandered so far from your village.'

'But he has magic!' the miller's wife blurted.

'Be silent, woman!' the cadre leader barked. 'Bring him with us, comrade,' he ordered the youth with the rifle and militia cap.

'Forgive me, but I can't go with you,' Jiang said. 'I stopped here merely for breakfast. I am grateful to the miller's wife for that. And now I must be on my way.'

'Our way is your way now, comrade,' the cadre leader said and nodded to the militiaman.

'I don't wish to hurt anyone,' Jiang said as the militiaman took his arm and guided him out to the courtyard.

'Then come with us without fuss and you won't be harmed,' the cadre leader promised.

In the courtyard, Jiang willed his speed back into his legs, and his body shrugged like a wild horse. The militiaman was flung into the bamboo wall so forcefully that the wall collapsed, and the crowd of gathered villagers gasped.

'Forgive me,' Jiang apologized and stooped to see

whether the young man was all right. But when the stunned youth shook off his shock and reached angrily for his rifle, Jiang bounded over him and skipped like a startled springbok for the path that led back to the railway.

The villagers whooped in amazement, and the sound of their cries paced him as the great strength in his legs carried him out of their sight in a blur.

Jiang was angry at himself for having stopped. This was not an age of marvels. This was the same world of tyrants and greed that he had always known. He couldn't barter magic for food without becoming a prisoner.

Jiang ran without stopping until he caught up with a freight train traveling east. Along the way he passed ox-driven carts, farmers in their fields, and fishermen on the river, but he didn't slow for their astonished shouts. Once he caught up with the train, he leaped onto the back of it, clutching the iron ladder at the back of the last car, and climbed up to the top. There he lay down and watched the bucolic landscape roll by.

The hills to the north looked laggard, and the river to the south was low, showing her boulders like bones. The brassy sun made the water shiver, and the shawls of her currents spread wide in the midstream and pleated toward the shores. The sight was restful, and the reverberant choir of the rocking train lulled Jiang to sleep.

The white devil was waiting for him in the lightning-colored dream. The dead were not there this time. The white devil looked as confused as he. 'Your name's Jiang, right?' the young man asked.

Voices were ruffles of echoes. 'How do you know my name?'

'I don't know,' the youth said. 'I guess, the same way you know my name – from these dreams.' He looked around with startled eyes at the hideous silver fire enclosing them.

Jiang thought and remembered the dream where his dead son had named the youth. 'Dirk,' he said, and his voice drummed in the lunar silence.

'Yeah, that's me. Look, you're Chinese, right?'

'Yes, I am from White Cabbage Village near the Yangtze Gorges.'

'I'm from Honolulu in America.'

'Ah, Golden Mountain. That is a place I've heard many tales about but can barely imagine.'

'Well, you'll be seeing it firsthand pretty soon.'

'Is that where this demon is taking me?'

'Yeah, I think so. There's some kind of thing from another dimension that needs our help.'

'Yes, A demon.'

'I guess that's as good a name as any for it. This demon needs us to help get it back home. That's about all I really understand so far. I'm sorry you've gotten caught up in all this.'

'No need to be polite. I am proud that the spirit powers have chosen me for this work. I had thought that my life was spent. I have no family, and so I had believed that my life had come to nothing. I am glad to be of some use. Only one thing disturbs me.'

'What's that, Jiang?'

'My children and wife. They are dead, yet I saw them in my last dream – with you. They were weeping pitifully. It hurts me to think that they are unhappy.'

'I know what you mean. My dad's dead, and I saw him in a dream, too. He wasn't happy.'

'Can you show me the demon that we must return to its home?'

'Sure.' Dirk opened a pocket among several pouch pockets with snaps on his beige pants and took out a silver coin. He held it up, and it disappeared against the mirrorgloss of the dream. Out of its invisibility, motion whirred, and a shadow of blowing whiskers and twitching hairs appeared and loomed closer.

Pincer legs and snicking mouthparts pounced out of the glare, and a spider face lunged into the dream. Jiang howled and thrashed awake.

He sat up into the rush of the wind and had to clutch at the shuddering wood planks of the train's roof to keep from tumbling off. What he saw displaced the fright of his dream with awe. Tiled roofs were jouncing by, and a cityscape stretched to the limits of his sight. The brakes hissed and squealed, and station platforms swung into view among cranes and trestles. A sign jogged by with the name **NANKING** in bold red ideograms.

As soon as the train stopped, Jiang climbed down the ladder and hopped to the platform. Porters and workers stared at him, and he ignored them and strolled wide-eyed across the trainyard. In the almost ninety years of his life, he had never once been to a city. The station's restroom at first confused and then amazed him with its flush toilet. After relieving himself, he ambled out into the noisy street, stunned by the crowds, the fleets of bicycles, and the paved roads shared by cars and wagons alike.

Looking up at the sky was like gazing out of a ditch. A few trees appeared on the wider boulevards with the joyous familiarity of old friends in this alien place of concrete and asphalt. He was tempted to sit under one and watch the bustle, but the very power that had carried him this far from White Cabbage Village was still urging him on through the stink and press of the city.

Where am I going? he wondered. The memory of his dream on the train circled back on him. *Was that truly a dream?* It had been more like a spirit visit, warning him of the danger but specifying nothing. Thinking about it, he realized that he had no choice but to relent to the power occupying him. That hardly seemed a chore since for the first time in many years he was not fatigued. He moved through the currents of people like driftwood, letting his body choose its own direction.

Sooner than he would have guessed, the clogged streets and towering buildings were behind him. Low buildings with red-tiled roofs jammed the flat terrain, and not far away factory pillars coiled thunder-clouded fumes into the sky. The railroad curved out from the factories, past the packed-together houses, south, in a splay of numerous rails. Jiang jogged along the tracks, waving at the railyard workers and the passengers on incoming trains.

With eerie speed, he watched the landscape rush past him. His legs were a blur, his feet like invisible flames, yet his arms rhythmically swayed at his sides as though he were a man out for a vigorous stroll. The engineers of the trains he passed blared their whistles at him and called ahead to the next station their sightings of the wind-running old man. But the eerie strength guiding Jiang outwitted all attempts to monitor him. He switched tracks, he ran through stations unobserved by paralleling passing trains, and, most effectively, he defied reason and so he avoided official scrutiny by not being reported to the authorities.

Cities, alike in their morose squalor, hopped by: Chinkiang, Changchow, Wuhsi, Soochow. The frazzled red and brown roofs, the soot-stained walls scribbled with scarlet ideograms, and the rickety fences and ramshackle trackside sheds looked to Jiang like autumnal litter waiting for the cold. An occasional flowering tree graced the desolate corridor of smudged walls and houses that had been worn ragged by the rushing trains.

The intoxicant of the blossoms reminded Jiang of his home and the great distance he had traveled in one day. A tint of horror suffused through him at the thought, and he glanced down at his body to see if the ghost fire he had seen around him last night was still there. It was. A transparently slim light enveloped him, spinning off in swirly tangles of energy. He stared hard at the indistinct streamers and saw again, with a stab of fright, the tiny, evil faces in the loose-flying flames. He put his attention back on the trackside houses, where clouds mopped the cluttered roofs.

By late afternoon, he had zipped through the massive switching yard at Shanghai and had arrived at the wharves. Huge ships under hulking derrick towers congested the harbor. Stevedores flurried industriously between warehouses and piers, gulls whirled and screamed, and the air was freighted with the effluvia of the sea.

Jiang's inhuman speed puddled out of him on the tracks, and he crossed the rails and the loading docks by his own frail effort. He slumped beside a tar-speckled, guano-streaked bollard and watched a cargo ship preparing to depart. The firm conviction that this was his destination swelled up in him, and he studied the busy wharf and gangways for a way to board the ship.

The gangways were being lowered and cranes swung aside, and there seemed to be no direct way to get on board. Jiang knocked his fist against the bollard in frustration and then noticed the thick rope that extended from the bollard to the ship. Without hesitating, for the other lines were already being cast off, he leaped up on the rope with a spryness that delighted and terrified him and, faster than a man sliding down a greased ramp, he scurried up the rope and on to the ship's deck. Delighted by his advantage over everyone, he peered down from the bulwark of the ship and saw men bent to their labors, too intent on their efforts to notice him. Terrified by the poise of the living steel coiled in the muscles of his legs, he almost shouted at the sight of the oil-green water sloshing below him, his black-slippered feet more like paws, gum-soled as a lizard's.

Voices chattered closer, and Jiang scurried along the deck in the opposite direction, seeking an open door. Everything was secured. In desperation, he threw himself at the nearest hatch and heaved at the lever handle. It wouldn't budge. The voices chattered closer, and in the last ravening seconds, he willed celerity into his muscles. Enraged strength kicked through his bones, flapping every muscle of his body, and the latch turned, lurching the hatch open and tumbling him into darkness.

He closed the hatch quickly, then looked to see where he was. A caseous light like moonlight tingled in a large vault of stacked crates and boxes and stuffed burlap sacks. With a stifled parrot's shriek, he noticed that the lunar glow in the chamber was seeping from his body. He sprang to his feet like a released genie, his splay-fingered hands on his chest. The pale glow was leaking through the fabric of his clothes, raying from the pores of the exposed flesh on his hands and face.

A porthole was situated on the far wall between stacks of lashed crates, and he went over to it, opened its latch with the heel of his hand, and admitted natural light into the room. The spooky flesh-shine vanished in the stronger illumination, and relief swelled in him. He paced the packed chamber and saw by the few stenciled ideograms he could read that the cargo of this hold was food. Sacks of rice slumbered atop each other, crates of canned peanut oil and boxes of dried noodles flanked the porthole, and cartons of various nuts, crackers, and dried fruits were neatly piled in wooden bins.

Jiang opened a container of crackers and one of assorted dried fruit and began to eat. That seemed natural. Why else would the demon have led him here? He was bound for wherever the ship was bound, and this was his next meal. He stood at the porthole, nibbling and watching as the big ship was tugged from the pier and guided out of the harbor. The sounds of busyness on the dockside dimmed, and the vibrant noise of the ship's engines came on like a giant's mutterings.

Clouds galleried about the sun, low over the retreating shoreline, and the last that Jiang saw of China was dazzled in sunshafts. He watched until the land was a black silhouette against the green shadow of the sunken sun. *Goodbye homeland*, he thought. *I gave you my life, but my death lies elsewhere.*

The hatch rattled as the lever was shoved open. Jiang ducked quickly behind one of the wooden bins, and the hatch swung aside. A white uniformed man entered with a clipboard in his hand. The overhead electric lights came on in a flutter, and Jiang was able to watch the man's shadow from where he crouched. When the shadow veered left, he skulked right, duckwalking around the side of the bin. The instant he saw the sailor's back, he dashed through the hatch on to the deck.

The sea air wound about him, and he let the excitement of his unknowing hurry him along the deck. Night reared ahead. A waterfall of stars glimmered in the direction that the ship was sailing. Behind, an emerald bar of dusk was fraying into wire whisks of red light.

The ship seemed almost abandoned. In Jiang's imagination, ships bustled with deckhands. The riverboats on the Yangtze Gorges were continually astir with people. Here, spindrift crossed the bare decks like ghosts. Jiang wandered to the end of the main deck where ladder steps ascended to a well-lighted pilothouse. A figure appeared at the top and hurried down. Jiang glanced about for a place to hide, but there were no hatches nearby. He would have to rush across the deck toward the cargo hold to find a doorway, but then he would certainly be seen. The sailor coming down the stairs turned to hop the last few steps, and Jiang ducked under the ladder. He urged his power to fill his body and reached up for the overhang of the upper deck. Invisible cables hoisted him up, and he clung to a steel support as the sailor reached the deck and walked under him.

Hanging in the dark, Jiang observed again the cold, wispy radiance about his body. The sailor was directly below him, talking into an intercom in the bolt-studded wall at the foot of the ladder. Jiang couldn't move, and he hung there in his cocoon of pallid light, hoping the man wouldn't look up or see the glow.

While he hung with his cheek pressed against the steel, his fingers and ankles clasping the support, the dull fire about him did a frightful thing. It pulled away and swirled into a bodylength of refulgence alongside of him. Jiang watched stupefied as the astral smoke bulged with definition and a being congealed beside him. It was horrendous. Its length was segmented like an insect, tightwaisted as an ant; its limbs were stunted buds cleaved and twitchy as claws; and its horrible head, inches from Jiang's sweat-pearled face, was an abstract mantis mask with vividly simian eyes, madman's delirious eyes, above fang-meshing mouthparts.

Jiang screamed. His grip relented, and he crashed to the deck. The sailor at the intercom leaped about with a shout, then stuttered into the voice box. He bent over Jiang, who was stunned, his eyes fluttering. He slapped the old man and sat him up.

Jarred by the fall, Jiang came around groggily. He searched for the monster and saw men charging down the ladder and stooping over him.

'It's just an old man.'

'A stowaway.'

'Better call the captain.'

'Don't be stupid. We were the ones who were supposed to be at the gangways during loading. You feel good about winning with your lucky dice now, dolt? It'll come out we weren't on duty, and we'll all be docked for this. We're not turning back for an old man. That means his food and the cost of returning him come from our pay – not to mention the penalty for gambling if that's found out, and where else would we have been, eh? We'll lose our jobs for sure.'

'Dog guts!'

'Throw him overboard.'

'Sure, who's going to know? Come on, He's just a peasant, a turnip-head. Look at his clothes.'

'You can smell the pig shit. Over he goes.'

Laughter swung hilarious loops in the air almost curling into howls, and hands grabbed Jiang and lifted him. He shook his head, trying to clear his jolted brain. He struggled instinctively, but the sailors' grips were firm. He felt the rail of the ship brush his back, and the white streamers of the ship's wake flashed phosphorescently in the darkness below him.

As he was flung into the air, Jiang's clarity asserted itself, and he reached within his will for the demon power. Too late. He sprawled into his fall.

His muscles thumped powerfully, wrenching him iron stiff, and then going limp as lint. His plunge into the sea stopped inches above the curling wake. Gradually, like a gull facing into the wind, he rose, grazing the sea-mist fuming off the dark swells. He laughed at the stupid shock on the faces of the sailors and pulled up toward the tapping stars.

With arms and legs outstretched to embrace the sky, Jiang sailed into the night, swooping once past the crouching men who had thrown him overboard. The demon power launched him far ahead of the ship in a tremendous lunge of speed that tugged back his hair and whiskers and smeared his features into a bulldog's frown. He shivered with the frost of space, his eyes wind-burned and weepy with

134

wonder, bright with the fury of wonder, as he tilted into the earth's curve.

His body was blazing with blue-black light. He could see his reflection in the sea below, flitting like the full face of the moon over the dark water and the lacings of wave froth. Yet even as he was watching his bodylight shadowing him in the sea, the lunar glow flared away from him. Jiang rolled to his back and saw a ghastly sight. The violet luminescence about his body had pulled away again and taken the shape of the demon he had seen on the ship. Its ravenous maw was stretched in a shark's gape, brambly with fangs, and the clasped hemispheres of its hairless head glinted with numerous spider-beaded eyes. Jiang willed himself faster, and he felt earth's hug tighten and abruptly relent, spewing him at bone-aching speed over the black span of the ocean.

The demon figure was attached by a hot green umbilical cord, and it trawled on its taut line behind Jiang. But the speed disfigured it. The thing was not as substantial as he, and its gruesome features bleared in the wind-rush like a torched wax figurine. As soon as it was reduced to a blob of blue luster with furry red sparks, Jiang slowed. The tremendous burst of speed had strained every muscle on his boneframe and rubbed the air around him into a hot flash of green fire. The nervous flames smoked away, and from a great distance thunder rolled across the star-splattered night.

Coasting on his back, Jiang studied the shapeless mass of ultraviolet glow shadowing him. He passed his hand through the glisteny strands coiling from his navel to the cloudy light, and nothing changed. Whatever it was, it was made of bright ether. He

135

could see swirlings in it, like alcohol immixing in water. Particles of shadow and flechettes of blue fire whorled in a busy pattern that with the gradualness of weather was beginning to take shape. The pincered arm buds were the first shapes to appear at the vaporous fringe of the billowing phosphorescence. The seamed head began bulging forth next, shiningly oiled, its fanged chewing plates and black dewdrop eyes lolling drunkenly on a tiny neck joint.

Jiang commanded his strength to burst the foetal mistings apart. The effort only speeded the monster's twitchy growth. The pleated gills along its dolphin-muscled flank webbed open, and a searing screech stabbed Jiang. The sharpness of the scream gored his brain, and the power snuffed out in him, plummeting him into the ocean.

Cold water ripped over him, and he flailed into the darkness. He didn't panic. He was a good swimmer. After all, he had lived all his life at the most riotous bend in the mighty Yangtze. What was a calm ocean, however deep, compared to the treacherous currents and whirlpools of his river?

In the moments it took him to rise to the surface, he kept his eyes open in the stinging water, looking hard into the utter blackness for the demon light. He saw it. It bristled with energy in radiant urchin spikes, and Jiang burst the surface and drank air.

He willed himself into the sky again, but the power was gone from him. Like a piece of the moon in the sea, the monster light circled him twice while he treaded water – then it too vanished. Darkness covered the ocean to the circular horizon where the stars were so bright they looked wet.

He wondered if he had killed the demon and with it his own power. *Is this all?* Jiang asked himself. *A demon has carried me away from my home to throw me into the sea? Or are there two demons – one of power and one of craziness?*

Silence answered him. Yet within the void – and with no more wattage than an imagined voice – was the demon. Jiang heard it with his inmost ear, apologetic as a bumbling monk: 'Am I not a grub? I can't even control myself. My craziness has run away with my strength and left you there to drown. What have I done?'

'Help me!' Jiang called. But the demon, or his imagination, had flitted back to silence.

Real or imagined, all voices made little difference now. The strength in him was crumpling and soon would tear, and then he would drown. Only the dreams of the white youth, Dirk, had led him to suspect that something more than an exotic death was in store for him.

He imagined Dirk vividly and tried to fly again. His will was empty as a wish. *A dream, after all, is just a dream.* He spat out the salt water and lifted his face to the cringing stars.

The painbuffers in the titanohematite brain were breaking down. Sporadically, Insideout's consciousness drained away to help bolster them. Without the buffers, the agony of its distance from the hyperfield would make human contact impossible. As it was, the four minuscule minds it was touching were fading in and out. And the lapses were going to get worse as its stamina wore down. Despair cancered through the alien. How could it hope to save itself among such tiny minds?

Insideout loosened its grasp on the humans, and 4-space widened around it. In a blackness shivering with inner motions, clusters of light cones were suspended. The clusters formed a brilliantly faceted gem shot through with smoky darkness. Every point inside the gem seemed the center.

The center that Insideout had just crawled out of was the human plane, a dull facet of the gem. The human dead were there as pale bristles of luminance, slender light cones, barely visible among the coruscations of other life. Only the flash of radio and microwave noise from human technology made this mind outstanding in the sparkling radiance of the tesseract range. Human space was small, and its smallness was acutely obvious so close to the cetacean minds, which glowed like a galactic splash.

Insideout longed to return to its ocean friends, to spend what little time it had left happily, in yes-out-of-mind. But it wasn't strong enough to leave the hole that it had crawled into. Its strength was bleeding away moment by moment. And its consciousness was wrinkling smaller – becoming more human.

The night sky was a skillet greasy with stars. Howard Dyckson sat in the passenger seat of a red convertible that was cruising eighty miles an hour into the desert. The driver was a slick-haired, narrow-faced man with a pencil-line mustache and a blue silk suit. His name was Tony, and he was taking Howard to a private card game at a desert ranch.

Where didn't matter to Howard. Where was always right here in the time-melt, minutes ahead of everyone else. Remorselessly ahead. In the tumble-hours was a clatter of scenes: He saw a green felt table and kaleidoscoping playing cards. Ahead. He watched a hurry of slow hands and crooked faces – and at the end of it all the loud neon of the city and

138

Cora laughing in their hotel room. Miles of time teetered before him.

Behind them, Las Vegas was a smear of light on the black horizon. Howard and Cora had arrived several hours earlier from Peoria. Cora was exhausted from exhilaration, weak with delight at the millions they had won, and as soon as they arrived in their posh hotel room, she collapsed in a euphoric heap on the immense bed. But Howard was too wound up to rest. He wanted to assault the Sleepless City, and Cora reluctantly agreed to tag along. Howard was popping like a street dancer when he exchanged his pocket money for betting tokens. She made him promise that he would stop after he lost them. He promised her with a smile as self-assured as a monk's.

Howard accepted a glass of complimentary champagne from an underwear-clad cocktail hostess and breathed in the carnival energy of the casino. He strolled among the one-armed bandits, frisky with the stupendous sensation of seeing just beyond the crested moment. The machines grunted and clanked in a loud frenzy that backdropped the dazing clangor of winners-yet-to-be. Howard could hear them across time. As he passed a machine about to pay off, he could hear the echo of its bells bounding back from the near future. Unerringly, he went from winner to winner. Roulette was the same. The upcoming winning number hung motionless before his eyes in the gauze of the wheel's spinning motion *before* the wheel was spun. Within two hours of their arrival in the city, they had visited three casinos, doubled a thousand dollars ten times, and won over a million dollars.

'Howard, why is this happening to us?' Cora asked

him when they were alone again in their penthouse suite. The ten million they had won in the state lottery was a shock – but here, lying on a lordly bed covered with a million dollars in cash, here they were beyond shock and in the demesne of Unknowing. The events of the last day were unbelievable, incredible, beyond understanding – she thought. And, in fact, she was right. Cora was smart that way. When life became overwhelmingly ridiculous, she knew how to stop thinking about it and sustain herself on life's primal simplicities: During the time that Howard was laid off from Caterpillar and he had gambled away all the money they had saved and she was actually feeling grateful that they couldn't have kids, she still kept up on the housework, made herself pretty, and wore sexy underwear for Howard. If she could rise above the stifling humility of poverty, she figured she could handle being unjustifiably rich.

The muscadine scent of all that cash was a pungent aphrodisiac, and Cora forgot her exhaustion. With her fingers in her husband's thinning hair and her mouth close to his ear, she asked, 'How can anyone be this lucky?'

Howard pretended ignorance. In fact, he *was* ignorant about how his blessing worked. Or even if it was a blessing. He'd seen enough horror movies about crazed fortune tellers and ill-starred time travelers to wonder whether his power to glean the future was possibly a luck-disguised curse. That's what kept him from telling his wife about his new power. After fifteen years of marriage, he knew her well enough to keep this secret. She was too conscientious: She recycled the paper of used matchbooks. Their last argument had been about her need to donate a portion of their welfare check to famine relief in Timor. If she knew that he could peek into the next moment, she'd insist that he turn himself in to some scientific institute for the good of humanity. And right now all he wanted to think about, after a decade of hard work and near poverty, was the good of the Dycksons.

Even during the rare spells of reckless honesty that swelled in him when he thought about his fortune and Cora's faithfulness to him during his years as a loser, he couldn't square with her. The timelines wouldn't let him. The timelines were the contours of movements and shapes yet-to-be that he saw fleetingly about everything he stared at. The overall effect was like a Cubist painting. Strata of images layered his visual field, and the scene of what was really before him was not so much clouded with possibility shadows as laser cut into actuality from time's cumulus: His sight was never sharper, and he noticed details that had always eluded him. Objects broke the space around them into a mosaic, a hyperbolic lattice of time echoes, so that within their busy auras, each object was louder in its clarity. When he looked into Cora's face, he saw her dimpling shyly at twenty-two on their honeymoon, he saw her old, her face eroded by her tirelessness, and most clearly of all he saw her now, her large dark eyes dream-fetched by whatever blessful thing she was thinking about his face. He wanted to tell her then about his new way of seeing, but as he thought that, the timelines shifted, and in the glass of her face, he saw himself, the flesh sloughing from his skull like a serpent's old skin.

Howard fobbed off his winnings as pure luck, and Cora, like the amazed casino cashiers who had exchanged his chips for bucks, believed him. What else could she believe? The hour was late – two in the morning desert time – and she was delirious with the suddenness of their wild fortune. They tumbled in the bed among the raw money like hyperkinetic kids. And for the first time in recent memory, they made love magically, hourlessly, until they were hollowed out, their bodies sweat-pasted with hundred-dollar bills.

Howard tucked in his exhausted wife, showered, and dressed in the cream cotton summer suit he had purchased when they first arrived at the hotel lobby's all-night garb shop. He collected a hundred thousand dollars from the heaped cash on the bed and stuffed his pockets with the bills.

'Where're you going?' Cora asked through the smoke of sleep.

'My luck isn't tired,' he said, kissing her eyes closed. 'I'm taking it for a walk. I'll be back for breakfast. Get some sleep. You're going to need all the rest you can get. Spending money is hard work.'

Cora let him go. He had earned his night on the town. She went with him in her heart, but her body was stunned silly by fatigue and giddiness, and not even the stupendous amount of money all around her was enough to hold her awake. She soared toward sleep contemplating the good deeds this money would buy for the old friends of her new life.

At the first casino Howard returned to, he met a thin-mustached, silk-suited gambler called Tony Robello. Money pastiched the time-quilt around him. They met at the revolving bar where Howard had gone to steady himself with a few drinks. Beer had been Howard's sustenance since he was sixteen, but on the flight from Peoria he had discovered that stiffer doses of alcohol helped him to control the jostlings and surges of his prescience. He had been stewing in a welter of ghostly images – sunlight-wincing glimpses of white sand beaches, criss-crossed palms, volcanic craters, and a punk with blond windcast hair and eyes like shattered glass. After a couple of Scotch and sodas, the distracting sun-washed images had disappeared, and he had been left among the brilliant spanglings and neon pulsings of his anticipation of Las Vegas. Since arriving, he had been careful to keep his intake high, much to Cora's consternation. The alcohol, however, had no apparent effect on him. He walked straight as a gunslinger, and the only doubling of his vision was the eerie superimposition of his future sight.

Tony watched Howard put away three double shots of whiskey, and he had to restrain a grin when he sidled up to him. He had seen the balding, Adam-appled hick win big earlier at the blackjack table, but he hadn't approached him then because he was with his hick wife. Now he was alone, and he was the ideal mark for the game his employers played. Tony was paid to round up suckers for private card games that were subtly rigged to favor his bosses.

Howard saw money, bundled stacks of old bills, in the diamond splinter light quilling about Tony's sleek head. He became interested in a friendly game of poker away from the brash environs of the city. In the short time that he had been in Las Vegas, his foudroyant winnings had alerted all the casino hawks, and he was uncomfortable with the crowds that had begun to gather at whatever table he visited. His outlandish enthusiasm for the games only drew more attention: He couldn't help but howl when he won. Anything less would offend the powers that were gracing him. When he won big, he did his chest-thumping gorilla dance. The gods were pleased. His light-webbed vantage on the future persisted.

On the ride out into the desert, Howard lifted his face to the flexing stars and for the thirty-ninth time in the last five hours questioned what was happening to him. Every time he had wondered how he could see the future, he had drawn a blank. But this time, an answer offered itself.

The sun-golden wastrel with eyes like chipped glass, whom he had seen before in his visions of Hawaii, appeared in a sudden tangling of rainbows. 'My name's Dirk,' the apparition said in a soundless voice. 'I'm your friend. I guess I'm more like your work buddy. We've been brought together by an alien – some being from a world we can't even imagine. This alien needs our help. Got that?'

Howard gazed up from the headrest serene as a cobble in a streambed, the cool desert air rivering over his face. The ghost before him was like all the apparitions gazing backward from the future – enameled in sun-gel, brighter than sight yet without the pressure of vision, as though the image were merely imagined. *You're different*, Howard thought. *You talk back.*

'I'm real,' Dirk assured him. 'But our contact is slim. It won't last long. Howard's your name, isn't it?'

A querulous expression darkened Howard's face. This was real. This was the answer to the why of his miracle winnings – this was the explanation for how he tasted the future. 'An alien?' he asked aloud. 'You're kidding?'

'What's that?' Tony asked. Howard looked looped

144

to him, but that was all right. The money he had seen in the rube's pockets was real enough.

'Nothing,' Howard responded. The vision of Dirk had been displaced by the plasm of stars suspended in the black night. He took out his silver pocket flask and swigged the sharp liquid.

When he looked at Tony Robello, time's lavings were translucent with glimpses of himself leaning across a velvet green table and hugging a heap of cash. But when he faced the sky, time was a plunge, lightning-silent, radiant and jagged with peeks at surf-smoking sea cliffs, green ocean, Dirk running across a cactus field sheathed in sunfire, and a horrid face – a mad-eyed, millipede-whiskered head with gnashing mandibles so viciously vivid that just staring at it was using up his life.

Howard hooted with fright at the abominable creature, and Tony swerved off the road and rooster-tailed gravel before righting the car.

'Hey! What's wrong?' Tony shouted.

Howard was clutching the dashboard and gazing bugeyed through the windshield. One hand flapped toward his pocket and found the silver flask.

'Keep your pink elephants to yourself, all right?' Tony grabbed Howard's flask and took a swallow. 'We're almost there.'

There was immediately here for Howard. Grateful to separate himself from the terrible being he had seen, he took back the flask, had another swig, and stared ahead at the road. He sat back in his seat and let time untangle its mesh of events before him. What could he do if an alien being were houseling its power in him? Was that monsterface he had seen the alien? Why was it showing him the yet-to-be?

145

Horror drilled in him, and only time's wildfire blotted the joyless implications of his vision.

Tony took sullen Howard to a ranchhome past a gatepost mounted with a coyote skull. From outside, the place looked ramshackle, sag-roofed, and blister planked, but inside the rooms were elegantly and expensively appointed with silk furniture and exotic potted plants. The slate floors were covered with lama skin rugs, brushstroke erotic art hung on the walls, and large-screen TVs playing sex videos lighted darker backrooms.

A sapphire breath of perfume made Howard turn to see a lissome young hooker in a fragile lace dress approaching him. Her angel-white hair feathered to her bare shoulders, and her hips rocked as if she were walking up stairs. When he stared at her slinky shape, blind depths stymied his clairvoyance, and he knew there was no future for him there. He shrugged her hand off his arm and followed her into the playing room. He nodded politely at the crooked faces he remembered from his visions on the ride over and sat down at a round table matted with smaragdine velvet..

In the raveling of time-currents across the green table, Howard saw the possible outcomes of each game as the cards were being shuffled. Scenes shunted before him, shadowy voices muttered, cards fanned and flurried, all in a billowy hush, white-hot as a full moon, almost blurring natural sight. Sometimes it did blind him, and he had to think of his shoelaces or the Cubs blowing the playoffs for the World Series or Cora dancing in her underwear to find his way back behind his face. Fortunately, there was no dearth of alcohol at the ranch, and he drank enough for the hustlers to think he was crosseyed.

But behind his numb stare, Howard watched closely. By dawn, he had won another million.

While he was packing the money into two shopping bags the amused hooker provided, the timelines shifted: In a Guernica of flashforward glimpses he benumbingly witnessed himself being clubbed with the butt end of a forty-five by Tony Robello and dumped in the trunk of his red convertible. Images coalesced of himself blood-gnarled, sprawled under a saguaro with the music beaten from his limbs, and his eyes like oysters. He looked about the room at Tony and the other grim men that he had played with. They were all slouching, sulking, pondering what went wrong. Tony was standing by the window watching dawn's yolk smear across the horizon. Howard glanced at the two doors of the playing room. Timetunnels appeared murky and torpid in all directions across the room except through one of those doors.

Howard picked up his bags of money and casually walked through that door. It was the bathroom. He unzipped his fly and noisily relieved himself while he let his second sight survey the small room. Only the window had the bright clarion curves that swooped toward the future. He unlatched it, hoisted his money ahead of him, and crawled out.

The future was a narrow path of lucid timelight: The shining trail ran with straight efficiency across the weedy yard beside the ranchhouse to Tony's red convertible. Electric smoke boiled everywhere else. Howard dashed with all his might down the blazing timeline and reached the car in a huff. The keys were in the ignition. He started the engine and was rolling toward the highway and dawn's green rags when a voice shouted at him.

'Hey, are you with it?'

Howard startled and turned to face Tony Robello behind the wheel. A chill of abrupt wakefulness seized him as he realized that he had been dreaming forward. Ahead, at the side of the road, a gatepost mounted with a coyote's skull appeared. Above, the night sky was black as a skillet and greasy with stars.

Window in the Blood

Only what is lost is truly free.

Reena Patai was alone in the courtyard in the purple shadow of the chestnut tree, and she crossed herself when she heard those words. The voice came to her from nowhere – not from the anemic thoughts of the mad, which continued to chew her hearing with their baffled mutterings though midnight peaked over the dark asylum – and not from the night matron, who was subvocalizing a paperback about a woman's second chance at love. The voice was Satan's own.

Though the other patients were secure in their rooms at this hour, Reena had gotten out by wedging a piece of cardboard into the socket of her door's latch to keep it from locking. She had used her telepathy to sneak past the matron and her staff, left the building through the open front door, and strolled into the courtyard. For an hour she had sat silently, watching the night fold its feathers, not listening to the patient's weeping terrors, thinking through the marvels of the day.

After deep consideration, she concluded that her miraculous recovery (Yannick himself believed it was impossible for the hippocampus to regenerate itself) was indeed the work of the Dark One. This was His world. She had heard that from the matrons time and again. There were no more holy miracles, because God had left this world to the demons. The matrons had told her this when she had asked them whether God could cure her sickness and make the stiffjointed trances go away and help her think like other people. Don't pray for miracles, they had said, pray for acceptance. God had pulled away in an infinite ebb that left the world empty of any sign of Her. Deep in the invisible, Her divine force mounted toward the world-smashing tidal blow of Judgement Day.

Of course the matrons had called God 'Him' – but Reena had known from her trances that God was a Woman nailed to a Giant Tree: In the jolting agony of her trances, she had seen the Tree filling the night with the phosphorescence of the stars, and her pain had briefly converted to its opposite. Staring into the trillion-mile-high sky, she experienced a muscular pleasure, the stars' contractions and the heavens' great expansive release. (Many shaky-kneed, goose-pimpled night fits passed before she heard about orgasms from one of the promiscuous old women in the laundry cellar and realized what she was experiencing had a name.) After one intensely hurtful and pleasure-cored seizure, her nerves still splattering pain in needle-jab flinches, she had morosely flipped the pages of an encyclopedia and seen the Tree in the bloodways and sparkways of the body, arteries and nerves ramose as oaks. On another page, she recognized the Tree in the cradle of female hips, and with her lips tediously spelling out the caption she traced the birth tube as it twin-branched into Fallopian boughs and the fruit of generations. She understood then that her pain was the rootgrowth of the Tree in the mud of her flesh. Her screams were the wind in the branches. And God was life Herself nailed into the Tree by atoms, stretched over the emptiness by pain. Life was pain. It was okay. Death made it okay. *The Mother gives and the Mother takes away.*

Reena had made her peace with the Mother then, and the magnet winds drawing her from trance to trance, meal to meal, day to day, on toward the leaf fall freedom of death was the Mother's sapforce. She went with it. The matrons were pleased with her (she ate better and complained less), and she was pleased with Her. That had been five years ago, when she was seventeen and wise. Now, at the end of her first tranceless, clearheaded day, she had gained clarity and lost her wisdom.

Nothing was certain to her anymore. And by that she knew she was in the shadow of the Dark One, breathing His confusion. The Mother was life and life was pain. She could plainly see that in everything that grew out of the dirt, bloomed into orgasm, and fell back into the dirt. Orgasm, chained in terror and hurt to the organism, was God's one gift of pleasure to life, to everything strong enough to live to maturity. The rest was suffering – growing pains and death throbs. Freedom from pain came from Satan, not God. *So!* she resolved herself and placed attention firmly in her surroundings. Fireflies glinted over the sleeping flowers, and the air was soft, starry, and fragrant with the dreams of the roses. Satan was approaching.

What had He said to her? *Only what is lost is truly free*, she repeated. She had been lost all her life. Had she been free? *Satan's arrogance*, she thought, staring up at the star-daubed sky. *He's given me wits in exchange for my soul.*

'Hey, it's not that way at all.' Dirk's voice bounded from the draggle of hedges at the wild end of the courtyard, and she jumped. 'I'm really not the Devil.'

Reena stared hard at those dense shadows, and a figure appeared. She gasped, though she could see nothing of Him but a tenebrous human shape. He

151

walked nearer but did not step out of the shadows. 'What do you want with me?' she asked out loud, tense with fright. The echo of her voice tripped through the black iron fence and into the dark hills.

'Reena, I need your help.' Those words appeared in her head with a sound like a rush of wind.

'What can I do for *you*?' she whispered, pulling her white sweater and green smock tighter about her.

'I want you to leave the asylum,' the gusty voice said, and Reena thought she saw the amber of flesh in the darkness, the glint of eyes.

'Leave?' Her hands fretted with a button. 'Where are we going?'

'To America.'

'That's not possible.' Her brain felt muscular with common sense. 'I have no money. No passport.'

'Anything you wish is possible now, Reena.' The shadow stepped closer, and shards of a face appeared – a fox-curve of brow, a pugnacious nose, small and snubbed like a bat's, the flint of an eye. 'I don't have much time to explain. I wish I could stay with you moment by moment and guide you. But I'm lost myself. I'm going crazy in this maze of worldliness, trying to make sense of everything I'm touching. Everything is so new. I'm not sure if I'm coming or going. And I can be gone in an instant, so listen, please, listen. You not only can hear other people's thinking, you can touch their thoughts. You can make them think – and believe – anything you want.'

A look of frightened aversion trembled on her face. She wanted to shout the demon away, but before she could speak, the air flashed hotly, and the figure was scorched to a retinal silhouette. Reena squinted, and as her numbed sight adjusted to the

152

flaring brilliance she saw tiny barbed faces snapping before her. Fang-gnashing snouts spun at her like hornets. She screamed.

The rat sneers burst into stardust, and she was alone again with the prophetic shadow. The bell of her scream rang in the hills, and shouts leaped from the dark rooms of the insane. She stood up, shaking with rage. 'You *are* Satan!' she said with exultant conviction, and the reverberations of her fixed stare shook her whole body as if she were being electrocuted in slow jolts.

'No,' the shadow almost stammered. 'You don't understand. These – demons are not mine. I mean they are but not really. Oh, how can I explain? I can't control them anymore than you can control a sneezing fit. Please, don't be scared.'

Reena was shivering with righteous wrath. Her vehemence confused the alien. Anger stymied its singlemindedness, and the continuum fractured into rheumatic branchings: Jiang jaunting faster than hawks over the ancient trails to a splashdown in a starlit ocean, Howard plundering timelines for treasure, Dirk absconded by killers. Wildness ached like a century of steerhood – cut into parts, blood drained into worldlines, body butchered into separate dimensions. The sacrifice was made in pain, and the alien felt what it was like to be human.

Until that instant, Insideout had touched but not felt the minds of these almost mindless animals. It was a 5-space being arcing through 4-space, yes-out-of-mind, entranced by the soft-eared songs of the cetaceans, forced against its loathing to reach into the dim space of humanity.

Waves crinkled the emptiness, meshing tighter as it entered deeper into the cellular narrows of their fisted brains. Only now did it fully regret that in its

153

distraught urgency to manifest, it had disregarded the earth's curvature. It had acted instinctively as though it were in point-reality, and now its parts were separated by thousands of miles. It hadn't the strength to withdraw and try again. Its confusion was a whirlwind.

'Oh, dear, I've really bollixed this whole thing, haven't I?' The shadow moaned, and its arms covered its head. 'Dirk was right. I *am* stupid.'

'You're not Dirk?'

'Heavens, no. I've used his shape in the past as a convenient appearance for your sake. To Dirk I look like this.' The shadow stepped forward, and Poe appeared in the electric light, grievous-eyed and sallow. 'This is a writer's face from a schoolbook memory of Dirk's. I thought it was appropriate.'

A chorus of howls and mooncurved cries from the asylum were answering Reena's scream. 'I have no time to argue,' Poe implored. 'In moments the night watch and the matron will be here with flashlights, drugs, maybe shackles.'

Poe stepped back into the shadows. When the alien came forward a moment later, it was as Dirk, adding a few inches to his stature, softening his belligerent sneer, and brightening the light in his glass-splintered eyes to a butane blue angel stare.

Reena gasped at the sight of him, and in her breath Insideout heard the withinside of wonder, the expansive release of hope and the acceptance of action. It jerked a thumb at the wands of light waving at the entrance of the courtyard and asked, 'Will you stay here with them – or come with me?'

She had only one question really, and in that squeezed moment she faced it: 'Will I be damned?'

Insideout had no answer for that, for all life was damned to die, but in that damnation was its own blessing. It had learned that with the blinking out of the dolphins' bodies and the union of their light cones. Consciousness was a pattern, like the shape of a fountain everchangingly the same, flow bonded to form, as change itself changed. 'If you mean, will you be saved – I can only say no. No one is saved.'

'But will I burn with you in Hell for eternity?'

'Hell and Heaven are carried by each of us – now. And there is no eternity, my dear. Not in this universe.'

The strength went out of her knees, and she sat down. 'Then I will burn in Hell.' She lifted her face to the sky and shrieked: 'I will burn!' And then softer, 'For the Devil always lies.'

Footsteps came running over the cobbles, and the beams of the flashlights swung across the hedges. Shouts caromed from the windows as patients banged against the screened bars.

'This is no lie,' Insideout told her. 'If you stay here, they will lock you up and drug you. If you come with me, I promise you will understand. Listen.' It held a hand to the side of her head, and its touch was bright as ice. 'The voices are gone.'

Reena's mind was clear. The ogreish voices *were* gone.

A flashlight blinded her. 'Here she is!' the matron's voice called.

The night watchman grunted from the other side of the courtyard, and his lightbeam swung toward them over the serrated shapes of the flower garden.

'Why are you out here?' the matron asked, keeping the glare of her light in Reena's face. 'It's sleeptime now.'

Reena looked away from the light and saw the cobbled path of the garden curve through the darkness and out of the courtyard. Dirk was standing there, watching her. He was handsome and tall as a prince, his hair tiger-streaked, his eyes set on her with soulful urging.

'He may be Satan,' she told the befuddled matron as the woman grabbed her by the arm, 'but here I am in Hell.' She stood up and said firmly, 'Let me go.' The inside of her head flexed as though her brain were sinewed, and the matron's grip relented.

The matron stepped back, alarmed. Behind her, the watchman appeared.

'Go back inside,' she commanded, and her words vibrated in her bones. The two turned mechanically and walked out of the courtyard and into the building.

'Wait,' Insideout said to her. 'Have the watchman open the gate. Tell him to lock it after you and to forget ever seeing you tonight. Tell the matron to forget she saw you tonight, too.'

Reena did as she was told, and when the great iron gate at the end of the long driveway was locked behind her, she edged out on to the wide country road under the sombrous pines and the sky chiseled with stars. She stepped like someone walking on contact lenses.

'Relax,' Insideout said. 'No one and nothing can hurt you out here. You have to affirm that.'

'Then what were those devil faces I saw floating in the air around you?'

'They're devils, all right,' Insideout confessed. 'I can't control them at all. They're wild energies set loose by the pain I'm suppressing. They're terribly embarrassing but not very dangerous, yet. Don't think about them. I'm trying to forget them, too.'

Reena looked about at the night-dense landscape. 'Which way do I go?'

Insideout pointed through the pines to a cluster of

stars in the Horse's mane. 'There's the plane of the galaxy, looking toward the core. We're closest to the core this time of year, you know. We're swinging past it now on our way around the sun. The earth's just glided three hundred miles in the time it took you to walk through that gate. The sun coasted four thousand miles in *its* galactic orbit, and half a million miles of space have expanded between us and the nearest galaxy. I can't get over that. Everything's just blowing up!'

'I don't want an astronomy lesson,' she said. 'Which way do I go?'

'I don't know.'

Reena turned her hands up to the sky as if to feel if it was raining.

'Walk toward town,' Insideout advised, pointing east. 'We'll stop the first car we see.'

Reena began walking, her muscles soggy with disbelief. 'I don't know why all this is happening. I don't know who you are. I don't even know who I am.'

'You could use your telepathy on me, you know.' Dirk's idealized face had a sweet and sad expression. 'Then at least you'd see what kind of Satan I am.'

Reena stopped and looked closely at Dirk. The balsam sighs of the pines filled the breeze. An owl hooted from the end of the world. Then scents and sounds fell away like dust, and she touched the alien. Its story rang coolly in the dendritic forest of her brain, an oboe recitative playing its tale into her nerves, and she experienced Insideout's wild leap out of 5-space, its plunge through the continuum toward the dolphin's song, its horror and pain as Donnie Lopes disrupted the arc, and its desperate need for a human alliance. It had to get back — and if it didn't, it and the hapless island where its body was trapped would be destroyed. But that was just a story. Even the experience of it was an hallucination. What made it real for her was that she could ponder it – she could actually think about it, consider it, weigh it against the rapturous abundance of her reason. For the first time in her life, she felt she had a mind of her own.

That was when the backwash of her telepathic push swelled over the alien, and it sensed her, clearly, for the first time. It felt the cellular exhilarations of her flesh before her mind had crystalized. Pure as a circle, her biokinesis had gone on, Krebs cycles, oxygen transports, and hormonal tides unwinding their molecular patterns, weaving a body that grew through girlhood into a fifty-four-kilogram woman. And all the while her brain was building its own world inside her skull – a world of little girl weepings, animal tenderness, forbiddings and screamings, and long tranceful hours with arms lifted, embracing emptiness, losing touch.

The pain at the start and end of those trances was as fierce as the wound between Insideout and its hyperfield. Maybe that's why its titanohematite brain had selected her. She was the perfect embodiment of its feelings – especially its hurt. In the instantaneity of choice, its titanohematite brain had chosen her for her emptiness. Of the four, she was the only woman. No doubt the double-x genetic structure of the female was more suited for accessing psychic fields, morphogenetic ranges, astrals, whatever a mind wanted to call it. It didn't know. Its brain did, and it sensed the truth of its hunch in thought sequences about the nuclear magnetic resonance of chromosomes, the electric field patterns of consciousness, and on and on. It had no time for that. Its life was frittering away, second by second.

Its immortality was decomposing. It didn't want to taste death.

'Only what is lost is free,' Reena told the alien with an elfin smile when she heard those thoughts.

'I don't want to be free anymore,' Insideout confessed. 'I was happy in 5-space. Replete. How could I ever tell you? I was wrong to push the map beyond itself. But I had no choice. There is no choice where I come from. I fulfilled the law, and now I'm going to die.'

Reena stepped closer to Dirk. She faced into the irreality of the ghost. 'I'm not afraid anymore,' she said, tenderly. 'I believe you.' The thoughts of Satan and God that she had learned from the matrons and that she had imagined in her trances hung in her awareness like numbers and equations. They were thoughts – nothing more. At the pivot of her mind, all thoughts were possible. And so none were true. She was lost among the possibilities. And when she saw that now she was free to choose her own thoughts, a regnant sense of well-being pervaded her.

'Then you'll help me?' Insideout asked with a heartleap of hope.

'I will help you,' she said, reaching for Dirk and watching in amazement as her hand passed through the holographic shape of him.

The hologram was in her brain, and she perceived that with telepathic swiftness. She walked off the road and sat in the aromatic leaf duff at the edge of the night forest. She sat there for about seven minutes, waiting for a vehicle to go by, and while she waited, she questioned the alien. 'Why did you select me . . . and the others?'

Dirk's pretty face was wrought with confusion. 'I

don't know. You must think me such a dolt. Do you?'

'No.'

'I'm so glad,' Insideout looked relieved. It pinched its chin, pondering. 'My brain was more strongly connected with the hyperfield when you and the others were selected. So, you see, it happened instantly. I wasn't at all human then. I couldn't have guessed you were all so — so different from one another. My considerations were a long way from causality and reason. I can't account for it now. I guess you would say it was the will of God.'

'Do you believe in God?' she asked in all earnestness, her back pressed into the rough hide of the tree, her naked body under her sweater and smock chilled to the verge of trembling.

For this question, Insideout let its brain search out a thought. 'I guess that there's always the Unseen,' Insideout replied. 'There are concepts vaster than the mind. At least as long as you stay in 4-space. Everything is so very partial here. It's distracting. But where I come from, everything is known. Everything is touching everything. God is not a thought or an exclusion, like here.'

'Your home is a place I'd like to visit,' she said.

'Oh no you wouldn't.' An ironic smile chilled Dirk's face. 'If you did, it would be for keeps. You'd become one with all else that is the Pith, the map, the knowing. You can't come back from that.'

A shrug tensed through her shoulders. 'Like you coming here,' she said. 'If the four of us fail and don't reconnect you in time, you'll be stuck here forever.'

'It's not a pleasant prospect,' Insideout admitted nervously. 'Especially since the agony of my rift from the hyperfield will probably continue. Maybe, if I'm lucky, the intensity of it will kill me. I don't know. And I don't care to find out.' It looked ready to cry.

Reena swelled with concern. 'Don't worry, we'll make it. We have to. The arc will kill thousands of people if we don't. So much is at stake.'

'Indeed.'

'And when we do get you back – ' She hesitated a beat. 'When it's time for you to leave – could I come with you?'

Her question startled the alien. Why would she want to leave? Then Insideout realized that she had perceived a truth that it, in its eagerness to get away, had ignored. She said it outright in her next question:

'I guess what I'm trying to ask is, what's going to happen to me when you're gone?' She pulled her sweater tighter. 'I think I already know.'

With swift certainty, the answer shot out from the interstices of the titanohematite brain where she had already perceived it. 'You'll revert to your former self,' Insideout told her. 'Oh dear.'

Her eyes closed, and the darkness under her lids was vertiginous. She snapped open her gaze. 'Isn't there some way to heal me? Can't you stop the sickness the way you stopped the pill Yannick gave me?'

'That was a self-catalyzing reaction,' Insideout replied through a thoughtful frown. 'You started it with my energy and it carried itself to completion. But – forgive me – the distortion in your brain is so complex, so pervasive I don't have the power to change it. I'm sorry. Truly I am.' It flashed her a fluorescent cross-section of her hippocampus, electrically etched to show a ravel of nerves like fire-frizzled hair. A pink ghosted overlay of an ideal hippocampal gyrus revealed a crossweb of exact nerve symmetries, precise and orderly as brush bristles. 'With this section of your brain tangled up, your sensations, emotions, and thoughts get confused. I'm sorry to tell you, but your schizophrenia is in the very roots of your brain.'

'Then why can I think clearly now?'

'I'm helping you. I'm overriding your damaged hippocampus with rectifying instructions from my own brain. As long as we're together, you'll be whole.'

'Then we really do need each other,' she said with a simplicity that moved the alien.

'Yes, we do,' it answered and was surprised by the warmth that this small mind had started glowing within it. 'I'll make you a promise, Reena. If I do get back to my hyperfield, I'll take you to an earth where you can be whole.'

'You can do that?' Disbelief clouded her expression.

'Of course. You may think I'm lying to win your cooperation, but I can assure you, there are endless earths.'

Earth without end, Reena remembered from her prayers. 'I don't think you're lying. But how can that help me?'

'When my arc is complete, I'll have almost infinite power. Enough power and computational potential to turn you into light with me and to put you back together again whole. On my way home, I'll take a short detour and return you to an earth where you don't exist yet and where you can live a normal life.'

She sensed the truth of this. Lying was impossible with her, since she was in a sense a part of Insideout, its most empathic part. And now that they had attained this exact degree of clarity between them, she was as comfortable with the alien as the crown with its dragon, the shell with its snail, the hand with its brain.

'There are that many worlds?' she asked with simpleminded awe.

'Time has no shores,' Insideout assured her. 'Past and future don't really exist. They're just different parts of the tesseract range, through which I can travel freely – when I'm free.'

Headlights pronged through the darkness, coming west on the highway from town. Reena stood up. 'What do I do?'

'You know,' Insideout said and said no more.

Reena stood in the middle of the highway, her arms reaching out for the approaching car. 'Stop,' she called into the binary glare, and the corpuscles in her brain twinkled.

The car slowed and came to a stop with its bumper touching her kneecaps.

Reena stepped out of the brilliance of the headlights. She already knew the driver was alone. She knew his name and the names of all his relatives and friends. She knew the details of his job as a paint salesman. She knew the glutful sensation of his illicit hours with his mistress. She knew the chest ache of his fibrillose ventricles. She knew more about him than she knew about herself. When she opened the passenger door and sat down next to him, her eyes were twin diamonds. 'Let's go to the airport,' she said.

A terrible black voice said: *To be is to gather from within.* And Dirk Heiser woke up. For a crazy moment, a doubleness of mind held him: He was still with Reena Patai as she set her will in the nerves of the paint salesman – and he was curled around a granite headache, jostling inside a speeding car.

'He's awake,' Limu grumbled.

Dirk clung to the dreamfulness of Reena, pretty Reena with her mountain lake eyes and hair of spun noonlight. 'Let's go to the airport,' the indigo sound of her declared in him, and his tendons twanged on his bones like strings on a bass fiddle.

'Eh!' Limu shouted from the back seat and pushed his huge body toward the front to grab hold of the wheel. 'Where you going?'

'Airport – no?' Chud replied in a voice like a ricochet of thunder.

'Airport? You crazy o' wot?' Limu tugged at the wheel, and the car fishtailed with the vehemence of a hooked marlin. 'Turn round, already! Peel off!'

Limu rapped the side of Chud's bald head with is knuckles, and the driver snapped out of his trance. He glared at Limu and eased the car through a lazy U-turn. 'Don't hit me, brah.'

'Fo' shu-ah when you get crazy. Why you w'en drive to the airport, eh? I tol' you, we take 'em to the shack.'

'Yeah, yeah.'

'Then why you w'en drive to the airport?'

Chud ignored him and rubbed the side of his head as he drove.

Limu settled back next to Dirk and regarded him. The youth looked trashed. The scarlet welt across his forehead where Limu had slammed his face against the car door was livid, and the kid's eyelids were droopy. 'Sweet dreams, hah?'

Dirk said nothing. He wanted to be back with Reena and the alien. Those two had found each other, and their union sang in him like a rock video,

164

hopping with crosscuts of Reena's sprite face, pin-wheel galaxies, and fluorescent brain parts. He flexed his arms and feet and was relieved to feel that he wasn't bound. The dense pain of his jarred brain clouded his thinking. Was the alien with him, too – or was he alone?

Stay calm, a windswept voice appeared in him, and his heart skipped as if for a lover.

Hey! Dirk shouted in his mind, and his headache pounded louder. *You've got to get me outta here. These suckers are gonna kill me!*

'Stop squirming, toilethead,' Limu grumbled and rammed his elbow into Dirk's side.

To be is to gather from within, a child's ether voice said.

Yeah, and what's that supposed to tell me? Dirk glanced to the door on his left and contemplated springing it open.

'Don't try fo' it, Mistah Romance,' Limu warned, 'or I'll put you out again.'

Dirk closed his eyes and tried to reach the alien telepathically, the way Reena had. But behind his eyelids he found only a headache. The memory of Reena and the alien together was vivid, and he continued to search in himself for Insideout.

I'm here. Insideout said in a baritone variation of Dirk's voice.

Yeah? Well what am I supposed to do now?

Get away from the people who are holding you. They mean you harm.

'Jesus, I know that!' Dirk said aloud.

'Eh!' Limu grunted and seized Dirk by the back of his neck in a grip merciless as steel. 'Wot you mouthin'?' He shook the boy to a blur of tousled hair and chattering teeth. The sensation of manhandling the kid was so gratifying he did it again and snorted

165

a laugh. He hated Dirk, and not because the punk had ripped off the Mokes. He hadn't. The coke had been fine until Limu had stomped it when no one was looking. That was his excuse to the Mokes for his rage at Dirk, since he couldn't admit his real reason without losing face. Limu was jealous. Dirk was a loverboy who was arrogant with his good looks.

Limu had wanted Sheila for himself since she was thirteen, but she had always spurned his advances. He had been friendly and generous with her and had even bought her a diamond ankle bracelet. She sent it back to him tied around a fish too dead even to eat. She was mean that way, and that, as well as her pert rump and pendulous breasts, was what he liked about her. She was as churlish as her brother, the leader of the Mokes, and Limu, who had been the leader a decade ago, before he went pro with the Japanese mob, absorbed a lot of backtalk from that kid hoping he would sway his sister for Limu.

But Sheila lived as if she had no family. She was a rogue bitch, a runaway slum kid, full of herself, ignoring local boys for army brats and the kids of transferred executives. She started going with Dirk a year ago, when she was sixteen and sweet enough for Limu to sweat like a diabetic whenever he was near her. He thought of raping her, but the Mokes would hate him for it – he was their legend, and so he writhed for her in the shackles of his reputation.

Limu grabbed Dirk's face in the splay of one huge hand and studied the fear there. He had heard that this rude boy was vicious, and he could see something of that in his tight stare eager for reckoning. But the boy was too stunned to act. Limu had hoped the kid would try something in the car. He liked killing in closed spaces. The kid sat still in his doom. This was Chud's car, and Limu had promised not to bloody it unless he had no choice. So he contented himself to gaze at the knot of frown in the loverboy's face, to feel the knot of bowel in the coldness of his skin. He was so scared he was corpse-chilled, and Limu shoved his face away with satisfaction.

To be is to gather from within, the alien slurred in a muddy intonation.

The knots of fear in Dirk's body tightened. *Listen*, he pleaded. *C'mon, please – you got to come through now. You got to help me. Do you hear me?*

You can help yourself.

How?

You know how to fight.

I already tried that. Remember? It's no good against these buffalo.

No, the muted voice insisted. *I held you back. Inadvertently. Remember, the strength went out of you during your fight. I finally figured out what happened. Your power was drained off by my shadow self. I can stop that.*

Why didn't you stop it before? I wouldn't be in this mess now.

I was confused before Reena. The alien sounded like a peeved kid. *This is all new to me, you know. Everything's so scattered – so separate. Even me! My mind is broken into four parts – and I'm still discovering what's what.*

You got it straight now? Dirk's viscera were trembling more with anger than fright. How could this being traverse light-years and yet blunder so stupidly? *What can you do to get me out of this?*

Nothing. My range with you is purely cognitive.

What about Jiang's strength? I could use some of that.

I can't give you that. And I can't give you Reena's telepathy or Howard's prescience. Those functions are as separately connected as width, depth, height, and time. That's simply the way 5-space prisms in your universe. Nothing I can do about that.

Great. Now what do I do?

Fight.

The car swerved into a turn, and Dirk was pressed against Limu. A smell like squashed gingko nuts soured the bulky man's aloha shirt. The car bumped over a rutted dirt road through curtains of palm fronds and fern boughs, and Dirk clutched the seat behind Chud to keep himself out of Limu's lap. His mind was racing for escape. He had come around in time to look out the window before the turn and recognize the verdant cordillera above Kaneohe Bay, and by that he knew he had been taken out to some desolate camp in the wilderness of the Koolau Range. Shouting and running were useless here. He would have to make a stand.

On the floor of the car next to Dirk was his duffel bag, clothes hanging out of it from Limu's search. Dirk let his hand fall into it and he felt for the arc. It was still there, but the power had gone out of it. It felt flat and lifeless as a coin, and he let it go.

When the last of the windshield-slapping branches burst aside, a a green vista of mountains kneeling at the sea came into view. Dirk's heart squelched: A black Mustang with two red hearts painted on the hood above the headlights was parked in front of an abandoned millpond shack. That was the Mokes' wheels and meant there would be others to deal with.

Chud swung the car to a stop under a wide-crowned monkeypod tree, and Limu shouldered open his door. Dirk quickly surveyed the terrain:

The shack was the back of a sawmill that had been abandoned a century ago. The cornerstone, cut free of vetch and cluttered with a collapsed pyramid of empty beer cans, was engraved 1856. The cascade that had powered the mill was etched into the greengrown cliff above a collapsed vine-enwoven hillock that was once a building. High up on the cliff, cars glinted by on the roadway that had diverted the stream and killed the mill. A giant gear, big as a Mayan calendar stone, leaned against one of the three standing walls of the shack. Downhill, a short way from the shack, the terrain curved through a couloir of hot green turf and scarlet-flowered shrubs before dropping into a hundred meter gush of emptiness.

Limu grabbed Dirk's hair and dragged him out of the car. 'Eat it,' he gruffed, throwing Dirk's face to the ground. 'Dat's all you are now, toilethead. Dirt.'

Gravel bit him and dust stung his eyes, and he slapped the earth with his forearms to break his skid. He lay still, hearing the car door slam and metal snick as Chud got out and a knife opened in his hand.

'No!' a woman's voice cried out.

Dirk looked up to see Sheila standing in the doorway to the shack. In her lowcut green blouse, tight blue jeans, and open-toed spikes she looked weirdly displaced standing among the weed-ruck and the sagging timbers.

'Get back in your brother's car and get out of here, Sheila,' Limu commanded.

'He told me you were gonna kill him,' she said, stepping out of the shade into the sharp light.

'Get in the car!' Limu barked.

'He's goin' with me,' she said and strode toward Dirk.

The sight of Sheila risking her life to help him anguished Dirk. He spit dust and rolled to his feet. He was suddenly spilling with rage; the gritty dirt in his mouth was the taste of his lifelong hurt, and he wanted to lash out. His heart rocked grimly. Yet he was afraid. His strength had faltered before. Could the alien prevent that now? What if he made a natural slip. They'd kill him. He backed off a pace and stepped into Sheila.

'Come on, Dirk,' she said in a gray tone, mastering her fear. 'We're getting out of here.' She took Dirk's hand and led him toward the Mustang.

Chud took two strides and cut them off, the knife in his hand chromed with sunlight. Limu stepped closer. 'Let the lady walk,' he told Dirk. 'This is our business.'

To be is to gather from within, a thought, slimmer than a voice called to him. *Inside you're a fighter*, he heard himself say. *Your father trained you that way. It's the way that killed him – but you, it will save.*

A laugh jumped out of him. His father was dead all right. And his mother was walking dead. The only thing they'd given him was his body and a fury that fit it well. He let Sheila's hand go and stepped away from her. 'Get behind the wheel, Sheila,' he said quietly. 'I'll be with you in a minute.'

In a sudden burst, Limu lunged at him, wanting to tear him apart with his bare hands right in front of Sheila's eyes. Dirk watched him with a mordant lucidity, unmoving until the massive man was an inch from tackling him. With gravity's complicity, he fell backward, kicked both heels of his western boots into Limu's midriff, and sent him flying over him into the dirt.

Dirk somersaulted backward with the momentum of this collapse and came up behind Limu. He

170

jammed a boot heel into the back of the fallen man's thick neck and viciously pressed his face into the earth.

Behind him, Chud had rushed up, thrusting his knife in an upward swipe. Sheila screamed as Dirk hopped aside and the blade slashed past his face. Dirk turned as if to flee, reversed into a roundhouse kick, and caught Chud squarely in the throat as he stepped into the blow. The impact dropped the bison-shouldered man and left him retching for air, spasming toward shock.

Dirk picked up the dropped knife and turned around with it poised to jab when he heard Limu charging him. Limu's hand flicked out faster than Dirk had guessed he could move, and the knife was slapped away. Dirk clutched his stung hand and retreated before the killer, dancing backward, surprised, staring at Limu for a limp, a lapse, a way in. There was none.

The ground sloped downward under Dirk, and he snapped a glance over his shoulder and saw a startling drop into a crag-spiked gorge. His strength coiled dizzily, rooting him to the spot. With grim intent, he fixed his gaze on Limu's hard stare and lowered his weight into his pelvis.

Limu did not charge as Dirk had hoped, and the youth swiftly changed his stance to strike instead of throw. The large man parried Dirk's eye-gouging stabs and caught a groin-kick with a wrist block so solid that Dirk was flung backward. He bounced over the hummocked turf and crashed into an ohia shrub, pulling its taloned roots from the thin soil and sending it tumbling into the windy drop. He was on his back, sprawled like a pentagram on the cliff edge, stock-still with both hands grasping the tufted grass. He stared up at the sky and watched the clouds carrying today into tomorrow while he ice-inched his body away from the ledge.

Don't panic, he heard the alien's childbright voice saying. *There's a ledge just below you. Go on. Don't be scared. Get up.*

He rolled to his side glittering with sweat and saw Limu over him. Limu's bare foot kicked for Dirk's head; Dirk lurched, and the blow caught his shoulder and flung him backward over the edge.

Limu grinned and with cat-wariness stepped past the gash from the uprooted ohia, wanting to satisfy the pornography of the kill and see Dirk's broken body. As he leaned over, Dirk, who was on the ledge just below the brink waiting out his certainty that Limu would peer over, grinned his mirthless shark's smile at the startled man. Limu gaped and frantically turned to climb back up the cliff edge. But Dirk grabbed his thick ankle and yanked with all his might.

Limu fell forward, slapped the cliff edge with his torso, and clutched at the serrated grass. The weeds tore away in clods of ferruginous red clay, and he dropped. Yodeling hysterically, Limu slid past Dirk and tumbled into the abyss. Dirk dug his fingers into the turf, pulled himself up, and clambered over the slope without looking back.

Sheila was watching from the top of the rise, fraught with alarm. Chud was still on the ground, but he was sitting up, and his gaze was baleful.

'Let's go,' Dirk urged as he came up to her.

Her face looked funny, anguished and almost laughing at the same time. 'No, I'm not goin' with you. I didn't want anybody killed. That's why I came.'

Dirk took her arm, and she flinched away. 'You're cold,' she whined and frowned at him with disbelief.

His hands *were* icy – his whole body was lithe with frosty power. Grappling at the cliff edge had infused him with chilled radiance. And in that boneheld light, he sensed the alien closing in on him again. He ran to the rust-mottled car that had carried him here and took out his duffel bag. He pulled out the arc. It was brilliantly markless and cold. Holding it in his palm, in the shadow of his bag, he noticed that his hand was sheathed in a violet luminescence so transparent that it would have been invisible in daylight. He crouched into the shade of the car; his arms and torso were also englossed in vapory light.

Fear, starker than his fright at the cliff's edge, heaved in him, and he dropped the arc back into the bag.

Ease up, son, his father said. *Keep your wits about you now.* The sound in Dirk's head molted to his mom's nag: *I can't hold back anymore, kid. I'm hurting real bad. That shadow self I told you about earlier? It's on me right now. I can't stop it. Get away from the others.*

Dirk's scalp was wet with fear. He ran both hands through the nest of his hair. His brain was darkening. 'Don't use those voices, Jack.'

'Sorry.' Insideout said in a stone flat female voice. 'I'm trying to get it right, Dirk. Really I am. Listen inward for a moment and you'll understand.'

Dirk placed both hands on the hot car roof and rested his face on them with an exasperated sigh. 'I'm listening,' he said, and as his cool breath misted back from the sun-charged metal of the roof, his mind veered into a trance.

A hulking gargoyle squatted in the sunlight. Its grotesque face a clasping of jaws, fangs, and slithering barb-tipped feelers. Its torso banded like a scorpion's thorax, it reared up on thick legs that slushed into the contours of the earth below it. The bandy arms it raised vibrated into waves of plasmic light, violet and oozy, streaking in the sunlight and looping in spirals toward the diminutive image of Chud.

'Isn't it grotesque?' a sonorous, polished utterance came from beside him. Poe was there, arms crossed, one hand fingering his mustache. 'I don't know if I'm more embarrassed or terrified. It's a collage of demon-destroyers from human history – dragons, gremlins, ouphes, bog queens, seraphim, wraiths. I have nothing to do with it. That's what's scary. It draws its energy, as I do, from the vacuum field.'

'What's that?' Dirk asked.

Poe tucked his chin to his shoulder. 'It's my shadow self – my death reaching for me from the future. I've decided to call it an orc, a word for monster from the roots of your language. It's a monster that wants to devour me in whatever form I assume, the way antimatter eats matter. I hate to say this. I really do. But you must know, it will kill you to preserve the cosmic symmetry.'

Staring at the orc as it writhed from fang and claw actuality to swerves of violet energy, Dirk was mesmerized. 'What is it?'

'It's just like me. It's pure energy, waveforms in the vacuum. But it's not conscious as I am. It's more reflexive – more bestial. It's reaching into the human psyche to stalk me. You see it here in the projective light of my mind. Soon you'll see this abomination in raw sunlight. Then God save you – and me.'

Poe folded into bent light, like a ruby's flaw, and Dirk was himself again, leaning against the roof of the car. He squinted into the stinging sunlight and saw Chud swaying to his feet. The air around him was thrilling to mirage-waves, and Dirk thought he saw the purple shadows of the orc in the giant's face.

'Sheila,' Dirk called. 'Get in your car! Get out of here! Fast!'

Sheila scurried to the black Mustang and got in. The engine rumbled, and the wheels roiled dust as the car curled around Chud and growled down the rutted road and through the hanging branches of the crowded trees.

Chud ignored her and came at Dirk in a stooped, linebacker's rush. Dirk got in Chud's battered car, found the keys in the ignition, and started the engine. Chud grabbed the tail fin as the car pitched into gear and swerved off. Metal shrieked, and the taillight came off in Chud's grip. In the rearview, Dirk shivered to see spark-points of blue light chipping the space around Chud as he threw the taillight after them.

At the paved road, the alien said in Dirk's father's voice, 'You did well, son.'

'Sure.' Dirk stared to the right, down the highway through the virid miles toward the bay, the sun-bashed windows of the town, and the road that led back to the orphanage. He turned left and drove the climbing curve into the mountains. 'Thanks for telling me about the ledge back there. Knowing about it helped a lot.'

'Knowledge is power,' Mitch's voice said.

'Do you have to use that voice?'

'I thought you admired your father,' Insideout said as a female telephone operator.

'Yeah, but he's dead.'

'Dead but proud.'

'Nah. Just dead.'

'I disagree,' Insideout said. 'I found his light cone. You know, the lost light of the past. He's a bit

175

scattered like you'd expect from someone who's been dead for twelve years, but coherent enough to be proud.'

'What're you talking about?'

'Your Dad.'

'You mean, even when you're not recreating him, he's still around – like a ghost or something?'

'Ghosts, astrals, the bardo – those are your species' intuitions about light cones in the vacuum field. They're fairly accurate, as intuitions go. You see, thoughts are things. They're electrical patterns, complex and precise waveforms. Yours are unique to you, unique as a snowflake. Everything you think and feel, even the sensations, perceptions, and dream patterns that you're unconscious of, are photonic shapes that are imprinting the vacuum field continually, your whole life long. You ought to think about this. After the waveform-generating system – the body – dies, the waveforms go on expanding with the vacuum field. They don't die – light is ageless. It never dies. So the waveforms of consciousness are always there. And they're always repeating themselves, endlessly. Yet evolving slowly as field particles interact with them. That evolution is the life of the dead. It goes on for ranges of time you have no names for. Mysterious as ghosts seem, they're quite common really. You can interact with them, too. The brain is designed to talk with the dead.'

'Of all the crazy stuff you've laid on me, buddy, this is the craziest.'

'Yet doesn't it sound right to you? Everything that ever existed, still exists. Nothing is lost. Right this moment the universe's explosive birth is tingling its warm echo in the freeze of outer space. The sky around you is filled with the lights of myriad worlds

– including this world at every instant in its past. The blackbody depth of the universe holds every waveform intact. Every photon that ever was is circling back on itself, circumnavigating the universe and – get this, because this universe is finite yet unbounded – lost light visits *all* galaxies as it returns to itself.'

Dirk sat up straighter. In the rearview he saw a figure galloping uphill at a tremendous speed. At first he thought it was a lunging animal – then the back of his neck prickled as he saw that it was a man. It was Chud running after him at forty miles an hour. 'Shit! That's impossible.'

'It's the orc,' the alien sighed. 'It's gained enough power to seize the people around you and use their bodies.'

'Insane!' Dirk wiped the sweat from his woeful eyebrows and floored the accelerator. The clunky car groaned and went no faster. 'The grade's too steep!' he wailed. 'What are we gonna do?'

'Whatever you do, don't try to fight the orc. That will just strengthen it.'

Chud was only a carlength behind him now, and Dirk could see the air around him prickling with light like a fuse. His face was gruesomely distorted by the inhuman effort of his run, and as he reached out for the car's fender the whole mask of his flesh flapped on his skull.

'Evade!' Insideout shouted.

Dirk stood on the brake. The tires screamed, shot smoke, and the car bucked to a stop. Chud slammed into the trunk and bounced off the rear window with glass-shattering force. Dirk squeezed the wheel with all his strength and rested his head between his knuckles.

'This is a nightmare,' he whispered, his insides squelching with fright. 'I don't believe this.'

A bellow yanked him upright, and he saw Chud standing beside him, his face stickled, scoop-cheeked, and blue as a prehistoric fish. His spark-whirring hand reached for the door handle.

Dirk threw the car into gear, and it coughed and stalled out. As he jangled the ignition, the door swung open, and the car screeched forward. Lightning banged through Chud, and the door ripped off in his fist as the leaping car careened off the road. The impact of the electrical discharge gonged through the car, and Dirk lost control and slammed into the trees. He was thrown out the torn-off door and lay in the leaf mulch watching Chud slump toward him.

The man was monstered: His hands and face were tarred with astral mucus, and his rabid eyes were fixed on Dirk. The sight of this ghoul paralyzed Dirk, but Insideout squeezed itself to one loud word in the boy's mind: *Move!*

Dirk sprang to his feet and ran to the car. He snagged the duffel bag with one hand and dashed for the highway, waving his arms in a freefall sprint down the mountain. Chud loped after him, smoking astral fire but moving slower, somewhat spent from tackling the car.

A black Mustang swung around the bend blaring its horn, and Sheila rocked to a stop beside Dirk. 'Let's ride,' she said, throwing open the passenger door.

Dirk dove in as Chud pounced up to the Mustang. Sheila put the car in reverse and squealed backward around the curve, jitterbugging with the spin of its wheels. She braked hard and shot forward, rocketing

178

toward Chud, swinging to hit him and missing by inches.

Climbing into the mountains at seventy miles an hour, Dirk allowed himself a sob of relief. 'I thought I was dead back there.'

Sheila turned toward him with a flame-quaking grimace.

Dirk screamed and cowered against the door. Landscape tinseled by at eighty miles an hour, and the car was streaking across a curve toward a rail guard. He grasped the wheel and pulled the car through the turn. Deft with terror, he snatched the keys from the ignition, and the engine stuttered and died.

Sheila, her hands and face suddenly tentacled in ichorous light, steered the Mustang toward an oncoming truck. Dirk fought her for the wheel, and the truck swooshed by with a roar of its horns. The car bulldozed through thimbleberry bushes and smacked into a stand of ironwood trees, renting open the hood and geysering steam.

Dirk braced himself for the crash and muscled out the door as soon as the car stopped. He collapsed in a sprawl among the shrubs and saw that Sheila was clasping the wheel, watching him with a terrified stare. Blue sparklers scintillated along the dashboard and vanished. Dirk scrambled upright and backed off into the woods.

The truck they had almost hit had stopped, and the driver was running toward them.

Dirk waved feebly at Sheila and hurried into the forest. As he hopped over fallen trees and crouched under flower-nettled branches, he felt for the arc. When he found it, he held it tightly, and the pluck of his heart quickened with the ice of its touch.

* * *

179

Time has no shores, someone had graffitied on the ribbon-curved wall of the airport concourse. Hula dancers in shivering grass skirts approached with necklaces of color-splashed flowers in their out-stretched hands. Howard couldn't take his eyes off the graffiti. Its message was so utterly appropriate to his predicament that he stood still in the throng of deplaning passengers while a lei was placed around his neck, and he read the words aloud. The scrawl had the color and line of Utah's red arches, implying the same timeswept bewilderment.

'You're dreaming, Howie.' Cora fluttered a sheaf of hundred-dollar bills over Howard's slackmouthed face, and he woke sputtering. 'Welcome to your first morning as a millionaire! How were your dreams?'

Howard gazed about baffled. It was still Las Vegas: Sunlight stood with archangel stature in the tall white draperies, and through the rufflings from the air conditioner, he saw the casinos' electric icons looking robotically simple in the morning light.

Cora held a bouquet of cash under his nose. 'Is any perfume sweeter?'

Money was spewed across the bed and scattered over the floor. *What time is it?* he had to ask – that's how the dream went. 'What time is it?' he asked, and harmonics of time chimed like a tuned piano.

'It's after eleven.'

He would stand now and go to the window where birds like black hands would wave from their plunge into the sky. He stood and went to the window, startling gray wrens into throwing their wild hearts to the wind.

'Honey, are you all right?' Cora had never seen Howard so – strange. He almost always was grouchy when he woke up but never sullen. But then, she had never seen him with so much money. The big lottery win had set something desperate loose in him. The million he had won in the casinos last night was crazy excess, manic luck. But the *second* million he had come back with at dawn, that was frightening. And that was why she had woken him. He was muttering in his sleep, and he only did that when he was scared. Something bad was up.

Howard waited at the window. Cora had to ask a second time before he replied. The wait was necessary, a part of the dream's blueprint.

'Howie, what's wrong?'

'That money I brought in last night?' On cue, the urge splurged in him to look at her, and he did. With the windowlight on his face she was startled by his tired, sunset eyes. 'I won all that money straight, Cora. But – shit. Cora, I won it off a mobster.'

She clutched him. 'A mobster? Howie, you're joking, right? Where do you know mobsters?'

'Some guy asked me to play. I smelled money all over him. So I played him and his buddies, and I won. I didn't think they'd try and kill me for that. Geez! When they got nasty I ran.'

'Give the money back.'

'No way.' He pushed her away from him and glowered at her. 'I won that money fair and square, Cora. They were trying to cheat me last night. But I got lucky.'

'I'm beginning to wonder – was it luck, Howie?'

That question wasn't part of the dream, and Howard felt the timelines shifting. A quag of uncertainty shadowed the patchwork transparencies on the periphery of his sight, and he felt a doomful chill. He forced his attention to the ivory-edged light of his wife's face. 'What do you mean?'

'What I mean is, you expect me to believe you beat

181

a bunch of mobsters who had set you up from the start, right?'

'It was a fluke. That's all. I would've let the hundred grand go – but I won. I doubled it three times! That was once-in-a-lifetime luck, Cora. So I ran with the money. I stole their car.' He smiled gloomily. 'I guess they'll be coming after me now.'

'You guess!' Cora shrieked. 'Why didn't you tell me this last night?'

That question rang true in the empty space of his precognition. 'What? And ruin your night in Vegas?' He offered this meekly, without meeting her stare.

'My night in Vegas.' She snorted. 'What about the morning after?' She stalked to the phone.

'Who're you calling?' he asked, already knowing, reverberating with the timelines that he saw motion-streaking past him as his wife dialed. He shut his eyes, and the rays connected into a uranium blossom, a radiance of time-to-come intersecting here-and-now in the smell of desert pollen and the glycerin sounds of traffic on the boulevard below.

'The police,' Cora answered shrilly. 'We're going to explain it all to them, and if we've broken some laws or something we can straighten that out right now.'

'For Christ's sake, Cora, the house was licensed,' Howard said angrily, waving at her to put the phone down. She pursed her lips and gave him a stern look, but she did. 'The whole thing was legal,' he added more gently. 'Except they tried to cheat me.'

'How do *you* know it was legal? It was somewhere outside the city, you said.'

'The guy who set it up said it was all right.'

'Oh, right. A mobster's word of honor. What was his name?'

'Tony Robello.'

'I'm calling the cops.'

'Cora.'

'I can't believe it – Tony Robello. You played cards with a guy whose name was Tony Robello.'

'What's wrong with that? It's a perfectly normal name.'

'Sure, sure, until he sets you up for a rigged card game in a private casino. Then it becomes one of Death's nicknames. Tony "Bones" Robello. Or maybe Tony "Neck-tie" Robello – like those Colombian killers we're always reading about in *Newsweek* who cut open their victim's throats and pull their tongues through like neckties.'

'Cora, honey, we're not calling the cops.' He came up behind her and took the phone from her hand. 'We're going to make love. Then we're going to pack up our money, go to the airport, and fly to Hawaii.' He embraced her in a bear hug, and she pushed away.

'You expect me to feel horny with Tony Robello lurking outside our door?'

'I thought you'd find that tintillating.'

'*Tit*illating.'

'I like it.' He put his hands on her breasts and guided her to the bed. The glaze of silk under his fingertips, the corolla-sheen in Cora's brown curls, and her tabid scent garaged his anxiety. This was the radium-petaled core of time, the timelessly symmetrical center of now. He had crossed this plateau of lovemaking before in his dream. And he knew Tony Robello was nowhere nearby. As long as he fulfilled his dream here on this bed, where the paper money made a glistening sound under their weight, they would be safe. Cora's worried face relaxed to a smile under his rapturous stare, and he knew then

183

they would find their way to the future and an airport wall that reminded, *Time has no shores.*

Howard and Cora's ride to the airport and their hop-flight to LA were uneventful, as Howard knew they would be. The timelines gridded the dark of his shut eyes with the calmness of terrazzo tile. But Howard didn't relax until after they had made their connection in LA. And their Honolulu-destined jumbo jet was bounding into the sky. By then the massive quantities of alcohol he had drunk in the last twelve hours finally overcame him, and he slept.

'Do you want to know why you can see the future, Howie?' a blond street kid with sweat-nested hair and razor-sharp eyes asked. Howie recognized him as Dirk, the tough from his first oneiric glimpse of Hawaii. He was dressed in black pajama bottoms and a sleeveless black shirt sweat-stuck to his muscular physique. A smell of oleander and damp earth lilted off him, and his smile was dark with pushed-back teeth. 'Because there is no future. Time is just the release of what's already there.'

They were standing on a sward of blue-eyed grass overlooking a spice-colored beach and a green sea. 'Are you the alien that lets me see the future?' Howard asked.

'There is no future.' Dirk took Howard's arm and turned him to face the ocean so that the wind was kissing him. 'The past and future are always here. All times, all minds, all screams and songs are here. But where is here?' Dirk bent close to his ear and said, 'Right inside the atoms that make up your brain, Howie. That's where reality lurks. Not as atoms but *in* atoms. Right inside the protons that make up those nuclei is all the time there ever was, is, or will be.'

'You're crazy,' Howard decreed. 'I don't understand a thing you're saying.' He tried to rouse himself from this dream. But the dream went on, calm as a stone.

Dirk showed his shadowy smile. 'Think about this,' he said. 'Protons are the bricks of the atomic nucleus. They're supposed to be "made out of" quarks. Cute name. A proton is made of three cute quarks – but one cute quark, Howie, weighs five times more than a proton. How can that be? How can you build a brick doghouse so it weighs less than the bricks?'

Howard strained to disrupt the flow of his absurd nightmare. But nothing happened.

'What's holding you in this dream?' The punk made a fist. 'Binding energy, Howard. Everything that sticks together is fisted with binding energy. The earth and the moon. The sun and the stars. Whole galactic streams. But the energy that stars, planets, and we need to stay together is really small. If you'd been paying attention to your physics teacher in high school, you'd know that gravity is the weakest force.'

'Give me a break – I took auto mechanics in high school. Can't you talk straight with me?'

'Forget about sense,' Dirk fleered. 'If nonsense explains nothing, it's already explained a lot. Listen. Three heavy quarks add up to one featherweight proton because *fourteen-fifteenths* of their mass is consumed as binding energy!' The kid laughed with zeal. 'You should be breathless, baby. And the punchline's yet to come. You see, the smaller you get, the more energy there is. And there's no end to the smallness! No end at all. Protons, atoms, and you exist because you have very little energy. You're cool enough to stick together. At the level of the

185

quark symmetries, reality freezes into atoms. Any smaller and there is no matter, only exotic super-short-lived forms of pramatter and photons. Smaller yet and spacetime breaks apart. The energy is so enormous that it wraps spacetime around it like a black hole. Nothing gets out. Everything moves inward into vaster and vaster energy ranges *endlessly* intensifying toward the point horizon of infinity.'

'Shut up, already,' Howard said in a tearing whisper, but couldn't remove his gaze from the kid.

'It gets crazier when you realize that all of creation, billions of cubic light-years of spacetime, is *made up* out of these furious fire-points blazing smaller than spacetime. You see, the universe is just the cold exhalation of a hotter reality – a truer, timeless reality you can't even begin to guess about, except to know, without any doubt, that it is here. You are intimately connected with it. You are made from it.'

The kid leaned nearer and poked a rigid finger into Howard's chest. 'With that much power, that close – anything is possible, Howie. Anything at all.'

Howard looked beyond the tomcat slant of the kid's head to a dune of jipijapa leaves resonating in the sea breeze. The motion broke into neon-edged fractals, and Howard reeled awake.

People were in the aisles, pulling luggage out of the overhead bins and filing past him toward the open hatch and a smiling stewardess. A narcotic scent of tropic blossoms wafted from the bright opening.

'You're awake,' Cora said cheerily. 'You were sleeping so soundly, I didn't want to disturb you.'

Howard groggily rubbed feeling back into his face. Having had no alcohol during the five hours of the flight, he was streaming with timeline perceptions.

Cathedral swoops of spectroscopic radiance overlay retinal sight. Worse, vaults of distance were dilating from inside him, expanding beyond his body, and swooning him with the mixed sensation of both flying and falling.

Let's find a hotel room, Cora would say presently. *You'll be more comfortable there.* Waiting for her words, Howard thought of her creamy belly and auburn-highlighted hair, and the dizziness abated. Root thoughts were as good as drink, he had learned from their sexcapades in Vegas. Food sometimes worked, too: He thought of an inch-thick steak in a puddle of mushroom gravy and a potato flayed like an exotic butterfly. Soon the timelines strummed into the soft vibrations of ordinary sight, and he opened his eyes to see his wife in her aqua pantsuit standing beside him and taking down their travel bag.

'Let's find a hotel room,' she said. And the plagiary of the future becoming the present was soothing for Howard. 'You'll be more comfortable there.'

He felt confident enough now to consider telling Cora what was happening to him. But like every other time when that urge rose in him, it was met by a fright like a child's scream. Naves and clerestories of rainbow tracery netted his vision, and he was suddenly whirling through a nautilus spiral of electric fire. At the hub, a basilisk of invisible force clawed for Howard, its dragonish human shape erupting blackly in the brilliance of the whole world falling into it and smashing to light.

Howard quickly suppressed the desire to tell his wife about his future-seeing power, and normalcy gelled into place. He huffed like a man who had just learned he could breathe unaided. *Okay*, he thought, apprehensive about not having heard this thought in his dreaming. *Let's see this thing through. Whatever that means. Hell, at least it's happening in Hawaii – and I've got bucks to burn.*

Sleep had revivified him, and he delighted himself by unfolding effortlessly from his seat and walking lightfooted with the crowd, holding Cora's hand behind him. Through the window of the boarding ramp, he saw palm trees and dim pavement. Ukulele music braced the air, and at the end of the fluorescently lit corridor, Polynesian dancers in brown tapa wraps were swaying. An exhilaration of *déjà vu* stretched through him, and he looked eagerly for the graffiti from his dream.

There it was – an exact replica of its foreknown shape, promising that beyond the world of stitched-together hours, beyond the endless pursuit of night and day, there was no tomorrow and there was no never – there was only whatever is.

TIME HAS NO SHORES.

Dirk Heiser had arrived an hour earlier and had zipped the words onto the concourse wall outside the passenger gate with a spraypaint can that he had found in a trash receptacle. At first, he had been reluctant – not about defacing public property (he'd often spraymarked bus stop benches, highway overpasses, and elevators with his street name **TENDER BENDER**, and the pithy insights that came to him during his classroom meditations, like **GOD HAS SUICIDAL TENDENCIES** or **MAMA IS MAW** or **NUDE IN THE GARBAGE**). Dirk was a willing street artist, but he had been reluctant about giving up his free will.

After totaling two cars in the mountains and fleeing orc-possessed Chud and Sheila, Dirk had huddled in a root cove of a banyan tree until Insideout's

Poe-voice told him that the orc energies had subsided. Reluctantly, he returned to the highway and hitchhiked to the airport as the alien directed. During the two rides that got him there, he stared at the drivers, looking for orc-fire in their eyes and in the patina of their faces, annoying one of them enough for him to say: 'Eh! I owe you money or wot?' When he was let out at the arrivals pavilion, Dirk was springy with relief.

'Get the spray can out of there,' Poe muttered as Dirk strolled past a metal trash basket in the airport terminal.

Dirk did as he was told and followed the alien's mental commands through the airport to Howard's gate. Understanding folded in him like mental origami, thoughts and sensations bending together into a coherent shape that perfectly fit the contours of his mind, so that he understood, without knowing how, that a man was coming who would help him get the arc back to where it belonged.

The flight monitor informed him that arrival time was an hour away, and Dirk sat down on the floor with his back against the wall even though he was facing a reception area of empty plastic seats. Dirk hated those seats. It was impossible to slouch in them without feeling uncomfortable.

The spray can he was holding tingled with effervescent energy, but he was resistant to the desire to use it on the wall behind him even though the concourse was empty. 'Why do I have to do every little thing you say?' he complained. 'I mean, I can understand cutting out on Sheila and hitching here to meet this guy I've seen in my dreams – but do I really have to spraypaint this wall? What if I don't want to?'

'You have no choice,' Poe replied with lugubrious

189

insistence. 'It has already happened on the timeline that leads me back home.'

'And if I refuse? What happens then?'

'The timelines shift and I don't go home.'

'Just because of some stupid writing on the wall? You gotta be kidding.'

'Why would I kid about my life?'

'But how can that be?'

'If the man we're waiting for doesn't see this sign, he will begin to doubt the absolute veracity of his visions. That doubt will prove fatal soon enough – when the orc finds us again.'

'So I've got no choice?'

'No.'

That syllable punched him like a trumpet blast, and in the riff of silence that followed, he stood up and stared at the white wall. What would he write? Nothing came to his mind. The alien offered nothing. *Screw it*, he thought and poured motion into his arm, slashing up and around in a wild, swirling gush of spraypaint, striding the length of his effort in an arm-waving monkeydance. When he was done, he cast a furtive glance about him to be sure no one had appeared during his reverie, and he regarded his mess with a puckish grin.

A jab of shock dropped his grin and made him stand back when he saw that his unguided arm had actually written a sentence: **TIME HAS NO SHORES**. He looked at its rust-red curves and turnings like a dog staring at a doorknob, impressed by the incomprehensible.

People appeared at the far end of the concourse, and Dirk wandered off in the opposite direction. Sunlight running through gray filtered glass patterned the curve of carpeted hallway with white trapezoids. The skewed squares of ruined light looked like steppingstones into the afterworld.

Dirk was shattered about losing control of his life. The strangeness of the alien poisoned him. He wanted to be free again. But his conscience stalked him: Had he ever been free? The Home was his kennel, the counselors his masters. Closer to the bone, he was his own prisoner, condemned by his defiance of fate and caged by his rage. He had even created his own executioners – damp-eyed and vicious Donnie Lopes and love-demented Limu.

What would it mean for him to lose his life? he wondered, and Limu's hysterical scream in the last moment of his life echoed in his mind. That reminded him of what the alien had said about ghosts as waveforms in the vacuum field, and sadness drizzled in him for the intense fragility of life. He wanted to make peace with the whole world.

His amble had brought him to a garden of raked sand, boulders, bamboo, and orchids, and he sat down on a stone bench facing the wave-patterned sand and cried. The brutal and utterly unreal events of the last day made all his memories, all his prior moods and vaunting hopes, appear trivial, vulgar, pathetic. He quaked with remorse for the mindless selfishness of his life. In mid-sob he noticed a family in matching aloha outfits strolling by, pretending to ignore him.

He got up and walked across the combed sand. At the exit to the garden he noticed that he was still holding the spraypaint, and before chucking the can he fired on to the wall: **PLEASE TURN OFF THE ORCHIDS**.

Dirk was slouching against the wall beside the alien's painted message when Howard arrived through the gate in a crowd of tourists. He was carrying a dull metal attaché, the kind bottles of rare blood might be conveyed in. Dirk recognized him from his precognitive dreams and nodded at him once to break his amazed stare. He was a stork-faced guy with a red mustache and question mark posture. The woman he was with had curly brown hair, sugar pink lips, and long legs. He waved at her.

'Howard, that boy's waving at us,' Cora complained.

'Yeah, yeah,' Howard answered morosely. 'He's probably our tour guide.'

'We don't have a tour guide.'

'I asked for one at the last moment,' he lied. 'Wait here.' He walked up to the kid. 'Dirk?' He didn't offer his hand. 'I'm Howard Dyckson.'

'Howzit?' Dirk flicked a nervous glance to each side. 'Let's get this thing over with.'

The boy's face was smudged and scratched, and he smelled of wet lumber. 'Look, Dirk, my wife doesn't know about any of this. We're going to keep it that way, okay?'

'Ask the alien.'

'You're not the alien?' Howard retracted his head in bafflement.

'Hell, no. You're supposed to help me get rid of it.'

'Howie?' Cora stepped in. 'Is everything all right?'

'Sure it is. Cora, this is Dirk, our tour guide.'

Cora eyed the scruffy teen and frowned fiercely at her husband.

'Cora – ' Howard didn't know what to say. His dream had ended here. 'Come on now, don't argue with me.'

Cora turned Howard aside. 'But Howie, he looks awful – and mean,' she whispered.

'Mm.' Howard plucked at his mustache, thinking.

192

'All right, Cora. You deserve the truth. He's not our tour guide. After what happened in Vegas I thought we needed someone to keep an eye on us. He's a bodyguard. I didn't want to alarm you.'

Cora peeked at Dirk with slimmer, wiser eyes.

'He comes highly recommended,' Howard added.

'By whom?'

'My bookie back home.'

They left the gate and walked along an outdoor rampway through pollen breezes and the grousing of air traffic to the baggage claim. On the taxi ride to the best hotel in Waikiki, while Dirk sat with the driver, Howard amused Cora by ogling the green garth of mountains and pointing out cloud-piled nooks and rainbow-linteled corries. He grouched about the traffic. And at sight of the white beaches, he goggled with sun-vexed eyes the girls in hip-cut swimsuits and promised to buy a bikini for Cora. By the time they stepped out of the cab and into the submarine shade of their hotel's elegant lobby, she was convinced that he was easing back into his old self again.

The desk informed them that the large suites were booked up months in advance, and Howard strode into the hotel manager's office. He opened his metal attaché on the manager's desk and revealed his Vegas winnings. They were taken to a vast, cool presidential suite. Dirk took a shower in one of the two bathrooms while Howard and Cora freshened up in the other. Afterward Dirk put on red briefs, color-drained jeans, and an apricot pullover with bevel-cut short sleeves. He was sitting on the balcony overlooking the beach, his cartooned duffel bag at his bare feet, the arc turning in his fingers like a lucky charm, when Howard, in sandals, orange swim trunks, yellow T-shirt and Cubs baseball cap, walked in.

The sight of the arc transfixed him. Timelines bundled around it: Red-gold cell clusters bubbling like roe.

Dirk saw the trance in Howard's eyes, and he palmed the arc. Howard blinked and rubbed his pink-whiskered chin. 'Let's go for a walk,' he said.

Dirk tugged on his boots, and Howard shouted at Cora, who was basking in the whirl of the jacuzzi, that they were stepping out for a spell.

In the lobby, Howard was tempted to duck into the bar for a drink. The sight of the arc had left a floater on his visual field, spiderwebbing flux lines that distorted everything he looked at. But he knew that the alcohol would only suppress the distracting visuals. The future-fusing dreams went on inside him anyway – and when he finally dozed he would see into the next room of time. Better to stay close to the experience, he figured, now that he could share it with someone.

'What was that thing you were holding upstairs?' Howard asked.

'That's the alien.'

They stepped out of the cooled lobby into the vivid afternoon, and Dirk turned toward the beach. Howard took his arm and guided him in the opposite direction. 'It looks better this way,' he said. Time gleamed more brightly in one direction that the other, and he didn't know why but he knew enough not to doubt it. '*That* thing is the alien? That thing that looks no bigger than a bottle cap?'

'That's right,' Dirk said, allowing himself to be led.

'Well, who is it? *What* is it?' In the panoply of timelines, Dirk glowed like no one he had ever seen before. The loom of possibilities was a wheel of light around him, visible even in the crashing sunlight. Luck shone in him.

Dirk relayed what he knew about the alien's trespass on earth as they sauntered under the sun-spinning palms on the streets of Waikiki. 'If we don't get the arc back in time, it'll turn into light. A lot of light. And heat. Enough to waste this whole island.'

Howard slowed almost to a stop. 'I've always felt the only way into Hell was assbackward – but this is too sad.' Backdropping all his timeviews was a diaphanous white luminance, which was easy to ignore. Maybe that was the nuclear glare of the arc's doom at the end of his visions. That thought quickened his pace.

Dirk didn't like Howard's sombrous expression, and he searched for something to say. 'You can see the future because where this thing comes from everything is happening at the same time. Weird, huh? What's it like seeing the future?'

'I don't see very far. But maybe that's best.' He told Dirk about the state lottery, Vegas, and Tony Robello. 'I'll tell you, kid, I've never been so scared in my life. Nothing like this has ever happened to me before, even in my nightmares.'

'You think any of us are experienced at this?' Dirk laughed soundlessly. 'We're all running scared. But what're we gonna do?'

'There are others?'

'Two more. An old Chinese guy – Jiang – and a woman, Reena. She's in France.' Dirk recounted how Donnie Lopes found the arc on the Big Island. He also related his horrible encounter with the orc.

Howard's insides crawled at the description of the alien's monster self. 'If all this creature from the fifth dimension wants is to get back to the lava fields, let's go. I've got plenty of money. We'll charter a plane. Hell, we'll buy one. If we leave now we'll get there before the orc gets any stronger.'

'You haven't been listening, Howie. The alien has to be returned to the *exact* spot where Donnie picked it up. Even the gimp won't remember that. That's why Insideout is becoming human – so it can find its own way back. The only problem is, we've gotta wait around for the others.'

'But there's only a day left before it's too late. The alien said it could only last three days away from its hyperfield. It arrived yesterday.'

'Yup.'

'Then we better go to the Big Island ourselves and at least try. The others will catch up with us there.'

'You see that happening in the future?'

Time shadows had darkened around them since they'd left the hotel. 'No,' he said. 'The only direction that looks good now is toward the sea.'

Dirk had a similar feeling. Something urgent had to be communicated between them and was moving them toward the harbor. The thought itself, whatever it was, was too big for his head.

'What about Cora?' Dirk asked.

Howard gave him a funny look. 'She's got Waikiki and almost two million bucks to spend. She won't miss us till dinner.'

For Howard, the walk among the long boardwalks of the wharf was narrow as a tightrope act. The path that led to the future desired by the alien was a crystal corridor; the peripheral view of banner-streaming boathouses and white yachts was smudged in the crosshatching of timeplanes. They meandered through sunbursts from high cumulus and a sweet warm wind damp with the scents of plumeria and the emerald reef water, until ahead, almost hidden from view by cruise boats docked on either side, Howard saw a clear, lens-rainbowed focus on a black speedboat. It was sleek as a shark and bobbing with the excited breath of the water. A sandy-haired man in oil-stained canvas pants and faded red T-shirt was lowering the shiny black bonnet on the engine. Howard stopped on the dock in front of him.

'Hey, buddy, how much for a spin in your row-boat?' Dirk asked.

'Forget it,' the boatman said, latching the bonnet. 'I just tuned the engine. I'm racing later today.'

Dirk stared up at terns circling in the wind, polished by waterlight.

'We're not going to take the boat for long,' Howard added. Not far ahead, he saw himself and the kid returning in the boat, gliding on the still water of the harbor. 'We'll be back in an hour.'

'Guys, forget it.' The racer grinned affably. 'This boat ain't for hire.'

Dirk rubbed his fingertips with his thumb, looked at Howard, and nodded his head toward the racer.

Howard removed his baseball cap, reached into it, and took out a wad of hundred dollar bills. He handed the wad to the boatman. 'Here's ten grand. Yours for an hour in your boat.'

Howard steered through the olive-green water of the harbor, ignoring other boats and following the brightest curve through the hallucinatory contours of Insideout's timesight. Boats honked angrily as they veered by in near collisions, and Dirk waved cheerily at them. Once out of the harbor, Howard opened the engine full throttle, and Dirk was heaved back in his seat. They sliced over the water wind-stroked in the belly of the engine's roar until Honolulu was a cluster of brilliants in the lap of the green mountains. Castles of rain glowed darkly far to the south. Nearby, the clouds were buffalo-headed and silver-furred. Sunlight studded the wavetips like topaz.

Howard killed the engine when the timefacets gumming his peripheral sight irised open. They coasted into an undulant, ocean-breathed stillness on the night-blue water. 'What now?'

'Damned if I know,' Dirk said, standing up and gazing back at Oahu swaying with the horizon. 'I was following you, buddy.' Mica flashes drew his attention to a burst of small fish leaping from the swells. Larger water shadows ghosted under the boat, and Dirk spun his head to watch them appear on the other side.

With a heart-punching shriek, a group of dolphins flew out of the sea and thrashed water in a ring around the black boat. Their synchronized cries ripped hearing and collapsed Dirk back into his seat.

The dolphins splashed away, leaving their stabbing scream quivering in the brains of the two humans. The cry was a greeting to Insideout, and the song reached the alien at the moment it was painfully compressing itself more vividly into the humans' nerve plexes. The sudden shout momentarily stunned Dirk and Howard. Insideout heard the cry from its 4-space niche within the curly brains of the humans, and it used the abrupt stillness of their thoughts to draw all of its power back into itself. The effort intensified the noise of its pain,but the momentary clarity was worth it: The cramped space of human consciousness lit up like a slim moon in a thick night.

Howard tipped back his cap and knuckled his tingling sinuses. His timesense was gone. 'What now?'

Dirk stood up again, his mind reaching for an explanation. But his thoughts were simple and uninformative. 'I don't know.'

The dolphins shoaled and swam in a tight circle on the starboard side of the boat. The water they corraled shimmered like peacock feathers or gasoline's water-furled streamers. As the two men stared, the irridescent circle of water bulged to the head of a surfacing swimmer. The head was bald and smooth-featured, masked in veils of water. Horror icicled through them when they saw the glassy shoulders and arms of the figure surface and realized that his human shape was made up of water.

Both men backed with surprise as the shiny humanoid lifted straight up until it was standing on the water. It was naked and lively but devoid of genitals, hair, or markings, like a person in a body sock. The dolphins broke their circle, and the sun-sparkling human shape of water walked to the edge of the speedboat and placed its foot on the rail to step aboard.

Howard panicked at the sight of the bizarre being approaching them, and he tried to start the engine. It choked like a rooting hog.

'Friends, friends!' the precise human shape of water said. Its voice was childlike and nervous. 'Don't be afraid. It's me, Insideout. I have to talk with you.'

'This is crazy,' Howard howled softly. He and Dirk had backed up against the windshield and steeringwheel.

Dirk reached down into the duffel bag and came up holding the arc. 'You want it?'

'Oh, if only I could.' The alien pouted and sat on the taffrail. It was colorless as a glass of water, and the rail and hull it leaned against were visible and looked warped. 'I wouldn't get a hundred yards

199

before this body broke up. It's terrible. Everything I do is fits and starts without the hyperfield. I couldn't even parametrize right with you people. Tell me you forgive me.'

'What?' Howard groaned.

'I think it's apologizing,' Dirk said.

'Yes, that's it. I apologize.' The alien's face looked like it had a stocking pulled over it, yet the despair in its expression was stark. 'I'm so needful of you, I don't want to upset you. But look at what I've done. You're both terrified. And I thought this shape would please you.' It sobbed and hung its head.

The two men's rigid stances unlocked, and Dirk stepped closer. 'Hey,' he said with forced casualness, 'I oughta apologize to you for moving the arc.'

'No, that wasn't your fault – or Donnie's. I should have been more careful. I was overeager. I wanted yes-out-of-mind right away, here with the dolphins. What a fool I've been.'

'Yes-out-of-mind?' Howard asked. He leaned against the side, ready to leap overboard if the thing got any closer.

'That's what I called you here for. You see, I'm dying. My mind is going first. And I was afraid I'd lose it before I'd brought all of you together. Jiang and Reena have been exalted by my intrusion into their lives. But the two of you – Well, to make peace with myself, I had to be sure I'd given back something for all I've taken from you.'

'You paid me off just fine,' Howard said with bold sincerity.

'Money,' Insideout sniffed. 'A mere token. A symbol. That's really your poverty as a species. You have an appetite for symbols that can't stomach experience. Don't you see that?'

200

'You can fork me some of that poverty anytime,' Dirk said.

'You really don't see, do you?' Insideout leaned closer with amazement. It pointed out the dolphins crowding the water around the boat's aft. 'These poor creatures, without tools, clothes, or houses – these beasts that your people kill with impunity know more about wealth than you do. Because they have a song you don't. They can sing, while all you can do is sign.'

'Huh?' Howard looked to Dirk, who was squinting at the alien, trying to grasp.

'Oh, I can't *explain* it,' the alien fretted. 'But I can show you. And in that way I will have enriched you.'

'What do we have to do?' Howard asked apprehensively when the alien rose and approached them. He tried to edge away but couldn't move any farther without going overboard. Fear frosted his insides.

'Do? Why, nothing. Nothing at all. That's the beauty of yes-out-of-mind. The glory of lusk. You don't have to do anything at all. It does you.' It reached out its shining arms and grabbed their startled faces with icy, magnetic hands.

A Xanadu feeling permeated them, and waves of wholeness and fulfillment radiated through their bodies like the lavings of a foetal dream. Howard was enraptured by the jeweled beauty of time, faceted instants clustering to planes of minutes, planes of hours, spires and minarets of crystal aeons. And he stood transfixed by the loveliness of its symmetries.

Humming with empty hearing and pleasure, Dirk vibrated with the alien's knowing. To be was indeed to gather from within: The very structure of the universe articulated itself violently through him. In a body-blinding flash of awareness, he saw to the pith of himself: The ruffled fabric of molecules that tailored his body unraveled into a teeming haze of star-pointed nuclei and blurry electrons. The inside of himself looked like outer space: Blackness held everything. His mind was stretched across that blackness, twinkling with the galaxies of atoms and *seeing*, close up, firsthand, that the pinpoints of hazy energy, the tiny electrons, were all the same. Not similar, like pennies or xeroxed pages, but indistinguishably the same. All protons, too. All neutrons. All neutrinos. At its core, the entire universe was made up of identical units, wholly devoid of individuality. The sameness of all the parts almost maddened him. And he understood then the glory of life with its frenzied hungers and rendings, its baffling diversities and genetic distractions. *Life is nature's need to be abandoned.* It was so clear: Life was creation's need to let go of the sameness of atoms and molecules and be free as the fields of force that began all matter. *To be free is to be lost.* A laugh ballooned in him. What was all this maniacle life, this abandon, but him? The same force that exploded into the universe was thundering in his heart, radiating his hair and his thoughts, working at his life as busy as the stars.

The song began for him then – the diamond grindstone of heaven's chiming music, bright as rock-and-roll, expansive and coherent as a Bach fugue. And for a second's orgasmic epoch, the energy of the song was his life. In the next instant the energy had cooled to personal thoughts and the comprehension that he had always been free. He had only been a slave to himself, a prisoner to his own illusions about history and time. The alien had opened a window in his blood, and he had crawled through. For a moment, gripped by Insideout's panoramic vista of his being, Dirk was the freedom of life. Terror sainted his awareness: He was but a mote of life in a swirling vacancy of motes. And though this gored him with loneliness, he did not rage against it as he always had before. Everyone, he realized, was an orphan. Everyone was a child of light locked in the night of spacetime. The crown of creation was as empty in the middle as zero. And what had been his torment became his truth, his joy beyond telling.

His body was too slim to hold it all. Knowing spilled through him and into the sea's tidings. Dolphin snouts poked from the water and sprayed amazement as pulses of human feelings beaconed over the sea.

Howard twitched alert. His trance cracked when he saw Dirk blinking toward blackout, swaying over the side. Time was wrinkling into desiccated colors around him. Howard grabbed his shoulders. 'Yo! Are you all right, kid?'

Howard's startled grip brought Dirk around. He clasped Howard's arm. 'I'm okay,' he said.

'You're sure?'

A smile widened Dirk's face. He was more than himself. 'Yeah, I'm sure.'

Howard lowered him into one of the seats and turned to face the alien.

Insideout was back at the stern of the boat, sitting down. 'Wild, no?'

'Beautiful,' Howard agreed. 'And spooky. This whole world is a flower of balanced energies. A dream.'

'That's the beautiful part,' the alien said and looked away, staring with its blank eyes toward the green altar of Oahu. 'The spooky part is that another orc bloom is building up.'

203

Howard's heart flinched. 'You mean the people around us are going to turn into monsters?'

'I'm afraid so. I'm terribly ashamed. And sorry. Oh, I am sorry. It's my brain, you see. It can't hold back the pain anymore. The hyperfield that sustains me is on the rack of your expanding universe. And I'm being stretched to the limits of my life.'

'That's horrible,' Howard conceded, 'but what's this about an orc bloom?'

'My painsick brain is becoming demented, Howard.' Insideout hid its face in a perfect mime of distress. 'My craziness makes orcs.'

'Dirk, are you hearing this?' Howard called, anxiously.

'Yeah.' He was buzzing pleasurably from the experiences of yes-out-of-mind, and he listened with his face turned up to the sky and his eyes filled with clouds.

'I can't stay with you any longer,' Insideout said, standing up. 'These shapes are terribly unstable.'

'How *do* you do that?' Howard asked.

'Electrostatic charge. The ocean's teeming with ions.'

'Come back,' Dirk called feebly.

'Trust yourselves,' the alien said. Dolphins scythed through the air behind it. 'I will – '

The watershape splashed into spray, the dolphins dove out of sight, and Howard's timelines clapped back into place. A roar shook seaspray from the stern, and the boat shot forward, flinging Howard to the taffrail.

Dirk quickly choked off the engine. Howard crawled into the seat beside him and lay back stunned. After a moment of breathless silence, he asked: 'What're we going to do?'

'We can't do anything until the others get here,'

204

Dirk said in a dreamy voice, his eyes half shut. 'Let's go back to the hotel and lay low. Wait.'

'With my wife turning into an orc in front of my eyes? No way, kid. Think of something better.'

'I can't think after that, man.' Dirk sat up and frowned to feel the euphoria of lusk diluted by the need to act. 'Okay, now we have to fit Cora into this mess.'

'Look, kid, she's my wife. I've always taken care of her, and I always will. If we're emitting some monster-making radiation, then I'm staying away from her until this whole thing is over.'

'Hey, don't get bent. We'll give her a call when we get back to shore. Right now, we got to figure a way to stay away from the orc for about another eighteen hours. By then, Jiang and Reena will be here.'

'Sure, but where can we go until then?'

'That's for you to figure out, Merlin. You're the guy who can see the future.'

Howard tried to quell his anxiety and analyze the timelines intersecting within him. But he was too nervous and the swaying of the boat and the liquid sparkles of sunlight on the swells were distracting. 'Take out the alien.'

'The arc?' Dirk asked, reaching into his pocket.

'Right. It'll help me see into time. Maybe I can find us a safe way through time to the others.'

Dirk took the cold shape out.

Howard flinched when he saw it. The arc was a piece of daybreak in his eyes, the blind tip of lightning, puncturing sight and leaving black blisters on his vision that glowed like embers under his closed lids. He turned his gaze aside, into the blunt glare of the sea, till the sting in his eyes relented; then he looked again through tightly squinted lashes. The light was alive. The light was declaring life. In the dazzling triumph, Howard felt its power reaching into the prickly points of his body, his cells, endlessly shattered and made, inventing him moment by moment. The light of the arc saturated him with its radiance. The ways of choice rayed through him like air-tracks in an icecube.

'Get us outta here alive, Howie.' Dirk's hot-hearted presence pressed closer, fragrant as pine resin. 'Find us a way to hide from the orc.'

Voices of silence intercut the noises of the sea. Howard surged free of his body and into the wave-light of the alien. Immediately, he was with an old dragon-whiskered Chinese man, Jiang, as he was at that moment: Running with demonic speed over rail ties past a cedar lake brown with the tannin of fallen leaves. Time buckled, and Howard soared with Jiang into his fate a few hours ahead. The railroad tracks sang a silver scream, trees snapped by, then sagging shacks, soured industrial lots, huddled buildings, and the frantic avenues and architecture of Shanghai. The flashforward speeded through Jiang's departure from Shanghai harbor as a stowaway to his discovery and plunge overboard and his mad flight across the night sea shadowed by an orc of luminous corpse gas. Jiang meteored into the ocean, and the timerush calmed to its ordinary flow.

Jiang's pumping legs held him up like an offering to the spectral night. He was strong, but his strength was vanishing into his effort. His old heart repeated its prodigal wish to keep treading water, to stay afloat. His body complied and cried with weariness.

He watched the star-pattern of the Lion plunge into the sea. Over two hours had passed since his demon power had abandoned him. He relaxed his legs and dropped his head back, wanting to float, but the black depths drew him down. He moved his arms before him in a tai chi sweep, kicked his legs, and rose to the surface again. He would not die here, the joke of some demon. Too much suffering had been endured, too many others of his own seed had gone ahead of him into the void for him to abandon himself so helplessly to an absurd death. The ocean would kill him, but he would choose the moment. He would swim until dawn and drown with the sun in his eyes.

Howard was snatched from this scene, bounced through intricacies of fire and emptiness, and emerged in the marmoreal expanse of an airport at night. Neon signs in French shone up from the depths of the marble floor, and Howard swung his attention, trying to orient himself.

He was hovering before the plastic colors from a fluorescently lit airlines kiosk. Reena was beside him – a tall, blond woman with green eyes in a fox-wide face. Behind her was a timeshaft, a tunnel of outer space glinting with opal light. In the jeweled light were events that replayed themselves as Howard studied them. The timeshaft behind Reena showed her journey from the asylum to the airport at Avignon and the flight from there to Orly international airport. Minutes before, a white-sweatered, green-smocked Reena in hospital slippers had entered a clothiers in the floodlit glass and marble mall and selected a new outfit. She picked out lacy underwear, gray denim slacks, amber-soled canvas-top shoes, blue socks, a lavender shirt, and a light-weight buff jacket with abalone buttons.

A security guard watched her step out of the dressing room fully garbed in her new clothes, smile at the cashier, walk out, and discard her old garments in a trash bin. The guard followed her to an airlines counter where she acquired tickets for a series of connecting flights to Honolulu, which she paid for with nothing more than a smile.

When Reena walked past other security guards and into the gate for an overseas flight without a passport, he intercepted her. This was where Howard's sentience had manifested, and he watched intrigued from his invisible stance beside the electric kiosk.

'Madam, may I see your passport?'

Reena faced the guard with a childlike smile and thought: *Let me pass. Forget you've seen me.*

'Your passport, please,' the guard insisted.

Fear spurred her, and she thought more forcefully: *Leave me alone. Forget that you've ever seen me.*

'I noticed that you walked in here without displaying your passport,' the guard said. 'I want to see that now, please.'

'Of course,' Reena replied and began searching through the pockets of her jacket. Fear trilled louder. She had lost her power. The alien was falling asleep. She sensed that. It was still there – her mind was clear, so it was still compensating for her malformed brain – but she could not longer push her thoughts into peoples' minds. She trembled with the thought that if Insideout went any further away, she would collapse into her sickness. She hid her shiver as a shrug and faced the guard with a jinxed smile. 'I lost it.'

Howard was lifted away as he watched the guard leading Reena off. Blinding effulgence gulfed over him, and to a chorus of raving screams he watched the ocean sheeting below and Honolulu's white modernity loom ahead. Beside him, Dirk was weeping. Howard offered his hand, and with a rush-smeared smile they rocketed forward together.

He was back on the harbor, walking across a

parking lot and away from the boats with Dirk. A shadow alighted on them, and they turned up their faces to see a pterodactyl-winged, millipede-segmented gargoyle swooping overhead. Spiderlegs stab-flashed outward, pincered him by his clothes, and hoisted him away from Dirk. He screamed and darkness snapped hugely.

He was back in the boat with Dirk. Reef fish flashed out of the water, clouds swelled in slow motion, and sunlight forked his eyes.

'What'd you see?' Dirk wanted to know. He had put the arc into the pocket of his jeans, and it was burning uncomfortably.

Howard tried his breath and at first couldn't speak. 'Jiang and Reena are in trouble,' he gasped.

'What kind of trouble?'

'Jiang's drowning. Reena's been picked up by an airport security guard. I think we've lost them.' Howard pressed his eyes with his fingertips.

'What about us?'

'The orc's onshore. I saw it.'

Dirk banged his fist off the fiberglass hull. 'We can't go back.'

Howard looked up, and his face was smoky with tears.

'We'll stay out here,' Dirk said. 'We'll wait for the others.'

'Forget it.' Howard wiped the fright-sweat from around his eyes with the heel of a hand. 'That thing I saw had wings. It'll fly out here.'

'So we're just gonna go back there and get taken out?' Dirk stood up. The buoyant rhythm of the boat made him keep his stance loose, and the frustration he was feeling had nowhere to go but into his heart. And there an answer was waiting. 'We'll go back. But we won't hide. The orc can't hurt us except through others. We'll keep moving. Whatever plasma shapes it takes just look scary, right? They can't hurt us.'

'Kid, the thing I saw carried me away.'

'Maybe what you saw is wrong.'

'It's never wrong.'

Dirk reached into his pocket and took out the refrigerated arc. Vapor wisps curled off it. 'Maybe you can look again. Find another future.'

The arc looked like a shiny compressor slug. Howard reached out and took it. His hand jumped to feel how cold it was. He held it up close to his face, but no timelines crystalized out of thin air. He shot a stare at Dirk. 'I think it stopped working. I don't see anything.'

Dirk took the arc back. It was warmer now. 'I think it peaked.' He searched his heart for the answer he had just known: *The orc can't hurt us except through other people*, he repeated to himself. *So? So what?* The comprehension and ecstasy that had flourished in him moments before was gone. 'Fuck it!'

'You feel normal, too, don't you?' Howard asked. 'I think we're all on our own now.'

'It punked out,' Dirk concurred glumly. The arc was as warm as any normal wafer of metal.

Howard started the engine. Dirk put the arc back in his pocket and sat down. The ride into the harbor was strangely ordinary. 'So you went on a class trip and picked up a spaceship. That's how this madness started.'

Dirk nodded and watched the afternoon sunlight glinting off the diadem of Honolulu.

'Your parents know anything about this?' Howard asked.

'I live in a Home,' Dirk answered in a flat tone. 'My dad died in Nam, my mom left.'

'Oh.' Howard tried to engage his stare, but the kid wouldn't look at him. 'What about the Home, then? Anybody there know about our troubles?'

'Some guys I owe money kidnapped me in front of about twenty other kids. I think the Home knows I'm in some kinda trouble. I don't know if they've called the cops or what.'

'They guys who took you were orc-infested. Is that right?'

'Right.' Dirk felt dreamlessly bland. What had he called it in his spell with Mr Leonard? Anomie. Anomie dripped in him. Without the influx of power from the alien, his life seemed futureless. Even if he survived the orc and got the alien where it was going, what then? Back to stealing stereos and running dope?

They sped on in silence for a while, and Howard remembered his vision of this moment. The ocean was sheeted with speed beneath them, and the engine's roar was like a screaming choir. He looked over and saw Dirk gazing listlessly at the scarves of high clouds. In the dream, he had been weeping. Maybe he was weeping. Howard spoke up: 'Kid?'

'Hm.'

'Until today, we were strangers. When I first saw you in my dreams, I thought you were a punk. But back there I saw our destiny. Everything perfectly balanced, tuned like an engine. It was so beautiful I just know we can get through this thing – if we stick together. I know that's true, kid.'

'Yeah,' Dirk responded without looking at him. 'I'm with you.'

'Okay, then we're buddies. I figure what you and I saw happen back there makes us friends for life. No one else will ever believe us. It's just you and me. Right?' Howard offered his hand.

Dirk saw the hand out of the corner of his eye and watched it hang there a moment before taking it in a quick shake.

'We're friends now,' Howard said, slapping Dirk on the shoulder. 'So don't call me Howie anymore.'

'Sure. And don't call me kid.' Dirk hung his head into the slipstream of rushing air.

'Since our lives depend on one another,' Howard went on, 'so do our fortunes. I'm not greedy. If we get out of this thing alive, I'm giving you one of those millions the alien won for me. That won't make up for not having parents, but you got Cora and me for that – if you can stand us.'

Dirk faced about with a slack jaw. 'You're goofin' me.'

'I'm not goofing you. And I hope to God you're not goofing me. I have a feeling we're going to need each other over the next twenty-four hours.'

Dirk grinned up at the highest contrails. 'You just made my life, Howard.'

Howard puttered slowly into the harbor, timid without the timelines to guide him. Dirk directed his approach and waved off skiffs and fishing boats that came too close. The sandy-haired owner of the boat was waiting at his berth among the wharves with a handful of friends and a cooler of ice-chilled champagne. 'You guys are ten minutes early. You want a grand back?'

'Keep the change.' Dirk beamed and boosted himself on to the wharf.

Howard helped himself to a bottle of champagne and raised it in toast. 'To Reena and Jiang. May they make it here safely – and quickly.'

While he swigged, Dirk watched the grinning boatman to see if the orc was on him. Howard handed Dirk the bottle, and he looked away from the

212

boatman and leveled his pale stare on Howard. 'To staying alive.' He gulped and put the bottle back in the ice. He and Howard walked down the pier attentively, scrutinizing everyone as they went along. Howard knew that the parking lot was where the orc had appeared in his vision – but timelines might have shifted since then. His insides were burnished with fear. Everywhere he looked he saw ordinary people absorbed in their acts and dreams: Crews setting sail and docking, open-faced tourists promenading the wharves, laughing friends, quiet lovers. The winged monstrosity from his vision couldn't possibly exist in a world as sun-rich and quotidian as this. But it had to be real. His prescience was never wrong.

In the parking lot, crossing to the boulevard that led back to their hotel, Howard had his eyes on the sky, but Dirk as usual was scanning the street scene. He heard the snick of a camera to his right and turned, expecting to see tourists. Three stout Japanese men with brushtop haircuts and crisp shirts and trousers stepped from the shade of the lot's huge mangrove tree. Two dashed toward the harbor to cut off retreat; the other strode purposively to meet them. Dirk observed that the man's forearms were thick as trout and blotched with tattoos. *Yakuza!* – the Japanese mob. He grabbed Howard's elbow in a panic. 'We got trouble, pal.'

Howard quit his sky surveillance and cast a troubled look about him. Beyond the mangrove tree, a black Mercedes with tinted windows was idling. Standing by the open driver's door, with an auto-reflex camera in his hand and wearing aviator sunglasses and a smile as thin as his mustache, was Tony Robello. Howard's prescience had been right after all – but the alien's dwindling strength had distorted the future view of this moment: Tony and the Yakuza had appeared in his vision as the winged monster, and Howard had been duped by his literal expectation. Too late, he realized that this trap could have been avoided.

'Make a run for it,' Dirk said, dropping his duffel bag. 'I can handle myself. I'll hold them off.' Dirk crouched into a defensive posture.

Howard was terrified of the muscular, tattooed men closing in on them, but flight seemed inappropriate. He'd already seen the orc snag him, and he'd just sworn his friendship to the kid. Only after Dirk shoved him did he dash for the street.

The man approaching them quick-stepped to block him, and Dirk lunged forward to confront him. With a yell, Dirk leaped into the air and descended on the assailant with one leg tucked under and the other heel thrust forward.

The Yakuza whirled and knocked Dirk to the ground. The kid tumbled and bounced to his feet, hands clawed to strike. He lashed out in two rapid viper-stabs. The Yakuza blocked both, punched one, and dropped Dirk flat on his back. His eyes gushing tears, his head clanging, he watched the Yakuza grab Howard and carry him to a waiting hatchback. They threw him in and drove off before Dirk could even sit up.

Swiping the tears from his eyes, he looked about drunkenly. The Mercedes was gone, too. Howard's baseball cap lay upside down on the asphalt. A group of chuckling fishermen, their strung catch of crevalles and yellowfin still bright with the sea's chrism, walked off the pier and into the parking lot. No one else was in sight, except the rush of cars on the boulevard, where no one stopped for anything.

* * *

Cora was waiting nervously on the balcony, tugging the sleeves of her pink caftan while watching the street for the first sign of her husband. He hadn't been gone that long, but she was frightened for him because of the incident in Vegas. If he wasn't back in the next half hour, she was calling the police. Twenty minutes later, she spotted the young body-guard Howard had hired. Her heart winced. He was alone.

Cora met Dirk at the elevator. 'Where's Howard?'

'Relax, lady. Howard's taking in some deep sea fishing.' He hoped he wasn't being literal: He figured the whip-thin guy in aviator glasses he saw with the Mercedes was Tony Robello. The brawn had defi-nitely been Yakuza. Dirk's prayer was that they had taken him to get his money, not his life. If he was right, they would be coming here next. The suite was in a fictitious name, but Dirk didn't figure Howard – or anyone – would be very tight-lipped with the Yakuza.

'Why didn't he call?' Cora complained. 'I taught him everything he knows about fly-casting. He'd want to take me along. I know it. Something's wrong.'

'Nothing's wrong.' Dirk walked to the suite and went in, but Cora hung back. 'Lady, I'm not gonna hurt you. I'm here to help you. Leave the door open if you're afraid of me.'

'If you want to help me, then you tell me the truth about my husband.'

'He's out at sea, fishing. We figured that was the safest place for him right now. He's concerned that we might have been trailed to this hotel, and he sent me back to move you to another place.'

'I'm not going anyplace without him,' she said

from the doorway, and a blue-silver sheet of flame flapped once over her face and was gone.

Dirk blinked, wanting to believe he hadn't seen that lick of orc fire. 'Your life is in danger here. I'm trying to help you.'

'Are you?' She paused, gauging him for truthfulness. 'Where's your ID? I want to call your agency.'

'I don't work for an agency.'

'Ha!' A rasp of ultraviolet sparks came and went behind her.

Dirk knew he had seen that, and his blood whipped faster in his veins. 'Howard needs somebody he can trust.' The words inspired a cringe of dismalness. He had already failed Howard. He had to do something now to help him, and the only thing he could think of was to get Cora out of danger and give Howard a chance to bargain. 'I'm not just some bodyguard like he said. I'm a friend.'

Cora heard the depth in his words, and she stepped into the suite. 'How does Howard know you?'

'Does that matter?'

'It would help me trust you.'

Dirk nodded and reached into himself. 'He knew my dad in Nam. They were military buddies.'

'Howard was never in Nam.'

'They met in the Philippines, in Subic Bay. He was my dad's best friend before he was killed.' A swell of emotion budged on his face, remembering the sadness of his father's ghost.

'Howard never told me.'

The memory of his father charged him with hurt, and he felt filthy for lying. 'What more can I say, lady? Either you get your stuff and I'll find you another place, or you stay here and meet whatever comes down the pike. I'm not gonna fight you.'

Cora gathered her clothes and Howard's in their suitcases and had Dirk carry the luggage to the front door for the bellhop to pick up. She carried the silvery, metal alloy suitcase that Howard had bought in Vegas to transport the twenty-thousand hundred dollar bills. In the lobby, she accepted the return of the cash deposit, settled her account, and tipped the manager a handful of the big bills for his promise that the hotel would continue to take messages for her and her husband and relay them when she called.

They left through the delivery entrance and had the bellhop load their luggage on a pedicab that Dirk waved down. He had the driver pedal them along the back streets to an equally opulent hotel.

'What happens now?' Cora asked after the luggage was delivered and they were alone in an oceanview apartment. Orc energies marbled the air around her, and she was beginning to notice them. Her eyes twitched to catch the shimmers of light she sensed at the edge of her sight.

'Have some food. Rest. Wait.' Dirk backed toward the door.

'And you?'

'I'll go meet Howard. I don't want you to worry about anything. We'll be back soon. Now that he knows you're safe, we may just lay low at sea tonight. We'll be in touch by tomorrow.'

'Tomorrow?' She surged with protest but then held herself back. Dirk looked anxious. 'Okay,' she conceded. 'But tell Howard to stay bundled up out there. Maybe I should give you some of his clothes. It must get chilly at night.' She went to the suitcases trailing a comet trail of diaphanous blue energies.

Dirk stopped her with a shout: 'Hey, no! Clothing's no problem. I thought of that already.' He opened

217

the door and backed out. 'Don't worry. Okay? Keep hanging out and hanging on.'

The door closed and he was gone. Cora waited two heartbeats, then went to the phone and called the police.

The day tilted. Night rose to the east. A planet burned in a teal-blue sky over the Pacific. And the vastness of the galaxy began to spill through the transparency of the night. Dirk sat among the boulders of Sandy Beach, his duffel bag a pillow against a slant or rock.

This was a favorite haunt of his, only two miles from the Home. He knew the beach's dunes and rocky coves well, and he had come here because if this was to be the night of the orc, he wanted to meet it on his own terrain. Other nights when he had crawled down the Home's wall of dented bricks, he had sat here trying to calm the craziness in him with the surf's noise. All that seemed childish now. What had he despaired? That his father was dead? Endless fathers were dead. The sea was a father. The waves of this beach had taught him everything he knew about balance, daring, surrender, and release. Body-surfing was more thrilling than a ballgame with the old man. And the girls he had met here were more affectionate than any mother could have been. He wasn't starved for love. So what was his gripe? He couldn't remember now.

He listened for the alien. All he heard was the surf's commotion. Far down the beach, a night fisherman's lantern came on, green as an eye. Since leaving Cora, Dirk had seen wafer faces of glare around other people, but he had kept moving and nothing had concentrated.

The black voice of an animal cried from the sea

rocks, and Dirk was blown forward on to his heels. He strained his eyes to stare over the boulders, which had become masses of darkness. He saw nothing unusual. The sex of night and day continued in the west, shining on the windcut clouds and the island's bluffs.

The melisma of a cat in heat sounded again, and Dirk sat back. His heart was staring hellward, anticipating the orc. He knew with the certainty of the alien's mastery that it was coming for him, but he kept his mind innocent. He had to. The night was a harvest of fantasies. He would not succumb as easily as he had to that Yakuza thug who had decked him this afternoon.

His hand went to the bone bruise where his jaw had absorbed the Yakuza's blow, and he stopped himself in midreach. He traced the ancestry of his motion back through the lineage of half-conscious associations to the achy absence his parents had left him. He gently but firmly placed his hand in his lap and drained his mind of distracting thoughts. He breathed the sea's omens and watched the constellations kindle. He wasn't his father's son for nothing.

Arc of the Dream

Jiang rose and fell in the steady surge of the ocean. His face floated on the surface in a tangle of wispy white hair and whiskers like the blown waste of a tubeworm. He was in a trance of exhaustion, his windburnt eyes flickering to the rhythm of his tread in the water, waiting for dawn to release him to death.

Moony blue light sheened the swells. The apertures of his body loosened with relief, ready to give up, but he exerted himself yet, swaying gently as a hydrozoan, turning to face the shadow of the rising sun. Slowly, he rotated toward the light, and the sea flashed brighter. Gleams of blue fire went off like fireworks as the light struck the rocking waves. Shock twitched the silver tufts that were his eyebrows, and his eyes opened wider. In crooked light, like a sheet of frozen lightning, his children were standing on the sea hills, rising and falling.

Jiang clapped his eyes shut and opened them again. His children were still there, watching him with slow faces, weary with grief. Their ghostly arms reached toward him. His wife was there, too, the spicy murmur of her voice calling the childrens' names. The names pealed across the ocean like the wanderings of a bell.

Exhaustion and sadness pulled him down, and he relented to the cold gravity of the sea. Water sloshed over him, and as his sinuses cramped with the bite of the salt water his sight ignited into fiery streamers. The sea banged away from him in a geyser of spray, and he was flung with outstretched arms and legs like a human star into the night.

The demon had seized him again. At the moment of his surrender, Jiang was suddenly flying through the sky once more. Dare he believe this was true? He clenched his hands to his body in the rising rush of his flight. He was solid. His exhaustion and bone-soggy coldness had sloughed away, and he was infused with the superhuman stamina that had carried him to the sea.

He relaxed into the buoyant embrace of the demon and looked about for the grisly creature that had fallen with him into the ocean. Sparks flurried behind in the draft of his soaring flight, and he did see gnashing, oiled faces in the blinks of fire. But the sparks were not gathering into larger shapes, and he was grateful for that.

The scalloped hem of the solar wind rippled in the east, and Jiang briefly saw the sun sitting like a lizard on the earth's curve before he dropped back into the night. A frail star appeared in the blackness of the Pacific. As Jiang swooped closer, the pinch of light blossomed into a web of lights, and he saw that he was being carried toward a ship. Closer, the white hull shone in the glare from the deck-lights, and he could see the ship's name in some foreign language.

Jiang's heart skittered. He was sailing through the air directly over the ship. He could see every small detail – the lightning rods on the steam stack, the parabolas of tiered decks, the two men in white uniforms standing together on the main deck, the red spark of a cigarette rising and falling between them. The men were not Chinese.

Whirling in a slow and invisible vortex, Jiang twirled gently down to the ship, hovered momentarily over a swimming pool lit with eerie gelatinous light, and collapsed on to the deck with a loud *oomph*. The crewmen, two cooks hot from preparing breakfast rolls, were sharing a cool break on the aft deck. When they heard Jiang land behind them, they jumped around, and the one who was smoking dropped his cigarette. 'Who the hell are you?'

'He's not crew.'

'No kidding.'

They bent over him and helped him to his feet. 'He's soaked. Must have been in the pool.'

'That's sea water. Can't you smell it?'

'Sea water? We're going fifteen knots. Can you talk, old man?'

'He looks Chinese. Feels strong as a horse.'

Jiang was allowing himself to be carried, but his muscles were tiger-packed with restless strength.

'You did real good, old man.' They bolstered him on either side and guided him toward a companionway. He swung his smile between them. They smelled flagrantly rich, scented with cooking oil and flour. 'Don't know how you did it, but you made it. We arrive in Honolulu after breakfast.'

The wide morning stretched through the tall windows of Orly airport. Reena sat anxiously in the security office, staring through the tinted sheet glass at the traffic of people and luggage. The guard who had picked her up was conferring with his superior, a portly woman with page-cut hair. The chief was glowering at Reena while nodding to the guard.

Reena ignored them and watched the churning crowd with longing for the mystic freedom she saw there. Insideout was still close to her, but it was drowsy and had withdrawn her telepathy. Without the mental noises from the throng in her head, she too was just a wanderer. The idea thrilled her. In all her life, this was the farthest she had traveled. Beyond the arched windows, in the tempest noise of the airfield, jets were launching into a dawn like milk, and the places they were scattering to she would never see.

Wake up! she cried to the godful presence within her. *If you fall asleep, I'll go crazy. They'll lock me up again!* For an hour, while calls were made to report her, she had been crying silently to herself like this, sitting here, watching the sky gray and the clouds brighted to curry tones. This time her cry for the alien was reflex, and she hopped in her seat when blue acetylene jumped from the tips of her body and her head cawed with psychic noise.

The glowering chief shouted with alarm to see Reena's hair lifting out briskly and shining like bright optic fibers from her spark-faceted face. And the guard toppled over a chair in his rush to back away from the fiery woman. The air in the room looked polished, and it was suddenly filled with a menthol fragrance of glaciers and conifer crags.

Reena stood, and the tremulous electricity spilled in curds to the floor where it splashed and skidded wildly. Troll screeches rasped like fingernails on a garbage can lid, and the electric blobs became pugnacious prehistoric fish faces snapping rabidly. The fiery, jaw-raving congealments gnashed briefly and were gone.

Reena put her attention deep into the stares of the two security guards and said. 'Forget you saw this. Forget me. Go about your normal routines happily and with kindness.' She brushed the static wrinkles from her gray slacks and walked out into the crowd.

'Where were you?' she asked aloud. In the cloud of noise both inside her telepathy and in the mill of passengers, she was too confused to hear herself think.

'It's almost too late for me.' In her scalded hearing, Insideout was a whisper. 'My brain is shutting down. I've been away too long from my source of power. Come quickly.'

Reena selected a Concord flight to New York. Once snug in her seat, she used an airline magazine map to plan the rest of her itinerary from New York to Los Angeles, and then Hawaii. The whole journey would take fifteen hours. To be certain that her travels were not interrupted again, before she got on the Concord she stopped a woman her age and asked for her passport. She accepted Reena's mental command to be happy and kind by cheerfully turning over her passport and walking spritely to an airport café. With her new passport, Reena booked passage for all her flights and got her tickets. She would arrive in Honolulu at 7:45 in the morning, island time.

For the next half day, she sat and listened inwardly for Insideout. The musings of those around her were all heard before, but the rainbow-colored thoughts within her were strange and compelling as an atonal nocturne. She cleared herself of thoughts, which she had learned to do simply by trying. When she heard the blood in her ears, she stared at the emptiness within her, waiting for the alien to appear.

What did she expect Insideout to say? Why it had gone away? How it had come back? It couldn't even tell her how it had come to this fragmentation blast she called a universe.

The answer to that was somewhere. All knowledge was sealed like a fossil in spacetime. Insideout, too, wanted to know exactly how it had come to this frightening place. But there was no time for its brain to go through the analyses that would bring that knowledge forward. And what good would it have done the alien? Some riddles become mystery just because there isn't enough time to think them through. Indeed, time was steaming away, and with it Insideout's strength. Most of its energy was spent sustaining its brain away from the hyperfields, buffering the remorseless pain of the decaying fields in the titanohematite matrix.

Insideout showed Reena what it was doing. It let her telepathy penetrate it, hoping she would understand. With what little power it had left it was reaching out to the humans. Yet even in its impuissance, it was too strong for them. Its most simplistic effort required four of their brains and bodies. Why? Was that somehow related to the coldness of this cosmos, which had frozen energy into four separate forces in four narrow dimensions? *Why me?* it wondered. What was this *me* that always seemed to be the center? Was it not the pith itself shattered into countless lives across the whole universe? The woe in that thought blew a bassoon-note of despair across its being. *Strange are the ways.* The alien marveled that any self-awareness had evolved in such dimwitted brains so firmly entrained to furious bodies.

'I'm an oaf,' Insideout said miserably, its voice childishly genderless. 'I don't belong in this wild place. I'll never make any sense to you. Why do you try to understand me?'

'It would help, I think. People like to understand.'

'My home is the pith. My center is the infinity of collapse. But that's meaningless to you. It's like – I – oh, it's all so *different!*' Its petulance sparkled a little in the dark of Reena's closed eyes. 'How can I tell you when there are no words?'

'What does it feel like?'

'Heaven,' the alien responded without hesitation. 'An effortless experience.' It thought deeper, and its brain found a kinder word for that in the tenuous waveforms of forgotten words whispering among the separating photons of the past: 'Lusk.'

'Excuse me?'

'Not lust, my dear, *Lusk*. It's an archaic English word I found in Dirk's verbal unconscious. It sounds simpler than yes-out-of-mind. That's my best translation for the click and whistle phrase my cetacean friends use.'

'Yes-out-of-mind,' Reena echoed.

'Lusk is handier. It means the same thing, you know. The primal affirmation of oneness beyond thought. The spell of wholeness. Your ancestors didn't think much of it. To them it was a kind of sloth – a sin. But what can we expect from the great-grandchildren of the rat? Humans are never satisfied unless they're toiling. But to stay close to me, you have to be languid. Lazy. Lusk.'

Reena communed deeper. The Oriental, Jiang, came closest to acknowledging yes-out-of-mind in his occasional imitations of his grandfather's Taoist meditations. But the brutal effort of his life to survive the aggressions of his fellow creatures allied him more with his rat ancestors than his meditative ones. Dirk and Howard had no meditative ancestors at all. And Reena was a casualty of the exploding universe, her brain broken into distracted selves by the violence of chance. Lusk was meaningless to them.

'What more can I tell you? You see now, don't you? I have nothing to offer you of my world. What can you *do* with yes-out-of-mind?'

'It's a way to be with you, isn't it?' Reena asked. 'Lusk is how I just reached you. I stilled all my thoughts – and I found you.'

'Yes, I see.' The alien was amazed. 'You're right. Lusk may be useful to us. I wonder if the others will be able to still themselves as deeply.'

'If they have to, they will.' Reena was elated with her communion with the alien. 'Tell me more.'

'About what?'

'You. The universe. Anything.'

Groping for a response to Reena's patient attentiveness, Insideout touched on thoughts close to the edge of her comprehension. One thought in particular fascinated her – the closed timelike line of her universe, the path of spacetime from its origin to its return on itself: Creation. *Of course*, the alien realized. After all the palaver the matrons in the asylum had fed her about God, she would be eager to see the Creation.

Insideout amplified that thought for her. The limitations of her brain didn't allow it to display anything mentally beyond the zero mass surface of the point from which the Big Bang began, so it couldn't show her its world or even the multiverse that connects all worlds. But she readily grasped the dramatic visualization of 4-space emergence: First – nothing. Then, from nothing, everything leaped out of 5-space, like Insideout, in an arc of energy, sphering out from the one point of the singularity and ballooning into the gaseous, fire-filamented, spark-whorling bloom of the universe.

'Soon enough,' Insideout said to her in its weightless voice, 'it will stop ballooning and begin to fall back in on itself. Eventually, it will collapse into the singularity and disappear. All vectors will have canceled. All mass and energy will have been conserved. Do you understand? Have you any idea what I'm telling you? Everything that is now – all people, cities, nations, stars, and galaxies are really ghosts.

Truly a dream. Ultimately nothing. The whole universe is a quantum fluctuation of the vacuum.'

Reena lost herself in the alien's mind-video. At the end of it, she had exhausted hours of her attention and had already arrived in New York. The import of that, which would have stunned her with delight at any other lucid time, was insignificant now. On the flight to LA, she wanted to know, 'If the universe is just a big balloon of energy blowing up out of nothing and dropping back into nothing, then what is it *in*? What's surrounding it?'

'Nothing,' Insideout told her. 'The universe is embedded in a true vacuum. This vacuum is forever. And because it is infinite, there are fluctuations of energy in every range, some as vast and complex as this universe. I come from one such fluctuation. But my universe has no future or past. I mean, from here, my home looks like magic. Its sounds unbelievable, but it's real. It's a real place, with no meanings there but itself. No cruelties trying to be kind. No mystery hiding in riddles. And, best of all, no death.'

'How?' Reena squirmed, trying to comprehend. 'How can that be?'

'My universe is just another fluctuation, like yours. Another throw of the dice. And like your world, it makes sense only to itself.'

'And you'll take me there with you when you go?'

'I'll take you. But not there. You wouldn't fit. It's a universe big enough for only one mind.'

Corrugated white light rippled the air. Howard sat at a formica-top table shuffling cards. Tony Robello and two of the Yakuza who had kidnapped him sat with him, playing poker. They were one ripple of the corrugation. Across the empty, shadow-strewn span of the vacant warehouse was another ripple where a thug was talking on the phone they had patched in to a passing telephone cable. A mile away was the harbor where he had left Dirk. The boy was gone from there now. It was almost night. Through the fluorescently lit wall of the warehouse, Howard's timegaze could see the molasses sky over the marina's boatlights and rigging, and he could hear the sluggish drone of the traffic on the adjacent highway. Farther west yet, the next warp of dream-seen light covered the Pearl Harbor anchorage where a luxury liner would dock the next morning. Gazing into the pearly texture of that vision, Howard could already see the next morning's sunlight slippery on the bay water and the liner tied off to its stage. Stepping down the gangway, among chic couples and sun-bossed travelers, was an old man with a long silver mustache and chin whiskers. He was wrapped in a blanket and bareheaded, and tufts of white hair glowed like smoke from his smiling face. Two police officers waited for him on the dock.

'Enough with the shuffling already,' Tony said, thumping his knuckle on the formica. 'Deal the cards.'

Howard turned his timegaze to the table. Close up like this, his perception of the future was hazier. He could see a granite glow to the game he had shuffled. It would never be played. He shrugged and lay the deck on the table to be cut. As Tony reached for it, the man on the phone hung up, and Tony sat back to hear what he had to say.

The Yakuza strode to the table and spoke to the others in Japanese. The one on Tony's right translated: 'His wife is not in the hotel. She checked out after we took him.'

'I told you guys,' Howard mumbled. 'My wife

skipped with the money. She doesn't care what you do with me.'

Tony dismissed his lie with a nah-look. 'The kid he was with musta tipped her off. It's been three hours now. Where's the make on that guy?'

'The photograph you took is still circulating among the gangs,' the Yakuza explained in his fluent English. 'If he was a gang member, as you think, we will find him.'

'As I think.' Tony rolled his eyes. 'The kid was a street fighter. In this hick town, every gang must have seen him before.' He picked up the cards and began shuffling them.

'Do you still pretend you don't know him?' the Yakuza asked Howard with a subzero stare.

'If I'd known you guys were on my tail, I wouldn't have hired a street kid. I'd have gone to the police.' He pointed to the table. 'That was my deal.'

'Then who was he?' the thug asked.

'A kid. I told you. I met him at the airport. He seemed to know his way around. He found us a good hotel. And he had a friend who let me joyride his boat.'

'Yeah, for which you paid ten grand,' Tony pointed out and began dealing.

'Hell, I can afford to be generous. That's why I'm here, right?'

Tony threw the cards down and thumped the table. The Japanese remained motionless. But Howard, even though he had seen the gesture in the future moments before it happened, jumped. 'Somethin's screwy here, Dyckson. You ripped us off back in Vegas, didn't you?'

The timelines were trembling. A scream like bending iron drifted through him from across a great distance. Anything could happen. 'How could I rip

230

you off?' Howard asked. 'It was your setup, your cards, your players. What could I do? Read the future?'

Tony bit his thumb and sat back. 'I'm in trouble because of you, asshole. The boys in Vegas think I used you to burn them. If it wasn't for my island friends here, I'd be dead now. You hear me? I'm bringing back their money, or I can't show my face in this hemisphere again. Now you know that. So why do you keep feeding me lines? You want ugly?'

'Tony, I was lucky that night in Vegas,' Howard lay his hands face up on the table in exasperation. 'You saw me at the tables. I was rolling.'

'Sure. But the odds against beating our fix were astronomical.'

'I was lucky.'

'Yeah, Dyckson, but it was bad luck.'

'You can have the money back. I've been telling you that since we got here.'

'Then where's the money?'

'I can't help it if I can't find my wife.'

'Well, I hope you like this decor, because you're here until we collect. And not just my money – '

'I know, I know. These guys are in for a cut of the lottery winnings. You think going over and over it like this is going to make it happen faster?'

'If your wife doesn't answer our messages at the hotel soon, we'll start sending your fingers.'

Howard covered his face with his hands. Was he dreaming this? They had had this conversation so many times, he wasn't sure. A white rose flourished in the blackness of his shut eyes. It was a time node, here and now, the photon-cut silence of spacetime opening its jewel. A whale's dripping eye watched him from the rose's center. That was the alien Dirk had told him about, he was certain.

231

The rose fluttered with time's wingbeat. He tried to push his vision forward, to see what was going to happen to him. But the wraith-rose showed nothing but the round, little eye.

A pounding boomed from the iron door at the far end of the hollow building. Howard dropped his hands and watched two of the Yakuza rush to the door. As they ran, their motion-shadows brittled into a crystal sheeting of luminous time scenes. The door opening, the Yakuza guiding in a hulking man with a cobra-sheath neck, bald head, bonesunk eyes.

Time slipped back into gear. Howard blinked and observed the glint of savagery in the huge man's iron stare.

'His name's Chud,' the Yakuza told Tony. 'He's one of our local contacts. He knows the kid.'

'What's the kid's name?' Tony asked with gleeful solemnity.

'Dirk Heiser.' Chud looked at Howard and the Yakuza with a ghastly vehemence. 'He killed my partner. Now I want to kill him.'

'Where can we find him?'

'The Mokes are looking for him now. They know his hideouts. When they find him, they'll call us here.'

'Fine.' Tony began regathering the cards. Time-lines became rubbery again, and Howard witnessed more card games in the transparent hallways of his timesight. Tony stared up into the underbrow darkness of Chud's face. 'Seven-stud high-low?'

Cora had spent hours answering questions for the police. They had put a trace on the phone messages being left at the hotel where she and Howard had first checked in, but that had led to a different payphone each time. Cora wanted to pay the two

232

million dollars that the messages demanded for Howard's release. The police had other ideas. They had her leave a message at the desk that she was willing to pay for his release but wanted to speak with him first. An hour later, the message came that her request was too risky. An envelope with conclusive proof was to be picked up under a streetcorner newspaper box. With a discreet police escort, she went out and retrieved the large manila envelope. She opened it with fright numb fingers and found Howard's orange swimtrunks and a small white envelope with the wire-red whiskers of his mustache.

The message waiting for her at the first hotel's switchboard instructed her to leave the suitcase of money at a wastebasket near the entrance to a nearby beach park. The police had her respond that she was too scared to go out at night. The final message required that the cash be dropped off at the wastebasket by eight the next morning.

When the police left, they took the money and posted a watch in the adjacent apartment with the adjoining door unlocked. Cora sat on the balcony and in the lunatic agitation of her fright began counting stars. An unfathomable night lay before her.

Howard watched his wife. He had found a way to peer through the corrugated light and see her. The view was bellied as if seen in a glass bowl. And it was fleeting. She smiled at him from the spring he had asked her to marry him, she scowled at him from the night he ripped her fancy dress in the car door. She sat on the balcony counting stars and weeping. The vision tattered to scraps of other scenes: The smiling old man in the blanket, the blonde lemur-eyed girl, Dirk scramming over black, jagged rocks.

Howard pluckied at his shorn lip, and the tattered glimpses vanished. He was sitting on the concrete floor in the baggy blue serge trousers Tony had given him. All lights but the one over him had been turned out. A Yakuza watched him from where he sat in the dark by the formica-topped table. That was the one that had shaved him with a sharp knife and no lather or even water. Howard's scraped nerves burned. But then he put his mind on the timelines that were constantly fringing his sight, and the hurt disappeared. He studied the simmering of shadows around actual objects, and he realized with expansive relief that no torment could reach him here. The Yakuza seemed to sense that, too, for after that they made no effort to hurt him.

Sleep, he commanded himself, but he couldn't remember sleep. He thought about Cora and the danger she was in. He hadn't asked for any of this – not the money or the grief – yet a spate of guilt boggled him. If he could have changed everything back to the way it had been in Peoria by handing over the money, he would have. The futility of his remorse was apparent in the hovering timelines. At the hem of his sight, watery ripple shadows came and went. By relaxing his gaze, he could see into them to patches of lucidity, lenses peering ahead. He was getting good with his sense of yet-to-be. If he could put aside his anxiety about Cora long enough, he knew he could find his way through this maze of clipped scenes back to her. He wanted to see that she was all right.

He stared up at the tubelight dangling from the girders, and the brightness tightened his irises. When he looked back into the darkness, his peripheral sight scintillated like the sweat on a jazzman's brow. One twinkle flared into a view of Dirk at the airport. The edges of the vision ruffled away, and Howard was inside Dirk. His heart muttered its mantra, his thoughts curled on themselves.

Dirk was waiting for Reena. The night on Sandy Beach had been empty of threat, except for a pack of Mokes who came clattering over the boulders around 3 A.M. Dirk had dodged among the tide pools and grass-shaggy dunes, keeping out of their sight. They shouted his name. 'Eh, no trouble,' a kid called out, whom he recognized. That was Sheila's brother, the Mokes' headman. 'When we want you for trouble, we can get you – jus' like magic.'

Sure, Dirk had thought and stayed hidden. He had the arc in his hand, its icy fire prickling his whole arm and thickening his courage.

'Limu's dead, Dirk. Chud say you dropped 'em. No problem, fo' shu-ah. He was bad on you. Dat was Limu's numbah. Dat was his t'ing ovah Sheila. She tol' us plenny. So its ovah now, brah. We not gone stalk you. Unnerstan'?'

Dirk had kept still. If what they had said was true, he was glad; if not, no sense finding out now.

'You go stay wit' you head in dah sand,' the Mokes' headman called. 'Sheila tru wit' you, brah. Cuz you crazy. Hear me? I w'en leave dis class ring of yours he-ah. Eh?' The voice trailed off, and Dirk heard the Mokes scuttling over the rocks back toward the beach's parking lot. 'Eh!' the Moke called out again. 'Chud's still on you. He's talkin' about killin' you. But dat's not us, haole. Watch it.'

Dirk had found his class ring on the boulder where the Mokes had left it. It was a red-stoned, brass knob of a ring, and he had given it to two other women

235

besides Sheila in the six months since he'd stolen it. For an instant, this reminiscence of his selfish past spurred him to throw the ring into the sea. But its unexpected return as a peace offering from the Mokes granted it emblematic significance. It had become lucky, and he pocketed it.

Afterward, he sat on the beach remembering his life as it had been. Dawn budged him from his memories, and he recalled that Reena and Jiang were arriving today. He freshened up in the beach park's public bathroom and took a bus to the airport to meet the woman he had seen in his visions.

Morning was a bronze shadow over the green mountains when he arrived. He stood before the arrivals monitor, trying to figure out which flight she'd be coming in on. 'It's the seven-thirty from LA,' Poe's sullen voice said.

'Where've you been?' Dirk asked to the air. He'd been reaching for the arc every few minutes since leaving the beach, hoping to get some clearer sense of what to do next. It was too cold to keep in his pocket, and he carried it in his duffel bag. Even through the thick material, he could feel the arc's cold glow.

'The less you hear from me, the less chance my energies will manifest as an orc.'

'Fine,' Dirk said and walked off, heading toward the gate where Reena's flight would arrive in an hour. 'We'll talk later.'

'The trouble is this,' Poe's glum voice went on. 'Airport security recognized you when you walked in. The Home reported your abduction yesterday. The police have already been alerted.'

Dirk spun on the balls of his feet and headed back toward the exit. A police officer appeared from around the pillars supporting the overhead rampway and stood waiting for him outside the automatic glass doors.

'Don't freak out now, Dirk,' Poe said. 'The time-lines that lead to my salvation lead you to jail. I'm sorry. Please, believe me. I didn't want it to be this way. But if there's going to be any hope for me, you must surrender.'

Dirk backed up and cast a look around the pavilion. Two other security guards were watching him from either end of the mall-like room.

'Just turn myself in?' he asked, incredulously.

No reply came. The automatic glass doors opened, and the police came for him.

Howard's greedy stare darkened all at once, and he twitched alert. The Yakuza had turned the tubelight off, and the warehouse was numb with darkness. The lit end of a cigarette floated in the dark where the table was, and its acrid smell sharpened the air.

The skylight cast its stencil of crossed shadows on the concrete floor, and Howard peered up at the bitumen of night, searching for a sign. Fatigue stretched through him. His eyelids batted, and he slept.

The red ash of the cigarette glowed hotter, and a glistening of blue fire smeared the watchful face in the dark.

Reena was peaceful and determined when the Hawaiian Islands appeared out of the red smoke of the dawn sea. Her acceptance of Insideout and of her own fate had allowed her to master the telepathy that was their bond. The alien was weakening by the hour and could no longer be reached by thought alone. Even through lusk, it was far away and very quiet.

As the blue shadowed islands turned below them and the giant yellow day swung its spokes among the jumbled clouds, Reena wondered how long her own clarity would last. The anguished thought of becoming again what she had been reminded her of the hospice. By now it was dinnertime in Avignon, and Yannick and the matrons had long before reported her missing to the police. They had already searched the forest around the asylum all the way up to the staggering pines on the ridge. They would search again tomorrow. After that, she would become for them one of the thousands that vanished tracelessly each year. Yannick would be troubled. After all, she had behaved differently just before disappearing. He would wonder, through the days of his life, what had happened to her, and each time, her mystery would turn him back on himself.

That thought left her shamed and angry. A note explaining that she was well would have solved so much, she thought. She was grateful that she hadn't revealed the alien's telepathy to him, for that would only have haunted him more deeply. As the plane descended into the bright morning of her new life, she considered going to a phone and calling him. Insideout would have dissuaded her then if it could have reached her. She was looking back to an unrecoverable past. If she had turned her telepathy on herself then, the myths of her species would have warned her: The look back at Hell is itself the return journey.

Reena had expected Dirk to meet her at the airport. No trace of him even glinted in the sluggish drone of the terminal's mental noise. Flares of emotion went off around her as people recognized each other and were reunited. She drifted with the glow of people, distracted by their flashing thoughts. The image in her mind of Dirk was the alien's idealized version, and she scanned the crowd for him, not realizing that there was no one like him in this world.

At the sight of a wall of public phones, her concern for Yannick swirled up in her again. She took off her jacket and leaned against one of the metal-faced phones, knowing she could never return, feeling that he alone had been a friend to her and deserved more than silence. When she picked up the receiver, her uncertainty thinned away.

The operator didn't understand French, and Reena's telepathy did not transmit over the telephone line, so she had to command a passerby to complete the call for her.

'Docter Lefebvre, I'm free,' she said when she heard him on the other end. 'It's all too wonderful' – *and frightening*, she thought – 'for words.'

'Reena, is that you?'

'Yes, yes, Yannick, it's me, Reena.' Her face was hot, and her eyes hurt to hear his voice. 'Don't worry about me. I'm healed.'

'Reena, where are you?'

'That doesn't matter. I won't be here long. I'm on my way to someplace wonderful.'

'Please – tell me where you are. I must see you before you go.'

'I'm already gone, Yannick. It's too complicated to explain, but you must believe me. I'm happy and well. My mind is clear. I feel I could write a poem.'

'Who are you with?'

'I'm with friends,' she answered, imagining Dirk with his kestrel-clear eyes and the two others the alien had revealed to her, seen more vaguely. Anxiety about their whereabouts twanged in her. 'I just want you to know that I'm all right – and that I'm

239

grateful for all the help you gave me. I'll remember you, Yannick. Please, don't worry about me.'

She heard his breath ebb toward words, and she hung up. A chill soaked her. She was alone. The faces of Dirk, Howard, and Jiang, which had floated in and out of her mind during the trip, were nowhere to be seen. 'Insideout?' she called. Nothing. She closed her eyes and tried to lusk. Soon she found the vibrantly still presence within her. 'Where are you?'

'Here,' a frail voice spoke. 'I think. I feel fuzzy.'

She pressed the back of her head against the metal face of the phone and stared into the crisscrossing of people as the crowd from her flight thinned. 'Where is Dirk?'

'Isn't he there? Ah – I forgot. The police have him.'

Fear spiked her. 'The police?'

'Reena,' Insideout said in a gasp of exhaustion, 'you'll have to free Dirk on your own. He has the arc.'

'But how will I find him?'

'The same way you'll find the others. Use your mind. I'm pummeled to pemmican. Can't talk anymore now. Oh – yes. Go to Jiang first. He needs you right away.'

That was all the alien could manage, and its last words yawed eerily with echoes. It dithered into silence.

Reena hugged herself and listened for Insideout's presence. It wasn't there. It kept itself transparent, watching her watch for it, so that she found the alien as the minds of the others. Howard was the first one she heard within her, his voice throbbing like a jellyfish: 'Time has no shores. Anything can happen.' He was mumbling to himself, unaware of her. She saw him in her mind's eye more sharply

240

than the tall, sunny doorways that led out past the baggage claim to the street. He was sitting on the floor with his back up against a wall in a warehouse. Huge, airy shadows filled the empty space, and he stared into the volume of veiled light with nimble eyes, tracing the shapes of things she could not see.

Reena walked with her head slung, listening deeper. Dirk was there, indistinct in the mauve shadows of his cell. She glimpsed sunrays slanting through a barred transom on to a gray wall where he was flaking the paint with his thumbnail, spelling words she couldn't read but understood by his thought: TENDER BENDER.

Deeper, she found Jiang. He was almost wordless, near to lusk, and his silence carried her directly into his surroundings. She saw the deck of an ocean liner, water loud with sunlight, the black piers of a large harbor, and the stained hulls of other ships. She knew looking at this scene, from the buzzing mentations of those around Jiang, that this was Pearl Harbor. Fighting an upwelling of brilliant sensations from Jiang, the noises and sights around him, she found her way to a taxi and ordered it to Pearl.

During the fifteen-minute cab ride, Reena watched the old Chinese man. He was wrapped in a blanket and smiled as two gleaming white sailors led him down a gangway to a squad car. A police officer and a plainclothes agent took Jiang from the sailors, and the officer put his hand on Jiang's head as he ducked into the back seat. The old man was confused but accepting. She felt his fortuity, his gleeful awareness that he had found his way to Golden Mountain – and she felt his heart like a circle of light sweating shadow, fearing the demon that had carried him here. *Strange are the ways*, a thought fitted in him.

In the middle of a busy street, the squad car with

241

Jiang in it approached, and Reena used her mind to make the taxi driver cut it off. Tires screamed, and the police officer jolted from the squad car with his pistol in his hand. Reena stepped from the cab and told him to put his gun away. Jiang was huddled in the back seat, watching her with amused eyes. Life-force spilled between them like the glow of cold rushing off a frozen pond.

'Ni hau ma?' Reena asked aloud, mimicking the sound of what she wanted to say from the echo of her thought in Jiang's mind.

'Bien, à tout prendre,' he replied, astounded to feel his muscles seized by strange nerve impulses. He knew no French. Her telepathy lit his body.

Reena told the plainclothesman beside Jiang to get out, and she commanded him and the taxi driver to forget her. Then she got into the back seat with Jiang and had the patrolman drive them to the police station.

Insideout followed from the fringe of love and pain, from the pouring sunlight, from the space between Jiang's callus-bossed fingers, from the moist creases of Reena's elbows, from the invisible pit of forgotten words, from the nonsense of nothing. The alien was in that psychoid realm between mind and a white scream. It saw what they all saw, each in their way – the future opening like a wound, paying out time in the shape of lives. It was only one of those lives.

In the oil-stained air of the car's exhaust, tiny bestial faces writhed in the smoke, sparkling like confetti, swirling like the glues of an hallucination.

Dirk was busy chipping old paint from a wall the color of peppered eggs into a sign that signified love and will to him. TENDER BENDER he scratched,

242

believing with that rhyme and without thought that love and will were not contradictions. The irony of etching this on a prison wall did not occur to him. Actually, Dirk was barely conscious of his industrious fingernails. He was listening to the diamond grindstone of heaven filling his head with sublime music as it crushed his questions to answers.

The moony music tranquilized his anxiety about the arc. Its chill had gone out of it when the police picked him up, and when the cigar-gnawing detective at the station had gone through his bag, he barely looked at the blank medallion. Dirk had briefly considered telling the detective that in a few hours the metal wafer he had dismissed would disintegrate the whole island. But the dreamy elastic sounds in his head had nightmared to a shriek, and he had let that thought go. Instead, he asked the arc's crafty noises to sing of other mysteries.

He was wondering about the blackbody of the cosmos and how it carried the light of all-time. He was wondering about his father's ghost. Mitch had never looked as real to him as he had in Insideout's presence. Dreams and memories distorted the past, but Insideout had brought Mitch back exactly as he had looked in all his forgotten details. Infused with the alien's mental strength, Dirk could see how the superstitions of the past had some grounding in actuality: Ghosts were obviously some kind of mental wave functioning, persisting in the photonic field, like lightwaves enduring in the vacuum, maybe even transmigrating by morphogenetic resonance with the antennae of DNA in the nucleus of a fertilized egg. *I really don't understand that*, he thought – yet he did understand; limitless knowledge hummed around him like an ocean, touching all of him except the iceberg-tip of his self-awareness.

His hands stopped flaking paint for a moment, and he replayed those crystalline notes in his memory, listening closely. Light patterns, bodies of energy, life fields migrated through the tesseract volume of the universe carrying consciousness endlessly through time. Consciousness spontaneously evolved across time in the form of lightwaves – cellular potentials, synaptic sparks –

All life emitted light. Each molecule of DNA acted like a tiny laser: Its atomic vibrations were synchronized by its superordered structure, and it generated coherent light in ranges from ultraviolet to infrared and radio waves. This biolaserlight contained the uniquely precise information of that genetic molecule. And even though the signal was ultraweak, its information was not lost. The vacuum field carried all light, from the enormous first flash after the Big Bang to the feeble biophotons of single-cell organisms an inch underground. Light timelessly propagated through the ubiquitous vacuum. The patterns of information within the light, being weightless, were immortal.

Some of the biolight was even reabsorbed by DNA similar to the DNA that first generated it. Each consciousness – plant, insect, or animal – was a wave bundle that had been emitted and reabsorbed many times, evolving in the photonic field over many lifetimes. All life was graffiti – atomic graffiti scrawling patterns on the blackbody depths – molecular graffiti scribbling nucleotides into DNA patterns on the wall of the biopause. Who was writing? The question opened like a lion's maw. The answer swallowed the beast: Implicit consciousness. Before the Big Bang, before the inflationary rush that swept the universe clear of monopoles, before the singularity, before the vacuum, was the empty set – the nothing. 'The map is there,' Poe's voice slurred. 'Mind is there.'

'What about Mitch?' Dirk asked, not really caring about cosmic limits. 'Where's my dad?' The crystal music chimed elusively. Where was the vacuum field that held the wave-wrack of all-time? Everywhere. But for Dirk everywhere was nowhere, because he lacked the power to tap it. Reena could talk with the dead and not even know how the dead endured. And Dirk, lightheaded with astonishment, understood but could not commune with the wavefield in the abyss between his atoms.

Now that he had begun to understand a little bit more about the universe around him, he could hardly believe that the world had ever seemed so dead that all he had wanted, without even knowing it, was to hurt it, to make it scream to life. Reality *had* suddenly come alive – new possibilities bloomed and the dreariness that had once owned him was gone.

Dirk and the alien were gnattering like this when the police brought in Donnie Lopes. He was enraged. After word had reached the Home that Dirk had been picked up by the police at the airport, where he was presumably attempting to flee the state, Mr Paawa conducted a thorough search of the Home, trying to find some clue to Dirk's behavior. In Donnie's locker, he found a car stereo and several digital wristwatches, and he called the police.

'I'm telling you,' Donnie was practically shouting when they led him into the squad room, 'that misfit Dirk stole all this stuff. He just makes me hold it. Am I culpable because I didn't want to get maimed?

245

Come on, use your heads – I'm not the guy you want.'

Donnie stamped the floor with his aluminum cane while he and the officer escorting him waited for the wire mesh door leading to the detectives' desk to unlock electrically. The anteroom with its walls of police posters was pungent with ammonia cleaner, and the bare, brash tubelight smeared away all shadows. The door buzzed, and they banged through it into a fluorescently lit room crowded with desks and the stale smells of cigarette smoke and coffee. Most of the desks were empty. A typewriter was clattering at one desk where a bald man gnawing a cigar was finger pecking a report. Near the mesh door, on a metal tabletop, was Dirk's duffel bag.

'I know my rights,' Donnie told the bald, sallow-faced detective with the cigar when he rose from his typewriter and sauntered over to him. The police escort jerked his thumb at Donnie, rolled his eyeballs, and left.

'Look, kid,' the detective said around his cigar, then referred to an index card in his stubby fingered hand, 'Donald – we don't think you stole the items we found in your locker. We just want your testimony, then you can go. Come over here.'

The glow of Donnie's rage dimmed, and he followed the detective to his desk, was offered a seat, and sat down. They chatted for ten minutes, and Donnie told the detective about Dirk's pattern of having him hold stolen goods in his locker in exchange for not being roughed up. 'The guy's a miscreant,' Donnie volunteered. 'He's a sadist. He likes hurting people. That's why I figure the gangs were after him. They were the ones who slaughtered our house mascots, Hunza and Peppercorn, and left their carcasses on Dirk's bunk. When I saw that, I

246

thought he'd done it. That's his style – utterly brutal and mindless. But it scared him. I saw him scared, and I should have known then that he was in trouble. He started acting nice to me. I couldn't figure it until I saw him get abducted by two gang members.'

'These the men?' The detective flashed two small mugshots of Chud and Limu from the file in his lap.

'Right. They carried him away in broad daylight in front of half the Home. You want the license number on the car? It was a beatup Nash Rambler.'

'We found the car.' The detective slapped the file closed. 'Okay, Donald. Thanks for your help. You can go now.'

'The least you can do is tell me what's going on,' Donnie said, rising with the detective.

'We don't know much more than you do right now.' The detective led Donnie to the mesh door. 'We found the car that was used in the kidnapping but the gang members are still at large. They're affiliated with island mobsters, so we have some leads to follow.'

'What about Dirk? What're you going to do with him?'

'We picked Dirk up at the airport, but he won't talk to us. Except to say that he did steal the stereo and watches we found in your locker. He admits that he extorted you into holding the goods.'

That suprised Donnie, but he was glad Dirk had finally been nailed and that he had had something to do with it. 'You're putting him away, right?'

'Juvenile court will decide that. Right now, we want to get to the bottom of his gangland affiliations. If you find out anything more, let me know.'

The detective turned and walked back towards his desk. Donnie shook his head with dissatisfaction at the laxness of justice and opened the mesh door.

From the corner of his eye, he spotted Dirk's duffel bag, and an inexplicable impulse opened in him. But Insideout wasn't calling to Donnie. The call was coming from the alien's nightmare.

Donnie looked to see that the detective's back was to him, and then he reached into the duffel bag, rummaged among the tangling of clothes, and found the hard metal disc that Dirk had shown him at the Home. He swiftly put the arc in his pocket and left.

On the bus ride back to the Home, Donnie examined the arc. It was dull and torpid to his touch, and holding it up to the sunlight and seeing a vague glint of rainbow, he suddenly remembered finding this object on the Big Island. He figured that the fall Dirk had tripped him into had jarred his short-term memory. Now, he recalled the scintillant energy that he had felt around it on the lava field and wondered if it had picked up some kind piezoelectric charge from the friction of the volcano's tectonic plates. He put the slug of metal back in his pocket, satisfied that at least he had redressed one of Dirk's crimes against him. The arc hummed a note beyond the range of his hearing, and Donnie's anger bit deeper.

How could a creature like Dirk Heiser have been tolerated for so long? Didn't everyone see what a monster he was? Or maybe it was just that anyone else with a busy schedule and two good legs had no time or desire to filthy themselves with Dirk's ugliness. They could walk away from him, but Donnie had to take it. He thudded his cane against the floor at him. He was glad the cops had finally nabbed Dirk. And if they let him back in the Home, Donnie was determined not to eat grief from him anymore. Somehow he would find a way to be certain that Dirk would never hurt him again.

Donnie limped down the steps of the bus when it

arrived at the Home and snapped at the driver, 'Stop it!' when she started the hydraulic lift that lowered the step to the curb. He hobbled as quickly as he could across the lawn, skirting the playground where kids were playing soccer, and headed toward the pond.

He didn't know where he was going just yet. He was mad – furious at the whole world. This happened to him sometimes, only this time his fury was untamable. He jerked forward at a pace that hurt his leg, and the more it hurt, the harder he pushed himself until the pain and his motion were one. 'Hurt goddamn you! Hurt me! Go ahead!'

Tears of defiance greased his sight, and he lurched to the edge of the pond. He stopped with the toes of his shoes touching the lace of green and brown algal scum. The pain in his bad leg was like a hot wire. He wanted to throw himself into the mud, to thrash out his rage in the sticky waste of life. He was edging forward, clenched with hysteria, when he saw the graves.

Donnie stabbed his cane into the mud and pivoted to face the site where Dirk had buried Hunza and Peppercorn. The earth there was torn open and sunken, and the blood-smirched linen they had been wrapped in was dragged half out of the hole. Bent over a withheld gasp, Donnie swung his body closer and saw a double set of pug marks pacing away from the open graves. At first he assumed some animal had dug up the corpses and dragged them off. But then, crouching nearer to the mud, he saw that there were no other tracks. The gasp in him widened toward a scream. The animals had dug themselves out!

The horror of his observation battered his heart, and he would have turned and fled. But he couldn't move. He followed with his gaze the trail of paw prints that wandered into the grass toward the hole in the chainlink fence that the strong-legged boys used to get out into the wild fields under the volcano. The urge rose in him to follow. But he resisted, and the thigh of his bad leg twitched with involuntary strength. He jerked forward one step and screamed a tiny, hopeless cry.

Cold smoldered against his thigh, and his hand clutched at the icy burn. It was the metal disc he had taken from Dirk's duffel bag. It was searing his whole leg with freezing fire. He yanked the disc from his pocket, and his hand pulled out a piece of the sun.

Nerve-aching brightness dazzled in his palm. His wrist, arm, shoulder, and whole body flashed into blue refulgence. Maniac strength fitted itself to his body, and he managed one last whimper of shock before the deep mightiness of the arc's power flapped the rags of his body sharply against his skeleton. He jerked like a tangled puppet, and his mind melted away.

A bellow like a mad bull's sounded from across the pond, and the kids playing soccer two hundred yards away stopped their game. They saw Donnie Lopes at the far end of the pond, walking without his cane. The few with the keenest eyes saw a shimmering hung over him like a glass bell. He budged through a sheared hole in the chainlink fence and disappeared into the sere brush of the bison-humped hills under the empty bowl of the volcano.

Dirk. His name glittered in him, and he sat up on his cot and looked toward the gray bars of his cell door. Sunlight sheeting through the skylight of the jail corridor hexed his sight, and all he saw was a figure with long hair and supple posture. He stood up, and his heart swerved.

'Reena,' he said in a gust of surprise. He could barely believe that he was facing her. She was more beautiful than she had seemed to him in his tranceful encounters with her, and he palm-wiped his eyes to be certain that she was standing before him.

The was really her. He stepped up to the bars and took all of her in with his surprised stare. He hadn't expected to see her dressed in gray crushed denim and silk. Her ash-blonde hair was a spill of pale fire over her lavender blouse, and the languor of her green gaze and the lynx-span of her face held him wordlessly before her.

She put an arm through the bars and touched the pollen down on his chin. He looked something like her vision of the alien but less pretty, more harsh. His pale eyes were like the insides of ice. There was a teeter of loneliness in his stare, but more strongly she perceived a varletry to the thrust of his jaw, the hollowness of his cheeks, and the surly curl of his mouth. He looked arrant.

'What're you doin' here?' he asked, and immediately felt stupid for so obvious a question.

The telepathy of meaning echoed simultaneously with the breadth of his voice, and she understood him as though she were fluent in English. 'Jiang is outside,' she answered in French, but she could see from the comprehension in his expression that he understood her in his own language. 'After you there is only one more of us to free.'

'Yeah – Howard. And we better get a move on, too, because the guys holding him are not notorious for their patience. I'm sure his wife has called the cops by now. Can you get me outta here?'

She turned to call the guard, and Dirk rubbed his chin where she had touched him. Her fingers had felt like points of wind, cool and electric.

The guard shuffled down the corridor and opened Dirk's cell.

'Now that's a way with words,' Dirk tried to kibitz.

'We have so little time.' Her idle eyes looked wearier, and he recalled the alien's urgency and the understanding that when it left, so would its powers. They would revert to their old selves. That was the freedom Dirk had craved since Mitch's ghost first appeared – but for Reena, of course, it meant madness. She smiled, hearing his thought. 'Insideout is taking me with it when it goes.'

'You're kiddin'?' he said, though the harmonics of understanding were already chiming in him: The arc had the capacity to translate a human body to wave function and shrink it with itself smaller than the fabric of spacetime, small enough to fall out of the continuum and into the infinite array of possbible realities. The mentations went on, defining the energy equivalencies that would be siphoned from the vacuum field into the upper atmosphere to preserve the conservation symmetries and allow Reena's exit from this universe – but he wasn't listening. Until now, she had just been an image in his mind of another babe, and his feelings for her had been slack. But here in the immediate presence of her with her fruit-sweet scent reaching into him and her features shining in the incandescence of now, muscular emotions wrangles in him. He tried to suppress the infatuation swelling in him, frightfully aware that she knew his feelings. But that was hopeless. To his relief, as they walked out of the cell block, she gave no indication that she was tapped into him.

In fact, Dirk's thoughts chivvied round and round Reena's heart. She had never felt love for a man before, and she wasn't sure that what she felt for Dirk was love. She didn't even know this boy. Yet his heart was transparent to her, and in it she saw a sort of grandeur in the athletic jubilance of his rascality, a brightness to his dark spirit, like a vampire's unearthly beauty. He wasn't sly or crooked. His crimes were all daring, almost selfless with danger, like when he had run drugs for his mother or when he disrupted the conformity of the Home with his chicanery. She liked that in him, because she would have liked that in herself if she had been whole.

Walking past police officers, clerks, and detectives, Dirk experienced a ribald arrogance, a dream-like silliness that almost provoked him into leaping on to a desk and dancing. Then at the periphery of his sight, he noticed ultraviolet gems dangling in the air, and when he swung his direct gaze toward them, they snapped into caustic sparks and were gone. Understanding nettled in him: The orc was mounting power from their unbalanced impulses. But the power wasn't fully manifesting here. It was draining away from them and pooling elsewhere, steepening toward an ultimately seismic encounter.

'I've seen the gargoyles,' Reena spoke to him. 'Jiang has, too. They're the alien's demons.'

'What're we gonna do about them?'

She stopped at the wire-mesh door that led out to the public corridors. 'I thought you would know.'

Dirk grabbed his duffel bag from the detective's desk where it lay and held it up. 'The arc knows. It'll come to me.'

Outside, Jiang was sitting in the driver's seat of a squad car, his hands on the wheel, pretending to

253

drive. He was dressed in the clothes that he had been given on board the liner – blue denim pants with belled cuffs, a wide-neck red and white striped pullover shirt, and his black slippers. He looked like an old salt just released from drying out in the drunks' tank.

Since collapsing on to the deck of the liner last night, he had been reluctant to use his special strength. He knew he was strong again because he felt engorged with vigor, but he was afraid to use the power. The demon he had seen on his mad night sea flight was still around. Glimpsed in windshield reflections, it was an insect-masked dragon, come and gone in an eyeblink. He hoped that if he remained still enough in his heart, it would go away. Yet how could he hope for stillness when he was spinning with astonishment? Golden Mountain alone was cause for excited exploration. Perhaps if he were still an old man he would be content to sit in the midst of this miraculous whirlwind and meditate (ch'ing mo), but moving so magnetically, feeling so weightless and fresh, he had no hope of containing his energies.

And so Jiang touched the world around him. He sat in the driver's seat and grasped the steering wheel, absorbing the tactile luxury of this stupendous machine. Furtively, he reached out with his strength and pinged the mirror-paned side of a skyscraper, feeling the resilience of the tempered glass and the opulence of the bronzed sash. The air was tainted with traffic fumes, a perfume of technology to his awed senses. He glanced about the mad glints and enamels of the dragon. In the rearview mirror, flame-shaped adder eyes watched him, and he hopped from the car.

'It's all around us,' Reena said to him, and he was

254

relieved to see her beside him again. On the ride
with her from the docks, he had observed how his
special vitality had coursed more intently through
him when they were touching. The boy with her was
Dirk, the wise youth from his dreams. But the boy
looked tougher in person, more earthbound.

'The dragon is watching us,' he said to her, and
Dirk, too, understood him. 'It's followed me here to
you.'

'It's called an orc,' Dirk said authoritatively, and
Jiang knew what he was saying because Reena was
among them. 'It's the alien's craziness. And it's
gonna get worse.'

'Forget the gargoyle,' Reena said. 'There's nothing
we can do about it, right?'

'The more we do, the stronger it gets,' Dirk confirmed, reaching into his bag for the arc. He felt the
round, brass button on a pair of rodeo pants and
thought that was it. He didn't want to take it out
until they were away from the police station, and he
threw the bag into the front of the squad car. 'And
when the orc zombies a body, it's unstoppable.'

'There's one more of us,' Reena said. In her mind,
Howard's thoughts were petals of radiance, the
bloom of time unclenching from the present.

'Howard was taken by some very dangerous men,'
Dirk said. 'The men who have him want a lot of
money. And I have no idea where he is.'

'Ah, money,' Jiang nodded knowingly. 'In China
now, they say to get rich is glorious.'

'I can find Howard,' Reena said, ignoring Jiang.
'Together we can free him.' She gestured for them to
get into the squad car. 'Dirk, you drive.'

'Hey, wait a minute.' Dirk slapped his hand
against the top of the car. 'We can't take on the

255

Yakuza. They've got guns. Why not use the cops to bust them?'

Reena gave him an askew look. 'Can't you hear Insideout?' She could. Whenever she faced Dirk or even called his image to mind, she heard the alien's thoughts. They were there inside Dirk, faint but distinct, brooding and sulphurous with hope of escape. But he was focused externally. The closest he came to the alien's interior was wanting to understand ghosts and how his father's consciousness persisted beyond death. Reena was thinking of her own survival. She was tuned precisely to Insideout's need, and she heard the alien through Dirk.

She put a fingertip on the velvet space between Dirk's eyes, and he saw Poe again in the ferrous shadows of his mind's eye. 'Don't, don't,' the miniscule voice whispered. 'The police are no part of the timeline that leads me back to the hyperfield. You have to get Howard out on your own. Please, trust me, even though it seems I've made a mess of everything else. Go, as quickly as you can.'

Dirk shivered. The thunderish expanse between him and the alien seemed too far to breech alone, and he trembled with the thought of falling into that depth. He blinked and forced alertness into his head. The lot of parked squad cars was burdened with sunlight. 'Okay, then.' He ducked behind the wheel. The touch of the ignition key displaced his unearthliness with a crude joy. He'd never stolen a cop car before. 'Let's roll.'

Reena and Jiang got into the back seat, and Dirk drove out of the lot. The old man sank into his seat and watched the modern landscape drift by. While Reena fed Dirk directions, Jiang lay his hands on his thighs and felt like the root's pulse in the grip of granite. His life was melting stone. Like a slow-growing cliff tree that cracks boulders, his frail being had been wedged into the marvelous. The impossible was shattering around him into the everyday miracles of life on Golden Mountain. *Try to speak to yourself*, he mentally pricked himself. But what was there to say? The sinewy energy in him was far from words. He smiled at the back of Dirk's head, noticing the dimple of a boil scar and the novelty of sun-streaked hair. 'You explained much to me in my dreams, young Dirk. You showed me the demon as a circle of metal. It needs our help, you said. Which is why we are together. But how can it need us when its own power is so much greater than ours?'

'That's the craziness of this whole thing. We're as far from understanding it as yeast are from us. It's all so weird.' He tossed a grin over his shoulder. 'Yet it needs us the way we sometimes need antibiotics. Without us the alien's wasted – and so are we and everybody else on this island.'

'Don't call it an alien,' Reena said. 'That makes it sound like something frightening.'

'You're not scared?' Dirk asked.

'I'm afraid of becoming what I used to be.'

'That's never going to happen again,' Dirk promised. 'If we don't make it, we're ash. And if we do – you're getting away. The old man, Howard, and I are gonna have to pretend this whole crazy trip didn't happen.'

Jiang twitched at the words 'old man.' 'You mean to say, I will return to being as I was?' he asked.

'When the a – When Insideout goes, the weirdness goes with it.'

Jiang clutched his knees and shut his eyes. The world seemed to convulse. Could he be old again? Could he endure the frailty, the aches, the heaviness again?

Reena placed her hand over his marbled knuckles. 'Don't be afraid. Remember, just two days ago you were willing to be happy.'

Her touch overpowered his anxiety. He *was* an old man. Of course. That was the way of the world. At least he had lived to be old. He remembered sitting before his straw fire in the evening cooking scallions and rice, alone except when one of the villages visited to honor their own lost grandparents. Wrung from the day's toil, his very bones were exhausted. He sat and watched the flames untangle themselves from the grass. Life became blank. Even the haunting memories of his wife and children that startled him every day in the field or on the road were motionless. Minutes crackled in the fire. Night whispered in the trees. This was the tangless taste of death. Yes, he remembered and was braver for it.

Reena experienced this transition with him and met his smile with her own. 'The five colors blind men's eyes,' she repeated a thought she heard deep in the well of his mind. That was Lao-tzu's admonition to Confucius – one of his father's favorite quotes. His father had used it whenever friends had tempted him to leave his farm and return to a scholar's life in the city. Jiang's smile broadened. The simple world was confusing enough, how could he hope for clarity in the grip of the miraculous? 'Let's finish quickly what we've begun,' he said.

Dirk pulled the car off Numitz Highway on to a factory road that curved through a compound of warehouses. Rays of Hawaiian morninglight buzzed on the metal roofs. Reena had Dirk stop the car in the shadow of a giant pineapple-shaped watertower. 'He's two blocks away. I think we should park the squad car here so we don't startle them.'

'Okay.' Dirk took command, turning around and reclining his seat so he could face them cross-legged. He put the duffel bag in his lap. 'Let's get this teeny little super guy out here and see what it wants to do.' He rummaged in the bag and looked up with startled imcomprehension.

'It's gone,' Reena said and closed her eyes.

Dirk dumped out his clothes and turned out the bag's lining. 'Friggin-A! The cops probably have it.'

'No.' Reena was gazing underbreathed for Inside-out. It was there, solemn as a salmon at the end of its climb. To link her with the whereabouts of the arc, the alien had to use all its strength. It did. She prickled with the loom of directions that would lead her across the island to the volcanic grotto where Donnie Lopes was waiting.

The alien's strength spun away. The last dazing image she saw through it was Donnie himself. He was squatting among dragonish cacti in the pelvis of the dead volcano. Gossamer veils of field lines shimmered like a vast spider's nest in the silver sunlight, and he was slung at the center, the air quavering around him. His boyface had sunken closer to the bone and looked wet as plastic. A chitinous varnish seemed to coat all of him, and his bulged eyes were locked open. On the ground before him, the arc shone in a needle-spiked blue glare. The image wrinkled away, and the brown darkness of her closed lids returned.

'The demon's gone again,' Jiang said, but he saw that they couldn't understand him because their words were making no sense to him. He crossed his hands over his suddenly dense body and stared stiffly at the others.

Dirk was yammering: 'Christ, it's punked out on us again!'

Reena was saying in French: 'This is the center of the earth and those are the clean, giant clouds of Greece.' She reached her arms out the window and up to the sky and sat rigidly motionless.

Dirk looked at her cross-eyed and then waved his hand before her face. She didn't stir. 'Okay, we're back to square one.' He got out of the police car and sat on the hood, fuming. All of the alien's sapience was gone from him, yet he knew what had happened. 'Insideout's out,' he told Jiang when the old man struggled out of the car and leaned against the fender with him. 'It's gone into a glide, and who knows when, or if, it's gonna come around.'

Dirk's head was hung in angry despair, and Jiang was the first to see the approaching man. The character looked sinister, and Jiang nudged Dirk's ribs.

A block of a man, huge as a linebacker, was crossing the street toward them, bald head slung like a bull's. Dirk stood bolt upright and almost yelped. 'Chud!'

When Chud had heard that Dirk had been picked up by the cops, he had gone to the station and posted himself in a saimin shop across the street to await developments. After Dirk and the others came out, he'd followed them here on his moped. 'You owe,' he said.

'Hey, Chud,' Dirk grinned weakly and backed away. The man did not appear orc-possessed, but he was threatening enough without supernatural strength. 'Don't want no trouble, man.'

Jiang moved to block the large man's way and raised both of his gnarled hands before him. 'We mean you no harm,' he said in his village dialect. 'Please, leave us alone.'

Chud shoved the elderly man to the ground, and Jiang tried to roll with his fall but was too stiff and hit the pavement with a hurtful thwack of his head.

Concern leaped in Dirk then snapped at once to rage. 'Hey! You Chinese Blood, he's just an old man. What kind of geek are you?'

'You're dead, brah,' Chud said and kept coming.

Dirk slinked backward into Repulse Monkey, palms open and shuttling with his retreating stride. 'I dropped you once, Baby Huey. And that was no accident.'

The insult goaded Chud forward, and Dirk suddenly lunged and leaped into a leopard kick. Chud dodged, and Dirk pranced past him. Sunlight grinned from the blade that opened in Chud's thick hand. Jiang, who was sitting up, groaned to see it.

Fear unclasped Dirk's knees, and he had to straighten up to conduct strength back into his legs. He took a deep breath, and as Mitch had taught him, he imagined the breath distilling to a point of ferocious intensity just below his bellybutton. The effort calmed him, and he sunk into his stance and waited for Chud's attack.

Chud danced forwards with a sprite agility that startled Dirk. The knife hacked the air, and Dirk traced its hysteric pattern with the fingertips of one hand. With the blade sweeping toward him, he stepped into its path, caught the big man's wrist in one hand and punched into his face with the other. The blow stunned Chud, but the force of the blocked knifehand sent Dirk sprawling to the pavement.

His knife hot with sunlight, Chud bent and stabbed. But the downsweep of his killing blow choked when Jiang, who had climbed to his feet, threw himself on to the giant's back and snagged his arm with both hands. Chud bucked, casting Jiang off like a heavy coat. And Dirk seized the momentary distraction to kick upward into Chud's groin.

The killer buckled, and Dirk hopped upright and

struck a devastating downpiling blow to the side of the man's head. Chud dropped faceflat to the sidewalk and lay unmoving. Dirk took the knife, clasped it, put it in his back pocket, and hurried to Jiang.

The old man was dazed but intact. Dirk helped him to his feet and led him back to the car. Reena was still reaching through the window to embrace the clouds. Dirk opened the back door and supported Jiang's featherweight until he was sitting on the shaded back seat. The geezer looked used up, sweat-streaked, and pallid, and the alarming thought whirled through Dirk that he might have to administer cardiopulmonary resuscitation if the old guy had a seizure.

Jiang patted Dirk's hand and nodded his head. He mumbled something in Chinese, and Dirk backed off.

What now? Dirk wondered and glanced to be certain that Chud was still unconscious. Disburdened of that anxiety, he went around to the other side of the car and stared into Reena's face. How fragile she looked now. Her green stare was mulling something over, but the porcelain of her face and her weightless arms were disconnected. He touched her cheek. She was cool as marble.

Overhead the morning was widening among rafts of blue-white clouds. That emptiness was what embraced the whole earth, and toward which Reena was grasping. He looked again at Chud, and fear muttered louder in him. 'This is crazy,' he said. He clapped his hands before Reena's face, and she blinked but didn't move. Jiang watched him with a feverish gaze.

'So what now?' he whined. He plopped into the driver's seat. 'Do we just sit here and wait to see if Chud or the alien wakes up first?' His body sagged, and he nodded to himself like a drunk. Jiang was just an old man. Reena didn't look so pretty with drool dripping from her chin. And he was just a snare for trouble and always had been. Nothing good could come from him. *Yet* – Blood flurried through his arms and legs, and a foxy optimism renewed itself. He'd always taken care of himself, had never yielded to fear or betrayed a friend. Somehow, he'd make this work, too.

He looked deeper into Reena's slack face and saw the dulled beauty of her features that would brighten when her alertness returned. The glamorous violence of their situation inspired him, and he turned away with the conviction that if anyone could succeed, they would.

'That's the strength we need,' Reena's gentle voice said.

Dirk curled about and saw Reena leaning through the open window, her chin resting on her hands. Jiang had hopped out of the car and was standing on the curb, his body erect as an ironweight.

'So how about answering your question?' Reena asked. 'What now?'

Jiang lifted Chud's unconscious body into the squad car and propped him over the steering wheel. Reena flexed her hands. They were prickly and bloodnumb from her catatonic posture. She got out of the car and squinted into the transparent brightness. The morning was twenty-two years deep: Her whole life was compressed into the wakefulness of this moment – as her lapse into her former state had proven. The lovelight in Dirk's face was dimmer now when he looked at her, and her telepathy mirrored the sodden stupidity that he had seen in her visage. Her life in this world was deadlocked. She had to get free.

263

'Insideout blacked out because we pushed it too hard,' Dirk explained hastily, following the contours of thought as they materialized in his mind. 'It was trying to find the arc.'

'It found the arc,' Reena said. 'I know where it is now. The way to it is inscribed in me. I saw it.' She recalled the cocooned boy she had seen squatting in ectoplasmic light among the cacti and superimposed that memory on her view of Dirk. The boy's name came to her. 'Donnie Lopes has it.'

Dirk put a hand to his forehead and paced briskly. 'Donnie. That twit'll throw it in the ocean to spite me.'

'I don't think so,' Reena replied. 'The orc has him. It's transforming him somehow.'

'Into something gruesome, no doubt.' Dirk ran a fretful hand through his hair. 'Now the arc is bait.'

'Put it out of your mind,' Jiang said. In this crux of sunshine, uncertainty, and danger, with his bones dutiful, his muscles strumming with might, he was ready to act. Today was the blossom of his life, and he was shining. 'Let's free the one we've come for. With his strength we'll have the force that we need.'

Dirk plunged his hands into his pockets to manacle his anxiety, and they walked toward the moss-colored building where Reena sensed Howard. On the way Dirk sketched out a plan of attack, suggesting that they approach from the shadow side of the warehouse where they would be noticed less quickly.

Strategies were unnecessary. What had to be done revealed itself as they went. Emerging from the shadows across the street from the green warehouse, the lookout at one of the large swivel-hinged windows spotted them and watched to see where they were headed. Reena pointed at him and told him to forget he had seen them. He turned as if to shout to the others, then sat down. At the door, a massive sliding structure, Jiang coiled his strength from the pith of his body, drawing force from the center of the earth. Reena found Howard's dreamy presence at the far end of the warehouse, and she nodded for Jiang to exert himself.

Jiang willed the force buzzing in him to extend into the steel and wood structure of the door. An ear-wrenching boom resounded, and the large door crashed apart and went hurtling inward.

Howard, who had been dozing at the formica table bent over the mound of chits he had won from Tony Robello and the Yakuza, jumped awake. He saw chunks of wood and twisted rods of metal spewing across the empty space, and the blurring tints and hot filaments of his timesense focused to a vortex eye of serene white light. He shifted his gaze to see into the actuality of what was happening and was shocked to watch Dirk with an old man and a young woman striding through the spinning splinters and rolling dust of the exploded door, heedless of the guns trained on them. Tony was agape, a forty-five wavering in his grip. The Yakuza were intent.

The old man raised his arms like a maestro, and Tony and the four Yakuza dropped to their knees like supplicants, their pistols flying from their hands. The guns circled the tall space like a flurry of crows before smashing through the windows and plummeting to the street.

The Yakuza stared dumbfounded; Tony was sputtering. The young woman shouted something, and the five men lined up like marionettes on parade. And then something weird happened. The air thudded rapidly like a breathless heart, and the space around the five kidnappers glossed blue.

Dirk ran up to Howard. 'Let's sky, Howard,' he shouted though the air had suddenly become as still as a cyclone's bull's-eye. 'The orc is coming down.'

Before they could move, they were shocked by a gale of withering cold. The five killers leaped like windblown sacks as the force of the Arctic blast funneled through them. Dirk grabbed Howard's arm, and they bolted for the sunny door. The Yakuza and Tony Robello pounced toward them adorned with ghastly body haloes of green-blue fire.

Reena skipped closer and commanded, 'Stop!' She was stunned the next moment when Tony Robello was staggered by the shout but did not stop. The watery fire about him writhed more sharply, and he grabbed her and slapped her to the ground.

Dirk hurled himself at the man, but a Yakuza grabbed him and they tumbled to the floor. Jiang was immediately over them, and he jerked the Yakuza off Dirk without touching him. The gangster flipped into the air like wind-caught laundry. Dreadful brilliance crackled around him, and he stopped, poised in midair, and grinned with an inhuman intensity. Jackhammer blows of radiance pulsed from the hovering man and kicked Jiang off his feet. The old man smacked the floor so forcefully all his breath gasped out of him, and he lay stunned.

Tony bent over Reena, lifted her by her blouse, and prepared to strike her again. Reena felt his mind, molten with rage, and as he unleashed his blow, she circled the intent back toward him. His arm rebounded, the air around his face swashed sparks, and he crashed to the floor.

'Don't fight them,' Reena shouted to the others. 'Turn the orc force back on itself. Lusk.'

Lusk, Dirk thought, receiving the alien's understanding in a rush of clarity. 'No effort,' he said aloud, and when the man who had knocked Jiang down from midair leaped to the ground beside him, Dirk rolled into him and knocked him over. 'Don't fight. It just gives power to the demon. Don't feed it.'

Howard didn't know what Reena and Dirk were saying. The timelines' vortex eye had scrambled into a hocus-pocus of jangled colors. He ignored that confusion and held his attention on the fracas around him. These killers were real with or without the ghostlights around them. He backed away from the fight, his hands open before him submissively.

Jiang had come around in time to receive Reena's directive. He leaped acrobatically to his feet and advanced on the two Yakuza that were closing on him. Instead of lashing out with his invisible strength, he surrounded himself with a rubbery force. When the bunsen-flamed Yakuza pounced on him, the air clanged with brilliance. Bewildered cries rang out, and the two men fell back in a snaggle of electric thorns and flitted sparks.

Dirk pushed upright and ran for Howard. A Yakuza blocked his way, the eerie blue emanations around him sticking to the air in tendrils. Dirk jinked left and ran to the right, skirting the man. A smoky tentacle lashed out and wrapped about his head. Dirk froze in midstride, and a frightfully familiar voice stippled with silence brimmed through him: *You're doomed, son.* It was Mitch. *The orc is stronger than the alien now. You'll be with me soon.*

Cords of ghostfire uncoiled from the thugs' bodies, and their faces sickened with the torment of their possession. Reena could feel their uncomprehending horror, their brains bouncing with fear, unable to escape the abomination growing from within them. They lurched like Frankensteins, and the blue flames of their bodies roared like a furnace.

267

A whip of fire struck from Tony Robello and snagged Reena's throat. She restrained her panicky urge to tear it away, knowing the effort would only tighten it. The small space of her mind was penetrated by the orc's consciousness – a darkness like the dungeon of a coma, a shimmering darkness like a meshing of insects. Here was her insanity, the brainwave of the wind, empty and full of meaningless noise. She had never been more than this before the alien came to her, and the encounter with it from the pivot of her clear mind was boggling.

Eels of blue fire stung Jiang and Howard, too. Jiang was fanged at the heart, and the orc's umbilicus was poisoning him with nightmares of his wife's and children's worm-riven corpses, their faces falling apart like wet tobacco. He released a silent shriek and withered.

Howard was already on his knees. A viper of green voltage was biting his forehead. The Yakuza from whom it reached was gray with pain. Howard saw him at the center of a lightning-cut whirlpool, dragging him into a maelstrom of abysmal darkness.

They would have died there, all of them, killed by their own pain. But Insideout couldn't let that happen. They were its only path out of this mad world. It needed them more at this point than it needed its own consciousness. So the alien gave them all that it had left. It pushed the limits of its human bond, and in doing so, its painbuffers collapsed, and it was smothered in a blat of suffering.

The remorseless agony stripped the alien's sentience to one electrified nerve, vivid with all the colors of pain. It became suffering's sorcery, endlessly damaged. Its shattered mindforce zigzagged among the four charging them with the binding energy that had held its consciousness together. A squall of whale chimes and dolphin music rushed into them, and Insideout was no more. The alien went on as an electrical pattern in the titanohematite brain of the arc. But its mind was gone.

Reena tolled with the inrush of the alien's force. Lightning strength burst from her, and the orc's tentacle shriveled away. A scream like an incoming rocket ripped from Tony Robello, and he charged at her in a blur of clawing ferocity. Reena didn't budge. She connected with the killer's mind and let it penetrate her. The orc's fury blurred past the clarity Insideout had given her and plunged into the blackness of her schizophrenia. The orc's violence had nowhere to go but back on the bodies that it was using. Tony's aura bruised red, and the charging man was lifted into the air. He whirled crazily, a swastika of arms and legs. The red light about him imploded, stabbing inward in scarlet needle-spikes, and his body burst like a blood bag, scattering viscera and bone chunks in lathed chips.

The other gang members were also yanked into the air and blasted to blood meal, one after the other, in an explosive wave that swept the warehouse as the alien's sentience was parsed among Jiang, Dirk, and Howard. Jiang saw the grisly phantoms of his family vapor into the emptiness that permeates all things, and the astral spear in his heart became a cable conducting the alien's power back to the orc. Dirk's father also whispered away, and the last words he heard from him in the echoey silence were, *You're everything I want my son to be.* Those words flew from him toward the orc like knives. Howard rose from his knees toward the whirlpool that had transfixed him. The Yakuza had fallen in, and the vortex collapsed around him. White blindness relented as the maelstrom shattered, and the radi-

269

ance quelled to a web-glisteny timeline, a Cubist fracturing of vision that led in the direction of the sun-filled doorway.

A quag of blood and minced body parts showered the warehouse, and everyone crouched beneath the wet thunder of the bursting bodies. Hot liquid splattered them, bone bits pelted them, and stillness lurched back into place. The four looked at one another garmented in blood and groaned with disgust. A fecal stence polluted the air. The floor was slick, and they slid toward one another like the raw remnants of apocalypse. Sirens cried from the street and several police cars pulled up to the crashed-in door, blue lights whirling.

Reena, Jiang, Dirk, and Howard, holding on to one another, gaped at the police jumping from their cars. And the cops goggled back at the four figures shawled in gore. None of the Yakuza had survived. The police approached in slow motion, shocked at the carnage around them.

Dirk bolted first. 'Come on,' he called, gliding over the pooled blood, and the others followed, sliding across the warehouse to a narrow back door. Jiang kicked it open without touching it, and they hurried into the sunlight. Two cops who had circled around to the back spotted them and gave chase. Reena stopped, and when they were close enough, she told them, 'Go back and forget you've seen us.' They obeyed.

Several blocks later, Jiang stopped before a fire hydrant and pointed at it. The valves spun free, and a geyser fountained over them. After they had washed the bloody swarf from their bodies, Jiang tightened up the hydrant. He imagined his power enveloping his body close to the skin and, with a vigor not strong enough to rip fabric, rushing off in all directions. The water and bloodstains soaking him shot away from his body and clothes in sun-glinting spray, and he was left perfectly dry. He grinned. One by one, he stroked his hands over the spaces around the bodies of the others, and the water jumped away from them, too.

When they were clean and dry, they looked at one another with stricken bafflement. Men had died. Sanity had been breached. And they were not yet done.

'Insideout's dead,' Reena said. Jiang's cleansing had scattered her long hair and veiled her face, making her pronouncement truly grim.

'I don't believe that,' Jiang said, flexing his hands before him in graceful circles. 'We have our powers.'

'Sure,' Howard agreed. 'I'm still seeing timelines.' The timelines now looked like the transparent con-tours of a streambed, carving space in flowcurves toward the high-way.

'Reena's right,' Dirk said. 'The arc is still real, and it's powering us. But Insideout's dead. Its voice is gone.'

'All that's left of it is pain,' Reena said in a drained voice. She had pulled her hair back from her face, and her eyes looked cloudy.

'Then it's over,' Howard responded. He stared at Jiang and Reena, seeing them clearly for the first time in real space. They both looked small, and when their lips moved they were saying different words than he was hearing. Jiang was more frail than he had looked in timelight. Reena was prettier.

'Insideout is gone,' Dirk said. 'But the arc is still bound to hyperspace. If we don't return it to its exit point in time, we're fallout.'

'How much time is left?' Jiang asked.

'Three hours,' Dirk answered after listening for an answer. 'A little more.'

'The Big Island's over two hundred miles away,' Howard quailed. 'We better use every minute. Come on. Don't worry about me. I'm fine.'

'Rein it in, big guy.' Dirk put a hand on Howard's shoulder. 'We don't have the arc anymore.'

Howard gave him a hard stare.

'It was stolen,' Jiang said. 'But Reena knows where it is.'

'The demon has it,' Reena whispered. She looked to Dirk, nervously.

'The orc's using it to lure us,' Dirk picked up. 'It doesn't care about the arc. It only wants to destroy what Insideout created. Us.'

Cora stood on the lanai of her hotel suite, staring down through palm crowns of nodding fronds at the lavish pools, the colorfully clad people, and the lustrous sunlight bounding off of everything. The brilliance of the scene was incongruous with her dark mood, which was good, for it reminded her that the world was going on despite her suspension. If she had been home in Peoria when this terrible thing had happened, she would have been bedridden with helplessness. Here the surf sounds of laughter, music, and the pools' splashy swimmers made it impossible to cower under her sheets. The tropical sunlight inspired her to put on white shorts and an airy, yellow blouse. And the sea-spiced breezes gentled the hysteria that was endlessly renewing itself and piling through her in waves.

The dropoff of money for Howard's kidnappers would take place this morning, and she prayed that the FBI would not get her husband killed. A harpy of doubt gnawed her with the fear that she had been wrong to call the police. To dispel it, she had wanted to find a church and light a candle for Howie's well-being, but the federal agents had recommended that she stay in her suite until after the drop was completed. She didn't like the agents. They were efficient, courteous, and sympathetic, and she was afraid they might be betrayed by their own strength. None of them had flashed even the strap of a gun holster in her presence. Were they wicked enough to be pitted against the hurtful minds holding Howie?

The agent who had been assigned to her and who had slept in the extra bedroom last night did little to assuage her uncertainty. She was a large, freckle-splattered redhead named Charlotte Traherne, and though she had a prize-fighter's brow, a neckless torso, and calves like bowling pins, she was as gentle and caring as a sister. She had comforted Cora last night with assuring tales of the agency's successes, and her hopeful attitude had eased Cora's fears enough for her to get a few hours of sleep and dream a very curious dream.

A knock sounded at the door, and Charlotte entered. 'I have some news.'

Cora scurried in from the lanai and met the agent at the rattan sofa. 'Was the drop made?'

'There won't be a drop now.' They sat down. 'The Yakuza aren't holding him anymore.'

'He's free?'

'I don't know. The police called us in on our way to deliver the money. Howard escaped from the Yakuza. He was seen running away with three other people, apparently of his own will. They eluded the police.'

'You mean Howie ran *away* from the police?'

'It looked that way. But the report isn't clear. The situation was a very grotesque one.'

273

'What do you mean?'

'All of Howard's captors were murdered.'

Cora groped for an explanation with grum sincerity. 'A rival gang?'

'No evidence for that.' She gave her head a bewildered shake. 'The whole report is very strange.'

'Who killed the kidnappers?'

'Everybody wants to know that. But so far not a clue. It's a sickening mess over there. The sight of the slaughter broke down a local hitman that the police found asleep – you won't believe this – in a squad car two blocks from the murder scene. He gave us the names of the four Yakuza and the mob man. It was Tony Robello.'

Cora felt like weeping at the sound of that name. 'What can we do now?'

'We're going to find the people Howard's with. We have leads. Have you ever seen this man before?' She opened the manila folder and showed Cora a black-and-white school photo of a youth with Arctic wolf eyes and put nose.

'That's the boy Howard said he'd hired as a bodyguard. He said he knew his father when they were in the Philippines. His name's Dirk.'

'Dirk Heiser's father was in Vietnam six years after Howard left the Philippines. They couldn't have met.'

'Who is he then?'

'Says here he's a ward of the state. He ran away from one of the state homes just before he met you at the airport. He's a problem kid, with a bully's reputation at the Home. A real defect case. Dead father, prostitute mother. The police picked him up when he was six years old for selling dope to prostitutes in Waikiki.'

'You're kidding I hope.'

274

'The case gets weirder. Dirk disappeared from police custody just before Howard was freed. Passersby saw him near the police station with two other people. One is a woman who matches the photos sent from Interpol of a runaway mental patient. A phone call from her to her doctor was traced to Oahu earlier today. The photos were telexed in an hour ago. Two witnesses spotted her with Dirk and an unidentified man.'

'Who?'

'We're not sure. He's an elderly Chinese man, and he fits the description of an illegal alien who eluded police earlier today. If that's him, he was a stowaway who was found aboard a luxury liner. He signed his name in the captain's log in Chinese. It's Jiang Cheng-yu. There's no record on him we can find. Ring any bells?'

'No. What does all this mean? What's happened to Howard?'

'We have no idea. I'm sorry, Cora. The police claim that he ran off with these three on his own. There were no visible weapons or coercion. What do you make of it?'

'I don't know. That's not like Howard. Now I just don't know.'

'Think about it for a while. Did Howard get any mail from France, from anywhere overseas?'

'No.' Cora tilted her head with the remembrance of something queer.

'If anything comes to mind, silly as it may seem, I want you to tell me.'

'There is something. I hadn't thought much of it until now. I thought maybe it was only something my anxiety needed. It's certainly odd.'

'Tell me.'

'I had a dream about Howard last night.'

The wattage of Charlotte's attentiveness dimmed.

'No. I don't usually even remember my dreams. I'm not saying I'm psychic or anything. But last night I saw Howard as clearly as I'm seeing you now. He was covered with something like cobwebs, silvery, shiny veils. But his face was clear. It was him. And over his shoulder, in the foggy spiderwebs I saw you and me driving a green Toyota – which I remember because it had a big dent in the roof of all places.'

Charlotte kept the surprise from her face when she heard about the Toyota. That was the coconut-dented car she had been assigned. It was parked in the underground garage. Who could have told her about it?

'We passed sea cliffs and golf courses and came to a huge volcanic crater filled with cactus and brush. I saw a sign for Koko Head Stables, then I was looking at Howard again. His mouth was open and his eyelids just barely shut and twitching, the way he gets when he's half asleep watching TV. Then I woke up.'

Charlotte nodded politely. Perhaps she had seen her car from the window – a stretch of street was visible, though not the street that she drove to and from the garage. 'What do you think it means, Cora?'

'I think it means we should go to that crater. Right now.'

'Now *you're* kidding.'

'I'm not. I'm a religious woman, and I think God sometimes uses dreams to tell us things. Besides, there's nothing for us to do here but wait.'

'Whatever news there is you'll find out here first.'

'Don't you have a police radio in your car? In the dream it was built right into the glove compartment.'

Charlotte turned her head and gave her a sidelong stare. 'Who told you about my car?'

'It's really green? With a dented roof?'

'And a police radio in the glove compartment.' Charlotte nodded and plucked at her lower lip contemplatively. What did it matter how Cora had learned about her car? That was no secret, and though it was an unlikely topic of conversation, she might have overheard an agent joking about it. No matter. The incident would make her work easier. Charlotte had been assigned to keep Cora calm and out of the way. A serene ride through a volcano park seemed an appealing way to kill a morning. And though Koko Head was within two miles of the Home where Dirk roomed, that was probably one of the safest parts of the island for Cora. Police there were looking for Dirk and anybody suspicious. She smiled, and the blueness of her eyes brightened. 'Let's go for a little spin.'

Reena stopped a maroon, air-conditioned Mercedes on Nimitz Highway, leaving the driver in her designer dress and fire-points of gems with the dictate, 'This is the happiest day of your life. Go ahead and share your happiness with others.' Howard took the wheel. As they drove off, they saw the driver grinning beatifically in the diesel wake of the highway, her thumb stuck out.

Reena believed she was doing some small good with her power, and she was pleased. That woman they had left behind was inconvenienced, yet how many lives would she enliven today? 'Do you realize what we could do if we had more time?' she asked the others. 'We could change the whole world.'

'Whoever touches is touched,' Dirk replied from beside her. He was sitting in the back with Reena, and to make his point, he put his hand on hers. She didn't object, and clarity sang in him like the smooth glide of the car. 'That's where the orc gets its power. From us. Whenever we use the alien's strength – even now as these thoughts broadcast words from the verbal field – the orc is strengthened. So let's face it. We're never going to change anything.'

'Only we are changed,' Jiang said. He was playing with the electric window switch in the passenger seat next to Howard and staring out the window at the blue-white clouds musing overhead. With his body comfortably bucketed in the deep upholstery of the car, his restless vitality churned in him. He wanted to fly again. He hadn't dared since his power had returned to him on the luxury liner because the demon's purpose was clearly here with the others. He couldn't articulate what had to be done the way Dirk could, but he could feel truth in his actions. The demon was guiding him. And in a few hours, his work would be done.

'Dirk,' Jiang spoke and turned to see the young man's face. 'Your gift is to understand. Can you tell me what becomes of the dead?'

'Oh, Lord,' Howard groaned. 'I'm trying to concentrate on keeping us alive and you want to talk about the dead?'

'Hush.' Reena pierced the back of Howard's head with her stare. 'Jiang's lost his whole family.'

'Insideout would say they weren't really lost,' Dirk answered. 'Nothing's really lost in this universe.'

'Then where are my wife and children?'

'Their bodies are gone,' Dirk said, 'but their life-force goes on in the form of light.'

'Goes on where?' Jiang pressed.

'All around us,' Dirk answered, 'in the emptiness that backdrops everything, even time. Insideout calls it the vacuum field. It even said that there are tiny antennae in human eggs that can receive these

278

lifewaves just like a radio picking music out of the air.'

'Reincarnation,' Reena culled the word from Dirk's mind.

'Reality turns out to be a lot like a movie,' Dirk continued. 'It's projected on to a screen made up of infinite energy. That screen's the vacuum field. The movie is us and everything in the universe from atoms to galaxies. We're just flickers of energy in the vacuum field. And, exactly like a reel of film, reality is made up of frames – spacetime frames, very, very small. Yeah. It's all we know of reality – these individually unique spacetime frames recurring so rapidly we don't see the vacuum field between the frames. We can't see it, because it's outside of time. But it's there, sports fans. It's really there.'

'Ghosts,' Howard said from the passenger seat beside Dirk. 'That's what we're going to be if we don't pull this off.' He was leaning forward on the wheel, following the clearest timeline through the weave of traffic. 'We've got to get the arc back – before we go nuts or die with this damned alien. Listen to me.' His eyes were slits, peering into the sun's weight and seeing the silence of the future shifting its shapes. The rims of his sight rippled like the hair-thread legs of a microscopic creature. The highway, the palm trees, and the verdant valleys sprawling with houses were a wraith. Only the highway directly before him was clear. Far ahead, the arc blazed at the core of Howard's vision, its rainbows tangling in the air with monstrous, fanged faces. The latticework of possible futures was crowded with abhorrent scenes of large pincers and insect mandibles rippling flesh from Reena's maimed body, snagging ropes of viscera from under Jiang's blood-drained face, severing Dirk's head. And there he was, his chest caved in and writhing with voracious monster grubs. One timehole floated among the bloodsmoke and the grimaces of their screaming faces – one sun-coin – one fiery aperture narrowing even as he watched, garroting the luminant scene of the four of them on a field of black, knife-pointed lava rock.

'There's only a short while left before it'll be too late to return the arc,' he interpreted aloud. His face was laminated in sweat. 'The orc doesn't even have to stop us, just delay us. And we'll be the ghosts you're talking about.'

Dirk's hand tightened on Reena's. 'We'll make it,' he mouthed just loud enough for her to hear.

The distress in Reena's face softened, and she squeezed Dirk's hand. She recognized the loveglow in his stare, and it meshed poorly with the urgency in her to reach the arc and her new life far from this world. Sadness lifted through her. 'I'll miss you,' she whispered. 'We've only been together a couple of hours – but I'll miss you.' Her words loosened all anxiety in her. There. She had said it. She had admitted her bond to this world, this life. It would have been a good life, if it had been whole. This love-drowsy face was the certainty of that. She smiled to think that she could be loved.

A pall filled the car, and Dirk's happiness dropped from his face. Reena had that stupid, soft-eyed look again, and Jiang jabbered something in Chinese.

'Oh, no,' Dirk whispered. He looked to Howard, who was sitting back and scowling.

'The alien's out again.' Howard rubbed his face vigorously and blinked at the highway. A beach park of wide shade trees trundled by on the right, and he pulled in.

'There's no time to stop,' Dirk said, anxiously.

280

'Balls!' he shouted and parked the car at the far end of the lot, nearest the sea. He turned off the engine, and his voice went flat with tension: 'Do you think we're going to face down the orc like this?' He jerked a thumb at Reena. 'We've got to stay calm, even if there is no time. Or we'll wind up like those suckers back at the warehouse.'

Dirk cast him a sour look, saw the grim insistence in Howard's wrung features, and restrained an impulse to give him the finger. With the alien out, Dirk's sapience had withered again to the anger of his hurt soul. His jaw pulsed

Howard blinked like a newt and got out of the car.

The old man nodded wearily at Dirk. He hadn't understood a word they'd said, but he knew from the distemper in the air that the ground was falling from under them. Reena was curled up on the back seat, mewling catgut whimpers.

Dirk cradled her. She felt large in his arms, long-boned. Her face burrowed into the timber scent of his shoulder, and her cries softened to sobs. Twitches flitted through her muscles. The hopeless-ness of loving this woman invaded him, and the tightness of his embrace relaxed. She could never be his. Yet she was all he wanted.

Howard walked away from the car, mounting a grassy dune and staring across the beach park to the sea. What was the last thing he had said to Cora? He couldn't remember. He breathed the emerald sea. He was both glad to be free of his timesense and frightened without it. The world around him, empty of implication, was deceptively easeful. Surfers careened among steaming waves, children splashed in the shallows, oiled bodies lay in the glamour of the late morning, all one with the moment. Yet namelessness stalked all of them with the tread of

281

their hearts. None of them could see it. It was just an understanding, as it had been for him, that life changes, accidents happen, people grow old, wars are made, suns die. Now that he had *seen* that namelessness in the mad infinity of its choices, he could never be the same. Every gesture was a signature now, every decision a testament.

He looked back at the car and saw Jiang scrolling the electric window up and down and Dirk hugging Reena. Her vapid, tear-bruised eyes and the confusion in her jarred features were facing right at him. He wanted more than anything to get this craziness over with. Dying was preferable to living like that, he thought.

The fragrance of the sea reminded him of the encounter with Insideout on the speedboat. Anything was possible, that's what the alien had shown him. 'Okay,' he said aloud, resolving to keep his anxiety under control. 'We're going to make it.'

'Talk about the orc,' Howard said, getting back behind the wheel and starting the engine. 'I sat through one timespell after another last night, and almost all I saw were you and the others getting chewed up by huge insects and the Yakuza when you came to get me. But that didn't happen. The orc should have killed us. I know that. I saw it. Instead, it killed itself. Why?'

Reena's closeness had cooled Dirk's anger enough for him, too, to remember what Insideout had shown him at sea. The abandoned euphoria he had known then could have faced death. What had the alien called it? 'Lusk.'

Howard glided across the traffic on Ala Moana Boulevard and turned off on to Atkinson to avoid the congestion of Waikiki. He frowned with incomprehension into the rear-view mirror.

'Remember Insideout showing us yes-out-of-mind on the speedboat?' Dirk asked.

'You mean that standing dream?'

'That's all we got to remember, Howard. When we stop struggling, the arc will beat the orc.'

'I didn't know what you were yelling about in the warehouse,' Howard admitted. 'I'm still surprised we're out of there and alive.'

'She's the only one that had to believe,' Dirk said, tasting Reena's hair. 'Her power is what really binds us. She's got telepathy. She's feeling us from the inside out. And what she thinks can influence how we feel. As long as she believes in the lusk, that's good enough. Her thoughts can carry us.'

'But what exactly is this lusk?'

'It just means we do next to nothing, Howard. An old man, a schizo, and losers like you and me don't stand a chance against most of life. What can we do against a mad alien? We gotta stay out of it and trust in the arc's power to get itself back to where it belongs.'

'Right. And if we blow it – we're blown up.' He snorted ruefully.

'So when your timesense comes back, don't put your thoughts into the orc's future. Hold on like a bronco buster to any future you can find that gets us free.'

'It's not that simple, Dirk. I can't *choose* the future.'

'You can't – but I think the alien can, or at least the arc can. The alien's humanlike mind is gone. It lost that to keep us alive back there. But it's still living, in an alien way. Your timesense comes from the arc. It knows the path of events that will free it. All the other paths are just emptiness, distracting

283

illusions. So don't you do anything. Be lazy. Lusk. Let the true path reveal itself out of the emptiness.'

'You sound like a Taoist,' Jiang said and laughed. The vitality bloomed again in him, and he was filled with jocular clearheadedness. A moment ago he had been once more at the shriveled end of life. Now his blood was crooning with enthusiasm, and his muscles were supple as an athlete's. What a flourish of life and wonder for his last days! He knew they were amazed and proud. He laughed again, with gusto.

Reena agreed with him. As the arc's power lifted her from her stupefaction, she soared to a new revelation. The dead watched the living. In fact, the dead and the living were interchangeable. The two created each other. Like light and emptiness.

She was happy to find herself in Dirk's arms. She felt the love in him, and she sat up with a clear smile. She sensed mental linkages in an unconscious corner of Dirk's mind. They were oracular echoes of her own thoughts about life and death, processed by the titanohematite brain and channeled to her through Dirk. She listened absently to the odd geometric thoughts, locked fingers with Dirk, and watched clouds gnaw the green crag-juts of the mountains. Her shifts between madness and telepathy opened her to the illogic of being's doubleness: Life and death intertwined like the pain of her madness and the ecstasy of her clarity. She was overtaken by the certitude that these were the same poles that were vertiginously spinning night into day, spinning time. Without duplicity, there were no dimensions. The universe *was* the dilemma of electrons and protons spinning atoms. Without contradiction, there could be no interchangeable opposites like man and woman. Only the infinite inwardness of a world alone with itself. The alien's world.

Dirk knew that Reena was tapping his rational access to the alien. And though he was concerned that this disregard for lusk was strengthening the orc, he didn't say anything. She had to work out her fate. She wasn't long for this world, whatever happened to the arc.

As for himself, he was as eager now as Jiang or Howard for action. He wanted to get this nightmare over, and he wanted to wake up intact, knowing Reena was whole. He refrained from seeking answers from the alien. Whatever he had to know would come to him.

Dirk watched Howard. The man looked torpidly sick. His head was lolling from side to side, evading some terror.

'How ya feelin?' Dirk asked him.

'Mint.' Howard's narrowed eyes looked foggy.

'No speedtraps, tire blowouts, or roadblocks up ahead?'

'Wish there were. I'm looking for anything human.'

In Howard's mind, leopard-muzzled humanoids with lobster eyes, scorpion bodies, and taloned limbs were ghosting among vistas of cactus, scrub brush, and black rock. Cora was there, too – tiny with distance, crying his name. He rocked among the paisley of hallucinations, keeping his attention on the slim path of the road. They drove past sea cliffs, a golf course, and grassy beaches where people were flying kites before his timesense guided him off the highway. A green mountain with its side and insides scooped out rose ahead.

'Koko Head Crater,' Dirk announced. The gravel

and dirt turnoff they were bumping over wended through a chaparral of dwarfed kiawe trees toward an extinct volcano. Half of the volcano was blown out, and the cone appeared as a massive, lopsided bowl.

Howard leaned against the wheel, amazed at the precise fit of vision and timelines. There was obviously only one way in. They drove past a horse stable to where the road ended at a tarred log. They got out and surveyed the expanse of the crater. Barrel cactus and pale-limbed kiawe covered the floor of the caldera, and the far wall of the volcano seemed a long way off.

'I guess from here we walk,' Dirk said and turned to Reena. 'Which way?'

'I feel Donnie and the arc in there, somewhere.' She nodded to Howard. 'He knows which way to go.'

Howard's vision blurred in all directions but one. He stepped over the log and hopped through a tangle of dead branches in the direction of his clearest sight. The timelines were steady now, as they had been before the Yakuza kidnapped him. His fate was empty of choices.

Jiang instinctively took a position beside and half a step ahead of Howard. He had willed his power to envelop them like a soft balloon, and it was gently rattling the shrubs and gravel nearby. Lizards squirted across the red sand, and myna birds big as crows flapped blackly from their coverts.

The footing was rough, but Howard matched Jiang's strong pace, and, with Jiang's force pushing the thorny branches out of their way, they moved swiftly. Reena reached for Dirk's hand to help her over a squabble of rocks, dead branches, and dodder.

His touch steadied her anxiety. From up ahead, a psychic pulsing ached in the air like a deep drum.

They scrambled farther into the crater and its woe of twisted trees and wormholed rocks. The drummed tautness in Reena vibrated deeper, making the joints of her bones ache. And she was about to ask the others to slow down, feigning exhaustion, when the fevered air suddenly chilled.

Jiang stopped short. The soft balloon of force bouncing around them had been stabbed a few yards ahead, and he sagged as his strength drained from him.

Howard caught him, and they knelt in the pebbly sand. 'It's just ahead of us,' Jiang said.

Howard peered at the wall of thorny shrub and saw nothing in the clarity of the converged timelines.

'I'll check it out,' Dirk volunteered, but Reena grabbed his arm. She shook her head. Psychic space droned like a hive, and she could barely hear her own thoughts.

'I'm fine,' Jiang said, standing. His body felt as though it had been rubbed all over with steel wool. The orc was draining his power through the pores of his skin. 'Whatever it is, it has already seized me. I must face it.'

He stepped quickly into the bush, the snare of branches snapping apart before his advance. The others hurried after him and almost collided with him when he pulled up short. He yelped once with shock, and when the others saw what he had seen, they too cried.

Volt-flames flashed bluely, and two animals lunged from among the rocks. Jiang caught them with his invisible strength. Sparks gnashed in the space between them, and the beasts lifted into the air and hung before them, straining among flitting corpuscles of blue fire. They were not animals but animal husks inflated with crackling orc-energy. Poised in midleap, they were the shaggy skins and greasy pulps of a cat and dog patched together with lightning. Dirk whelped a scream when he recognized that the beasts were Peppercorn and Hunza.

'Hurry!' Reena called against the scream of the electrified air. She stared with horrified fascination at the suspended animals, and she felt Jiang's mind lock with the screeching force that was shredding into sparks and raving the jaws of the carcasses. He was immobilized by his strenuous effort, and she knew with him that he could not last long. 'Find the arc!'

Howard faced away from the blur of voltage and found the timelines lensing clearly, with only a hint of rainbow, toward a gully fifty yards away. He ducked under a bower of thorns and clambered over a spill of boulders, Reena and Dirk scrambling behind him.

Sliding and jolting down the other side of the spill, they heard a voice flap from a far distance behind them. 'How-ie!'

Howard stopped and cupped his eyes against the sun. The timelines smeared, and he could see nothing. But Dirk and Reena made out two figures at the distant mouth of the crater. One was a large woman with red hair, hot as a flag, and the other was Cora. They were waving.

Cora and the federal agent, Charlotte, had arrived at the site of Cora's dream to find a maroon Mercedes parked at the end of the road. Charlotte used her radio to describe the car to the police, and Cora stood on the log with her hand shading her eyes like an Indian. When the report on the car came back clean, Charlotte took out her binoculars and joined Cora.

Charlotte spotted movement in the scrub right away, and when Cora took the glasses, she recognized her husband and Dirk. 'It's them!' she squealed and hopped off the log. Charlotte ran back to her car and called her operations chief with the news. After signing off, she removed her thirty-eight from under her seat and followed.

'That's Cora,' Howard said, hearing her call a second time. 'How'd she find us here?'

'It might be some orc trick,' Dirk warned.

'No, it's your wife,' Reena knew. 'We must really hurry now.'

Howard faltered. Was the orc drawing Cora into this? He wouldn't allow that. But he couldn't go back for her. He couldn't even see her. He swung his vision toward the one direction in which he could see, and his blood thickened like jelly.

A disfigured man was shambling toward them out of the brush. Its face was smashed beyond recognition, a disjointed arm swung at its side like a club, and its whole body was caked in dried blood. The orc's ultraviolet aura outlined the body.

'Limu,' Dirk whispered, his insides twisting coldly.

A bull-bellow shook the thick-hulled corpse, and it charged them.

Howard cowered, seeing only the hulking mass of the blood-gouted thing. Dirk crouched, readying himself to leap at it. And Reena stepped forward. Her mind was already within the corpse, engaging the clear, dark, ancient creature there. She remembered the lusk she had learned in the warehouse and did nothing to touch the power waves reverberating

289

through the animated body. Instead, she linked herself with her telepathy to the corpse, and its one good arm reached out to embrace her, its candescent flesh brightening.

Dirk leaped to intercept her but didn't touch her. Sunlight jerked in her eyes, and she was entranced. Just watching her, he was aware of her mind in the tightening spaces of the clotted body, miming nerve flickers in the dead muscles, fixing her memory of life and will into the dead meat.

Limu's corpse bellowed again, and the skim light of its outline spiked to burning needles. Even Cora and Charlotte, struggling through the dense and thorny weed growth, heard it and saw the sharp flash. 'What was that?' Cora asked.

'I don't know,' Charlotte admitted, all her alarms clanging, 'but we're going back to the car and waiting for reinforcements. Come on.' She grabbed Cora's arm and pulled her back toward the road.

Cora yanked her arm free and skipped away from Charlotte. 'You go wait for reinforcements,' she said, clattering over rocks and dodging the claw of a thorn tree. 'Howard's down there.'

Charlotte cursed and dashed after her, her broad shoulders immediately snagging on the bramble.

Limu's corpse had straightened from its charge, and it stood swaying heavily, its mask of smashed-in bone and crusted blood crawling with green wattage. Reena stood facing it, the space around her tensed with stretchmarks of violet light.

'It's you and me now, Howard,' Dirk said, grabbing his shoulder. 'It's on us. Find me the way to go.'

The way was clear: Narrow goat-stairs climbed down past a stand of ohia bushes into the gully. Howard walked with Dirk as far as the floral bushes, where the ground broke into a rocky descent. There, in the spalled shadows, the timelines closed in. Vision was chirpy, and his hearing shivered like an Arctic cross-wind. This was the timewall, hackled with horrifying visions that had almost smothered him at the warehouse.

Dirk recognized the stricken look on Howard's face. Howard dropped to his knees and held his arms up as if against a glass wall. A mane of fiery blue marblings sheathed him, and Dirk stepped away. 'Lusk, Howard,' Dirk almost shouted. 'Lusk!'

Howard heard him – and Reena – and Jiang. Their voices were an insistence of will, a human sodality wavering like wind-kicked flames against the noisy force of the orc. Demon faces trolled closer, and their stench poisoned the air. The screaming became a roar, and the smallness of his strength trembled. In moments, he would collapse.

Without hesitating, Dirk brushed past the ohia bushes and hopped and skipped down the lava rocks into the gully. Donnie was waiting for him below, hunched on a scissure of rock. Dirk's descent staggered when he saw the transfigured shape staring at him. Donnie's semblance was flattened tinily on an insanely disproportionate shape, insect-contoured, lizard-spiked, slithery as a squid.

He stopped, and the orc rose, its triangular head cocking to face him. A sizzling noise like a torrent of ants or the rasping scales of heaped vipers came from its cleft jaws. In the split rock between the thing's legs, the arc burned like a keyhole to the earth's core.

'Lusk,' he spoke to himself and began again down the stony steps. 'It's just Donnie, kid. You can handle him. Let the arc worry about the orc.'

The orc screamed, a piercing meteor-whistle, and the rocks under Dirk's feet crumbled like cheese and sent him tumbling down the steep scarp. Rocks punched him, gravel clawed, and horror whirled as the earth beat him closer to the demon. His arms and legs flailed and kicked vainly, and in a bruising avalanche of stones and dust he fell all the way to the hatched rock where the orc squatted.

Spidery arms seized Dirk and hoisted him toward the munching mantis head with Donnie's pitiful facemarks painted on it. Dirk howled. He wedged his legs on to the cracked boulder and desperately braced himself. The green head, translucent to its hinging mouthjoints, ticking veins, and membranous skull, dipped, and its slavering jaw plates fanged his chest. Pain collided with his effort to hold back. He buckled and was carried upright in the ravenous embrace of the orc.

Dirk's murder-scream shocked him to alertness, and the agony of his snapped ribs and gnawed lungs distilled him to a drop of sentience, dark with pain. Reflected in the drop was the underbelly of the sky, hard blue and spongy with clouds. The excruciating stab-flashing of the mouth at his chest slashed muscles and triggered spasms that curdled him inward and then vomit-wrenched him straight. Blackness battered him, and he would have succumbed if his attention weren't anchored in the dewdrop reflection at his pith.

Clouds surged across the glacier film of the sky, and the radium point of the sun led him away from his death. He went willingly, with stolen release from the agony of his chewed body. Was this an endorphin dream opiating him with the pain-products of his gnawed body? Weirdly, he recognized the alien's reasoning – and the cruelty jolted stronger. *Lusk*. The word calmed him. He ignored the alien's presence and let the scene he saw reflected in the bauble of his life absorb him.

He was standing groggily, staring down at his boots in the tawny sand. He swung his head up and saw Donnie beside the cracked boulder. He looked alert and furious. In his hand was Chud's butterfly blade, white with sun like a sliver of ivory.

Dirk slapped his hip for the blade and felt the torn fabric where his pocket had ripped during his fall.

'I've got the knife now, Dirk.' Donnie strode forward, caneless and springy. 'And it's you that's going to be hurt this time.'

'Donnie!' Dirk blurted and staggered back. 'Look at yourself, man. You're moving without a cane.'

Donnie looked down at himself and hobbled with surprise.

Dirk lurched forward, but his grogginess slowed him. Amazement slipped off Donnie's face, and he swerved into a half step and slashed with the blade. Dirk leaped back and almost collapsed with weakness.

Ferocity squeezed Donnie's stare. 'I've wanted this for years.' He pranced forward, taking full advantage of Dirk's faint. By the time Dirk responded, Donnie's knife arm was swiping up to gut him.

Dirk grabbed Donnie's arm but wasn't strong enough to stop it. The point of the blade pierced him above his stomach and glided off a rib. Donnie's other hand punched out and socked Dirk squarely in the mouth, knocking him down.

Donnie pounced on him, and Dirk caught the blade as it gashed for his throat. For a moment he was able to hold him, his weakness just matching Donnie's strength. 'Donnie!' yelled at him. 'What're you doin'?'

'I'm killing you,' his clenched face said. 'You're never going to hurt me again.'

Dirk's grip slipped, and the knifepoint needled his

larynx. His arm was trembling – words were trembling in him, too: 'Donnie, look at you! You're crazy. This isn't you, man. It's some demon. How can you walk without your cane?' But those words came out huffed and garbled as animal grunts. In the end, all he could cry was, 'Donnie, don't kill me!'

The piety of terror in Dirk's voice reached Donnie. This was the satisfaction that Donnie Lopes had always wanted from Dirk, and the sound of the tough's abject submission softened his savage will. The press of his knife slackened, and Dirk pulled the blade away and dashed it into the rocks. Donnie slumped forward, and his surprised face met Dirk's upthrusting fist. His head snapped back, and his startled eyes flapped white.

Donnie collapsed, and the air whomped with brilliance, blinding Dirk. When sight squeezed back into his eyes, he saw globules of turquoise plasma wriggling over the sand and rocks, splattering into frenzied amoebas of energy, and finally drizzling into glints of stardust speckling the gully for a few moments before evaporating.

Dirk sat up, his hands on his chest. He was intact. The world was luminously normal. Donnie's crumpled form was undistorted, and the only pain in Dirk's body was the constellation of bruises from his tumble into the gully. His weakness was also gone, and he stood up with buoyant relief.

A wild shriek swooped from overhead, and Dirk crouched around to see Howard splashing dust in a jubilant gorilla dance. The lusk had really worked. The arc had collapsed the orc.

Dirk found the arc in the fissure of the boulder where the orc had sat. It came away hot as ice, and when he held it up, a halo of colors wreathed it. The alien was still in touch with him. It was distant and weak, but it was still there.

Howard whooped again, and Reena cheered beside him. Their laughter rippled in Dirk's mind. Thoughts from the feckless alien fit themselves to his awareness, and he understood what had happened. He put the arc in his pocket and scaled the shattered face of the gully.

'Don't put yourself in my mind,' Dirk said to Reena, 'or anybody else's. Listen to your telepathy idly. And Howard, ignore the timelines much as you can.'

'That'll be easy,' Howard smiled. He looked about for Cora. 'I feel almost normal.' The gauze of design, which had veiled his vision since before his kidnapping, was weaker. Trickles of light came and went. 'But why worry about it? The orc's gone. I can feel it.'

'The demon is gone,' Reena agreed. 'But so is Insideout. I hear only our own thoughts.' She had faced into Limu's corpse the way she had faced into the gangsters at the warehouse, with her own darkness – the void of catatonia and the surging fear of her madness. *That's the past*, she was glad to remind herself, and tears pooled just behind her eyes.

'Insideout and its demon are weakened.' Dirk hurried past the red-flowered bushes. 'C'mon, let's find Jiang. He's got to hear this, too. If we can stay close to our perceptions and not use the alien's power too much, the arc will remain an object. We can drive to the airport, get on a plane, and bring it back. No miracles. No orcs.'

Limu's cadaver lay facedown in the dirt where it had dropped when the orc was canceled. The limbs were awry and the head tucked under so that it looked more like a heap of dirty clothes than a body.

295

The sight of it sent a draft through Reena, and she remembered the caulked blood and shattered muscles of the zombie. She took Dirk's hand as they climbed up the spill of lava rocks and heard the white notes of a silent music. That was Insideout, far away, on the other side of its journey, singing the song of its return, singing it backward from the future. And she was hearing it because she was going there, too. The antiphonal whisper of her own song lifted through her from the stag-antlered center of her brain. Her body was rejoicing in the wholeness that would soon be hers, without the angelic power of sifting thoughts from other minds – and without the abysmal numbness of her malformed brain. This prospect of normalcy was stranger and more enchanting to her than the magical and terrifying presence of the alien, and she squeezed Dirk's hand to renew her bond with the moment.

Dirk thought she was still unnerved by the orc and was searching for something soothing to say when Cora's voice hailed them from nearby. 'Howie! It's me, Cora!' She was struggling through a brake of thorny, fern-leafed kiawe a pebble's throw away.

The giant, red-haired woman she was with held up a wallet and the sunflash of a badge. 'FBI!' she shouted. 'Stay where you are!'

Dirk pushed Howard. 'Skip.'

Howard waved to Cora. 'I'm all right,' he yelled. 'I'll explain everything later. Don't worry about me, Cora.' He ducked under a lean of spindly boughed thorn trees, following Dirk and Reena. Cora called after him, and the agent shouted more commands. But he ignored them. Explanations knotted as he tried to imagine what he was going to tell her. Her cries were frantic by the time they reached Jiang.

He was atop a natural cairn of rocks that had fallen

from the tattered rim of the crater. He had gone there after the orc imploded and the dead animals plopped to the ground. His strength was impaired from his strenuous standoff, and he felt momentarily soggy with fatigue. But the relief of the orc's collapse had carried him to the top of the rockpile to see the others. Kiawe shrubs blocked his view, and he had thought of levitating over them when his strength returned – until he spotted Cora and Charlotte. He watched as they laboriously meandered the labyrinth of thorn trees, rocks, and cactus. With his telekinesis he probed the texture of the terrain around them and found what he wanted in a ledge high up on the rim.

'Jiang,' Dirk waved as he rounded a rise finned with prickly pear cactus. 'Are you all right?'

He nodded and pointed toward Cora and Charlotte, who were closing in across a field of swordgrass.

'Yeah, we gotta move.'

Jiang smiled. 'Don't worry.' He hooked his mounting strength into the crater rim wall and tugged free a herd of black rocks. The boulders somersaulted down the scarp, trailing a caterpillar of furry red dust.

'No!' Reena bawled in a voice that rang from inside his bones.

Jiang was bewildered. What was wrong? Did they think he was going to crush the two women? He had delicate control of the stampeding stones, and in a sway of outflung power that lifted him two inches off the ground and tilted him backward like a water skier, he brought the wall of rocks hurtling across the path of their pursuers.

Howard ran to the top of the cairn and peered into the roiling dust until he saw Cora and Charlotte backing away from the avalanche. He leveled a harsh stare at Jiang, but his ire faltered when he saw that the old man had slumped to the ground, breathless.

Dirk rushed to his side and scanned the crater for orc signs.

'I don't feel anything,' Reena said.

'It's there now,' Dirk replied in a hush of certainty.

'Maybe it's not strong enough to reach us yet,' Howard hoped. He gently took Jiang's throat in his hand and felt the feathery pulse. He looked to Dirk and shook his head.

Jiang looked like he was solving a riddle. He was concentrating on where his strength had gone. Deeper. He was surprised. When he had been toe to toe with the orc, facing into the rabid muzzles of the dead beasts, he had thought life moved outward. All his life he had believed this. The dragon was outside. And while he had waited for the others to battle the dragon, he had been content – and strong enough – to hold it and contemplate it. In its four mad eyes he had seen the perfect light. In its rage to kill him he had experienced the wrath of neverendingness. All experience was holy. His father had been right all along. Poet or farmer, angel or demon, rock or human – each was a midget earth, each was whole. There was no real comparison, except within the heat-lightning of the mind. And with that thought, he willingly let all comparisons go. He wasn't afraid to die now that he saw that it was a falling inward into the rising light where memories and thoughts came from. His family was there. And it was comforting to sink toward them.

'Jiang?'

The time to let go had not yet come. The withhold-ance was outside of him in the lateral world. He had to undo it himself. The actions required were already enciphered in him. He only had to open his eyes.

298

Reena laid her hands on his face and insearched for his life. It was rising toward her out of a pencil-sketched vagueness. As it drew closer, serenity pervaded her, and all lightness fled her body. She was a stone leaving its zeroes behind on the surface of the sliding light. She would have plummeted out of her own body right then, except Jiang's willingness to surface to life buoyed her, and they both bobbed awake.

'Are you okay?' Dirk's hands were at the sides of her face, and the concern in his voice was rift with fear.

When she came to, her mind-touch felt the release of his fear followed by joy mothering an impulse in him to embrace her. Jiang sat up between them. 'I'm okay,' he mumbled. 'Stand aside.'

Jiang soared to his feet, the dust spiraling about his ankles.

'Don't do that,' Dirk warned.

Reena used her telepathy to inform Jiang about the need to restrain their powers so that the orc would not feed off them, and he frowned with concern.

Dirk felt her silent energy like a whiff of glacial air. 'Cut it out, Reena,' Dirk looked back toward the gully and saw glints of light that could have been dandelion fluff lofting in a breeze or – 'Let's get outta here.'

Howard led the run back to the car. The timelines had brightened. The optimal path back to the car was highlighted in neon white, a softglow ecru that unmazed the desert forest. At the gravel road, Howard stood on the log and stared back through the gunsmoke tint of shrubs to where Cora and Charlotte were picking their way up the slope. He waved.

Dirk went into the green car with the dented roof

299

and ripped the wires out of the radio he found in the glove compartment. He was hoping that the agent hadn't called them in yet, but as he was getting out, two cars came barreling down the rutted road toward them. The cars spewed gravel, swung sideways to a stop before them, and unsprung men with drawn guns. 'Federal agents!' they announced. 'Put your hands over your heads.'

Reena looked to Dirk, and when he nodded she raised her hands and said, 'Get back in your cars and forget you've seen us.'

The agents complied. As Reena drove past the two cars of mannequin-faced agents, she rolled down her window and added, 'Have the happiest day of your lives. And share your joy with others.'

'For the benefit of all beings,' Jiang added, raising a hand in benediction. A few moments later, while he was laughing, a sickening lassitude bled through him, and he exclaimed in a Chinese dialect.

Dirk and Howard looked back with anxiety. Reena was studying the whorls of her fingerpads, a spindle of saliva drooled from her lip. Jiang opened his hands in a feeble shrug, his muscles leathern again.

In the rearview mirror, Dirk looked for the agents. He couldn't tell whether they had noticed the Mercedes driving away from them, and he restrained the urge to floor the accelerator. He also searched for the orc. There was no sign of it out there. Deprived of the alien's imagination, Dirk was his angry old self. 'Where are you, fucker?' he asked into the mirror as the FBI curled out of sight, and he was cursing both Insideout and the demon. At the paved road, he breathed easier and let himself believe that they had gotten away clean – while under the heel of his right boot, a grub of a snow-blue energy, packed and glimmering, hoarded strength.

Dirk drove to a nearby high school, and in the parking lot they ditched the maroon Mercedes. He hot-wired a tan station wagon and they pulled out on to the highway, westbound toward the airport. Moments later, Howard tapped Dirk's shoulder and jerked his head to the rear. 'It's Cora.'

Dirk craned his neck and saw the green Toyota at an intersection with Cora half out the window, pointing at them. The Toyota shot into the traffic, causing several cars to swerve and jam their brakes. 'Shit.' Dirk accelerated. 'How'd they find us?'

'Maybe the orc is helping them,' Howard volunteered.

'Now I'm glad I cut their radio.' He pulled up to the tail of the truck ahead of them. 'If we can lose them, we might make it. Hold on.' He swung on to the embankment, gunned past the truck, and cut in front of it a few yards from where the shoulder of the road ended at a concrete abutment.

'Christ, Dirk!' Howard shrilled. 'You're as dangerous as the orc.'

Dirk's risky driving put distance between them and the Toyota. And twenty miles later, when they glided up the off-ramp toward the airport, the green car was out of sight. They banked a curve and came into view of the conning tower, light aircraft hangars, and in the distance the jumbo jets. Dirk drove directly across the grass field and on to the concrete apron before the nearest hangar.

'How're we gonna handle this?' Dirk asked.

'Lusk, little buddy.' Howard got out of the car. 'We hitch a ride on my laurels.' He strode into the hangar. Mechanics were busy overhauling an executive-class jet. Howard stooped under a dismantled wing and confronted the pit boss in front of the wire mesh windows of his office. He was a narrow man, like

Howard, but short and gray-haired. Howard smiled when he looked through the window and saw a newspaper on the man's desk, open full page to the sports section.

Howard guessed that the pit boss would have a plane of his own to charter or sell, and when the wiry man announced that he had a Piper Seneca at the far end of the field that he'd go for thirty-nine thousand, Howard introduced himself as the kidnapped Illinois lottery winner. They walked into the boss's office and ruffled through the paper. Howard's photo, from Cora's wallet, as well as his story, up to the kidnapping at the boat harbor, were on the front page.

'I need your help in getting away. I'm being chased. I don't have any money on me at all. But if you'll give me that Seneca, I'll give you a hundred grand from my first lottery check.'

The pit boss's lean face impassively assessed Howard. 'You make it one twenty-five, put that in writing, and the plane's yours.'

By the time Howard had filled in the agreement of sale, the green Toyota appeared on the off-ramp from the highway, and Dirk began shouting. Howard thanked the pit boss and ran for the station wagon. Dirk had the engine running, and as soon as Howard leaped in, they peeled away.

Howard directed him down one of the crisscrossing airstrips, past a line of small planes, to the blue and white twin prop that he had just purchased. The Toyota had cut across the grass of the airfield and was rushing down a runway parallel to them when they reached the plane.

Dirk threw open his door and helped Reena get out. 'Get Jiang. Let's go.'

Howard carefully guided the old man's legs free of the door and lifted him upright.

'Come on!' Dirk was already walking on the clay-hard earth toward the plane, pulling a reluctant Reena. The green Toyota appeared from behind a line of small aircraft on a strip a hundred yards away, and Cora was waving from the window. 'Chop-chop, Jiang,' Dirk beckoned. 'Please, Reena, don't fight me.'

Reena was confused. She knew Dirk, but she couldn't recall from where. The urgency in his face was frightening her. Everyone was shouting in a strange language. She panicked and twisted free of Dirk's grip. He scowled with batlike ferocity and snatched at her, and she gambled all her strength on her feet and ran down the airstrip.

'You're scaring her,' Howard yelled at Dirk and hoisted Jiang into Dirk's arms. He ran after Reena, and she lunged into the tule grass that surrounded the airport. Charlotte was braking at the edge of the airstrip where the bramble was too thick for the Toyota, and Cora was barking with anger, 'Howard – stop – right – now!'

Howard caught up with Reena, his legs straining with the effort to pace her. 'Please, Reena,' he chattered. 'We need you. And I can't run anymore. I swear my liver's ready to burst.'

Howard's earnest plea touched her though she didn't know what he was saying. She was running and frightened and didn't know why. She slowed and looked with fawn-jittery eyes into his face. He took both of her hands. 'Trust me.'

He pointed to where Dirk was helping Jiang into the plane. 'Go there with me – please!' He urged her toward the plane, holding both of her hands. Charlotte and Cora had leaped out of the Toyota and

303

were screaming toward them. Howard and Reena bolted hand in hand, and only after Cora pulled up short with a wounded cry did Howard consider how this must have looked to her. He glanced back with a stricken heart and saw Charlotte kneeling into a firing stance.

The gunshot cracked loudly as hammered rock, and the bullet zipped a foot over their heads. Reena almost fell to the ground as the slug sucked by. Charlotte pulled the revolver back to her shoulder. She hadn't intended to fire that closely. She just wanted to scare them into stopping, but they ran faster.

Dirk helped Reena on to the plane from the inside. After Howard entered, lit the control panel, and started the generator, Dirk asked him, 'Can you fly this thing?'

'I was trained to build them,' he said, powering up the engines. 'But I don't know if I can fly it. Buckle up and we'll find out.'

Dirk didn't bother to buckle up. He was pressing his face against the side window, looking for the agent who had shot at them. She and Cora were just climbing out of the field and on to the strip as the plane began its run.

Howard had never flown anything before, but he'd had pilot friends in the service who had taken him up. He tried to remember what he had learned from them as the plane accelerated down the runway. The headset that had come to life when he had flicked on all the gauge lights was squawking something from where it dangled above the floor. Howard's hands were white-knuckled on the yoke, and his eyes were watching the speedometer climb toward the magic green bar that signaled he had enough lift.

'Look out!' Dirk yelled.

Howard raised his gaze in time to see a mammoth jet liner streaking toward them on an adjacent runway. He wailed with shock and pulled back on the yoke. The world slanted sharply, heaving everyone deeper into their seats, and the six-seater jumped into the air. The jetliner loomed ahead like a wall, and they could see the crew in the cockpit, aghast to watch them converging.

The small aircraft skimmed past the prow of the jet, and its rivets rattled like castanets from the turbulence of the near miss. Everyone on board was shouting, and when blue sky snapped into sight, their screams went dead, and they pushed their faces to the windows.

The jet lumbered into the air below them. The green peaks of the Waianae Range fell away, stepping down into the brighter green sea; the plane gained altitude. Mottled shades of aquamarine and cerulean patterned the coastal waters with the lacy outline of the surrounding reefs. Honolulu sparkled in the noon sun like a necklace of tech art strung along the throat of the bay. Clouds gasped by, and when the earth was visible again, they could see beyond the headless sphinx of Diamond Head to Koko Crater.

At the sight of the place where they had met the orc, Dirk touched the arc in his pocket to be certain it was still there. It felt dull, lifeless as a coin. His head felt blunt, too. No superpowered brainwaves were peaking in him now, only the cold memory of fear. He reminded himself that the orc, with all its gluey blue lights and demonic shapes, was all in their minds. The Yakuza had been real enough – and Donnie. But the orc's appearances were just electrical patterns in their brains imprinted by the arc.

'So which way do I go now?' Howard asked.

Dirk shifted fretfully, orienting himself. He pointed southeast through a surge of cloud steppes. Hands touched his neck and shoulder, and he turned in his seat and faced Reena. She was airsick. She had a corner of her hair in her mouth, and she looked ready to weep. Beside her, Jiang, empty of strength, was sitting back with the side of his face against the window as though listening.

The racket of the engines and the bounce and shudder of the plane had rubbed the velvet of her mind the wrong way, bristling and darkening her feelings. She had wanted to hold on to the man with the red mustache, who had asked for her help before. But he was flying the plane. And the old man next to her was tired, the amber of his scarab-lined face pale with fatigue. Only Dirk, the sullen, silver-eyed boy who had scared her with his anger, was left. He didn't look sullen or angry now. His face looked careworn and boyish.

Dirk put his arm around Reena, and she tucked her face into his neck and drooled on his shoulder. He smelled of bare oak, like the groundkeeper's lumber shed at the hospice. And that reminded her how far away she was from that familiar and hopelessly sad place. And that made her happy.

Cora was heartshattered. She believed Howard was running off with a younger woman, and her desolation drained her of strength. Charlotte, who was eager not to lose her quarry, had an arm under Cora's arm and was hurrying with her down the runway. 'You don't know that he's run off with her,' Charlotte said, breathlessly, not taking her eyes off the small plane as it dipped and bucked into the sky.

Cora knew. In the last two days she had seen how old she looked, how frumpy she had become.

'Howie's a millionaire now,' she said. 'Why would he want a frump like me?'

'You're not a frump, Cora. Besides, he loves you. You told me so.' A police van was speeding toward them, and Charlotte took out her badge. 'Don't judge him so quickly. I'm sure there's a perfectly reasonable explanation for all this.'

Charlotte officially commandeered the van and left the police driver behind to drive in the abandoned station wagon. She drove full speed down the runway. Cora clutched the dashboard. 'What are you doing?'

'I'm going after them.' She searched all directions with frantic intensity and cut across several runways to a helipad where a chopper was winding up for flight. She braked just outside the stroke of the rotorblades and darted for the helicopter, waving her badge.

Cora hustled after her. If Howard was leaving her, she would at least face it. Charlotte tried to shoo her off, but she was adamant and clung to the hatch until they lifted her in.

The pilot was a private operator about to take several tourists up for a sightseeing cruise. He acquiesced to Charlotte's request when she showed him her badge. He was a white-bearded, crinkle-eyed man who had flown helicopters in Korea and Nam, and the sight of Charlotte's gun tucked in her belt didn't alarm him.

They went up in a roar and, using a police emergency priority, got permission from the tower to cut across the airspace over the landing strips directly to the ocean. Because of that, Charlotte never lost sight of the twin-engine plane. Her work was full of uncertainties and unsolved cases, but this was one mystery she was willing to pursue to the ends of the earth.

'We're being pursued,' Howard told Dirk. They had been flying for over an hour, and the foam-webbed sea ranged landlessly below them. Howard kept the plane on a south-southeast bearing, full throttle, banking only occasionally to avoid massive plateaus of cloud so that their sight of land when it appeared would be unobscured. While making such a slow curve, he spotted the insect dot of a helicopter behind them. 'Nothing we can do about it,' he said to himself. 'But we better start thinking about what we're going to do when we do reach the Big Island.'

Reena was still hugging Dirk, and he had turned sideways in his seat to accommodate her. Jiang seemed asleep, but he was staring inward, waiting for the strength to come back to him. He was the first among them to sense the darkness within unraveling to light. The nerves in his eyes brightened, and his body was replenished. He opened his lids and saw Reena and Dirk holding each other and looking at themselves with sudden, bashful clarity.

Reena released her hold, but her fingers lingered at the back of Dirk's neck and on the wet patch of his shoulder. 'Thank you.'

The warmth she felt radiating from him eased her embarrassment, and she sat back in her seat and straightened her hair.

Howard watched tiny moths of fire flutting outside the cockpit, and he thought they were reflections from his timesense. He fixed his eyes on one and with a frisson of switched perspectives recognized that the flickering sparks were *inside* the cockpit. The spark he had fixated on looped nearer, and he was shocked by the fire-fanged face glaring at him with eyes of glory. He cried out and jerked back. 'Look!'

The flurry of volt-faces swirled hotter. 'The demon,' Jiang breathed.

Reena wasn't breathing. She was listening to the thoughts in Dirk's head, sifting past his fright to the translucent, latticed frost of the alien's mind. Panic encircled a core of scorching pain. No thoughts. Minutes remained before the hyperfield collapsed and the arc became an eternally sealed capsule of pain. Winnowings of consciousness blustered within the terrible hurt, and her body screeched like a drill-bitten nerve. She shook alert.

'Don't anybody try to do anything,' Dirk said, following the mazy flights of the specks of light, trying to trace their source. 'Lusk. Like we did in the volcano.'

Timelines spewed into Howard's sight like flung spray and spume. He tried to ignore them, keeping his eyes trained on the horizon, which was now dayglow purple. He flicked a glance at the control panel, to keep his gaze loose, and was stunned to see the fuel gauge needling empty. A half hour ago it had read almost full. He tapped it, and the needle fell flat to empty. Pressing his face to the side window, he saw the spray of leaking fuel and spotted the corrosive hole just under the wing where the tank was punctured. Tiny blue flames ate the edges of the hole. 'We're out of gas!'

A hoot of fear spiked Dirk as he understood why the orc was beginning to appear now. It would manifest at the first cough of the choking engine and harry them right into the sea. Reena felt it like a wave of nausea mounting in the cabin. Jiang was cold with its immanence, and Howard was staring into miles of sky and seeing nothing. 'I'm blind,' he cried.

'You're just scared,' Dirk said, hopefully. He daggered his fingers before Howard's eyes, and the staring face didn't flinch. He reached inward for understanding, feeling the drain of awareness, the thickening lethargy as the orc drew strength. Comprehension came: Howard's blindness was mesmeric fixation induced by the orc. The foveas of his eyes had been licked on to one point, and the neural flux from the retinas had stalled. He needed a gentle boost to snap out of it. Dirk looked at Reena, who was already away, and she pushed into Howard's mind, right through the rigid hysteria that had frozen the micromovements of his eye muscles. His eyes jiggled freely again, and his field of vision opened up.

'I don't think I should be flying,' Howard said. He brushed aside the flitting demon-headed gnats and squinted through a shredding of cloud. Ahead a whale-blue, humped shadow appeared on the horizon. 'Am I hallucinating or is that land up ahead?'

Dirk leaned into the windowshield and rapped his knuckles against the glass. 'It *is* land.'

Jiang sat up. He was shivering, and his face was bright as a drunk's. With a hand on Howard's shoulder and one on Reena's, he smiled kindly at Dirk. 'The journey is over.'

The engine coughed. Dirk was thrown to the ceiling, his right leg kicking straight out at the windshield. A blowtorch of star-blue light blasted from the sole of his boot where the orc had hidden. The windshield plate on the right side exploded outward, and the cabin dervished with icy air.

The plane yawed wildly and dove. The yoke pulled Howard out of his seat, and he fell forward

310

over the dashpanel. On the nose of the plane, an eel shape of gummy, azurous light reared a starfish-spiked head, its moray grin widening as the plane screamed toward the sea.

Dirk crashed back into his seat and was whipped by the wind buffeting through the shattered half of the windshield. Prismal tongues of astral fire licked over him, pinning him with the inertia of the spiraling dive and lighting up the inside of his skull with flame-quaking shadows. In the bright darkness, he saw his father. Mitch was necrotic, his face a rag of flesh against a hard grin of bone. Death had never been more articulate.

Howard, too, was entranced by the orc. Pressed face forward into the scream of their dive, he was seeing chromatic timelines funneling directly into the frog-gaping mouth of the orc.

The surge of the wind gunning through the shattered window had cast Jiang and Reena into the back of the plane. They clutched each other and watched the orc entwining the plane's nose press its lizard head into the cockpit. With ravening fury, its dinosaur jaws gripped Dirk, then Howard, leeching the vitality from them.

Reena heard their suffering from within, both of them mewling with unscreamable agony. She hid her face in Jiang's chest, her consciousness twisting around his with the urgency to do something. He embraced her in the meteorcry of their plunge, and he closed his eyes and groped inward, toward the heaviness of gravity. He found his strength in the stomach-squeezed cramp of their fall, and from there he extended his telekinesis, stretching his power through his body outward and into the crucified shape of the plane. He shoved against the earth's pull and felt his invisible force buckle. Empurpling strain almost blanked him out, but he exerted himself with bone-brittling insistence, willing the plane to fly.

The sea was close enough for them to see the swells when the nose lifted. The pitch of the plane's plummeting siren modulated lower, and the aircraft swung through the belly of the dive's parabola. Howard was flung backward into his seat. Dirk hollered with dismay. And the orc erupted into shards of ectoplasmic trolls that palsied in the wind like mescaline vibrations. The imps whooshed in with the bashing airflow and charged to the back of the plane.

Reena instinctively curled up in the seat where she had been slung by the plane's abrupt pullout, and the menacing imps swarmed over her. Jiang was flat on his back on the floor, his muscles popping like veins under his skin as he sustained the plane's flight. None of the ball lightnings lighted on him. Reena was magnetizing all of them to herself by using her telepathy to merge with them.

Inside was pain. It was the drilled nerve pain she had jumped from before. This time she held herself there, in the tireless suffering of the orc, and her body thrashed to a fit. She convulsed in her seat, her bones hammering to break the straps of her muscles.

Dirk barged into the back and grabbed Reena to steady her. The phantom flames eating Reena rushed up Dirk's arms in a snaggle of claws and teeth, and he let go and banged into the seat beside her. 'Reena,' he bayed against the wind's cacophony. 'Let the orc go! Lusk!'

In her anguish, she could hear nothing but the whirlwind mania devouring her. The roar of the furnace, the storming torrent consumed her, uncoiling her torment into greasy smoke and brittle ash.

312

The smoke and ash clotted to form her physical body, a pain-marrowed ogress writhing with the orc's hurt.

Dirk backed up to the windrushing cockpit, keeping Reena's wracked body under his gaze. 'How much farther?'

Howard's brain had been peeled open to the time-swept ranges of yes-out-of-mind. Iridescent shadows tattooed the sky and shirred to a geodesic funnel that dipped behind the mountain range below them. 'We've been over land since we came out of those clouds back there.'

Dirk glanced out a side port. A holocaust of clouds mushroomed over hummocky green fields and forests. Off the starboard side, ribbed with enormous jade chasms, was a mountain with a peak of glassy snow. 'Mauna Loa. We're almost there, Howard.'

'Where's there?' he shouted back.

Reena rose from her seat, resplendent with fiery flickers and comet dust. Her flesh was corpse-tinted, and her eyes were flame-cored. She bent to strangle Jiang, and the plane rolled.

'Geezus!' Howard yelped. 'I'm losing it. We're going down!'

The pit of Dirk's stomach trapdoored as the plane plummeted, and he threw himself at Reena. Their contact sprayed green light across the cabin, and the air soured with the stink of burnt flesh. Dirk hauled Reena back from Jiang, his arms and chest pierced by quills of fire. He tackled her into the empty seats, and his flesh was sliced with mincing razorstrokes. He wailed to the brink of blackout.

'Hold on!' Reena shouted. And he understood. The pain tattering his nerves and curdling his blood was the alien suffering its endless dying. That was the strength of the orc. By their willingness to

313

conduct that anguish, they weakened the orc enough for Jiang to regain control of the plane. Each second, they flew closer to where the hyperfield waited, and the arc intensified. Yet each second was a torment, and they burned like filaments in an electric current, their lives vaporing away from them.

Dirk clenched his life against the battering pain, forcing himself to feel his being, to touch the hurt, to remember – ah! At last, life came, returning to him with the memory of lusk on the ocean, when Insideout was a watershape and being was the abandon of life. That freedom soared in him again, and he rose above the swamp of his pain.

As Dirk lofted on a wave of pain-induced exaltation, the suffering lifted with him. The orc writhed over their clutched bodies. Howard, who was looking back with frightened eyes, not wanting to face the upswelling fields of ash and cracked soda, saw the orc as a mantis-jawed specter twisting violently. Its shape ruptured into flashes of discontinuous spectra that smoked away, passing right through the hull of the plane with a bellow louder than the dive's scream.

The plane righted itself and climbed with a soaring peal. Howard whooped like a bronco rider, and Reena came to underneath Dirk. The last thing she recalled was calling the orc into her to keep it from Jiang. Her telepathy searched for the demon and found it fuming with rainbow streamers like a borealis in the contrail of the plane. She refrained from probing Dirk's unconscious body with her telepathy. She was afraid he was dead, and she couldn't bear to touch that with her mind. Instead she shoved him upright and pressed the palms of her hands against his face. He was pale and fever-glazed.

She put her ear to his chest and gasped when she heard the trip of his heart.

'We're going down again,' Howard yelled.

The plane bellied back toward earth, the mountainous terrain swayed, and the sea shone like sapphire. The plane was gliding down in a gentle descent, drooping past snow limned crags, swooping above tundra fields and sprawling forests. Ahead, Kilauea Volcano twined a purple thread of gas into the luminous strata of the sky. Sere ridges of shrubs, silver deadwood, and straggling trees fell away, and the black lava fields came into view.

Jiang was seeing it all. The crater highlands crawled beneath him as though he were flying again in the embrace of the demon. He *was* flying, more nakedly than he had flown before. The currents of the wind nerved him, guiding him through streamers of clouds and the rinsings of heat draining from the lava fields. He saw everything the sun saw. The airplane at the pivot of his gravity was silver in the noon glare, jeweled glints dusting in its wake to the arc of a rainbow. Not far behind was the helicopter that was pursuing them. And below, yellow-plumed with fumaroles and black with frozen lava was the site he had journeyed from his ancestral land to reach.

Jiang was awed and delighted with his disembodied flight. The plane swayed to his slightest gesture. But there was very little need for adjustment. Where he was going thrummed tautly in him like a kite's guide thread drawing him down toward the scorched landscape and the ominous exaltation of the mountains. He looked around a last time at the cloud cascades, the sky with its layers of light, and the dragon-scaled land, sloughing toward the sea.

Beauty saturated the day, and he smiled as he bowed toward the horizon.

Reena was crouched over Jiang's body, and she saw the smile on his face even as she sensed the punchdrunk undertow of gravity competing with him for control of the plane.

'Better strap yourself down,' Howard called back as he frantically harnessed himself into the pilot's seat. The yoke was dead. The plane was flying itself. And the broken, wrathful terrain of Hell was rising toward them.

Dirk bent beside Reena and took Jiang's arm to help him into a seat. Reena stopped him. 'It's okay,' she said. 'He's flying the plane. The landing will be easy.'

Dirk peeked out the window at the tortuous rills and craggy outcroppings. 'Maybe just to be sure – '

She shook her head. 'No. It's going to be all right. Go ahead, strap yourself in. I'm staying here with him.'

Dirk shook his head as if he knew better and knelt beside her. Out the windows, the sky slimmed away and black ridges past. The plane slowed, the landscape steadied, and Dirk gripped the armrest of the seat beside him, anticipating their impact.

With a grating crunch and a loud whine of ripped metal, the plane touched the earth, rocked like a subway car, and stopped. Dirk unclenched his remorseless grip on the seat and stood up to see out the windows. The pitted, steaming fields of cooling lava surrounded them.

'We made it!' Howard exulted and flung off his seat harness.

Reena didn't rise. Dirk bent down again and noticed her hand trembling on Jiang's chest. Jiang was pale but smiling. 'Is he all right?'

Reena lifted her face, and her eyes were hot with tears. 'He's dead.'

Dirk put his fingers to Jiang's cold neck. There was no pulse. He hovered over the body for a moment in dazed suspension, then he double-fisted his hands and brought them down sharply on Jiang's chest. He pressed the heels of his hands on to the old man's sternum and press rhythmically as he'd seen on TV.

Reena put her hands on his. Her eyes were pure and stared him to stillness. At the back of Dirk's mind, in the ebbing and rising sentience of the Other, she heard the words she had to speak. 'Like the swan flying from its lake, he is serious, he has left home.'

Dirk relented, put his right hand softly on the old man's heart. Howard joined them. The air was a smoke of their individual motions and positions hazed the cramped space of the cabin – yet Jiang was fogless. His clothes were soaked with light, shining like petroleum-stained water, and his features appeared carved of aged ivory.

The monotonous thunder of a helicopter thudded closer. 'Get the arc out,' Howard said and clambered for the door.

'Can we find the right spot without Jiang?' Dirk asked.

'I'm seeing genies,' Howard answered and opened the door. The pounding, roaring wash of the copter bleared his face. 'Move it,' his mouth mutely said. 'We got to try.'

Dirk and Reena followed Howard out of the plane and into the sand-stinging gust from the churning blades overhead. The helicopter was bobbing over the downed airplane, dicing the air, hesitant to descend. When the three of them crawled on to the wing, they saw why. Jiang had brought the plane

317

down in the middle of a spiky, uneven field. The helicopter rose and canted over the nearest rise, looking for a safer place to land. They found it on a sward where the magma had forked, and they went down between the two lithified currents.

Dirk took out the arc and almost dropped it. The silver skin of the ovoid had tarnished to a strangely luminous ebony, like black milk. Only minutes remained before it would seal itself off and die inwardly forever. Reena grasped that with him. She also partook of Howard's prescience and saw as he was seeing the specter of the future coagulating into actuality: A glass well formed before her. Dirk's faraway thoughts told her it was the drop into the singularity. It began here with one step forward. The bones in her feet itched. She stepped down from the wing of the plane and began walking over the churned surface of the cold lava.

Howard escorted her and witnessed the hallucinatory mosaic of time blinking over the terrain. The one direct path that led to the hyperfield was unblurred; at the end of it he saw the three of them, their faces twittery as white leaves, walking past pitted lava boulders that looked greased in the dry light. Dirk followed their trancewalk, squeezing the arc in his fist, wanting to feel the raw cold of its power, feeling only dull metal.

Ahead, beyond the rise where the helicopter had landed, was the peak of a shake roof building. That was the ranger station, Dirk realized. Ohelo bushes glittered with crimson berries along the rise, and not far away was a gray planked walkway that disappeared among the skeletal shrubs. Recognition flashed, and Dirk stared past pocked boulders glazed by manganese oxides and spotted the pit where he had taken the arc from Donnie. A sulfur stench wafted as the wind curled across the cinder-waste from the smoking vents in the distance.

Howard and Reena skidded down the scarp hand in hand, and Dirk bounded after them. At the bottom, Reena took his hand. Dirk held up the arc. Less than a minute remained. Howard let go of Reena and touched the black disc in its web of light. Reena too put her fingertips on the arc. The crystal interfaces of all the minutes and events that had led them here pushed their hands down with a dowser's insistence. They knelt, the arc in the their hands swirling above the volcanic tuff like the planchette of a Ouija board.

A silver-gold charge leaped from the ground to the arc, and the three hands snapped away. The arc fused to the spot beneath it in a shock of galvanic fire. A dowel of energy the color of moonlight rose from the arc and disappeared in the sunlight among biscuits of clouds. The arc strobed silver, and its argent luminosity filled the grotto with lightning-shimmering air.

'My friends!' The windspun voice came from everywhere. 'Strange indeed are the ways. I've found my way back!' Poe appeared, naked and youthful, in a nimbus of white radiance that trembled like sheet lightning. Its large-eyed, mustached face was transfigured with joy. 'Oh, I can't tell you how happy I am – so – so yes-out-of-mind! You've actually saved me! I'd given up hope. Oh, glad fortune! No time left to thank you with the intensity I've learned to feel for you. No time – '

'What about Jiang?' Dirk called to Insideout, and the white-hot refulgence around Poe huffed brighter. 'He's dead.'

'Is that what you think?' Insideout's drafty voice asked. Its eyes were jeweled with tears of joy, the

319

flesh around them crinkly with merry assurance. 'I thought for sure you understood by now. Certainly you must know, Dirk. Poor dears. It's all inside of you. If only there were time to show you. Time has no shores.' It reached out its arms, and fire-dots appeared overhead, dew-webbing the forcelines that domed the basin. 'A moment of song,' it said, and the fire-dots spun like spirochetes.

Lavish waves of well-being rocked the three terrestrials, and the straps of their muscles and buckles of their joints loosened. Gravity unspooled a little, and their bodies hung effortlessly in space. The wave-bundles of their minds drifted free of their brains and floated into the charged air outside their bodies. Colors brightened to sheer vibrations, and a deep quiet fell toward the sun. Drifts of heaven flowed into them from where the future grows, reaving the last shreds of their past. Life splurged.

This extrahuman passion bloated the three of them with nostalgia for their humanity. In synchrony with this feeling, the fire-points in the air stopped spinning, and they were immediately back in their bodies – Howard, Dirk, and Reena again, snug in the loops of their blood.

'You've all learned to be more human since we first met,' Insideout said, bleary-eyed with bliss. 'Me, too.' Poe iced to a still image, hand raised in parting. 'Goodbye, my friends.'

'Goodbye,' Dirk said.

'Where can we say you came from?' Howard asked, urgently.

'Go in happiness,' Reena cried.

'Ah, more light – '

The radiance staggered, flared brilliantly, and Poe and the geyser of light vanished. The arc that was left behind pulsed like an ash-white coal. The space above it was cracked with wiry voltage, and a tense silence shrined the pit.

'You gotta stand over the arc now,' Dirk said, feeling Insideout's call for her.

Reena was sad and smiling. 'I know.'

'Right.' Dirk touched her cheek with the tingling tips of his fingers where the arc had shocked him. He had angel strife in his look. 'Good luck.'

She kissed him on the lips and stepped away into a distance he would spend the rest of his life crossing. Howard waved. He saw the glass well turning in the air, twisting, gathering her in. He took Dirk's arm and pulled him backward.

Dirk abruptly pulled free and leaped to Reena's side. 'Take this,' he said, digging his class ring from his pocket. 'I want you to have it – from us, your first earth. We'll remember you. I'll never forget you.'

She took the ring with a touch sticky with extreme cold, and a voltaic spray drizzled from the ring as it passed between them. She was speaking to him, but he couldn't hear her. Her face was happy and slippery with tears.

Dirk backed away. He stopped with his heels against the rocky incline for a last look at Reena as she stood over the white fire of the arc, the visible force wavering like tufts of bleached grass around her ankles. She raised her hand, and a rainbow dropped from it like a shooting star.

Dirk turned and climbed up the face of the scarp after Howard. Howard had already crawled out of the basin, and he saw Charlotte running toward him on the boardwalk that led from the ranger station. She had her gun out.

Halfway up the slope, the black rocks under Dirk glared white. He flipped over and scowled against the luminance. Reena's hair had ignited like a matchhead, and streamers and gushes of magnetically looped radiance wreathed her. The image fragmented into chips of chrome — solar phosphenes that twinkled briefly in the outline of her body before scattering like silver leaves on the lance of the wind.

Dirk scrabbled to the top of the scarp in time to see Cora appear on the boardwalk that led out to the lava. Charlotte was running ahead of her, gun drawn. Howard already had his hands on his head. Dirk raised his hands.

Cora budged past Charlotte and hurriedly picked her way over the sharp lava to Howard. She confronted him with worried alertness, looking for signs of lack-love, and he swooped her up in a staggering embrace that almost toppled them into the pit. Charlotte lowered her pistol and stepped out on the lava.

Cora's and Howard's laughter uncoiled joyously and echoed from the volcanic cones. Dirk, smudged, scratched, bruised, his clothes in tatters, gazed beyond them toward the distant brimstone outcroppings, the crater mists, and the sea. He was listening as far as he could for the diamond grindstone music of heaven. But that had disappeared. He was utterly himself again. He placed his raised hands against his head and laughed to feel the snugness of his bones. He looked into the basin. The air lifting from the pit had the smell of apples and twilight. A rainbow circled the space where Reena had stood and then was gone.

Epilog

Jiang soared through the thriving azures of an endless sky to Sandalwood Mountain, the land of the dead, with its cascades of shimmering gold and its slopes of transparent fire. He became light itself, sheer energy in a möbius bundle of complexifying waveforms, free of flesh and boundaries. A wordless understanding accompanied him, like Dirk's special awareness, and he knew that he was expanding at the speed of light into the luxurious emptiness of the quantum field. The sky around him was the eternity of all energy, the interior of light.

Howard's prescience went with him as well, for he saw his future pearling ahead of him to geodesic linkages of mass, phosphorescent circuits of matter. He was able to watch himself in the near future tunneling into a shining gridwork, his intelligence showing him the nacreous vibrations folding in and out of each other like water shadows and harmonizing to nodes bright as full moons — spirals of DNA, the youngest possible human body.

As the vast, elegant structure of opalescent light narrowed around him, and the edge of space closed in with a swirl of faces and places from his new life, he realized that he was reentering the genetic crystal of human life.

Dirk had been right: There was no end. Already his mind was folding into a new molecular bondage as the chromosomal antenna absorbed his wave pattern from the quantum field. And in that instantless zone between being and oblivion, a cinematic flurry of cross-cut images and vivid scenes rushed before him, spangling with color, revealing the achingly familiar features of his wife and children merging with the shadowy, backlift futureview of the family he was entering somewhere on a suburban slope of Golden Mountain.

Before relenting to this love that reconciled everything, Jiang looked for the others from the end of his last life. Howard and Dirk were there on that slope – with Cora. The timeless lensed. And Jiang saw that they would become a family, adopting Dirk in the last year of his childhood.

For her part, Cora believed not a word her husband and Dirk told her about the alien. In fact, no one did. The police were convinced they were lying, despite the fact that polygraph tests supported their lunatic story. Dirk was outraged by the detectives' incredulity and demanded truth serum. Some of the police wanted to oblige, eager to find the weapon that had pulverized the Yakuza kidnappers. But no such weapon was ever found – and experts insisted it couldn't exist. Howard posted their bonds after he and Dirk were charged with flying without a license and the near miss with the jumbo jet, and they were released from police custody.

Donnie Lopes woke up in Kolo Crater remembering nothing from the time he left the police station. All memory of the orc was gone, to return in the years ahead only remotely, between the acts of his dreams where it souled whimpering, teeth-grinding nightmares. The police found him crawling out of the gully, and they guided him away from Limu's broken carcass. The sight of Hunza's and Peppercorn's fly-busy bodies punched him, and the horrible undoing of the alien budged closer to memory. He was hysterical when the police carried him from the crater. Later, Dirk told him the whole story, but Donnie dismissed it as another ruse. He was overjoyed when the Dycksons adopted Dirk and took him back with them to Illinois.

Cora's interrogation and doubt would last longest. Who was that sharply dressed blonde she had seen running hand in hand with her husband? And where had she gone in that black desert? People did not simply disappear into thin air. Howard told her the truth, again and again, without once losing his temper, and she accepted that *something* had happened. But she didn't relinquish the last of her anger and suspicion until she found out that she was pregnant.

The child to come was just one cell in the gaze of Cora's blood when Jiang's waveform was received by it. Thirty-eight years before, Jiang had lost his wife and youngest son in the violence of the revolution and had not once dreamed they were on their way back – let alone that they would take the dissimilar forms of Howard and Cora. And he never would dream it, since the waveform's collapse into the spiral antenna of DNA also collapsed Jiang's link with the alien and the knowledge they had shared.

In the mothering gravity of his new body's first cell, Jiang's flight through the void that holds all things ended, and he became a thing again, spectral with happiness, full of blood and sleep.

Howard and Cora would never guess. Howard was content to have his wife back and a few million dollars in the bank. He accepted his bizarre fortune for the cosmic glitch that it was. The weirdness had left him with a lifelong exuberance for the ordinary. Baseball, food shopping, car engines, and changing diapers were all equally savory now, and he lived each day with gratitude and happiness.

In time, Dirk would come as close to happiness as his adoptive father – but from the other side. His encounter with the unknowable left him starved for the stature of his curiosity. What had really happened to him and the others during their three days with the arc? That question guided him back to school and eventually to the quests of science and the elusive dream animals of mathematics. One day he would even write down Insideout's story, wanting to touch again, however obliquely, the supernal knowing that had once possessed him. He could remember but he would never again know more than any of us know about the enduring mystery of our lives or the spell of our departure. That wouldn't matter. Knowledge became for him the good faith that understanding is possible – even as answers return to their questions and what is explained remains concealed.

And what of Reena, the only one of the four who could not be complete in the earned world? Insideout kept its promise. The last act of its titanohematite brain before collapsing into the perpetual rending and rapture of the pith was to use the energy of the vacuum field to rebuild Reena's body from her waveform. Molecule by molecule, it amended the distortions in her brain and released her on the far side of the sky, on another earth. Wherever she woke, her life would at last be whole enough to brim with her own dreams.

Dirk correctly figured out all the details: The arc, he theorized, had conserved its inertia and the cosmos' total quark-number by using its hypertubes to draw enough energy from the vacuum field to equal Reena's mass. If that energy had been released simply as energy, much of Hawaii would have been vaporized. Instead, Insideout condensed most of the

4.86×10^{25} ergs of Reena's mass-energy to atoms and fused those atoms to a molecular lace of naphthol ethers, oleo-resins, and cinnamic acid – several hundred cubic liters of a harmless gas. Reena had disappeared in a puff of colorless smoke.

In the lava kettle where the arc had come and gone, autumn's substance lingered. The wind frisked over the basin, and the smell of exhausted leaves wafted across the ash slag, pumice beds, and tar fields. By the time the sky wore away west to night, the fragrance from the edge of the universe was gone. Most of it was simply washed away in the rivers of air that endlessly circle the earth. But some of it, like some of us, the heat of the earth lifted above the night into the emptiness of space where the dark holds everything and the galaxies wander deeper into their loneliness.

Appendix:
An Excerpt from *Invasion from Inner Space*

by Dirk Heiser

Once upon a space – a very tiny space, tinier than an atom, tinier even than the quark symmetries – there was a world. It was a world of enormous power, with energies far exceeding the gamma ray ferocity of the hottest quasars. Any *one* photon in that world packed more energy than the largest stroke of lightning of our cold planet. To be small enough to fit into this world of subquark space, a photon had to have a wavelength no larger than 10^{-33} centimeter, which meant that its energy was about 1.9875×10^{16} ergs – more energy than the sun radiates over Manhattan in an hour![1] And that was the *dimmest* photon in this microdimension!

Physics had new rules at these extremes of energy – mysteries and mercies wholly beyond human consciousness. Because here, in the fifth dimension, spacetime did not exist. Space itself existed – and time itself existed. But they existed separately.

Space had no fields. Time had no sequence. Instead, space was a point, and all directions went nowhere except back on themselves, pressing across an inreach of narrowing distance.[2]

Space wasn't black distance, either, like the void of outer space, but iridescence, a shimmering frenzy of color: Here all quanta were really one quantum existing as an infinite variety of waveforms and creating a reality as complexly varied as ours. Varied yet exquisitely unified since time in this refulgent

328

world was all-time. That is, time was simultaneity: Every change happened everywhere inside the point-world at the same moment. Here everything was truly one.

And in this oneness, as this oneness, there was life: One life, one being, alert to the infalling splendor of its contractive universe. Mind existed as pure being. Awareness emerged from the resonating waveforms of this world's vast energy. As the consciousness of the one infalling quantum, mind stared comatose with fullness at the whirlpooling wholeness of itself.

Within the concave simultaneity of the point, mind matched reality perfectly in this being, down to the most extreme diminution. Mind sang the shape of its own being, the very extent of its collapsing world. Inward toward the shortest wavelengths and highest energy was the pith, core of everything and the central meaning of mind. The pith was the fullness of song and the joy of life. Outward was impossible. Mind moved only inward, matching reality in its collapse. Outward was impossible.

Or was it? In reality, wasn't there only one? One mind, one song, inward and outward the same?

Those questions represent as much as we can know of evolution in this nucleonic reality. Mind contemplated its wholeness. Beyond the one was the many. Mind knew it – by ending. In and out. Here and there. More than one. The many. The mystery of more. The unknowing of other. Could that really be? Mind folded in and in, singing forever, but nothing folded out. Outside was nothing. What was this nothing that was outside? It was beyond thinking, beyond the one. It was the many.

Mind stalled when the song pushed outward toward the many. Mind kept singing anyway.

Though the song splayed and wobbled, mind kept singing. It was singing to what was never seen – as sometimes we sing. It sang with all its might – until the giddy superabundance of life within its integral extent strobed once and was gone.

Megauniverses opened, and timelines spread like crystals across the interface of the singularity and the continuum. The One burst apart, and infinities of shapes unraveled inside the swooping parabola of an event horizon. Mind surged helplessly through these mazing patterns in the form of energy, bewildered and dazzled by the expansive awareness of radiance – radiation! – quanta streaming *outward*!

Behind was the contractive world of mind's origin – ahead, the multiverse billowed its mad tapestry. And here, where point became field, energy whelmed with furious outflung power.

Mind plunged into a universe – our universe – emerging through a quasar and gelling instantly to a tiny (for us)/huge (for it) photon-bundle (about 10^{-21} meter) of complexifying waveforms, a being of extremely high energy quivering with the sensation of I.[3]

Virtual particles pumped from the field vacuum flared blue-white along the axis of the being's flight. Everything else was a shimmering black, a kaleidoscopic black, endlessly unfolding.

The hypertube that had carried the mind from its dimension through the multiverse to this continuum was still there – infinitesimally present – and the mind sensed the majestic wholeness of its origin in the direction that led back into the glare of the quasar. *Direction!* The concept was outlandish to it, because direction implied sequence – multiple spacetime frames, manyness on an incalculably vast scale. Already the mind existed in numerous spacetime frames, a corridor of mansions tunneling from the quasar to now. Each spacetime from was one flicker of the continuum, one instant of its trespass through the cosmos.[4]

It willed itself slower, compressing quanta of action into each new spacetime frame, squeezing more momenta into each instant –

The being's intricate energies slowed and out-folded to mass, flashing X-rays in a tremendous needle-spiked tiara of black-purple light. The alien instantly molded into a four-dimensional presence with mass, spin, and charge. The instantaneity of its appearance was its 5-space heritage. The energy, mass, and information that patterned them was the spillover into 4-space of the 5-space song. As soon as the song manifested, it disintegrated into X-ray burst, a physical form, and a mind.

The shape that appeared was 3×10^8 Å in length and half that wide – about three centimeters across, the size of a quarter but oval-shaped. It was made of pramatter – a superhot plasma of free quarks – but as it slowed down the pramatter crystalized into stable, superordered matter. Its shell was an iridium alloy, and its intricate interior was composed of titanohematite, a magnetic metal capable of self-reversing electric fields, like neurons. The mind's consciousness was preserved in this structure's ability to conduct a field current: Within the daedal interstices of the metal atoms, hypertubules connected the 4-space body of the alien with its 5-space home, and the mind throbbed with sentience of its new universe.

The alien didn't think of itself as a physical form – which is why this story has taken place at all. It was ignorant of shape – ignorant, in fact, of most of the implications of mass. To it, matter was merely slowed

331

down light: After all, $M = E/c^2$. The alien's self-image was of a flare of energy, a trajectory that looped from the point of 5-space, through the cool, billowy cloud of 4-space, and then back to the point of its home – a fiery arc.

But the mind needed to stop the arc, to match the inertial contour of the 4-space continuum and begin its homing collapse back into the perpetual implosion of 5-space. Like a ball thrown upward, the arc could not return to where it had started until it first stopped. Somewhere in this vast reality of bloating emptiness, madly spinning fire whorls, sheer veils of tattering gas, and seething immensities of evanescent neutrinos it would have to find a place to stop – a place where it would experience concrescence with its surroundings. That moment would be the ghostly peak of the arc, the empty range where vectors were nullified and the mind's trespass and the shape of spacetime would briefly be identical. The hot physics of stellar interiors or the cryogenics of the cosmic vacuum seemed the only two options at first. But that was before the titanohematite brain sensed a flux of eerily nonrandom radio noises from a rock orbiting a nearby yellow star.

And that's where this story finds its beginning.

Once upon a time, an alien craft no bigger than a twenty-five-cent piece splashed into the atmosphere in a gush of cosmic rays and thunder. Colossal lightning bolts lashed the stratosphere, windy curtains of auroralfire gusted above India, the Amazon, and the Hawaiian Islands, and the arc flashed toward earth.

[1]At 10^{-33} centimeter, spacetime – our reality – breaks up into bits that are continually vanishing and reappearing like individual bubbles in a glass of champagne. These monads appear spontaneously from the all-pervasive vacuum field and very quickly disappear back into it. Anything tinier than this distance is not actually in our universe because it's compacted by a boundary similar to a black hole's event horizon. Within that boundary is the fifth dimension, where space, time, and physics mean very different things. The mathology for a photon with a wavelength of 10^{-33} centimeter is astounding:

$$\text{frequency} = \text{velocity/wavelength}$$
$$f = \frac{3 \times 10^{10} \text{ cm sec}^{-1} \text{ (speed of light)}}{10^{-33} \text{cm}}$$
$$f = 3 \times 10^{43} \text{ sec}^{-1}$$

$$\text{Energy} = f \times h \text{ (Planck's constant)}$$
$$E = 3 \times 10^{43} \text{ sec}^{-1} \times 6.625 \times 10^{-27} \text{ erg/sec}$$
$$E = 1.9875 \times 10^{16} \text{ ergs!}$$

The sun radiates 1.4×10^6 ergs cm^{-2} sec^{-1} on the earth's surface. For it to deliver 1.9875×10^{16} ergs to midtown Manhattan's 38.61 km^2 would take 3,676 seconds – about 61 minutes.

[2]This is not as bizarre as it at first seems: We live in an expanding space that increases by an amount equal to the volume of our galaxy each *second*. All quanta for us are moving out, carried by the expanding field of the universe. Yet – in the puny domain of our earth – light, noise, and physical bodies are moving with freedom in all directions. So in the subquantal world, where all space was a point, there was freedom, too.

333

[3]What actually entered our universe from 5-space was not the energy or mass of the alien. No conservation laws were violated, since all that crossed between universes was information – the alien's song. The song took on the characteristics of 4-space metrics by shaping the spacetime and photonic fields around it into an energy form that preserved its identity – including its consciousness.

[4]We understand that flicker as h, Planck's constant, the quantum of action, which shows what there is (E) at any one time (T):

$$h = E \times T$$

With gleeful surprise, the alien saw that what-there-is kept changing, frame by frame. Even more astounding for the alien was realizing that the rate (f) of flickering (h) was directly related to its form:

$$hf = E = mc^2$$

The flickering spacetime frames (hf) could appear as energy – which the mind was now – or matter.

The quantum of action is the smallest unit of wholeness in our round universe. And it, too, is round. Action comes in circles. The quantum of action, h, is equal to angular momentum – the momentum of a weight spinning in a circle:

$$hf = E$$
$$h = E/f$$
$$h = mc^2/f$$

Frequency is the inverse of time, so

$$h = mc^2T$$

The speed of light is a length (L) covered in a period of time (1/T):

$$h = m(L/T)^2T$$
$$h = mL^2/T$$

– the formula for angular momentum, the smallest package of action.